AF572718

THE FORTUNE TELLER

A novel by

GRAHAM STULL

Published by Ribbit Books

The Fortune Teller: a novel / Graham Stull – First Edition

Print ISBN: 978-0-99326-5-020
eBook ISBN: 978-0-99326-5-037

Text edited by Bernadette Kearns

TO MY GIRLS

JO, ANNA AND DAPHNE.

I LOVE YOU ALL.

AND TO DANIEL, MY MAIN MAN,

WHOM I SHALL NEVER GIVE UP ON.

NOT UNTIL I'VE DRAWN

MY VERY LAST BREATH.

PROLOGUE

It was a cold, damp morning in October and Fergus Maloney was late for school again. He took the shortcut across the two fields behind his house. On the other side of the far field was the lane that ran behind Smyth's hotel and on towards *Scoil na mBuachaillí* National School in the heart of Clonakilty town. This route would save him a few minutes, and that might just be enough to spare him a whack from Mr. Clancy's leather. Or it mightn't, depending on how wrecked the oul' bastard was likely to be from last night's session at the pub, it being Monday.

Fergus wouldn't have been late at all only for the fuss caused by his brother, Darragh, running off in the middle of the night and not coming home. Darragh had done it before, but he'd always come skulking back at midnight or thereabouts after *You-know-who* had gone to bed. Not this time, though. This time he'd stayed out all night. At quarter to nine in the morning, as Fergus thundered down the stairs and scoffed down his Weetabix, Mammy was hard by the kitchen window wringing her hands, and it seemed to Fergus she might have been standing there all the night through.

The electric school bell rang out across the outskirts of Clonakilty, unchallenged in the still October air. *Feck it*, Fergus thought. He wasn't even as far as the high beech hedge that separated the two fields. Nothing short of a sprint could save him now. The teacher's big, fat, red face appeared in Fergus's mind's eye, the fleshy neck protruding over his buttoned-up collar and spilling out towards the lapel of his tobacco-infused tweed jacket. Mr. Clancy was like an overstuffed turkey. He would shout "*Moille!*" in his stupid-sounding Connemara Irish and his face would turn even redder with the rage. Then he'd rise and walk ponderously over to where the weapon hung on a nail on the wall. It was the eternal waiting, the standing against the wall with every boy's eyes fixed right on you, that made the punishment as awful as it was. And then the leather would snap down on Fergus's outstretched hand and a flash of pain would light up his entire being.

The very thought of it spurred Fergus on and he jumped the muddy ditch between the two fields in a single bound. But his worn shoes—hand-me-downs from Darragh with no profile left on the soles—lost their grip as he landed and he fell heavy into the sodden earth of the next field. His fingers dug at the wet soil, out of which poked the stubbles of last season's hay.

"Feck," he hissed, scrambling to his feet, gathering his canvas school satchel and breaking into an open run. Now he'd be whacked twice. Once for lateness and once for having dirt on his knees. *That fecker Colm O'Reilly better not snigger, or I'll get him at small break, so I will,* Fergus vowed.

And that was the last thought he had before the crow cawed. Fergus stopped dead in his tracks. The field disappeared. The backs of the terrace of houses and the car park on the edge of town disappeared. The cold wet of the muddy earth on his knees disappeared. A tingling ran through his body.

He turned and looked back at the branches of the beech hedge lining the ditch he'd just crossed: they were bare and shivering like black shapes cut out of the October cloud with a sharp stencil knife. No other sound or movement permeated the icy air. Fergus watched the puffs of his own breath and listened to the sound of his own panting, and the pulsations of his heart. His blue eyes scanned the hedge behind. The bird's caw echoed, sending chills through him. It was a crow, only a crow, and yet it *wasn't* a crow at all. It was like nothing he'd heard before. This crow had a *voice*. Where was it? What did it want?

He'd begun to think it was all in his imagination when the crow called a second time. A long piercing caw rent the still air asunder. It was a physical force, and yet, it was also as if the bird was inside his own brain. *Come to me,* it said to him.

That was when he saw it. It was sitting on a branch in the beech hedge. The black-winged beast fixed its beady eye on Fergus for only a second before beating its heavy wings and taking flight. Fergus could but follow, clutching his satchel to his chest. On they went like that, Fergus chasing and the bird leading the way, hopping from bough to bough along the hedgerow. They reached the top corner of the field, where a thin rill of water trickled along the bottom of a deep ditch, covered over by thickets and brambles from the opposite embankment. Only then did the crow break off its hopping and, looking back one last time at the boy in pursuit, it disappeared down into the blackness where the water ran.

Fergus clutched a long, spindly, bramble branch to hold his weight as he peered down into the ditch. The tension inside him was so great he barely felt the thorns of the bramble piercing his pale fingers, as he clung onto it for support. He needed to find the bird. And there, underneath the canopy of overripe blackberries, a beady eye looked back at him with a sneer. The black beast let out a final, almost melancholy, caw.

"Get off of 'im, ya BASTARD!" Fergus bellowed and threw himself down into the abyss with all the recklessness of rage. The bird took instant flight. Fergus heaved his satchel into the air after it. He wanted to knock the fucker down; to tear its wings out and thrash the rest of its mangy oul' self into a tree. But he missed and, instead, the satchel got caught in the branches overhead. The strap came loose. His school books and tattered copies fell out and landed all around him, splashing into the icy-cold stank beneath his feet, its waters blackened by human blood.

New Treasury of English 2 landed open on Darragh's face and neck. As Fergus lifted it, he saw the reddish-blue discoloration that ran in an uneven line across his brother's throat. Similar gashes marred his wrists. And the blue eyes—so very like Fergus's own—stared up.

Up through the canopy of brambles, and into heaven.

1

Summer hung over Elizabeth, New Jersey, like a woollen blanket: heavy and unmoving. The sun, lost high above the endless wooden-framed houses, was shrouded in a film of haze and pollution which magnified the glare without providing the least bit of protection. Down on street level, the shadows cast by the three-storey buildings were no longer deep enough to permit the old-timers to languish on their stoops in the shade and those of them who could afford to do so had already retreated into the comfort of their air conditioning. The others sat on folding chairs inside open doorways, with only their bare knees and sandal-clad feet signalling their presence. Not a single grey squirrel stirred in the heat. Not a single cat upset the metal trash cans that lined the chain-link fences of the back alleyways, waist-deep in ragweed. Not a single dog barked, because there was nothing lively enough on the street to bark at.

Anyone who was paying the slightest bit of attention would have noted that there were, in fact, only two sounds to be heard in Elizabeth that day. The first was the intermittent drone of airplanes sweeping overhead from nearby Newark Airport, taking off from the south runway with eerie regularity and heading to the West Coast, where the thought of summer was somehow much less oppressive.

The second was the Irish construction workers. Shirtless, they stood on the scaffolding which covered one of the 'three-fams'—the three-storey/three-apartment houses that were being bought up and modernised for yuppies who could no longer afford to live in Staten Island. One crew banged pale-green roofing tiles into place, while another ripped off the tattered, old asbestos siding with crowbars and, heedless of protection, inhaled its carcinogenic dust.

There was no one there to admire the tenacity with which they worked. Their pale, milky skin was seared in the unforgiving North American sun. The copious amount of beer they had drunk the night before oozed from their open pores, forming a sheen around the red, baking flesh: a halo of perspiration which the humid air was never quite capable of evaporating. They could not work like that for very long, of course. No human being could. Most were young and would leave at the end of the summer, returning to Ireland to continue their college studies. Those who stayed would gradually be promoted to more skilled trades, or would find work in the bars in Manhattan. Some would become the foremen who would lead the next batch of illegal Irish immigrants and students the following year. A subset would manage the difficult transition to legal alien status, either through visa sponsorship or by marrying American girls. And increasingly, significant numbers were returning to work in Ireland, as tales of well-paid construction jobs in Dublin made their way across the Atlantic. The 'Celtic Tiger' they were calling it.

No, there was no one there to admire them except Fergus Maloney, a tall man with long black hair, cut-off jeans and a faded Coors Light T-shirt who stood on the opposite side of the chain-link fence in one of the alleyways and watched the monotonous hammering of the roofers. He'd come to the US as a student originally, though a student of what not even he could say any more. At one time or another he'd worked for most of the Irish construction crews in New York. There was even a time when Fergus had worked hard, possibly as hard as the sunburnt youths he was now observing. But he'd grown too wise for that shite, he reckoned. Too wise by half. The suits who made all the money on these deals never left Manhattan. The Irish, meanwhile, were being exploited, as they had always been. Part of a system of piss-taking of the proletariat, run first by the British, then by the Americans. A sucker's game. Getting fired from the building sites had been for Fergus an act of protest against capitalism: a statement of his belief in the fundamental principle of rewarding labour over unproductive capital.

He slunk towards the three-fam, positioning himself against the back of the house, out of view of anyone who might happen to look down from an upstairs window.

"Godzilla! C'm'ere!" he hissed at a topless young man with a bad farmer's tan who was in the process of wetting his faded T-shirt under the hose tap on the side of the house.

"Maloney? What the fuck—"

"Shhh! Shut up the head on you and c'mere, would you ever?"

The young man wrung his T-shirt over his scorched blond head and used it to mop the remaining asbestos dust from his face and shoulders.

"Didn't I tell you before not to call me that," he muttered, when the two of them stood face to face.

The young man's name was John Mulvihill. He had been one of the last construction crew Fergus had worked with before being sacked, the very day they had started on the house in Elizabeth. Mulvihill was stocky and a tad slow. The nickname Godzilla had been haunting him for ages now, ever since Fergus had dubbed him with it after he'd been observed on a building site stomping on the plywood of some old shelving units, like a monster crushing miniature skyscrapers.

"What you are doing here, anyway?" said Mulvihill. "Didn't Lar tell you to feck off and never come back onto his site?"

Larry Fuckin' Cullen, as Fergus inevitably called him, was the foreman of this particular construction crew. He was the man who had personally sacked Maloney, after describing the Corkman as "a lazy, worthless fucker, with a shovel full of quick-dry cement stuck up his arsehole". Cullen was a prick of the highest order as far as Fergus was concerned. He was, in Fergus's own words, "that rare breed of Cavan cunt, who wouldn't spare a brass farthing for his own grandmother's funeral".

In response to Mulvihill's question, Fergus Maloney put his hand to his heart and sang solemnly "*The working class / can kiss my ass / I got Lar Cullen's job at last!*"

"Right well, if the *céilí*'s over," Mulvihill said, in a tone that was meant to be dismissive, but somehow didn't fully hide his amusement, "some of us still have work to be gettin' on with—"

"Wait, listen, Godzill— I mean, John, I have something for you. A gift."

John paused and eyed Fergus skeptically. "What?"

"Duignan's Bar. Lower East Side. Do you know where it is?"

"Vaguely. Why?"

"They're lookin' for a new barman. I found out last night. I said I knew just the man. Said he worked like a *monster*. The owner's name is Barry. He said call in to him quick if you were interested. Pays seven dollars an hour. *Plus* tips. I'd go over tonight, if I were you. A sweeter little number than that you won't find this side of Rodeo Drive."

"If it's such a sweet little number why don't you do it yourself?"

Fergus screwed up his face into a pained expression. "I *would*. If I lacked any self-respect and I was willing to bend over and allow the capitalist system to fuck me hard up the arse, that is exactly—and I mean, exactly—the brand of sodomy I would subscribe to. But, you see, I believe in *Destiny*. The Fates speak to me, Godzilla. And they tell me 'Fergus, you are not to be a barman. You are on a journey that will take you to Cuba, whence you will discover true love. This is the first waypoint on your journey, Fergus.' And that's the other reason I'm here—" Fergus pointed down towards the side of the house.

John 'Godzilla' Mulvihill followed the direction of Fergus's finger and found himself looking at the storm door leading into the basement.

"I need you to go in through the front and down around and unlock that door from the inside," Fergus explained.

John considered the basement door as if he were seeing it for the first time. "Why?"

"Because I can't do it myself and I need to get into that basement. It's locked and if I walk around the front, Lar Fuckin' Cullen will see me. Isn't that much obvious?"

"But why do you need to get into the basement of this particular house? There's nothin' in there but old shite."

"What you call 'old shite' is what I prefer to call 'Destiny.'"

John stared at him uncertainly, trying to make up his mind whether Maloney was taking the piss, or whether he'd finally gone completely bonkers.

Fergus put a hand on his shoulder. "I'll explain. Last night, just after Barry Duignan told me he had an opening for a new barman, I started chatting up an American girl at the bar. And then, you know, I had a few jars, and one thing led to another and next thing you know, I was reciting poetry and staring her deep in the eyes and all that. And then the horny bugger in me took over."

"I can see where this is going."

"Yeah, well, fade to flames and all that. Anyways, I wake up in her bedroom the next morning. Wrapped up in girly sheets, and there she is, trailing kisses down the side of me arm, all lovey-dovey. Barely knew where I was, for starters. A knowing smile appears on her face. 'I'm not letting you go until you remember my name,' says she. But try as I might, I could not remember her fuckin' name. And I'm thinkin', *fuck*, they hate it when you forget their names!"

"Jennifer," John offered helpfully. "Half of them are named Jennifer. Gives you a fifty-fifty chance."

"Well, I was hoping to escape without having to guess at all. I mean, I'd made it as far as her kitchenette, Pop Tart in one hand, downing the rest of me orange juice, and I was just about to make my escape when she blocks the door. "

"Oooh, that's bad."

"You don't know the half of it. The next thing her eyes fill with tears, like, and she says 'So I guess that means you weren't planning to call me back. So much for taking me to visit the William Butler Yeats grave.'"

John winced at this. "You mean you promised to take her to Ireland?"

"Well, like, in my defence, I was drunk. Anyway, the next bit is the important part of the story. Because at that very moment—"

Fergus's blue eyes flashed with intensity and his voice dropped. Instinctively, John drew nearer.

"—at that moment something really *special* happened. I took her hand, just to calm her down a bit. But when I ran my fingers over her palm I had this ... this *vision*."

"Vision?"

"Yeah, it's a thing a get. A feeling inside me, like. A tingling that runs through me body. I've had it all me life. I can't explain it. Sometimes it's just sensations. Sometimes it's conveyed through the presence of familiars."

"Familiars?"

"Animals that serve the spirit world. And this time, in the girl's flat, it was like a voice calling out inside my head."

John frowned and scoffed, but he was clearly still curious. "What did it say?"

"It said '*Elizabeth*' and '*basement*'. And I knew that was the voice of Destiny calling me. So I said it to yer one. 'Your name is Elizabeth, isn't it?'"

"And was it?"

"The fuck it was! Caitlin or Maureen or some shite like that. Irish-American. She called me an asshole and threw me out."

"Jesus, Fergus, so much for your destiny. What a rubbish story."

"No, wait! The point is Destiny spoke to me; it said the words '*Elizabeth*' and '*basement*' to me. At first I thought Elizabeth was a ride—a girl, like. I mean, I could be forgiven for jumping to that conclusion. But you have to be able to read the signs. That's when I remembered the conversation with Barry Duignan and how I'd thought right away of Godzilla and where was he working now? And I remembered you were out here in *Elizabeth*, New Jersey. And that's when it came to me. You see, you were meant to get the job in Duignan's. And there's something in that fuckin' basement which I'm meant to get too. It's all part of the plan."

"This isn't your way of going back to that voodoo, fortune-telling shite again, is it? You remember how well that worked out for you last time around?"

"It's not shite. Or else, it sometimes is. But sometimes it's real."

John stared at him and shook his head. "Fergus, you're the loopiest fucker I've ever met, do you know that?"

"Well, be that as it may, will you open up the basement door for me or not?"

"I will in my eye!"

"Now listen. I gave you a tip for a good-paying job. At least do me this much. Go to Duignan's and see is there a job there, after all. If there is, you'll owe me one, whether I'm loopy or not. I'll come back tomorrow and if Barry's given you the job, you'll let me in then. Is that a deal?"

John eyed him suspiciously. "On one condition."

"What?"

"Never call me Godzilla again. Do ya hear me?"

When Fergus returned to the site in New Jersey the next day, he did so entirely unnoticed. Under cover of the roar of a jet engine overhead, he hopped over the chain-link fence, kicked his way past the trash cans and across the weed-strewn backyard. He pulled open the creaky storm door that led into the basement. Everything was unlocked. Godzilla had been as good as his word.

Downstairs was cool. As his eyes adjusted to the darkness, Fergus espied a treasure trove of junk. Every conceivable bit of rubbish the former owners had ever possessed had been heaved down there, presumably awaiting collection or disposal at some later point. Old brass lamps were piled on boxes of magazines next to a disassembled swing set and worn truck tyres. Fergus counted at least five washing machines. Idly, Fergus ran his hand along the sides of a stack of cardboard boxes piled three high.

And stopped.

A tingle, ever so slight, had come to him. It was weak and he almost missed it altogether. But it was there and unmistakable. He returned to the spot he'd felt a moment ago. The top cardboard box. He tipped out its contents onto the concrete floor. Old worn paperbacks and out-of-date volumes of New Jersey statute spilled out under his feet. A silverfish darted out and ran between his shoes. *That's it.*

The insect was the smallest familiar the Fates had ever sent him. But it was nonetheless clear for all that. Fergus followed its path with his eyes as it scurried across the basement, behind an old bicycle and underneath a—

Fergus found himself smiling wildly. What he saw was an object, about four feet off the ground, made of cast iron, with two adjustable cooling racks and a hinged iron door. On the back, a gas bottle could be attached. And crucially, it was mounted on a wheelie frame, making it fully portable. A bit rusty, yes, and the rubber feed-hose from the gas bottle would need to be replaced. But the vision was there, and already it was becoming the shiny future he had been searching for. A coarse file, some paint and a lot of elbow grease was all it would take.

There was no mistaking it! This was what Destiny had called him to retrieve from the basement in Elizabeth, New Jersey. This is why he had scored the Irish-American girl from Duignan's bar. This was why he had copped a job as barman for Roscommon Godzilla. He grabbed the portable oven and pulled it back over to the storm door. Fergus had just found himself a new profession.

He had been called upon to bake bread.

2

Maria Da Silva stood at the hall mirror in her apartment and brushed her shoulder-length, black hair. Her hair was down and cut with razor-sharp precision in gradated layers towards the back. The silk blouse she wore had been chosen to contrast with her red-patterned skirt; the make-up applied to her high Latin cheekbones just enough to accentuate her olive complexion; the red lipstick a studied shade of sexy; the high heels that awaited her at the door the right height and style to impress.

To anyone else, it was a killer look which projected power—yes, even sexual power—over her all-male corporate audience. Yet that was not what Maria saw when she looked in the mirror. What she always saw—no matter how good the make-up—was a 13-year-old girl with braces and acne, insecure and hungry for approval. It was the girl who had, once upon a time, sat on her own in the corner of the lunchroom in Talbot Middle School. A girl without a father, whose half-brother hated her and whose mother never understood her. The same girl that had followed Maria into the front row of every lecture hall in UMass Boston and from there right into Harvard Law School. A girl who, no matter how many A's she got, no matter how many scholarships, no matter how far she climbed the corporate ladder, was somehow *just not good enough*.

On the side table below the mirror was her briefcase containing the contracts, together with her latest presentation to the board of Peterson Investments. Maria resisted the temptation to take them out and review the contents one more time. Pointless. She knew it all by heart. The contents of that briefcase were, after all, her bread and butter. Her grasp of mergers and acquisitions law had made her the top candidate for a senior partnership at the corporate law firm of Rosenthal, Roberts & Sleete. That was the part of her job she mastered effortlessly.

As she applied her red lipstick with robotic perfection, Maria's focus now was on that part of her job she always had to work at. The banter. The studied small talk. The casual smiles. And, yes, the flirtation. All of the stuff that required inner confidence. The secret ability of professional seduction which her mentor and boss, Seth Rosenthal, had summed up in a phrase, "*Intelligence is knowing that your client's silver wedding anniversary is next Wednesday. Wisdom is knowing not to remind him he's married.*" It was this kind of wisdom that Maria struggled with. And it was this that seemed to come so naturally to everyone else. For instance her boyfriend Jeff. His grasp of technical details was inferior to hers. But that somehow never seemed to matter. He was the one in the limelight. The one the clients talked about. With a sigh, Maria took a final look at the 13-year-old girl in the mirror and put on a bit more make-up.

By the time she had finished getting ready, the desk clock displayed 7:20 a.m. It was time to get going. At the front door of the brownstone row house in which her Brooklyn Heights apartment was situated, she paused for a final check to ensure she hadn't forgotten anything, then strapped on her heels. There would be no time to get to the office, so all her material, including the draft contracts, had to be taken directly to the client.

Outside, the torpid air swamped her. These were the dog days of late summer, when every professional New Yorker fought to stay sweat-free, while at the same time keeping pace with a city that never paused to catch its breath. Halfway down Hicks Street, Maria glanced at her watch and sped up. As a rule, she hated walking in anything other than sneakers and almost always took her heels to work in a plastic bag. God had given her strong mental faculties, but weak ankles. There was a particular coffee hut near her office at which she would stop and change out of her sneakers so that her appearance in the office would never be compromised by this slight flaw in her biology.

No time for that today. Today, she was going straight to the client. And therefore, as she strode briskly towards the subway, she made a mental note to watch the cracks in the sidewalk. *It would be just like me to twist my ankle on the way into the most important meeting of my career*, she thought.

As she turned the corner onto Clark Street, a delicious aroma assaulted her senses and made her remember she'd skipped breakfast once again. Was there time to stop at the bagel bar on the next block? Depended on the how long the line was, which depended on—

Before that thought had been fully formed, a voice called after her, "Beautiful woman in the red-and-cream skirt and tasteful pin-striped blouse! Stop this instant!"

Maria turned in alarm and saw a man, wearing an apron, waving at her frantically with an '*I love Canada*' oven glove. Maria decided he was probably insane, and resumed her path towards the subway.

"Wait!" The voice called again, this time from right behind her. She turned again to find the oven-glove man sprinting after her. It was a public street and lots of people were around, so no immediate danger. She was about to tell him to bug off, when he said, "You can't go to such an important meeting on an empty stomach."

"What?"

"I said you need breakfast. To calm the nerves, like, for your big meeting. I sell bread rolls. Two for three dollars. And a complimentary palm-reading is included."

"I haven't got ti— Wait, how did you know I had a big meeting?"

The man smiled. He had a winning smile that made his whole face come alive. The eyes smiled, the cheeks smiled. Even his chin smiled. It was the sort of unreserved joy you see in small children. Maria indulged in a brief scrutiny of his features. He was handsome and tall, with a strong, wiry frame that moved with easy grace. His pale skin, scorched in places by the sun, was the perfect contrast to the shock of black, shoulder-length, curly, hair. And those smiling eyes flashed a brilliant blue.

"Psychic powers," he said in answer to her question. "Didn't I just tell you I do palm-readings? And you've buckets of time. Sure, it's only quarter to eight."

Only then did Maria realize the man spoke with a brogue. She wasn't one to fall for accents, but there was something soothing in how the words danced off his tongue. Almost like he was singing.

"Gwan an' have a roll. You can eat it on the subway." He turned and pointed back to the corner, where she now noticed a pot-bellied stove on wheels and a sandwich board on which he'd written *'Organic bread rolls and free fortune telling $3.00—'* So this was where the delicious smell had come from.

Maria found herself following the street vendor back to the corner. Normally she never bought food off the street, but, on reflection, this would be quicker and easier than standing in line at the bagel bar. And he was right, she did need something to calm her nerves. She watched him as he deftly packed the bread rolls into a paper bag and made change for her five-dollar bill out of a fanny bag which doubled as a tie for his flour-stained apron.

"Thanks," she said. "Um, don't you have any condiments?"

He frowned. "What'd ya mean?"

"I don't know, like, butter or jelly or cream cheese?"

"I sell good bread. Wholemeal organic. Bread like mine doesn't need any crap on it to be enjoyed." The smile returned to his face. "Now for your palm-reading."

"I'll take a rain check on that."

His features fell as quickly as his smile had risen.

"But it's free."

"OK, but you already profiled me. You know, with the 'big meeting' thing."

"That wasn't psychic power at all. It was pure deduction. I've been here three mornings in a row and you haven't even glanced at me, but I noticed you. And every morning you leave at 7:25 a.m. and you wear white runners—*sneakers*—and white socks. You have a Macy's carrier bag with your high heels in it. Only this morning, you're wearing the heels and instead of the Macy's bag you have an extra briefcase. Because you're not going to the office. You're going straight to a meeting. Also you're walking faster than usual. And you look nervous. So all's I did was put two and two and two together. Six. Elementary, my dear Watson."

Maria eyed him suspiciously. Was he some kind of stalker? Her instincts said no. Still, there were so many crazies out there you couldn't be too careful.

"Thanks for the bread," she said, and turned to leave.

"Good luck with the meeting!" she heard him call, as she merged into the swarm of pedestrian traffic that ran towards the subway.

Maria and Jeff sat just outside the sweep of the giant oscillating fan in the sweltering heat of an open-air rooftop restaurant in the Lower East Side. Jeff had opened the knot of his tie and the top button of his tailored shirt revealing a triangle of bare, hairless chest which glistened with a sheen of sweat. A single bead escaped his preppy bangs and ran down his angular forehead. Jeff Laurence didn't do well in the hot weather, as he always told Maria. *Your people are genetically made for this kind of heat. My people hail from a freezing cold Norman keep in Northern England.*

"So, how'd it go with old Peterson?" Jeff asked from behind his menu.

Maria looked up from her own menu and caught Jeff's grey eyes, which immediately darted away and back to the list of food. It was the question she had been expecting him to ask, but there was something in his tone that made her feel like he was mocking her. She decided to ignore it.

"Pretty good, actually. I mean, I was totally panicking at first, especially when it came to contract negotiation. I was dreading the moment when Peterson would turn to the other board members and be, like, 'We're going to have to speak to someone in the firm more senior about this.' But he didn't. They really seemed to accept that I was the go-to person for the firm. That felt good, you know. It was a real vote of confidence in me."

"So did he sign the contract?"

"No ... not yet. But he said they'd get back to me soon."

"What he means," Jeff's lips curled into a smile, "is that he'll get back to Rosenthal. It's not like Peterson doesn't talk to Rosenthal in the Harvard Club every Tuesday night."

Maria dropped her menu and stared at him. "What's that supposed to mean? The men do the real deals after hours in the club and I'm just there with my PowerPoint as ... what? Eye-candy? Is that what you're implying?"

Jeff sighed and looked up. "No, honey, of course not. I know you're good. And so does Peterson, I don't doubt it. But you know how these old-timers are. They've built long-term relationships going back ... forty years. You can't just come in and expect to wow them with a presentation and undo their whole network. That's not how things work." The waiter was buzzing at Jeff's shoulder now. "Um, we're gonna need another minute."

Maria thought about that invisible network of old men in law firms, stock brokerages, industry boardrooms. Men who had gone to Harvard together. Played golf together. It was the last place in America where a handshake was still better than a written contract. Jeff was right, of course. No matter how good her presentations were, what mattered to Peterson was the fact that he could still pull Rosenthal into a quiet corner of the Harvard Club and secure that handshake when it really mattered. She had gone to Harvard Law School too. But hers was the class of '96. Another generation. And she was from Fall River, Massachusetts, the daughter of a working-class, single mother. Though she had grown up closer to Harvard's campus geographically, socially she could hardly have been further away. And she was a woman. Nobody could convince Maria that that wasn't still a barrier to success at the top.

But in another sense, maybe that's what gave her the drive to succeed. Maybe it was the very challenge that impelled her to do the things she knew deep down Jeff was incapable of doing. After all, the easy, comfortable way in which Jeff had approached his career had a lot to do with his own male, WASP background. He'd grown up playing ball in the halls of privilege. As she often reflected, he had no clue how much she had sacrificed and fought to make it even as far as she had come already. It's easy to forget about glass ceilings when you're already standing on top of them enjoying the view.

Maria looked up and saw Jeff smiling across the table at her.

"I'm proud of you, honey," he told her. In that instant, a feeling of shame struck her for the thoughts she'd just been having: for wanting to outdo him, to beat him, yes, even to humiliate him.

The waiter was back again to take the order before Maria even realized how far past the menu she'd been staring. He tapped his pen impatiently on the side of his order pad. It was lunch hour in Manhattan. Table space was a premium. Even outdoor tables in 90-degrees heat.

"I'll have the ricotta and spinach rigatoni," she said.

In the background, Jeff was busy explaining in meticulous detail how he wanted his steak cooked. Absently, Maria picked at the bread roll on her starter plate. It was doughy and left a bitter taste of raising agent in her mouth: inferior bread to the rolls she'd had that morning on the subway train. She found herself thinking about the Irish baker, with his little portable oven, his flour-stained apron and the childishly-rendered script on his sandwich board.

Maria glanced down at her pin-striped blouse and thought, yes, it was quite tasteful.

Seth Rosenthal, the guru of corporate law in New York City and Maria's big boss, had never before come into Maria's office. Not once. And so her assistant Barbara must have been caught completely off guard when, that very afternoon, the man himself appeared at her desk. He entered Maria's office with an air of quiet authority and a generous smile. He extended his broad, perfectly manicured hand with the oversized gold ring. Maria shook it without hesitation.

"I just got a call from Rudolf Peterson," he said. "Looks like you nailed it. I have to say I am really impressed. Ball & Wentworth pulled out all the stops to beat us on this one, even flying Peterson to their golf course in Scotland by private jet. But we won it. And we won it on quality."

"Thanks, Seth."

Every part of Maria's body filled with a warm glow. She could almost have cried when he added, "I should say, *you* won it on quality, Maria."

"Well, it's not in the bag yet," she muttered. "They still haven't signed."

Seth laughed indulgently. "And that's exactly the kind of thing I would expect someone with your thoroughness and attention to detail to point out. Anyway, I got to go. I just stopped by to give you my personal thanks."

He paused again at the door and turned back. "You know, when I first interviewed you for the internship, I saw in you someone with immense talent. But I also saw that you needed direction. I flatter myself in believing I have given you that direction. From here, Maria, the sky's the limit for you. Really."

When he left, she had to go into the bathroom to compose herself, wipe away the tears of joy and freshen up her make-up.

She even whispered to the girl in the mirror: *I am good enough.*

3

"**Get your fresh bread rolls and a free palm-reading.** Psychic powers and nutritious organic whole-grains. Just what your morning needs. You, sir! Have you had your fortune told recently? Ma'am, do you want excellent bread and a glimpse into the future? Only three dollars."

A steady stream of New Yorkers pushed past, their eyes all fixed on the subway station one block ahead. It was as if Fergus didn't exist. Still the Corkman carried on with his antics, gesticulating himself into a parody of a sales pitch, more for his own amusement than in any hope of attracting custom.

Even at seven in the morning, convections of heat rose in waves through the smog-filled air. And not just from Fergus's oven, but from the very pavement on which he plied his sweaty trade. It was going to be another long, hot morning.

In fact, if Fergus were being honest with himself, which he rarely was, he would have admitted that the only reason he persisted with the Hicks-Clark Street junction was because of the olive-skinned girl with the Macy's bag, and some strange idea he'd managed to work into his head that she was somehow related to the whole "Elizabeth-in-the-Basement-Destiny" thing. He had to know: was she the Elizabeth of which the voice of Destiny had spoken? If not, well, he could let her go and set up shop in a more profitable locality. But first, he'd have to find out, even if that meant another morning or so of crap sales. So far today he'd sold six bread rolls out of two batches of twenty. And the third batch was nearly baked.

Scratch that. Overbaked. *Burned to shite, in fact.* All twenty of them. He slammed the oven door closed, knocking several rolls to the ground. As he turned to pick them up, his gaze fell on a pair of white socks in white trainers, out of which rose a couple of shapely legs in black tights. His eyes followed upwards, admiring the curves that undulated under a tight-fitting, sleeveless, blue dress. It was the woman with the Macy's bag. She wore her straight, black hair down again today and the aggressive red lipstick had been replaced by a milder pink. Her light-cocoa skin was youthful, even if she carried herself with a mature, almost stern, air. She was about thirty, he thought, though over or under, he couldn't quite say.

"Hi," Fergus greeted her with his best grin. *Big brown eyes*, he noted as he stared into them. He liked girls with big brown eyes. So much so, that the music—Van Morrison's 'Brown-Eyed Girl'—kicked off in his head.

"Hi," she answered, also with a smile. "So ... are you gonna stare at me or can I buy some bread?"

"Uh, yeah, o' course. But not these ones. They're a bit wrecked, I'm afraid. Here, these ones are still warm in the middle."

As she tendered the three dollars, Fergus made a point of overreaching and touching her hand. The contact lasted at best a fraction of a second. It was the sort of innocent touch you might have with a shop assistant or a colleague ten times a day and never notice. Yet for Fergus, it was a carefully orchestrated contact, on which he focused the whole of his attention. He needed to know if the tingling he felt was a genuine psychic revelation or just raw sexual attraction. Because she was hot, like. There were moments when the whole psychic thing seemed like a hoax, even to himself. Passion and confusion ripped through him in equal measure. He needed to know.

"The rolls you sold me on Friday were really good," the woman said. The pink lipstick danced a friendly smile.

"'Course they were. I wouldn't have sold them to you if they weren't. Now for your palm-reading."

He reached for her right hand, but she deftly dodged him.

"Maybe not."

"Why not?"

"Well, first of all, I don't believe in that stuff ..."

"Well, if you don't believe in it, sure then you've nothin' got to lose. Gwan an' give it a go."

"... and second of all, I have a boyfriend."

Fergus laughed. "Oh, is that right?"

"Yes," she said, with a frown. "That's right."

"He keeps you on a tight lead, that fella' does!"

She frowned harder. "He doesn't keep me on any 'lead'. It's a question of trust and mutual respect. He trusts me. And in return, I don't flirt with guys on the street."

"Oh, and you're very right not to flirt with guys on the street. I suggest we take our flirting to an indoor venue. Half-eight tonight at *Darcy Toners*?"

Despite herself, she laughed at this. "I have to go to work."

"What kind of work do you do?"

"The kind that's absolutely none of your business."

"So you're a lawyer?" Fergus grinned. The slight flutter in her eyes and parting of the lower lip told him he'd guessed right, and Van the Man sha-la-la'd and la-dee-dah'd in his head.

"See how good my psychic skills are? And that's just a taster. You should experience the full power of my clairvoyance. C'mon, I owe you a free palm-reading!"

"Sorry, I'm out of time. Maybe tomorrow."

"Wait, what's your name?"

She turned back to look at him over her shoulder. "You're the fortune teller. You tell me."

"Elizabeth?"

"Wrong," she said, with a carefree smile. She waved the bag of bread rolls one last time over her shoulder, before disappearing into the throng of commuters pushing their way into the subway station. He wanted to shout, "*Have a nice weekend!*" but it was too late.

Fergus stared after the girl whose name was not, after all, Elizabeth. He stared for quite some time, until the heat of the newly-risen sun baked the music out of his brain.

Once the morning rush to the subway was over, Fergus betook himself to the Promenade, where tourists and other people of leisure strolled along the waterfront of the East River, admiring the Manhattan skyline across the water, and, to their right, the view of the Brooklyn Bridge which connected the two boroughs. The sun had now risen high behind them, reflected in the glass of the skyscrapers Downtown. The surface of the river sparkled and danced in the breeze. This was what Fergus loved about New York. It had its own special kind of beauty.

Away from the tightly-packed streets of Brooklyn, the air felt less oppressive, and although it was hot, sales of bread rolls and clairvoyance were much better on the Promenade. The brunch set also had more time to idle and be amused by the Irishman's antics. When a brief lull came, he found himself reflecting on the girl with the Macy's bag. He'd completely abandoned his resolve to give up on her if her name weren't Elizabeth. Now the opposite had become true. The fact that her name was *not* Elizabeth only confirmed his belief that she was linked to his destiny. In a twist of logic all his own, Fergus interpreted this to mean that Destiny was attaching particular importance to her. The reasoning went like this: if the Macy's bag girl had turned out to be an Elizabeth, it would have meant Destiny considered her too obvious, and, hence, just another ride. But the fact that she *wasn't* Elizabeth meant that she was somehow significant. Destiny was making him work harder to figure out the link. Which proved how important she was.

The creeping desire for a drink, that uncomfortable thirst which nothing but a few pints could quench, hit him at around lunchtime. It manifested itself physically, in a sort of tightness that began in his thighs and stomach, then worked its way up into his chest and as far as his clenched jaw, then finally into his frowning face. He still had enough flour for two more batches, but the pouch with the dollar bills was stuffed full, and the thirst was on him and too great for him to resist any longer. As well as which, the heat had become unbearable at this stage. It was time to hit the pub.

"Well? What's the craic?" John 'Roscommon Godzilla' Mulvihill asked as Fergus wheeled the bread oven into Duignan's and placed it in the corner, out of the way of the crowd that would soon start gathering. For the time being, the place was empty, with bar stools upside down on the tables and the counter clear of any glasses. This wasn't one of those Irish pubs that had gone all 'gastro' and set out shitty little sets of cutlery on napkins and bottles of Heinz ketchup for lunch. That's what Fergus liked best about Duignan's. It specialised in the one thing Fergus felt bars were meant to serve: booze, and lots of it.

"Parched," he said in answer to Godzilla's question. "Give us a pint of whatever pours quickest."

"You're in early. Not many sales today?"

"*Au contraire*, ye of little faith! I've enough greenbacks tucked away to stay in here the rest of the afternoon and all night."

"Sounds like a wise investment of your profits."

"No sounder investment this side of Wall Street."

"Wall Street's only down the road."

Fergus answered by taking a long, hard swig from the Sam Adams that had appeared in front of him. He could feel the tension in his body being massaged away, as the alcohol seeped through every vein. It loosened his tongue and he began to chat with a couple of middle-aged tourists who'd come in asking for directions.

When he found out they were from Germany, he began telling them a humorous story about a German U-boat lieutenant in West Cork who was part of a secret IRA submarine refuelling operation during the Second World War. According to Fergus's version of events, the German fell in love with a local farmer's daughter, and stayed ashore far longer than was good for him. His U-boat left without him, and he ended up on the lam from both the shotgun-wielding farmer and a British secret service agent who had been tasked with uncovering the IRA operation. In the end, he craftily stole both the farmer's daughter and the British spy's sailboat, sailed with her across the Atlantic to Cuba, where he opened up a successful casino in Havana and eventually ended up becoming a leading figure in the communist revolution.

Only after finishing a second pint and clapping the bemused Germans on the back did he admit—with a mischievous twinkle in his blue eyes—that he'd made the whole thing up on the spot. They left without knowing what to make of him.

"What's with you and fuckin' Cuba, Maloney?" Godzilla asked. "You're always on about it."

"It's the place, man, I'm tellin' ya. Beautiful senoritas, big mad cigars, crystal white beaches. Mark my words, once I get meself sorted out here, I'm gonna go to Cuba."

"You are in your shite!"

"Give us another one, there, Godzilla, would you?" Fergus shook his empty glass at John, still laughing inside at his tale about the German submarine officer in Cuba.

Roscommon Godzilla gave him a cross look and was about to say something sharp when another thought altogether seemed to strike him. "Oh, here, I nearly forgot. I went down to the site this morning to pick up my final week's pay and Lar Cullen gave me this to give to you. He said to tell you this was the last time and that he wasn't your personal postal service." He handed Fergus a letter which had been tucked under the cash register.

"What the fuck does that gobshite want n—"

Fergus broke off speaking when he saw the handwriting on the envelope. The shiver came to him again, and with it the harsh voice of a crow calling out to him. It recalled an image of a dark, blood-filled stank and it seemed to him that the edges of the letter turned wet with blood, corrosive, spreading towards his fingers. He quietly slipped it into his back pocket, avoiding Godzilla's inquisitive gaze. Yet even from there, he could feel the letter's power. He looked out the window to see if the crow was there, or a rat, or some other dark familiar, watching him.

"What is it?" the barman asked.

"Nothing. At any rate, none of your fuckin' business."

John seemed to know better than to pursue the point and left well enough alone.

Fergus set to his next pint at the same fast pace. But the pleasure was gone out of the booze. Only its power of intoxication mattered to him now: its power to fight back the tension which was gripping his body, building inside him like a cascade of urgent whispers that rose ever louder into a shout.

The letter was from his sister, Clodagh. Without opening it, he knew from his body's reactions what it would contain. Detailed information about their mother. Reproaches to him for not being a better son. A homily about how hard she, Clodagh, was working to put things right. How she'd kept the family together. And then she'd tell him things about Mam's health. Things designed to make him feel guilty.

Well, she could fuck off, could Clodagh. He drank the pint hard, forcing the bitter liquid down his gullet as an act of defiance against his own body, and of the trials that body had endured. What did Clodagh know about it? She'd escaped the worst of things; went off to Dublin where she could sit in judgment from the lofty heights of her middle-class semi-detached perch.

The pub was beginning to fill up slowly, as the Friday after-work crowd began to arrive, but Fergus remained hunched in his corner at the bar, his head stooped low towards the pint, thinking black thoughts. How he'd like nothing better than to fuck the letter in the bin and be done with it, but knowing that, once back on his mattress in Harlem that night, he'd end up opening it and reading it.

And he'd cry like a baby.

4

Nearly a whole week went past before Fergus went back to the spot in Brooklyn Heights to try once again to make some kind of connection with the Macy's bag girl. The week was spent doing odd jobs for his flatmate, Karim Saunders, who, although he was a Muslim, spent a lot of time volunteering with the local Christians at the Mount Zion Baptist Church. The work kept Fergus busy enough that he forgot all about the girl whose name was not Elizabeth. But it all came to a head as the Thursday night session ended in the Purple Shamrock, and the lads were packing up their instruments. Voices, small whispers, began to call to him. Fergus downed the last of his eighth pint and let the buzz of it ride with him on the subway. Destiny wasn't letting go, wasn't letting him have any peace, not until he'd copped the score on this girl. Was she just meant to be another ride or else ... Or else what? Did he have the *grá* for her?

Fucked if I know, he thought, then fell onto his mattress, and into immediate drunken slumber.

On the Friday morning, despite the eight pints, he woke up with hardly a head on him. The tattered sheet he'd put over his window as a makeshift curtain was set aglow by the breaking day, its moth holes sparkling like stars. He drew the sheet aside and looked out at the buildings across Broadway. Their red-brick façades, with the black iron fire escapes, were still in shadow, but at their edge, the newly-risen sun streamed along 163rd Street and directly into his eyes, its rays almost horizontal at this early hour. Overhead, shifting clouds moved in a pleasant breeze. It was a turn in the weather, suggesting summer might finally be on the retreat. Better weather for selling bread, Fergus decided. The dog days were disastrous on the appetite. All people seemed to want was iced coffee.

Heaving a sack of flour over one shoulder, he went into the kitchen to fill his gallon jugs with water for the first few batches of the morning. He whistled a Christmas carol as the water hissed into the plastic bottles. The electric cooker was almost completely broken, but one ring and the digital clock still worked. It was 6:35 a.m. No time to pinch a cup of Karim's instant coffee, he'd have to rush if he was going to get to Brooklyn in time for the girl with the Macy's bag. And so he hitched the water and the flour to his oven, tied the sandwich board around his neck and began to haul the whole bread-making jalopy down toward the 163rd Street subway station.

On the train, Fergus was still whistling the Christmas carol, which for some reason was stuck in his head. A fat lady, dressed in her security-guard uniform, sat across from him. She gave him a sour look, to which Fergus's smiling reply was, "Good King Wenceslas".

"I know what it is," she answered bitterly. "But it ain't Christmas, 'cos it ain't even October yet. Hell, it's still summer! Don't be singin' y'all crazy songs in mah face, th' wrong time a' year."

"Well, you see," Fergus explained. "I'm from Ireland. Which is five time zones away. Therefore, we celebrate Christmas early, usually in September; August, if it's a leap year."

She did not dignify this nonsense with a response, but instead curled her lower lip further and continued her angry stare. There would be no convincing her to join the festive cheer.

Why that particular song? He hadn't a clue. Maybe the change in weather had suggested the image of the saintly king's snowy march with his page to bring flesh and wine to the poor man by St Agnes' Fountain. Maybe it was the expectation of seeing the Macy's Bag girl again. In the confusion of his mind, nothing was clear and linear. Associations were forever a jumbled mess.

It was 7:23 a.m. before Fergus had put the first batch of bread rolls into the oven. The Macy's bag girl arrived exactly on time at 7:25 a.m. and her gaze fell on the empty airing racks where the bread rolls should have been.

"You're back."

Fergus grinned. "Did ya miss me?"

"I missed your bread. Yet I see you don't have any today."

"I sold out already," he explained. "But not to worry, there's another batch just gone in. Give it two minutes."

"You did not sell out, you liar. You just showed up late."

"How do you know that?"

"Firstly, you never sold out before. Secondly, the racks don't have any flour on them, 'cos they haven't been used today. Thirdly, and most incriminatingly, your fanny bag where you stuff your grubby dollar bills is open and I can see that it's empty."

Fergus grinned and threw up his hands. "Oh, you're a top rate lawyer, you are. Must be why they pay you the big bucks."

She laughed. "Why? Because I'm observant?"

"So now, Miss Eagle-Eyed-Legal-Eagle, while we wait for the bread to finish, I'm ready to use my psychic powers to guess your name."

A strand of her jet black hair came loose and caught a draught, as if from a breeze that broke through the still humid air, a wisp of autumn. It wavered in the wind, captivating his attention. Somehow, the smell of the sea filled his nostrils, causing a tingle through his body.

"Go ahead."

"I need your palm."

"No you don't. You're just flirting."

"I'm not! And even if I was, would that be a crime, Miss Legal Eagle?"

"I already told you I had a boyfriend."

"Ach, where I'm from a little bit of flirting is allowed."

"It's a question of--"

"'Trust and mutual respect', I know. You told me before. But listen, I promise this isn't a come-on. It's the best way to create a psychic channel between us. Honestly."

Fergus put on his best, most innocent face and waited for her resolve to melt. In the end she threw her eyes up to heaven and sighed. "Fine."

He took her hand and worked his thumb across the delicate flesh. She had finely sculpted hands, thin bones and very sensitive nerve endings. He could feel her fingers respond to his touch, all the while he held her gaze in a way that almost dared her to look away. But she did not.

The tingling grew more intense. Waves crashed on wet sand, and a crisp breeze split the clouds, spilling sun down upon their bare, salt-caked skin. A seagull sang out in the wind, and Fergus listened to its voice, echoing over and over in his brain. *I'll never leave you, Fergus.*

"That's enough," she told him. "So now, what's my name?"

Torn from his reverie, Fergus was drawing a blank. The strength of the vision had been so great he forgot all about her name. Her name?

"I don't know," he told her simply, and fought back the surge of emotion. The girl who was not Elizabeth smiled faintly and shook her head.

"So, is the bread ready yet?" And in fact it was. An aroma was wafting around them. Fergus pulled himself together, put on his red-and-white Maple Leaf oven glove and took the batch out. Browned to perfection.

"They'll be hot, now. Mind you don't burn your mouth."

"I'll be careful." She was offering him a five-dollar bill.

"Eh, I haven't got any change ..."

"Consider it a down payment for Monday."

"All right then."

She looked like she was about to say something, then stopped herself, turned to walk away, but then stopped again and turned back. "My name's Maria, by the way."

Fergus tried his best to answer, but for first time in many years, he was left speechless.

That weekend saw Fergus in rare form. He drank and partied and made merry on other people's money, and did what he could to forget all about the girl whose name was Maria and not Elizabeth. He certainly wasn't about to tell any of the lads about her when they met at Gaelic Park in the Bronx, where he played centre forward in a hurling match on the Sunday afternoon. And what a hurling match it was! Fergus took part with an energy that surprised and delighted his team. Seemingly immune to the oppressive heat, he danced the *sliotar* down the pitch, balanced perfectly on the flat ash *bos* of his hurley stick. Match over. Job done. Time to shower up and hit the beer.

It was all the usual banter as the lads filed out of the stadium and marched, their hurleys slung over their shoulders with the helmets dangling, as far as the overpass of the elevated railway line that ran above Broadway in the Bronx. Lifts back to New Jersey and to Brooklyn were being organised. Paddy Flynn from Fort Lee was climbing into the back of another lad's Chrysler Van who was heading as far as Harlem on the Major Deegan. He shouted for Fergus to hop in.

But the Corkman was no longer listening. He was in his own world, walking away, only vaguely aware of Paddy Flynn's voice calling after him. Soon it was lost behind the rush of New York traffic. In front of him was the gateway entrance to Van Cortlandt Park, and he couldn't have said for the life of him why he was drawn to enter it. But he did. And music played. And time passed, though he was clueless as to how much.

Fergus looked about and found himself in the middle of the park, on a path. To his left, through a veil of drooping, late summer foliage, he saw there was a baseball game going on. All around him, up and down, New Yorkers jogged, ran or roller-bladed past him, in that angry, anxious way they all had of spending their leisure time.

The trail continued through the park's woods. On the left there was now a lake, whose banks fell sharply away from the verge. In the death of the afternoon, the low sun caught the surface at an acute angle, transforming water into gold. Evening was coming on earlier and earlier now. As the oppressive heat of the day waned, the number of joggers increased to ridiculous proportions. On the right, through the trees, he could make out the sound of tennis balls echoing against racquets. An angry voice shrieked out a solitary "FUCK!"

The curse came from the tennis courts. Fergus looked over to his left but couldn't even see them from the path. He beat his way through the foliage towards the tennis sounds. Before the courts came into sight another screech had erupted. "BULLSHIT! GODDAMN!" Fergus pushed on through the bushes and came to the courts by the back of the fence.

It was a man's voice, though a bit on the squeaky side. Through the fence Fergus could see a player on one of the courts, dressed in immaculate tennis gear, making a holy show of himself by smashing his racquet against the net. He'd clearly just hit the ball into the net and lost a point. Fergus looked across at his partner and his jaw nearly dropped. It was *her*. Maria the Lawyer! Destiny was not letting go.

She had stopped play and let her racquet fall to her side, clearly disgusted at her partner's outburst. But before she could react, one of the two lads playing on the court next to them turned to Maria's partner and said, "Hey buddy. Why don't you cool off? It's just a game."

"Why don't you mind your own goddamn business?" came the retort, in that uncertain way of men who want to show themselves to be braver than they really are.

The other guy was bigger, more athletic looking and more confident. He took a step towards Maria's partner and said, "Do we have a problem, pal?"

"I don't know. You sure seem to."

Maria called across the court, "Jeff, forget it, ok? Let's just go."

"Maria, can you just...I *got* this, ok?"

"No you don't. You need to calm down."

The other guy turned to his own partner and they shared a chuckle, clearly enjoying Jeff's discomfort.

"Listen to your girlfriend, Jeff," the other guy said. "Go home and cool off."

Thus outnumbered, Jeff's face turned an unfortunate shade of crimson. He snatched up his racquet and stormed away, without even glancing at Maria.

"Where are you— ...Jeff, wait! I don't even have a ride."

That was Fergus's cue. He put on the helmet, tossed the hurley over the fence and scaled it, a demonstration of his own athleticism. When he dropped onto the court Maria turned and noticed him.

"You!"

Fergus grinned. "I was just in the neighbourhood." He pointed back to the left. "Gaelic Park. It's where we Paddies play our 'tennis.'"

Maria scowled. "Are you, like, stalking me?"

Fergus frowned. "No more than you're stalking me. It's Destiny who's after stalking the both of us."

"How did you...?"

"I never question Destiny. I just obey her call."

Maria mouth was still open.

"So that fella just gone, he was the boyfriend, was he?" Fergus asked.

"What? Yeah."

"Trust and mutual respect?" Fergus grinned.

Maria was about to reply and stopped herself. She shook her head and grabbed the sleeve of her tennis racquet. "You know what, this is...I gotta go."

"Wait!" Fergus exclaimed. "You can't just leave now. Destiny... I mean, will you not give us a game of tennis at least? I promise I won't lose the rag if you beat me." Grin.

Maria stopped. "What?"

"Tennis. We'll play a game of tennis. You and me."

"You don't even have a racket."

"Au contraire," he said, and held up his hurley.

"That's not a racket. That's a ... actually I don't know what that is."

"It's a hurling stick. G'won and serve, you'll see," he answered, positioning himself in the returner's stanch, a step in front of the baseline. "G'won!"

Both the lads in the next court had stopped to watch, with big smiles on their faces. Maria smiled too. She shrugged, took up a ball, stepped behind the baseline, bounced it twice, tossed and belted a spinning serve onto Fergus's forehand side. It was a sharp, well placed ball, and no doubt she fully expected an ace.

But Fergus was a skilled hurler. He caught the tennis ball at shoulder height and whipped it back over the net. Maria's backhand couldn't reach it. The two lads burst into applause.

"Love - Fifteen!" Fergus grinned. "See, you're in love with me already. G'won again. If I win the set you owe me a pint."

They played on like this for several more points, until Maria got the measure of his game and started to hammer him. She wasn't a bad player, it turned out. He joked at every opportunity, engaging in banter the two lads, who had finished their own game and were watching. As the lads waved goodbye, the ugly scene with Jeff was long forgotten.

"I really have to go," Maria told him.

"How are you getting home?"

"Taxi, I guess," she said. "You?"

"Well I missed my lift. On account of Destiny. And then I was gonna walk. But seein' as it's the best part of ten miles, and I was meant to be playin' Irish music tonight, and your cab would be goin' my way..."

Maria buried a smile and shook her head. "Wait. Just one thing. Are you really telling me this was a coincidence? You just *happened* to be in a park two boroughs away?"

"It's not a coincidence," Fergus insisted. "It's Destiny."

Her soft brown eyes stared at him hard, looking perhaps for a lie that wasn't there. "I don't even know your name."

"Fergus. Fergus Maloney. I live in Harlem."

"Ok, Fergus the Breadman. I'll drop you off in Harlem. But that's it, ok? It's a friendly gesture. So that we're clear."

"Ah, you're a star! I'll pay you in bread. That's three more rolls I owe you."

He spent most of the cab ride explaining the game of hurling to her. So impassioned was he about his sport, he forgot all about the job at hand, which was to flirt shamelessly. When the taxi stopped to let him off he hesitated, caught off guard by the sudden ending of their chat. She sat with her arms crossed, waiting for him to get out.

"Do you not want to .... I dunno ... come in for a glass of water?" The line felt so cheesy he was sure it would fail before he even finished speaking it. He asked the question with a nervousness that was completely foreign to him in the company of girls. Maybe this was what it meant to have the *grá* for someone.

"Thanks for tennis, Fergus. It was fun."

"Right, so. Well, I'll see you tomorrow for that bread I owe you, then?"

Before shutting the cab door, an impulse struck him and he leaned back in and told her, "You are good enough, Maria the Lawyer. You're good enough without having to be with a guy like that."

Night had fallen, and so inside the back of the cab it was too dark for to see her reaction, but Fergus thought he could feel the impact his words had on her, as the taxi pulled away and sped south along Broadway.

When she appeared in front of him the next morning, wearing a white dress with a navy belt, Fergus had ready her prepaid rolls and presented them with a broad grin and a Shakespearean flourish. She smiled and shook her head.

"Right, now you get your fortune," he said.

"You already tried that last week. And failed."

"Ah, you see, that doesn't count."

"No? Why not?"

"Because that wasn't a proper fortune. I was trying to guess your name. That's not the same thing as telling your fortune."

"OK, fine, but I'm not giving you my hand again."

Fergus sighed. "I don't know how Destiny expects me to work under these conditions, but all right, I'll give it a lash." He adopted an exaggerated meditative stance and held a hand above her silky black head of hair. He noted how she wore it up in a ponytail today, which showed off her elegant neckline to best effect. An understated piece of jewellery adorned her olive skin.

"The key to your future is ... the thing that will unlock your destiny and entwine it forever with my own is—

"With *your* own?!"

"Shh! I'm concentrating ..."

Through his half-closed eyes he could see she was grinning. Whatever about the battle of psychic wills, he was winning the war of sexual attraction.

"Is what?" she asked.

"... is *Elizabeth in the basement*!"

"Elizabeth in the basement?"

"That's right."

"What does that even mean?"

Fergus shook his head. "I'm not entirely sure." And he truly wasn't. It had come out of nowhere, as easy as if another voice had taken control of his own. Destiny's voice, for certain. But why? He had no idea. "All I can tell you is this: it is the key which will change your life forever."

"Really?"

"Yes. Because of Elizabeth in the basement, you will quit your high-powered legal-eagle job, cash in your pension fund, and eventually end up running away to New Zealand with a broke but loveable Irish street baker and make loads and loads of babies with him."

Fergus could tell she was trying to be offended, but in the end she let go of her tough-girl exterior and had a good oul' laugh.

"New Zealand?"

"Yeah," he said. "It's full of mountains and beaches. With islands of seal colonies and forests full of little kiwi birds. Great place to raise children." Her mock incredulity spurred him on. "We'll have a little white house down a lane, near the beach. With goats. And chickens. And a broken oul' wheelbarrow in the yard, which we can plant up to the rim with flowers, and the cat will sleep in it on sunny days."

"And I'm supposed to run away with you to there? As you know, I have a boyfriend. And even if I didn't ..." She shook her head, possibly out of embarrassment for what she was about to say.

"What?"

"Well, frankly you're just not ..."

"Not what?"

"Not in my league."

"Oh yeah? Which league is that?" he called after her. She was halfway towards the subway station by the time he thought of a reply to his own question.

The Ivy League.

5

Maria strapped on her blue-and-white Prada heels at 7:35 a.m. the next morning. It was a Tuesday, the morning of the "Deal" with Peterson Investments Inc.—the day when they had finally agreed to sign a contract for services with her law firm, Rosenthal, Roberts & Sleete. If ever there was a day to wear Prada, it was today. In theory, this was the biggest moment of her career so far: her first major haul for the firm which would lead to dozens of merger deals. Maria knew everything about Peterson Investments. She had studied her prospective client's annual accounts, the organigram, the stock movements, even the names of old Peterson's grandkids. This contract—this deal—was her baby. More than that, it was her ticket to becoming partner. Even more, it was her opportunity to prove to Seth Rosenthal, to Jeff and his family, and to herself, that she really was good enough. As she applied her reddest lipstick, she told the 13-year-old girl in the mirror that in a few hours' time she would be sliding the contract out of her briefcase and onto the table of Peterson Investments' boardroom. And old man Peterson was going to sign it.

Yet, oddly, as she glided out the apartment door, her thoughts were on Fergus, the Irish street baker who could hit tennis balls with a stick as if it was an actual racket, and the fact that she was about to buy his bread. He'd know from her lack of sneakers that she was going directly to a meeting, as he had done the first time they'd met. Would she let him read her palm today? She hadn't decided. If so, would he guess anything about the deal? Probably not. Part of what made him so charming was that he was a terrible fortune teller. Or was he? She recalled his final words to her as he exited the taxi and a chill passed through her. You are good enough, Maria. Yes you are.

It was only after leaving the apartment and walking a few paces that Maria realized she had forgotten her briefcase with the contract in it. She had left it on the hall floor beside the shoe rack. *How in God's name—?* That contract was the pinnacle of her entire life's ambitions thus far, and she had simply walked out of the house without it.

Annoyed with herself, she scurried back up the red sandstone steps of the building. She'd never done anything like that before. *What's wrong with me?* Was it just nerves? *No*, she realized with double annoyance. *It was the Irishman.*

"Fergus, I'm sorry, I'm kind of in a rush now," she found herself saying five minutes later, as she approached him and his little bread oven. She knew it was unfair to be annoyed at him, but she was anyway.

"What? No bread?" he exclaimed in indignation.

"No time."

"Ah, sure, you're always in a rush!"

"Welcome to my world." She glanced at his disappointed face. After their tennis 'date', he'd clearly been waiting for her to arrive all morning, and, like a little boy, he seemed unable to hide his emotions.

"But you said—"

"Tomorrow," she answered over her shoulder, in what she hoped was a more conciliatory tone.

"Wait, Maria!"

The suddenness of the command made Maria stop in her tracks. He hadn't exactly shouted at her, but there was an insistence in his voice, an authority that took her by surprise, and stirred something deep within her. Yet when he spoke again he was almost pleading with her.

"The first time we met you were too busy for bread. And I made you stop for some. And weren't you glad you did?"

"Yes," she admitted.

"Well, then. You'll be glad again."

Maria glanced at her watch: 7:43 a.m. It was only a fifteen-minute train ride to Park Place. The meeting was scheduled for 8:30 a.m. and Peterson was always five minutes late. Perhaps she had time, after all.

The Irish baker was already packing her rolls into a paper bag with his big, powerful hands. There was something gentle and shy about him, and the way he moved his body touched her in a place she had never felt before. This strange manner of his was also what made it so difficult to guess his age. If he was over thirty, he moved and behaved like a much younger man. She glanced at the sandwich board and suppressed a giggle at the naïve writing. He'd misspelled '*destiny*' as '*destuny*'.

"Now for your fortune," he said, with a certain delight. His characteristic grin had returned.

"OK, but quickly."

Once again he took her palm and stared deep into her eyes. It was impossible not to notice the fact that he had the most beautiful blue eyes. They were the sort of eyes a girl could get lost in. She recalled an image from Sunday evening, of his lithe, muscular body lunging across the court in a vain attempt to return the tennis ball. Despite herself, she felt a thrill running from the pit of her stomach up into her chest, and forced herself to flex her toes until the pinch of the high heels brought her back to reality.

"Difficult choices lie ahead. You must listen to your heart, and to the advice of someone who cares about you."

"Oh, I suppose that's you, right?"

"No, 'tisn't Miss Smarty-pants! It's nothin' to do with romance. It's something else." Then he grinned, "I'll get to the romance bit in a second, so just hold your horses there!" As he said this, his fingers tickled her palm.

A pang of regret hit her. What in hell was she doing, openly flirting with another man? Jeff might have behaved like a real asshole on Sunday, but he didn't deserve this. Whatever way she chose to package it, Maria knew she was teetering on the edge of cheating. A mild version of cheating, yes, but cheating nonetheless.

That thought got no further in her mind. For in that very moment a change came over the Irishman's face. Whereas a second ago he'd been gearing up for some kind of silly joke about her falling in love with him, now his face was dark and foreboding. She felt the change too, an urgency in his touch, a palpitation, a shiver. His lips trembled. His eyes were looking past her further along the sidewalk.

"Maria," he said, still holding her hand, his voice something close to a whisper. "There's something wrong."

"What?" The rest of her smile faded away completely.

"It's the crow," he answered.

"What crow?" She turned her head and followed the path of his eyes towards where a pigeon bobbed up and down, scratching for food. "You mean that pigeon?"

OK, this was getting weird. She tried to pull her hand back, but he held it tight. She could feel a sort of coldness pour into her from his body, making the physical connection strangely uncomfortable, scary even. "Let go," she muttered with no conviction.

"No, you don't understand," he said in a tiny voice that shook with fear. Horror was in his face now. Pure horror. "It's calling to me. It's screaming out. If you go to work, something terrible will happen. You might even die."

"What?"

"Listen to me, please! This isn't a come-on. Take a sick day and ... I dunno ... go to the beach or something."

With the full force of her body, Maria wrenched herself free of his grip. "Seriously? Is that your idea of a joke?" Her voice was much louder than she'd intended.

Her shout had the desired effect. Fergus's face changed from grave concern to innocent shock at her reaction, as if he'd snapped out of a trance. "What? I only meant—"

But Maria was beyond forgiving him his childish antics. "I don't care what you meant! Today happens to be a big day for me and you don't have a right to scare people like that, you dumb-ass *Paddy*!" She threw the bag of rolls at him as hard as she could. "Keep your fucking bread!"

He was shouting desperate apologies after her, but she didn't hear them. The blood was pounding too hard in her head. What annoyed her most was the fact that she allowed this jerk—this *nobody*—to get under her skin.

He caught up to her and tried to say something to her, words to the effect that he was only trying to save her. Panic seized her altogether and she screamed, "If you come near me, I'm gonna call the police!" A man in a suit intervened, telling the Irishman to back off. Maria didn't stick around to see what else happened. She ran towards the subway.

At the turnstile inside the Clark Street station she melded into the crush of commuters, turning back one last time to make sure he wasn't following her. Once past the turnstile, she exhaled slowly and tried to calm herself. Waiting for the crowd to clear, she realized what was causing the logjam of people around her. *Of course*, Maria thought wryly, as she saw a long line of office workers waiting for the elevator at the end of the passage. Two of the three elevators were out of service today, causing a jam in front of the only one that was operating. Clark Street Station was deep underground, and there was no staircase access down to the first subterranean level.

In the crowded elevator she took a moment to glance at her watch. It had somehow turned 8:05 a.m. already, which meant she was now officially cutting it fine. *Damn it, damn it and damn it again!* The elevator descended to a passageway, deep underneath the waterline of the East River. Maria joined the throng in the passageway to where a final flight of stairs descended to the inbound platform, her heels clicking loudly on the tiles of the tunnel's floor. Fergus's words echoed in her head with each click: "*You might even die.*" God, how had she allowed herself to get sucked in by this crackpot? This obvious stalker. Who 'accidentally' bumped into her in a park on the other side of New York City. He was probably a psychopath. New York was truly a zoo.

Suits pressed and shoulders crushed. Perfume, hair products and the pungent odor of human stress mingled in the stagnant subway air. The clip of heels formed a cacophony with the rustle of fabric: it all merged into a single pulse of angry energy. Everyone seemed to be running late. As Maria shifted her weight onto the very first step of the stairs leading down to the platform, a man bumped into her from behind, hard. The briefcase was in her right hand, otherwise she would have caught the guide rail and stabilized herself. Equally, if she had been wearing her white Nike sneakers, she would have found safe footing. But as it was, her left foot missed the top step completely, and came down awkwardly on the one below it. Her body spun with the force of the shove she'd been given and the back heel of her right foot caught the very edge of the next step, propelling her downwards. Instinct made her twist her body to avoid falling backwards on her head. Down she went through the air until, two steps from the bottom, her left foot touched the ground to break her fall: heavily and at a slight angle, heel first. The ankle twisted. For one eternal split second, Maria could hear the crunch and scrape of tendons and ligaments being torn apart as the full weight of her body came down on her left ankle. Next thing she knew she was lying in a heap on the ground. Then the pain set in.

It was the most excruciating pain she had ever endured. So bad, she was only vaguely aware of the stream of commuters brushing past her without as much as a backwards glance. A patent leather shoe stepped on the floor only inches from her face. Another man jumped over her prostrate body in order to board the train that had just opened its doors. Maria watched helplessly as the doors closed and the train drove off. A second was just coming in when she made the stoic effort to get back up onto her feet. It was 8:14 a.m. She would hobble. She would crawl. But she would not miss the meeting with Peterson Investments.

It was only then she realized the briefcase was gone. Some motherfucking shitbag had stolen it. Tears welled up in her eyes but she fought them back. There was still a chance to make this right. Sinking back down on the ground, she tore open her handbag and fished out her cell phone.

Her assistant's extension rang through to voicemail. *Dammit.* She tried another number.

"Jeff?"

"Hi, baby, what's up?" They had not spoken since the incident on the tennis court, and the tone of his voice was too sweet to be genuine. Maria knew he was holding out for the apology he expected her to make. But there was no time for that now.

"I need you to do me a favor. I've just had an accident. My briefcase has been stolen—the one with the contracts for the Peterson deal. I need you to print out fresh copies and bring them in. Take a cab and hurry!"

He paused before answering. "I would, except I have a meeting myself."

She was just about to ask what meeting he could possibly have that was more important than the deal with Peterson when she realized she was wasting her breath.

"Wait, you said you had an accident," he said in a voice that had turned sweet. "Are you alright? Did you get attacked?"

Fuck! His faux sympathy was worthless to her now. What she needed from him was swift action. "No. I'll be fine. I—It doesn't matter what happened. The main thing is we get the contract to Peterson."

"I'll call them and we can reschedule. As long as you're ok—"

"Christ, Jeff, I can call them myself." She jabbed at the red button on her cell with a curse and fished around in her bag for Peterson's business card, before realizing that too was in the briefcase. She tried to ring Jeff back, but he wasn't answering. He was sulking because she'd hung up on him. And now it was 8:25 a.m.

When she finally connected with Peterson's personal assistant, a camp German named Christoph, it was already past the meeting time.

"Hold, please," he told her in a voice heavy with passive-aggressive overtones.

Peterson was always five minutes late himself, but he hated, hated anyone else showing up after he had taken his seat at the head of the boardroom table. Maria felt a lump forming in her throat; this stupid accident would cost her months of trust-building! How hard she'd worked, only to have it all unravel in a single moment of dumb luck.

"Ms. Da Silva? Mr. Peterson cannot zee you before zree o'clock, I'm afraid. And even then he only has little time."

"Three's fine. I'll be there. Please tell Mr. Peterson I'm very sorry for the—"

"Zank you, bye!!" The poisonous German secretary rang off.

Christoph was the last straw. Maria sank back and allowed herself a moment of quiet despair. She was still on the ground, with a throbbing pain pulsing up her left leg. More people walked past, and still no one stopped to offer her help. When she looked down at the left leg, she could see the bruising and swelling beginning to spread along her foot. She pried the Prada heel off the rapidly swelling appendage and threw it in disgust against the wall. It was a good fifteen minutes before she managed to get herself upright and hop over to the green, metal pillar. It was 9 a.m. and she still hadn't made it out of Brooklyn.

She took out her cell phone and instinctively dialed the number that was most familiar to her. For some reason the phone line was busy on the first, second, third, and fourth attempts. Finally, on the fifth attempt, she managed to get through.

"Mom," she said when it answered.

"Oh my God, Maria are you alright? I've been trying to call you. Are you hurt? Where are you? Are you at home? Are you somewhere safe?"

For a brief second Maria imagined Jeff had called her mother to say she'd had an accident. Which would have been out of character, and frankly weird, as they did not get along.

"Yeah, I'm fine. It's just my ankle—"

"Wait, something's happening! Oh my God, they hit the other tower! Oh my God. Oh my holy God! "

"Mom, calm down. What are you talking about?"

"They hit Tower Two! I'm watchin' it live. On TV, right here. They're flying airplanes into buildings in New York. Our country is under attack. Oh my baby, please tell me you're safe!"

At that moment an announcement from the speaker overhead drowned out the panicked voice on her phone, and Maria realized this wasn't simply her mother's paranoia. All train services in New York City were being suspended. The station was being evacuated.

In a state of uneasy contemplation Fergus looked out across the East River. His eye was drawn to a distant speck in the sky over Manhattan, bearing in from the north. From this angle, it looked to be right over Gaelic Park in the Bronx. Its flight path struck him as odd: it was too close to be heading to Newark, and wrong altogether for JFK. On it went, down the length of the Hudson, before finally disappearing into the cluster of downtown skyscrapers behind the World Trade Center, in what he assumed was a trick of the angles in his sightline. Fergus waited for it to appear on the other side. Nothing. Instead smoke billowed up into the sky from behind the Twin Towers. A man next to him muttered something about an accident, but Fergus's mind was too busy to really register it. He was still thinking of what had happened an hour ago. Of Maria the Lawyer.

The effect on Fergus of telling that sombre fortune had been so great it had placed him in shock. In that strange way in which shocked people can carry on with routine tasks, Fergus had continued selling bread rolls. Ironically, it had proven to be one of his best sales days. He even managed to sell out. He was as far as preparing the dough for a second batch, before he realised how tense his body was: so tense he couldn't as much as flex his fingers properly to knead the dough. That was when he'd given up, clapped up the sandwich board, folded up the oven and wheeled it off to the Promenade.

It didn't make a whit of sense. None of it. Why her? Why here? What was this voice, this dreadful insight he had into things he could never control and could never do anything about? *I don't want it*, he thought in a sudden flash of anger. In the past, Fergus had always made out like it was his 'gift'. *To fuck was it a gift!*

"It's a curse," he whispered under his breath, still watching the plume of black smoke rising from downtown Manhattan. *There must be a big fire somewhere*, he thought. More and more people were gathering on the railings, looking across. Some were taking pictures.

Another plane approached, this time from the south. It crossed the Upper Bay right in front of the Statue of Liberty, and struck the other tower, in full view of the spectators in Brooklyn. It didn't so much strike the tower as disappear into it, triggering a giant fireball like something straight out of a Hollywood action film. Another plume of smoke erupted out of the gaping hole that had appeared in the South façade.

Holy Christ. Instantly, Fergus snapped out of his reflections.

"Maria," he whispered and thought of his brother. Only this time he would not arrive too late. He had to save her.

Fergus jumped the railings and lowered himself as far as he could, until he was dangling from the lowest point of the overhanging platform that supported the Brooklyn Heights Promenade over the highway below. His had to lift up his legs to avoid getting hit by the lorries as they whizzed by beneath him. As onlookers leaned over the railings above and shouted down and gawked, he waited for a gap in the traffic. When it came, he dropped the seven or eight feet down onto the southbound road and bolted between the two other lanes of traffic, until he reached the margin railing. Horns blazed. Someone shouted a curse out their open car window. But Fergus continued, climbing once more over the railings and lowering himself until he was dangling again over the northbound lane of the highway, which was a level below.

This time he only narrowly avoided getting hit by a car, before making it safely to the railing, from where he could drop another level into the abandoned shipping yard of the Brooklyn pier. There was one more fence to climb before he made it to the big harbour rocks against which the black water gurgled. He took off his sneakers and tied the laces together. Slinging them around his neck, he plunged into the water and swam with all his might.

Twenty-five minutes later he pulled himself up the lichen-encrusted ladder and onto Pier 11. He put on his soaking sneakers and took off without stopping to catch his breath.

Under normal circumstances, the sight of a man emerging fully clothed from the East River would have caused a stir. But today no one noticed. Sirens were blazing all around him. Desperate faces passed him going the other way. At Legion Memorial Park, Fergus paused and stood for a second with a group of people, looking up through the gap in the high-rise buildings. What they saw was a great billow of smoke rising from the South Tower. In that very moment, it began to fall. A voice called out in terror. Everyone's eyes were glued to it, as storey after storey, the building collapsed upon itself.

Fergus continued running. At Wall Street, the cloud of ash caught up to him, swirling around him like soft, hot snowflakes. He pushed passed a barrier of parked ambulances. A confused-looking policeman made a half-hearted attempt to stop him, but got distracted and bolted off. Dazed people passed him by, heading in the opposite direction. Their eyebrows and hair and clothes were white and covered in ash. One woman, blinded by fear, or perhaps with her eyes scorched out of her head, walked into a US Postal Service mailbox and fell heavily to the ground. Twenty yards further on, Fergus passed a burly man with a military appearance and blue plastic gloves, who was carrying an unconscious woman to safety. Everywhere the ground and the bonnets of cars were covered in a snowstorm of white ash, and visibility was obscured to a few feet in front of him. Onwards he went. The heat and the ash and the burning grew more intense.

Fergus was forced to close his eyes against the power of the heat. Even the coolness afforded him by his dripping wet clothes was no longer a protection against it. Two firemen emerged from the burning blizzard, carrying the lifeless body of one of their comrades between them. Fergus went on.

"Maria!" he shouted with what little air was left in his lungs.

"You gotta get back! Get back!"

It was another fireman. His ashy-white face was streaked with blood. He held Fergus by the arm and together they turned away from the intensity of the heat wall and the impermeable, immense swell of soot and ash. Only then did Fergus realise how desperately his lungs needed air. Together they made it back to the barrier of ambulances and collapsed on the ground. The fireman was almost unconscious.

When Fergus looked up he saw that right in front of him was a woman, sitting on the stoop of the ambulance, clutching to her chest a golden retriever. She was crying, rocking the animal back and forth in convulsions of panic. Fergus closed his eyes and, once more, he could feel the gentle sea breeze and smell the salt air.

Somehow he had saved her life.

6

First Lieutenant Brandon Zeiss, Tactical Support Unit of the Operations Division of the 11th Wing of the United States Air Force, sat at his office desk at Andrews Air Force Base in Maryland reviewing his charts. They were flight paths for logistics hauls: support missions bound for South Korea and Japan. The work was neither urgent nor particularly interesting, but it still needed to be done accurately. Therefore, it required a copious quantity of coffee. In short, this was shaping up to be a morning in September like any other Brandon had known in his six-year career with the Air Force.

In fact, the only thing that was in any way different to every other Tuesday was the desk photo of his new-born daughter, Linda. He had added it only that morning to the existing pictures of his wife Mandy and his son, Scott.

He had no radio, nor was his computer connected to the Internet. In his isolated wing of the base, there were few fellow officers who came down the corridors. And so there was nothing and nobody to tell him that his world was about to change. Nothing, that is, until at 0935 hours the phone rang.

"Zeiss, get to Secure Control. Code Red."

He bolted down the corridor, pausing only to flash his ID at the MP who guarded the emergency stairwell. A minute later he emerged into a room he had only seen during practice drills. But this was no drill. The Brigadier General was already present, with the red phone to his ear.

Holy shit, Brandon thought.

"Yes, Mr. President," Brandon overheard General Lanare saying, as he scrambled over to his control stations. Other stations were rapidly filling up.

Behind him the Brigadier General's voice bellowed, "Scramble all fighters. We're tracking any commercial aircraft which break from FAA approved flight paths."

Screens lit up. Officers grasped phones and belted instructions into them.

"Listen up!" the General's voice called out behind him. "America is under attack. We're dealing with an unknown number of commercial aircraft being used as weapons by an unknown enemy against—"

"Sir?" It was the voice of another operations lieutenant. "The Pentagon's been hit, sir—"

This was real. Maybe even World War Three.

Brandon focused. He picked up his own phone and called his units to their battle stations. Within five minutes the two F-16s for which he provided tactical support would be scrambled. His responsibility now was Sector 15, a thin wedge of air space that stretched north-west from Washington DC, up over Maryland and into Pennsylvania. Sector 15 covered air space just west of his own home town of Carlisle, which lay about halfway between Pittsburgh and Philadelphia.

Brandon spoke rapidly to the two pilots, giving them flight paths which would allow them to fan out and perform loops over this patch of space.

"Keep your eyes open for anything out of the ordinary. Specifically, any commercial aircraft flying erratically."

Their mission at Andrews was to protect key tactical targets in DC from any incoming aerial assault, starting with the White House, the Capitol, even the Pentagon. During wargames, they had simulated an attack from Russian MIGs flying off a carrier. But commercial aircraft? *We've been caught with our pants down,* Brandon realized as senior officers dashed out updates of the situation in real time, and he did his best to update his pilots.

Scrambling the F-16s was the easy part. Much harder was tracking the goddamn commercial jets. The FAA data came through piecemeal, mapping it was imprecise and quickly broke down to guesswork.

"We've got a stray bird at 39.2 and -78.4 northbound," Brandon's neighbor, Lieutenant Pryce, called out. The Brigadier General was looming over his shoulder as Pryce pulled his own two birds into tracking position. They followed the big lumbering jet—weapons ready—for five minutes before contact was made with the commercial pilot, patched in from the FAA. Why the delay? No one knew.

"*This is Captain Geoff Bryant, Continental Flight 82 from Orlando on route to Chicago. We are safe and on pattern. Repeat. Safe and on pattern. All passengers are seated. There is no visible danger on board. Awaiting instructions for emergency landing.*"

The FAA controller responded, putting the plane on a pattern into Dayton Airport.

Brandon heard Pryce let out a sigh of relief before ordering his pilots to make safe their training rounds. Yet this false alarm had taken Sector 14's fighters nearly a hundred miles off course.

Brandon was in the process of adjusting the flight path for his top wing—whose name was Lieutenant Hutchinson—to cover the empty airspace, when another call came through. Radar had picked up a commercial bird which had done an abrupt U-turn over Cleveland and was heading back east. It was just passing south of Pittsburgh.

"Zeiss!"

"I'm on it, sir! Hutch, I need you at 3 ticks west."

"*Roger that.*"

In the background, Brandon could hear the FAA controller: *United Airlines Flight 93, we have lost contact with the pilot. I repeat, lost contact with the pilot. USAF, be alerted; Flight 93 has broken its pattern.*

"Tell me something I don't know," Brandon hissed. Brigadier General Lanare was at his shoulder now, watching as Hutchinson's F-16 closed onto the civilian target.

"*I've got visual,*" Hutchinson's voice came through the radio. From the FAA feed Brandon could see Flight UA93 was a Boeing 757, which he knew could carry up to 220 passengers.

"Hutch, get your training rounds ready," Brandon said, and prayed to God Almighty they would not be needed.

"*Roger that. She's all over the place, Bran!*"

"If it turns towards Pittsburgh, you open fire," General Lanare said.

"Yes, sir," Brandon answered over his shoulder.

For a long minute, they watched the blips advance south-eastwards along the radar screen, until Hutchinson's voice called out across the intercom unit.

"*She's losing altitude fast.*"

"What's down there, Lieutenant?" the Brigadier General demanded of Brandon.

Not Pittsburgh, at least. But beyond that, Brandon had no idea. Frantically, he ripped open a paper map of Pennsylvania, and traced with his forefinger the spot on the map, calculating in his head the speed and trajectory of the jet plane. It was near India Lake, a place his father had taken him and his brother fishing when they were kids. An isolated spot.

"Where is it, goddammit?" Lanare asked again. "Where is it?!"

"An abandoned strip mine. No civilian targets, sir," Brandon said, and shut his eyes, praying to God his memory was not letting him down.

"Then stand down," General Lanare ordered. "Just keep on her tail."

Brandon passed the command through to his bird.

"*Roger that.*" Hutchinson confirmed. Even over the radio the relief in the pilot's voice could be heard. A second later Flight UA93 disappeared from the radar.

"*She's gone down.*"

It was 1006 hours. The final attack of September 11, 2001 was over. But for Brandon Zeiss, the war was only just beginning.

7

"Secretary Wolfowitz, according to the polls, the *American public supports military action against those who committed the attacks on Tuesday, but what do you hit and where do you go after it? There doesn't seem to be any comparable targets, so what kind of war do you wage?"*

"We're still too early in the process to determine an exact action plan but one thing is sure, you do it with the full support of the military, our allies, and with the intelligence community. I think everyone understands that we have unfortunately entered into a different era. We've seen evidence that resources will be ready when called upon and, believe me, they will be called upon. Next question, please."

"Mr. Secretary, the President has said the United States intends to find those responsible, that he and others, including you, today have indicated that there will be a broader campaign that will go beyond the authors of Tuesday's attacks. What form will that campaign take?"

"Well, I think the President's words were pretty good, so let me say these people think they can hide, but they cannot hide forever. They think their harbors are safe, but they won't be safe forever. I think this has to be a broadened and sustained campaign. It's not gonna stop if a few criminals are apprehended. Next question ...yes, please ... second row ..."

"Secretary Wolfowitz, my question concerns the budget, the additional twenty million allocated to New Yo—"

Maria silenced the television. She could not bear any more of the coverage. Every station had been broadcasting 24/7 since Tuesday morning. Over and over, the same TV camera shots. She must have seen the Towers collapse fifty times already.

It had been two days since the attacks. Two days since, in panic, she had hobbled down the streets as sirens blared and police cars raced passed her. When she had finally made it to the hospital, she had been forced to wait hours for her X-ray, as case after case, all more urgent than hers, arrived across the Brooklyn Bridge. Here she witnessed, first hand, what had happened. Some of the people were scarred and bleeding, some were wheezing from the dust. Others stared blankly as they sat on the plastic bucket chairs and waited for care. Still others cried and consoled each other.

Meanwhile the live coverage blasted from the television in the ER waiting room where they all sat together. It showed the moment when the billowing caps of the towers erupted and, layer by layer, the buildings collapsed into nothing. Dozens of times they watched it happening, until someone had the presence of mind to switch the damn thing off. The strangest part of the ordeal was seeing all those people covered in dust and thinking: that dust is all that remains of the mightiest buildings in America's mightiest city.

When Maria's mother came back inside from the fire escape, where she had been smoking a cigarette, Maria resumed their earlier conversation. Now, with the TV off, she might finally get her mom to listen.

"What about Benji?" Maria asked. She hoped the question was posed with a tone of concern. "He'll be pining away without you. You said you're like his mother, his whole family even. He needs you." It was the last in a long line of arguments designed to convince her mother that Maria was alright, and she could now return to her house in Massachusetts to walk her toy dog, Benji, and smoke cigarettes at the hairdressers with the pack of gossip-mongering divorcees she called friends. Maria glanced at the wall clock in the kitchen. If Mom packed quickly she could still make the last Orient Point ferry.

"Maria, Benji's a dog! You're my daughter, fer Chrice Sake! What do you think is more important to me?" Her mother dropped to one knee next to the armchair, leaned in close to Maria's face and grabbed her arms with hands that still stank of the cigarette smoke. Mom knew better than to smoke in Maria's apartment. But that didn't stop the stench from following her in from the fire escape, clinging to her tacky, multi-colored, overly-revealing clothes. "I *know* you're tryin' to be tough about this. That's the woman I raised you to be, after all. But you need *support*. You're in shock, honey! I saw a show about this, people sufferin' from trauma and I recognize all the ..."

Maria was aware that, yes, on some level, she probably was in shock. The problem was she had no way of processing it all with her mother there. And, yes, she did need someone to talk to, but although her mother talked constantly, she was not that person. Not only was she not a confidante, in fact, she was an obstacle to Maria reaching out, because it was impossible to pick up the phone and call her girlfriends with her mother listening in.

There were things she needed to share with another human being. In order to fully comprehend it, she had to tell another person that the meeting with Peterson Investments had been scheduled at 8:30 a.m. on the 93rd floor of Tower Two. She had to hear herself saying—out loud and to another human being—that everyone on that floor of the building was now dead. And that if she had not twisted her ankle, she too would be dead.

Rudolf Peterson III was dead. His personal assistant, Christoph, was dead. Half the people whose biographies Maria had memorized: they were gone. Everything was gone. It wasn't even clear if Peterson Investments would continue to exist as a company. How could something like this happen?

"... that they need to provide more than just medical attention, they need to also provide counsellin' for people like you who suffered injuries in the terrorist attack ..."

"No, Mom! I didn't suffer injuries in the terrorist attack, OK? I fell down the stairs in the subway station. I wasn't even in Manhattan. I was right here in Brooklyn. The accident I had was completely unrelated to Osama bin Laden or the Taliban or whoever else. Got it?"

Her mother paused in her pacing and stared at Maria, a hurt expression creeping across her face. "You know, you don't gotta scream at me."

"I wasn't screaming."

"I'm only here 'cos I care about you. I put my own life completely on hold, you know; I cancelled bridge night; I cancelled bingo night; I put Benji in a kennel, 'cos I know how you're allergic, even though he hates the kennel; an' actually it's a bit *selfish* of you to make him suffer in that way. I made a lot of sacrifices because I care about you, and what do I get in return?" She broke off and tears exploded across her face in answer to her own rhetorical question, and snatched at the box of hankies on the ottoman next to Maria's elevated left leg.

With the aid of her crutch, Maria hoisted herself up and took her mother in her arms. As she whispered apologies and little words of appreciation for everything her mother had given her, she found herself wondering how—once again—Mom had managed to turn this to be about herself.

"I'm sorry, Mom, I guess I'm just a bit edgy. I do really appreciate that you've come. I know it's not easy for you to drop everything like that—"

"No it's really not. Especially as I hate drivin' in the city. The traffic in New York scares the hell out of me. You know that."

"Yeah, I know. And thanks. But, I think I just need some time on my own right now. To gather my thoughts. So please, go home."

"Are you sure you'll be OK?"

Maria smiled, "I'll be fine. I'll call you." They hugged again. "If you leave now you can catch the last ferry off Long Island."

"I never take the ferry, honey, it's too expensive. I'll go through New Haven." She had recovered and was looking at the gold watch that dangled from her wrist. "And you know, not only does Benji hate the kennel, but it's actually really pricey. On top of which gas costs a fortune."

Maria suppressed a sigh. "How much?"

"Don't say it like that, Maria, you make me feel like a beggar."

"Mom, I'm not—" But it wasn't worth the argument. She hobbled over to the breakfast bar and fished the check book out of her handbag. "Will four hundred cover it?"

A pregnant silence filled the space between them. "Five hundred?"

"Five hundred's wonderful. Thank you, honey. You are the world's best daughta', don't think for one second I'm not proud of you!"

It seemed to take forever for Mom to pack her things and leave. When she was finally gone, Maria collapsed back into the armchair and inhaled the sweet silence. She looked at the dirty dishes left piled in the sink, the crumpled hankies casually discarded on the arm of the sofa, caked with a film of pinkish beige from Mom's generous layers of foundation. Maria would tidy up later.

Right now, she just needed space to think. To think how remarkably close she had come to dying. If the elevators had not been out of repair, she probably would not have slipped on the stairs and missed the train. If someone had not stolen her briefcase, she would not have cancelled the meeting. If she had not been so shaken by the encounter with the Irishman selling bread rolls, none of those things would have happened and she would have been sitting in a board room on the 93rd floor of Tower Two at 9:03 a.m. when Flight 11 struck.

That was when it hit her for the first time. The images of the injured people in the hospital had pushed out of her mind the scene with the Irishman, and now it came back to her. This Fergus guy had told her not to go to work that morning. And that encounter, more than anything else, was the reason why she had been so flustered. That was what had made her late. That was why she had slipped and fallen.

He had told her if she went to work something terrible would happen. She might even die. Her heart leapt into her mouth. Had he really said that? In the confusion of what had followed she was not certain, and so she allowed herself the mental space to carefully rewind through the events of two days ago. Yes, she decided, that's what he had said. A terrible catastrophe would befall her if she went to work. Or at least, words to that effect.

So the fortune teller had saved her life. She sat with that thought for a long time. The evening sunlight danced through the leaves of the oak trees that lined the street outside, throwing speckles of light across her swollen ankle resting on the ottoman. The ice pack had long since turned to tepid water, and the throbbing pain had returned once again. She popped the last three of her Tylenol into her mouth and swallowed them dry. She was in too much pain to hobble back over to the kitchen for water. It was only a sprain, but God it hurt. This was the price she'd paid for her life. Had the fortune teller known that she would sprain her ankle too?

"Ridiculous!" Maria said out loud. She didn't believe in magic. But did that mean this Fergus—if that was his real name—had known these attacks were going to happen ...? *No*, she thought to herself, and began for a moment to doubt her own memories. It made no sense.

Maria picked up the phone and dialed Cindy's number. Cindy Jackson was one of her two best friends, whom she had known since college.

"Hey, girlfriend," Cindy's voice came through.

"My mom's gone," Maria told her. "Finally."

"You want me to come over?"

Yes, Maria did. But she also knew Jeff would be popping by later, and she didn't want a confrontation. Cindy and Jeff disagreed on everything: politics, race relations, abortion. Jeff was the epitome of 'greed is good' and a white libertarian, while Cindy was a black girl from Over-the-Rhine in Cincinnati, who had gone from Harvard Law School into civil rights law, protecting mostly penniless African Americans who got screwed by the criminal justice system.

"No need to come over," Maria replied. "I just wanted to hear a friendly voice."

Cindy laughed on the other end of the phone, as if she could read Maria's mind. "Tell Jeffrey I said hi."

They chatted about comfortable nothings for a few minutes. If the conversation had gone on longer, Maria would have spilled her guts. But at this stage the drugs started to kick in and drowsiness forced her off the phone. Cindy wouldn't let her go until she'd agreed to breakfast with her and their other best friend, Sam, next Saturday. *Pancakes in Queens, yum*, Maria thought as she hung up the phone and let her eyes fall shut.

The doorbell rang and Maria awoke. A shock of fear ran through her, and she realized she'd been dreaming about some terrorist coming to silence her. A second later, Jeff's smiling face appeared at the window. He always did that, leaning over from the wrong side of the railing and peering in. Maria labored to her feet and hobbled to the door.

"Wake up, Sleeping Beauty," he greeted her with a smile and a kiss.

"Hi," she mumbled, as he slipped inside. A welcome aroma of MSG followed him in.

"I brought Chinese." His head scanned back and forth. "Where's your mom?"

"Gone home. I managed to convince her I was fine."

"Thank God," he muttered. "How much did she hit you up for this time?"

"Jeff!" As annoying as Mom was, Maria hated when Jeff said stuff about her mother; mostly because she knew Jeff was right.

"I'm sorry, sweetheart, I didn't mean it like that. I was just trying to be funny. Hey, I got sweet-and-sour shrimp and chow mein. You hungry? C'mon, why don't you relax and I'll serve us up?"

Maria realized she was starving. She'd had half a bagel that morning and nothing else besides coffee and orange juice. When the plates arrived she found she was cheering up.

"Thanks, honey."

He had already started on his food. "You're welcome. I realized what a jerk I was about the tennis, and I wanted to say sorry."

With all that had happened, Maria had forgotten entirely about their little spat. Her groggy brain tried to replay the scene, but all she could see was Fergus's face as he got out of the taxi in Harlem.

"So how's the ankle?"

"Huh? Oh, painful. I swallowed a whole Walgreen's worth of Tylenol and it still hurts."

He smiled sympathetically. "Oh, I nearly forgot. Here!" He handed her a Hallmark card. It had a picture of a dog dressed in a three-piece suit with a broken leg hobbling into a court building. Inside the printed words *'Get well soon or I'll sue you'* were surrounded by a few dozen signatures.

"Everybody in the firm signed it," Jeff told her. Maria could see this was not so. A number of the senior partners had delegated the task to their personal assistants, and her own PA, Barbara, had craftily filled in the rest, using different colored pens. Maria forced a smile and said her thanks with as much sincerity as the card had been written.

"It was a pretty close escape, huh?" Jeff asked.

"You don't know the half of it." And she proceeded to tell him the whole story, including how the Irishman had told her fortune.

Jeff sneered, which was really annoying.

"Psychic powers, huh?" he said. "Honey, I think you've been taking too many of those painkillers. Sounds like a hallucination to me. Not uncommon in situations of intense trauma."

She could feel anger mounting inside her. The rush of blood focused her mind and she forced herself to remember the details. The palm-reading. Fergus's facial expression. The moment he turned and looked at the pigeon, but said it was a crow. Then how he ran after her and was restrained by the man in the suit.

"No," she said with conviction. "It was real. It happened."

Jeff shrugged and shoved half a spring roll into his mouth. "What, you think he's on the inside? Allied to bin Laden, maybe?"

It sounded absurd. "Well, I don't think he can see into the future, so what other explanation is there? Coincidence?"

Jeff pondered for a second. "What'd you say his name was? Fargo?"

"Fergus. Fergus, something... Murphy? Mulligan? I don't know, something very Irish."

"So report him to the FBI."

She cringed inside as he spoke the words. "You think I should?"

"Sure, why not? He's probably an illegal alien anyway. New York is crawling with illegal Micks. They're like roaches, only they drink more." Jeff cracked a smile and looked at her. "What? It was a joke, all right?"

"Racism doesn't amuse me. It must be on account of my dry, Spic-Dago personality."

"Oh, c'mon! I have nothing against Irish people. Some of my favorite breakfast cereal mascots are Irish."

"The thing is," she said, ignoring his puerile humor. "Our office is like eight blocks clear of the Twin Towers. And there was no way, absolutely no way, he could have known I was going to Peterson Investments that morning in Tower Two. So even if he was a stalker and he knew where I worked, how did he know—"

"Maybe that part was a lucky guess."

"Maybe the whole thing was a lucky guess," she countered, feeling an inexplicable desire to defend the Irishman against Jeff. She was lost in her own private thoughts and only half heard Jeff's answer.

"OK, then don't report him. Honestly, I don't think it matters. We're gonna go after the top guys here. I'm talkin' Osama bin Laden and his chief lieutenants. And we're gonna pull out all the stops. You know Bush's approval rating jumped to 90% today?"

"Really?"

"This is exactly what happened after Pearl Harbor," Jeff continued, now with his mouth full. "I talked to my dad on the phone today and he was giving me the inside scoop. He says with that kind of support Congressional approval is gonna be a cinch."

Maria looked up. "Congressional approval for what?"

Jeff looked at her like she was dumb. "For finishing the job in Iraq, of course."

"Iraq? You mean Afghanistan."

"No, I mean Iraq."

"What has this got to do with Iraq?"

"That remains to be discovered. But one thing's sure, we're not gonna leave any place standing where it's safe to hate America—not a mosque, not a hut, not a goddamn cowshed. We're gonna bomb every America-hater right back to the Middle Ages."

Maria's thoughts flew back to Fergus. She pictured his naïve little sandwich board with the uneven letters scrawled on it, advertising his skills as a clairvoyant. Did he hate America too?

Jeff was filling her in on the latest developments at the firm when he paused, clearly sensing that she wasn't listening.

"I think you should report him," he said.

This caught her attention.

"Look at it this way," he continued. "The mood in America is growing violent. Uncertainty breeds fear. If this ... um, Forrest ... guy is involved, a quick heads-up to the appropriate authorities is only going to help remove some of that uncertainty. The faster we can figure out who was and who wasn't behind these attacks, the less likely it is innocent people are going to get hurt. That's what you want, right? To save innocent people?"

"What if *he*'s innocent?" When she said it, a surge of something went through her. It was as if she was convinced he was. Or was she just trying to convince herself?

"If he's innocent, it's up to the Feds to figure that out," Jeff argued. "Then they'll let him go."

Maria nodded in agreement, but it was a lie. She refused to believe the Irishman was a terrorist. In that very moment she made up her mind that she would not, after all, be calling the FBI.

Jeff's voice had turned sweet now, telling her how much she had been through. He was caressing her leg in an obvious bid for sex.

"I ... I'm really tired, Jeff. I think I just need some 'me' time right now."

Jeff sighed. "You're telling me to go home."

"I don't mean it like that."

"Yeah, actually, you do."

She watched as he flung his arms into his jacket sleeves and yanked on his shoes.

"What did you say that guy's name was again?" he asked at the door.

She looked up, startled. "Why?"

Jeff shrugged. "I dunno. I mean, the IRA thing is still happening. They had a peace deal a couple of years ago, under Clinton, but not all of them signed up for it. Who knows, maybe there is a link to al-Qaida? I can run it by my dad and he can get it looked into it."

Maria watched her boyfriend in silence. Something prevented her from answering. They locked eyes for a very long second, before Jeff flashed a knowing smile and said, "Fergus? Wasn't that it?"

"I'm not sure," she mumbled and looked away. When she looked back up, Jeff was gone.

8

The Mount Zion Baptist Church in Harlem ran what it called a 'Homework Club' for the kids from M.S. 326. When Karim had asked Fergus to do the Thursday evening shifts, the Irishman initially said no, on the basis that he'd failed his Intermediate Certificate, which in American English meant he was a high school dropout. "You want them to learn from me? I'm rubbish at maths; I'm rubbish at English. I've no head for history." But then Karim had explained that the Homework Club was less about doing homework and more about getting kids off the street, away from the drugs and into a safe place, where they could hang out, get some nutritious food and play games.

"Ya'll got ping-pong over there in Ireland, right?"

"'Course we have. I was the undefeated champion of Clonakilty. Two days running."

"So play ping-pong with them."

Fergus was a star from day one because he never talked down to anyone and always came at everything with a sense of fun and adventure. When Pastor Richards thanked him for his work with the kids, Fergus truly hadn't a clue what the old man was on about. He himself enjoyed the Homework Club so much, he failed to see how Richards could call it work.

But Fergus's true acceptance and admiration among the kids began the day someone found a violin in a box of stuff that had been donated to the church. Fergus—just for laughs—started playing a reel. The little girls immediately gathered around and began to dance, the colourful beads in their braided hair bouncing to the beat. This got Fergus onto the idea of teaching them Irish dancing. This, in turn, was such a success that by the time the school term started back, he was halfway to organising Harlem's first ever *fèis*.

"Jaysus!" he proclaimed. "Yous are feckin' amazing. We're gonna give *Riverdance* a run for its money, at this rate."

The ultimate accolade came when he overheard his not-so-secret admirer, Peaches, correcting another kid who had referred to him as 'white', which was anything but a compliment. "Fergus ain't white," she said. "He jus' *light-skinnded*, is all!"

On the Thursday, two weeks after 9/11, the Homework Club finished early, for no other reason than because there was a general sense of panic about public gatherings, and the board of Mount Zion Church were being extra careful. It annoyed Fergus, because by now he knew that half the kids wouldn't or couldn't go home until ten o'clock at night. And once it got dark, it wasn't safe outside in the parks or on the streets. There were dangers much more immediate to them than the vague threat of Islamic terrorism.

After waving goodbye to the last kid to leave that night Fergus knocked off the lights, locked up the church basement and turned onto Amsterdam Avenue. The smell of autumn was in the air. It was only just after eight, but already evening was closing in. A flight of birds cut the azure above, stirred by the changing of the seasons. They could not pass without whispers of the spirit world echoing in Fergus's brain like cannon fire. They spoke the name '*Maria*.' As he crossed Broadway, his mind was still on her. Despite his best efforts, he had been unable to let go of her. Destiny was calling with a thousand murmurs and as many tingles, but the coward in him refused to listen. He wanted it to stop. He wanted them all to leave him alone, and so he would tense his body and brace himself against the voices to block it all out. Then, when he could bear the tension in his body no longer, he would start to drink. Tonight would be no exception.

Dusk was giving way fully to nighttime as he climbed the stairs up to his building door. Absently, he went to unlock it, only to find it had been forced open. This was not such a surprise, as their building was regularly being raided by junkies and dealers seeking refuge from the cops or a place to shoot up. Equally as unsurprising, the light in the hall was out. Fergus fumbled for a lighter but, of course, he didn't have one. And so he groped his way up the stairs. Just as he reached the landing he was aware of red dots wavering against the wall in front of him, then disappearing. The door into his apartment was ajar. He pushed it open.

A blast of light blinded him. He instinctively raised his arm to screen his eyes.

"Freeze! Put your hands in the air."

The red dots danced across his field of vision. A strong hand gripped his wrist and attempted to force his arm back into a hold. Instinctively, Fergus twisted free and was about to swing a left hook back at his attacker when someone else caught him from the other side. He felt a knee to his groin and hands under his armpits. He fell to the ground and they gained control of his arms, twisting them behind his back. Cold metal pressed into his wrists as a knee pinned him to the ground.

"Fergus Maloney?" a voice asked from above him.

He couldn't have answered if he wanted to. The pressure from the knee forced his head into the crack between the floor and the wall, so firmly it almost dislocated his jaw.

"You are under arrest."

The room they put Fergus in was entirely featureless. Its only ornament was a torn and tattered copy of the Miranda Warning taped to the wall beside the closed door. Apart from a table and some chairs, there was nothing else in the room. Except silence. Footsteps would approach the door and, with them, the hope that someone or something would break the monotony. But no, the footsteps would retreat again and the waiting would continue as he sat on a hard plastic chair and tapped his foot.

The tension in his body began to manifest itself slowly again. He clenched and unclenched his fists, rubbed his sweaty palms into his jeans. *I need a fuckin' drink*. Yet there was no relief and the tension grew worse. He tried to swallow, but his throat was seizing up.

And in the silence the memories came. Silence. Silent.

"You have the right to remain silent," he mumbled to himself, his eyes scanning the text of the Miranda Warning because there was nothing else to look at. Anything to dislodge the threat of the silence. He repeated the words, adding the next line, "Anything you say or do can and will be used against you in a court of law."

He repeated it again, slowly working the words into a sort of rap, banging his fingers into the table and chanting louder and louder. He turned the line "If you cannot afford an attorney, one will be appointed to you" into a full-fledged hip-hop chorus, sung in falsetto.

The door opened, just as he had imagined a thousand times that it would, and Fergus cut his song short. A man and a woman entered.

"I want to talk to a lawyer."

"Mr. Maloney?" the man asked, taking a seat.

"I'm an Irish citizen. I want to see a consular officer."

The man folded his hands and leaned into the table, staring at Fergus. Fergus, in turn, took the opportunity to look at the two of them a bit more closely. Both were dressed in dark suits, meticulously groomed. Although they were a man and a woman, they both seemed to belong to the same, sexless gender. If the woman was wearing a skirt, Fergus had not noticed. She had thin, brown hair pulled away from her sharp features. Not someone who enjoyed tucking into a big steak dinner, Fergus thought. It was she who spoke next.

"My name is Agent Liseki," she said. "This is Agent Jaas. We're with the Federal Bureau of Investigation."

"I don't give a fuck who you're with, unless you're with the Irish *fuckin'* Embassy."

"There's no need to curse, Mr. Maloney," Agent Liseki said.

"*Au contraire*," Fergus said, himself leaning into the table. "There's every fuckin' need to curse. I was taken from my home by a pack of fuckin' gorillas in uniform, who nearly broke me arm in the process. No one told me what was happening or why. Now I've been sittin' in this room for hours. No food. Not even a drink of water. And what about my right to a lawyer? Amn't I entitled to a lawyer? I might not have a visa, but I know the law. Even illegal aliens are entitled to a lawyer." He pointed at the Miranda Warning on the wall.

They paused, and eventually the man, Agent Jaas, asked him, "Would you like a glass of water?"

"No. I'd like a glass of let-me-the-fuck-out-of-here."

When Agent Jaas spoke again, Fergus noticed he had a sort of mid-western accent. Not quite a southern drawl, but definitely not from New York City. "Why do you think you're here, Mr. Maloney?"

"Why?" Fergus paused, wondering perhaps if this was a trap. A minute ago he would have sworn it was because he hadn't got his visa sorted out and was, therefore, an illegal immigrant. But there was something in the man's question that made him pause. "You tell me why."

The woman, Liseki, asked, "When did you first find out about the planned terrorist attacks on the World Trade Center?"

"When? When I saw it happen. I watched the planes crash in from across the river in Brooklyn."

"What about before that? During the planning stage. Who told you the attacks were going to happen?"

"What? No one told me. I hadn't a clue—"

"Mr. Maloney, where were you on the morning of Tuesday, September 11?" Jaas asked.

"Sure, amn't I after tellin' ya I was in Brooklyn? And then I swam to Manhattan once I saw the planes hit the towers. Why?"

"You swam?"

"Yeah. I wanted to help. Why?"

"What about before that? At approximately 7:45 a.m. Were you—" here she broke off and scanned a paper in her file, "—were you at the interchange of Hicks Street and Clark Street, in Brooklyn Heights?"

Fergus narrowed his eyes. These were coppers, and coppers asked questions they already knew the answer to.

"Why?" he repeated.

"Did you warn anyone, at approximately 7:45 a.m., that it might be dangerous to travel into downtown Manhattan that morning?"

Maria the Lawyer! That was when it began to dawn on him what all this was about. A smile swept across his face. He uncrossed his arms and extended his hands generously. "Ah, I see what's happened! Listen, I think I can sort this out. What I think we have here is a simple misunderstanding. You see," and he leaned in conspiratorially towards the FBI agents, "I have a gift. Well, it's sort of a gift. Destiny speaks to me. She whispers things. Animals, mostly. And feelings. A sort of vague sense of the future, like a puzzle I have to piece together myself. And sometimes the pieces are difficult to place and sometimes they're dead simple. And that morning with Maria, well, ..."

"Well what?"

Fergus looked into the cold, prosaic faces. It was only then the reality of it hit him. "You won't believe me if I tell you."

"Tell us what?"

"Was it her who told you?"

"Who?" the woman named Liseki asked.

Fergus felt a surge of anger at the little game they were playing. "You know very well who. Maria the Lawyer. That's who."

"Tell us about Maria the lawyer, Fergus."

A whisper ran through his body. He thought of Darragh. And the vision went further, and he saw Clodagh, standing with her suitcase, saying goodbye forever. And then she was crying as the leering face of the Geegaw Man loomed above them. The voices grew louder and to stop them Fergus cried, far too loudly, "I don't give a shite if yous believe me or not, it's the truth! I had a vision. I didn't know what, but I just knew she couldn't go to work. So I told her as much."

"You don't have to scream, Mr. Maloney—"

"I had a vision. The voices told me she'd die if she went to work. I had to save her, that's all."

"Are you claiming," Agent Liseki asked, "that you used psychic powers to predict that if ... Maria the lawyer ... went to work on the morning of September 11, she would be in danger of her life?"

"Yeah."

The two FBI agents paused for a moment, examining their notes.

"Mr. Maloney," Agent Jaas resumed the questioning, now reading from his prepared notes. "Are you a member—or have you ever been a member—of the Irish Republican Army, the Irish National Liberation Army, or 'Sin Fine.'"

"*Sinn Fein*," Fergus corrected.

"Excuse me?"

"It's pronounced 'shin', like the front part of your lower leg, plus 'fane'. As in ... um, 'fane'. And the answer is no. I've naught to do with them fuckers. Never have done. I'm an independent thinker. I don't trust politicians and I hate terrorists." He paused to look at their faces and felt despair, because it was clear to him now they'd never believe him. "Listen, honestly, you're making a mistake. I can see why you might think it. I understand you're following every lead, *et cetera, et cetera*, but I'm not who you're looking for. Jesus, look at me, would you ever? Do I look like a terrorist to you?"

He paused and waited for his words to have some kind of effect.

Agent Jaas turned the page in his file and continued, ignoring Fergus's question. Liseki was taking careful notes.

"It says here you're a street vendor. Of what?" Liseki asked.

"Bread rolls."

"And what else?"

"Nothing else. Just bread."

"No sausage? No egg? No cream cheese?"

"I sell good bread. Good bread doesn't need any crap on it to be enjoyed."

"Do you have a vendor's license from the City of New York?" Jaas interrupted to ask.

Fergus glowered back. "Is that what the FBI's arresting me for?"

On they went, writing their notes and studying their files.

"Tell us about your home at 3887A Broadway. How long have you been living there?"

"Four months. Five, maybe."

"You don't seem to be registered as a tenant. No utility bills. No credit cards at that address. Do you pay rent?"

"Let's just say, I have an arrangement with the landlord."

"What sort of arrangement?"

"I clean around the place and keep an eye out when he's away."

"And this landlord is ... Mr. Karim Saunders? He lives at the premises as well?"

"Yes."

"You said, 'when he's away.' Does he go away a lot?"

Fergus paused. "He goes away, yeah. Is that a crime?"

"To your knowledge," Jaas asked, "is Mr. Saunders a Muslim?"

"What's that got to do with anything?"

"Did Mr. Saunders tell you anything about planned terrorist activity, in particular the attacks of Tuesday, 9/11?"

"Not a chance! Sure, Karim's the last person on earth who would—"

"Mr. Maloney," Liseki interrupted him, sliding a piece of paper and a pen across the table. "We would like you to take some time right now to write down a list of all the people you have been in contact with in the last year. People you work with. People you live with. People you associate with when you socialize in the Irish bars. Where possible, provide names, their addresses, and the nature of the contact you had with them. Take all the time you need. We'll be back in a few hours to check on your progress."

"If I do this, can I go?"

Agent Jaas looked back at him with indifferent, grey eyes. "It's likely we're going to have some more questions after that." The two FBI agents rose and were about to leave.

Fergus slammed the pen down on the table, causing them to turn back, almost in synchrony. "I want to speak to my lawyer."

"Mr. Maloney, I would advise you that it is in your best interests to cooperate with us. That will make everything go much more smoothly for you," Agent Liseki said, before wrapping with a single knuckle against the door. A uniformed officer opened the door for them and they disappeared. The door closed with a thud and a bolt was drawn.

Fergus looked down at the blank paper and thought about the FBI woman's advice. He had never cooperated with anyone in his life. Therefore, things had never gone smoothly for him. And he'd be damned if he was going to start tonight.

As the rebellious thoughts swirled, slowly working him up into a fury, exhaustion was banished and he felt the stirrings of a fresh rage welling up inside him. Maria had done what for him would have been unthinkable. She had grassed on him to the coppers. And if that was true, every feeling he had had about her was wrong. Not only had Destiny cursed him, but she had lied to him— something she had never done before. And *she*—this Maria—had betrayed him, just as Clodagh had betrayed him. Just as his mother had done. Fergus fell to his knees and gripped his head in his hands, as the dark thoughts pulled him downwards.

9

As Maria turned, the breeze whipped her brightly-patterned beach cover-up tight against her legs and body. Heading east along the beach, she had barely noticed the breeze because it had been at her back, and so she had walked on despite the pain in her ankle. Lost in wisps of daydreams, she had continued far beyond where the beach houses ended and now the water of Mecox Bay loomed to her right, blocked from the sea by a single barrier of dunes. Heading back towards Southampton and the Laurence family beach house, the headwind pushed against her, blowing fine sand into her face and slowing her progress. She could really feel her left ankle now, and was aware of how she was beginning to limp. A chill ran through her body, despite the sun still hanging in the sky above the Atlantic Ocean. She pulled the beach towel across her shoulders and wished it was the cardigan she had left back at the house.

It was late September, and most of the heat was gone out of the year that was 2001. In one way, this changing of the season felt like any other. The kids had all settled back into the dull routine of school, fall was swooping in with sudden temperature drops and a steady erosion of daylight, and the yellow, orange and black of Halloween decorations had made its way onto supermarket shelves—the first beat in the monotonous 4/4 rhythm of Hallmark holidays: Halloween, Thanksgiving, Christmas, Easter. Break for the summer, and then repeat. It was a rhythm she had known all her life.

But in another, more profound, way, Maria felt as though nothing would ever be the same. It was already clear that September 11 was the event that would define America's place in the twenty-first century. In 1998, Maria had voted for George W. Bush, though with no real conviction. Back then, Bush Jr. was a nonentity whom everyone had assumed would prove to be nothing more than a slightly dumber version of his dad. Likely a single-term president with no policy vision and even less personality. Yet now he was rapidly rising in stature to become the face of a new America.

This change in the national mood bothered Maria in ways she hadn't expected. She had never really been politically minded, and, if anything, would always have leaned towards the Republican side of things. She was, after all, a self-made woman. Growing up in corrupt, Democrat-controlled Massachusetts in the 1980s, she had seen lots of examples of poor people who really had only themselves to blame. They wasted their welfare checks on scratch tickets and junk food. They bought cars and televisions on credit, which they could never hope to afford. And they refused to make the sacrifices she herself had made to achieve her goals. She spent her teenage years in a remote corner of the public library, quietly despising them all, studying harder and harder in order to get scholarships, escape Fall River and never return. Her own success, she had always felt, was proof that the American Dream was still possible.

This was exactly what Jeff's father, William Dale Laurence, made a point of saying at every family gathering. "Take, Maria, here," he would pronounce from his place at the head of the table. "She represents everything that's good about America. Coming from modest means, she has shown us what immigrants can achieve with hard work and sacrifice in this great country of ours."

Immigrants. He always referred to her as an immigrant. Not only had Maria been born and lived her entire life in the United States, but her mother and even her Portuguese grandparents on her mother's side had all been born in the US too, while her father, whom she knew only from her birth certificate, was Puerto Rican. Puerto Ricans had been US citizens since 1941. So for William Dale Laurence, the word 'immigrant' was shorthand for 'darkish skin, jet-black hair and Latina features.' But whatever. Let him say 'immigrant'. It only served to reinforce her image of herself as a self-made woman.

So why was the sudden snap to the political right troubling her so much? Was it because she had a contrarian streak to her? This was what Jeff had claimed during the car ride out, when she protested against all the American flag bumper stickers they saw on the cars streaming along Interstate 495.

"It's like some kind of weird patriotic cult, with Bush in the role of Jim Jones," she had said.

"Would you be happier if people displayed the Hammer and Sickle? Or the Crescent Moon?"

"I'd be happier if people thought for themselves," was her mumbled reply.

Maria's thoughts were cut short by the sight of the white rails of the widow's walk atop the Laurence house. A few steps further, and the blue shingles of the rest of the house came into view. It was a Dutch colonial style mini-mansion, with a massive front deck extension that afforded an unrestricted view of the sea. The deckchairs still had towels on them. Half-empty glasses of lemonade had been left out on the wicker side-tables, but there was no sign of the human occupants.

Inside she heard the voices of Jeff's niece and nephew, and that of his sister Carol micromanaging the children in her persistent, but totally ineffectual way. The bustle of it all, the tribal sense of unity the Laurences possessed always struck her, perhaps because it was such a stark contrast to her own completely dysfunctional family. The Laurence family with its petty squabbles and its strict patriarchy was safe, secure and stable.

"Maria!"

"She's here."

"Thank God! I am, like, literally, starving," Nathan, Jeff's nine-year-old nephew, said without actually greeting her. His pale belly wiggled and jiggled under his polo shirt as he bounced over to the dining room table, which was heavily laden with food. Nathan's rotund chin hung out over the serving dishes as he expended what must have been his last remaining calories of physical energy on surveying the feast, presumably before starvation caused him to collapse altogether.

"Maria, honey," Jeff's mom, Candyce, said, with just a hint of reproach in her voice. "we didn't know where you were! Jeff tried to call you on your cell, but it didn't pick up."

"I'm sorry," Maria smiled. "I lost track of time."

"Nathan Payne! Get your hands out of that bowl this instant, young man! No one eats in my house until everyone is seated at the table, and Maria is far from ready," Candyce turned to Maria with a smile, "Do you want to have a shower, dear? We can wait for you."

"No, we can't!" Nathan moaned, still licking mashed potato off his guilty little fingers.

"It's fine, I'll shower later."

Over dinner Maria sat braced for when the conversation would turn to the inevitable subject: 9/11. Sure enough, it began as dessert was being served.

Jeff described in detail, and not for the first time, the dust, the confusion, the panic.

"Were you scared they were going to attack your building too? 'Cos it could have happened, right, Uncle Jeff? I mean, you were, like, totally close, right?" his twelve-year-old niece, Tracy, asked.

"Well, our office is about eight blocks away, so we were pretty safe. And Maria wasn't even there—"

Apropos to nothing, Nathan cut across the conversation and said, "Imagine you would be, like, in the tower and it was coming down and you, like, jumped out the window at just the right time. So you could, like, surf down the rubble and land on the ground and, like, run away before the explosion got you – KABOOM!"

"That's totally impossible, loser," Tracy told her brother.

"Tracy, don't call your brother names!"

"It's not, 'cos it totally happened to this one guy. Double-loser."

"Nathan, don't call your sister names!"

"Did *not*. Triple-loser"

"Did too, triple-*quadripple*-loser. I saw it on TV."

As the children argued over whether or not 'quadripple' was a real word, the conversation went on, with everyone adding accounts of miracle escapes that had been documented with varying degrees of authenticity. But Maria wasn't listening. She was already recalling the faces of all the people from Peterson Investments who had died that day, thinking how it might well have been her.

"The main thing now," William Dale Laurence pronounced from his place at the head of the table, "is that our response is sufficient to ensure the safety of American citizens. And more than just *being* protected, Americans have to *feel* like they're being protected." He had a quiet authority that forced everyone's attention on him, even the children.

"Is that what this Patriot Bill is designed to do?" Maria asked.

William Dale turned to her. "Why, yes, Maria, I think it is. You sound as if you disagree."

"I don't know if I disagree or not," she replied. "What I do know is this. The biggest reform to our criminal justice system since the Civil War is being shoehorned through Congress in a matter of weeks. They say the House will pass it on Tuesday. How many congressmen would you say have even read the Bill?"

"You can't blame the State Department if the politicians don't do their job," Jeff interjected.

"Have you read the Bill?" William Dale asked her.

"I've read some of it," she conceded. "In particular Title VIII, which redefines 'terrorism' in a bunch of ways that essentially makes anyone and everyone a terrorist, if the State Department decides to call them that. Even financing terrorism makes you a terrorist. So if I give money to someone who gives that money to someone who, for example, 'attempts to communicate information which might endanger the safety of an aircraft'—well, let's suppose I donate to Green-peace and they're blocking a military jet from bombing a rainforest—all three of us are now terrorists, 'enemy combatants' and can be detained in military custody indefinitely. And that's not all," she continued. "Title X allows the Attorney General to pay bounties of up to a quarter of a million dollars to anyone, anywhere, under any circumstances, to bring such 'terrorists' into US custody. No Senate approval required."

Maria paused and looked around her. Many of the Laurence heads were ducked, playing with their food, while Jeff was treating her to an angry stare. The contrarian in her flared up and she went on.

"But the worst part is Title V, which allows the FBI, CIA and, as far as I can see, any other federal agency appointed by executive order—including I suppose this new Department of Homeland Security—to seize bank records, school records or whatever of a 'suspected' terrorist, from any institution without a court order and without presenting any probable cause to do so. Then there's a gag order, which says the institution being forced to give up the information can't even mention that this happened, much less appeal the decision in a court of law. It's all flagrantly unconstitutional."

"You can't fight terrorists with the same weapons as we use against ordinary criminals," William Dale said. "They're working from a different playbook to us. They hate our way of life. They hate freedom. They want to destroy everything we stand for."

"I thought due process and the rule of law were some of the things we stood for? If we destroy that ourselves, haven't we done the job for them?"

"Is this about civil liberties, or is it about apologizing for terrorists?" Jeff asked.

"What are you talking about?"

"You know what I'm talking about," Jeff replied. He and his father shared the briefest of looks, which only added to Maria's bemusement.

"No, Jeff, I really don't. Why don't you tell me?"

William Dale broke the ensuing silence with a slap of his authoritative hand to the table.

"All right," he said. "Enough shop talk for one day. Let's agree to disagree about this one. Maria's entitled to her opinion, which is one of the great things about the very freedom we're trying to defend. It's a freedom her family has benefited from, coming to the United States and working hard so that one day she could become a lawyer in one of the country's top firms. I don't know about everyone else, but I'm willing to drink a toast to that. To Maria and to the freedom she enjoys!"

Maria lifted her glass along with the others, and even forced a smile. But the wine tasted sour in her mouth. She felt like the token minority: a sort of mascot who had been tolerated as long as she kept her mouth shut and accepted her place. But if she tried to raise up her head in disagreement, that was the moment she would be told—in the nicest possible way—that she was nothing more than an immigrant and an outsider. And most of all, it was Jeff's final comment that stuck with her. Apologizing for terrorists? What the hell was that supposed to mean?

The debate went on in her own head, and followed her into the living room, right the way through the family game of *Trivial Pursuit* and into the lounge, where the fire was lit. Her thoughts swirled and danced like the flames she studied, slowly burning down as the Laurence men went off for their customary father-son chat in William Dale's study, and the rest of the family drifted up to bed.

An hour later, Maria was lying in bed in the guest bedroom reading when Jeff came in. She could sense right away from his body language that something was up.

"Your shoulders are lobster-red," she told him.

"I burn easily," he mumbled, looking at her in the mirror. The anger in his eyes burned hotter than the skin on his shoulders.

"Do you want to tell me what's going on?" Maria asked. He froze. She reached a hand towards his arm and he snapped away.

"I'm not stupid, Maria. I can see what's going on here."

"What? What are you talking about?"

"That's why you're getting a PhD in the Patriot Bill. Because of him."

"Him? Who is 'him', Jeff? What on earth are you talking about?"

"Don't lie to me, Maria, you know exactly who *he* is."

"No, I don't, Jeff, I have absolutely no idea what you are talking about."

Jeff's answer hit her like a bolt of lightning. "The Irishman."

"What? Are you crazy?"

Jeff stared at her sulkily. "Tell me the truth, did you sleep with him?"

"I ... no ... that's not true."

"Isn't it? Then look me in the eyes and say it." His eyes were blazing and his lips quivered as he spoke. He was wounded and she felt her heart swell for him.

"OK," she began, and took his two hands in hers. "I did not sleep with him. Or anyone else. I'm not in love with him, and I have absolutely no intention of cheating on you. OK?"

He nodded. She took his head and coaxed him forward into kissing range. "Now why don't you let me put some aloe vera gel on that sunburn?"

As she applied the lotion to his shoulders, his hands reached behind and began to stroke her thighs through the lace nightie she was wearing. He turned abruptly and kissed her.

"Wait," she protested, "I still have gel on my fingers."

"Damn the gel, I want you."

She broke away from his embrace. "Jeff, no. We can't. Not with Nathan and Tracy right next door. I'm afraid they'll hear something."

"We'll be quiet, I promise," he protested, putting a hand on her breast.

She removed it and said, "No, Jeff. Sorry, but no."

He heaved a sigh. "OK. I get it. Just don't try and tell me it's about the kids in the room next door." He threw on a T-shirt and, climbing into bed beside her, lay with his back to her, facing the wall. Maria wiped her hands with a Kleenex and tried to resume her book, but she was getting nowhere. She read the same sentence six times before finally giving up and turning out the lights.

It was only in the safety of darkness that she allowed herself to reflect on Jeff's accusations. She lay awake, staring at the vague black form of the ceiling fan, listening to Jeff's rhythmic snores. But she was thinking about Fergus. There was no possible way she could love him. She barely knew him. She hadn't lied to Jeff— not exactly. And yet, she hadn't exactly told the truth either.

What's happening to me? Maria asked herself. It was as though everything in her life was suddenly in question. Her job, her beliefs, and, yes, even her relationship. Maria had had her head down for so long. She'd studied through the night. She had waited tables, sucked up to professors. And all the time, she had never stopped to wonder if the goal she was aiming for was something worth reaching.

Everything had been thrown into turmoil by September 11. And, more particularly, by the Irishman named Fergus. The very thought of him sent an unexpected thrill through her: a genuine emotion that was so badly lacking otherwise. He had awakened in her something she had perhaps not even realized she was missing. And then he just disappeared. What had become of him? The man who had saved her life.

Maria rose, put on her robe and crept out of the room. The hallway was silent. She went downstairs and pushed open the screen door leading to the front deck. Waves crashed and the wind whistled through the dune grass. She sat on one of the wicker deckchairs and watched the sliver of moon cast a rippled patch of yellow onto the otherwise black pit that was, by day, the Atlantic Ocean.

Here, with only the stars and moon as her witness, Maria felt free to indulge in the thoughts she had up to then forbidden herself from thinking. She allowed herself to acknowledge that she wanted—no, that she *longed*—to see Fergus again. And if she couldn't, she at least needed to know that he was alright. Had he taken his little portable bread oven and pushed on to another location, like an Irish gypsy? Maybe he'd gone south, chasing the warm weather?

A shiver ran through her and Maria realized she had been sitting on the deck for over an hour. She went inside and crawled back into the warm bed beside Jeff. But not before deciding that, first thing Monday morning, she would track down Fergus and find out what had happened to him.

10

The buzz of the neon light overhead, which Fergus had not noticed at first, was amplified by the silence. It seemed to waver up and down in volume, creating its own kind of melody. The smell of the cheap office carpet filled his nostrils. He ran his fingernail over the canvass seam on the edge of the folding bed.

When the door opened, Fergus opened his eyes. One of the guards had entered, with his police baton at the ready.

"It's clear," the guard called to someone behind him, and a blurry figure in a suit entered, advancing to the foot of the bed.

"Mr. Maloney, are you awake?"

Fergus rubbed his eyes and the man in the suit came into focus. It was Agent Jaas.

"We'd like to continue questioning you now."

Fergus rubbed his eyes some more and hoisted himself up to a seated position on the bed. It felt as though he'd hardly slept a wink. He wondered how the FBI man could look so fresh after only a few hours' sleep.

"Am I not even allowed breakfast? Or is this part of the interrogation—you starve me into submission?"

"It's eleven-thirty. You slept through breakfast, Mr. Maloney. That was your choice."

"Are you prepared to cooperate with us today?" It was a woman's voice. And Fergus saw that Agent Liseki had been standing right behind her partner. She spoke in a kindly voice. "Because if you are, I'll see to it that you get some breakfast." Clearly she was playing the role of the good cop here.

Fergus heaved a sigh and rose. "Right, let's get on with it, so."

Jaas ran his cold eyes over Fergus's crumpled clothes, which he had slept in. The agent twitched his nose, and said, "Officer Cunningham will escort you to the interrogation room. You can eat your food in there."

As he was being led to the interrogation room, Fergus craned his head and tried to peek through the small wire-meshed windows atop the doors along the corridor. They were too high to see inside, but from behind a few he could hear voices moaning or speaking rapidly in a foreign language he did not recognise. *Where in fuck was this place?*

He glanced at the uniform of the guard who held him firmly by the elbow as they walked. The uniform was not that of a prison officer, or any cop Fergus had seen before. The shoulder patch bore the image of a pyramid with an oversized eagle perched on a column in front of it. It did not say 'Federal Bureau of Investigation', nor NYPD, but rather the more cryptic 'General Services Administration'. In his fatigue, Fergus had failed to notice any of these details the night before. Now he began to realize how strange this all was.

They brought him to the same room as the night before. Agents Liseki and Jaas were already seated, waiting for Fergus to take his place. There was a Styrofoam coffee cup waiting for him, and a six-pack of powdered doughnuts. *Breakfast of Champions*, Fergus thought. Still, he was hungry enough to eat a horse, and stuffed the first doughnut in his mouth, even before sitting down.

"Uggh, the fuckin' coffee's stone cold!"

"Regulations stipulate we are not allowed to provide hot beverages to detainees."

The white-powdered dough stuck to his dry mouth, sweet and full of chemical preservatives. Fergus winced as he washed the gloop down in a putrid gulp of cold, tasteless, instant coffee. Only then did he realise how empty his stomach had been. And how the shite they were trying to pass off as food was sticking in his gob. His own standards were low enough, but this was bloody torture. The Geneva Convention had to say something about three-hour-cold Folgers' Decaf without so much as a drop o' the oul' *bainne.*

"Have you made any progress on the list of contacts we asked you to produce last night?" Agent Liseki asked.

"Have you made any progress with the list of 'go-fuck-yourself' which I asked you to produce last night?"

Lowering his head, Jaas spoke rapidly into a pocket Dictaphone. "Despite repeated requests, the witness has refused to cooperate by providing the names of his contacts and associates."

Fergus picked up a second doughnut and pretended it was his own Dictaphone. With the same head motion, he spoke into it, "Despite repeated requests, the prick in the suit refuses to be anything other than a wanker."

The agents ignored him. They had a new file now which they were studying.

"It says here the High School you attended was called the Community College in Clonakilty County Cork," Jaas read from the file.

"Is that what it says?" Fergus answered. The same thought came back to him that he had had the previous night. How in fuck did they know so much about him?

"What subjects did you take in school?"

"Ah, you know. The usual. English. Maths. Geography. Bomb-making. Koran reading. For sports, we mostly went to the shooting range and fired off our Kalashnikovs."

"Mr. Maloney," Jaas said. "This can go on for a really long time, if you keep refusing to answer our questions."

Fergus slammed his fist on the table. "What fuckin' difference does it make what subjects I had in school?" In an instant the guards closed in on him, but Liseki waved them back.

"The fact is," Liseki leaned across the table with an air of complicity, "you are not our target profile. Ideally, we would like to be able to clear your name and move on to other files. What we are trying to do here is rule out any link between Irish terrorism and the September 11 attacks. But in order for that to happen, you have to cooperate. You've had food. You've slept. Now I'm going to give you a fresh paper and ask you, once again, to provide us with a list of the names and contact details of everyone you associated with since your arrival in New York. In particular, we would like to know the names and descriptions of any associates or friends of your roommate Karim Saunders who might have visited your place of residence. So, no more obscenities. No more jokes. Just give us the names." She forced her even-featured face into a smile which fell as quickly as it had risen. Liseki's manner was so cold and humourless that playing the part of the good cop wasn't coming easy to her.

As if on cue, they rose simultaneously and headed for the door. "We'll return in a few hours."

"What about my lawyer?" Fergus shouted before they closed the door. "I have the legal right—" He glanced at the wall where the copy of the Miranda Warning had been hanging. The torn pieces of tape marked out the spot of bare wall. The Miranda Warning was gone.

"Just cooperate, Mr. Maloney. For your own sake." The door closed and he heard once more the sound of the bolt sliding into place.

At some point in time more food arrived—this time a Styrofoam cup of lukewarm tomato soup with packets of cheap crackers—and Fergus forced it down. He took care to spill a little of the tomato soup on each of the six pages he was working on, and generally make a mess of it.

In his own sloppy, haphazard way, he wrote out a number of names of very random people he'd met, then kept it going, adding in more and more names. He started making up names, just to fill out the list. The longer and more irrelevant, the better. Further down the list, when another surge of outrage took him at having to do what essentially felt like a primary school detention punishment, he wrote the name *'Sheldon Horowitz, my new lawyer'*, then, in the column labelled *'Where I met them'* he wrote *'In this manky, shit-arse prison cell'* and under *'When'* he wrote *'pretty damn soon, or I'll be suing your asses from here to Beverly Hills.'*

The one thing he did not give them was any solid information on Karim. He'd be damned if he would grass on Karim or anyone he called a friend. Fergus was from Cork and he was a Republican, in the Irish sense of the word. And that meant his first rule of life was you never tell the coppers anything that's worth knowing. The second rule was you never betray your friends.

He finished the list, and ate the last of the crackers which he had saved as his reward. He rose and banged on the door. It was opened by the same guard who had been there that morning.

"Tell Agents Jazz and Lucozade I finished the list."

The guard looked at him blankly and closed the door again. Fergus kicked the wall in anger.

There was nothing to do. What felt like hours went by, without sign of another soul. Fergus felt sure the day must have passed entirely and night had fallen. He thought of the fact that he'd miss his Friday evening Irish music session at The Purple Shamrock, where for the price of pounding on a *bodhrán* like an eejit, he was given free pints and the right to call himself a musician.

He ran his fingers along the walls, traced the pile of the carpet, tapped his knees, shouted random bits of music or poetry, anything to avoid the nothingness that would bring with it the one thing Fergus could not abide: his own memories. Once or twice he tried knocking on the door again, but after a while the guard stopped opening up for him.

Eventually, gazing at the floor, he noticed that in places the carpet had been imprinted with heavy objects, likely furniture, which had only recently been cleared out of the room. He moved the table and traced the shapes made by the imprints. A filing cabinet had been against the wall. Here a shelf. And there a photocopier. Fergus realised he wasn't in a prison at all. He was in a fucking office building. *What kind of a hack operation is this?* He thought to himself. No phone call. No lawyer. *How do I even know they are the FBI?*

When they finally returned, Fergus's heart lifted in joy at the sight of them. Hated though they were, the boredom and silence of the interrogation room had grown intolerable. He hastily shoved the paper over to them and watched them read it in silence.

"What about friends of Karim Saunders?" the FBI man asked after a while.

Fergus shrugged. "Wouldn't know much about what friends he has. I never met any, anyway. But, like, in fairness I go out most evenings so I'm hardly ever around."

"Have you ever attended any social events with Mr. Saunders?"

Fergus paused. "Not really, no."

The FBI agents stared blankly at him.

"What about the 4th of July? Were you at a cookout organized by the Mount Zion Baptist Church?"

"Oh, yeah, I forgot about that."

"Was Mr. Saunders present at that event as well?"

Fergus frowned in a pretence of remembering. "I had a few jars that day ... I couldn't be sure whether he was there or not ... no, actually, I don't think he was."

"Mr. Maloney, you're lying to us. We know for certain that he was there. And that you socialized extensively with him and with a Mr. Shawn 'Mustafa' Troye and with a third, unidentified man."

Fergus looked hard at them and said. "Do you wanna know what I know for certain? I know I haven't been allowed see a lawyer. I know I haven't been let talk to my Embassy. And what's more, I'll tell you what I *don't* know for certain. I don't know who the fuck you even are! Because I haven't actually seen your fuckin' badges, have I? And what else I don't know for certain is where the fuck I am, because this isn't any kind of a prison building. And you've been asking me all the questions, now I'll ask you a question. What am I being charged with? What law is it you're holding me under?"

Jaas curled his lips in contempt. "You are being held under Title 18 of the United States Code as a 'material witness' to the planning and execution of terrorist attacks against this country which took place on September 11 and which claimed the lives of thousands of American citizens."

Liseki calmly gathered up the pages Fergus had written and, once again, the two FBI agents rose to leave. "We asked you to cooperate, Mr. Maloney, and you refused."

The door swung open and Jaas said to the guard, "Return the detainee to his cell. You can let CT Division know he's ready to be processed."

"So what happens now?" Fergus asked.

"We're done with you," Liseki answered, before disappearing into the corridor outside.

Thank fuck! Fergus thought to himself. A quick sniff under the armpit confirmed his suspicion that at this stage, he stank to high heavens. He wondered would he still have time for a shower before heading up to the session at The Purple Shamrock. *Better late than smelly,* he decided.

The door opened and the big guard with the 'General Services Administration' sleeve patch entered the cell.

11

The bar was practically empty when Maria entered. An old man in a tweed cap sat at one end of the counter nursing a glass of Miller and reading the sports section of the newspaper. He looked up briefly before returning to his article: 'Yanks set to clinch AL pennant'.

Maria scanned the rest of the pub to see if the barman was somewhere down the back. The bar stools were turned upside down on top of the tables for sweeping. The sound of a newscast made her turn and look up at a television suspended from a bracket above the door. Attorney General John Ashcroft was being interviewed on CNN.

"… the American people do not have the luxury of unlimited time in correcting the necessary defenses to future or further terrorist attacks. The danger that has darkened the United States of America and the civilized world on September 11 should not pass with the atrocities committed that day. Terrorism is a clear and present danger to Americans today …"

"You lookin' fer Barry? 'Cos he ain't here." It was the old man. He was watching her watching the television.

"Well, is there anyone working here?"

"Ya, the kid's here. HEY, BLAWNDIE!" he shouted into the backroom at the end of the bar, raising his voice so sharply and so suddenly that it caused Maria to jump. "There's some dame here who wants to talk to ya' and she looks pretty good. So hurry up before she leaves. Might be yer only opportunity to get laid!" The old man chuckled, revealing a mouthful of missing teeth. "That'll get 'im running. And he can run fast. He's fresh off the boat. I can say that 'cos I'm Irish myself."

She forced a smile of thanks and acknowledgement. He fixed his myopic stare upon her.

"How 'bout them Yankees, huh? You think Joe Torre can make it fouwr outta fouwr?"

Maria smiled and shook her head. "I'm sorry, I don't watch baseball."

When a young, blond man finally appeared out of the back room, he was carrying a plastic tray loaded with beer glasses and had a dishrag slung over one shoulder. He nodded a greeting to her as he placed the tray on the counter and began slotting the glasses into the rack.

"Excuse me," Maria asked. "I'm looking for someone and I was wondering if maybe you could help me." She paused, expecting a reply. But the young man with the blond hair just continued his work.

"He's Irish and I thought maybe someone in the community might know where he went."

"Who is it?" the barman asked.

"His name is Fergus. Fergus Malone or something like that. He sells bread. On the street."

With the rag, he wiped the remaining moisture out of the glasses, then put them away. He considered each glass with care in a way that was either profound or profoundly idiotic, Maria could not tell which.

"Sorry," the young man eventually said. "I'm fairly new here myself. People come and go. I rarely catch their names."

She watched him wipe another glass. "He's tall," she insisted. "With dark hair. And blue eyes. Very blue eyes. He tells fortunes."

The barman shrugged and wiped another glass dry. "No, sorry ..."

A sigh escaped from her. "I've been to ten bars so far. No one's heard of him. It's like he's a ghost."

She waited for the barman to say something in reply as he stacked the glasses in his ponderous way. When he did eventually speak, he did so without looking up.

"If you like you can leave your name and number on this, and if I hear anything, I'll pass on the message." A beer mat and a pen appeared on the counter.

By the time she finished writing he was already on his way into the back room with the empty dishwasher rack. "You can just leave that on the bar," he told her over his shoulder.

Maria left the pub in bitter disappointment. This was turning into a quest for the Holy Grail. If she had found a trace of Fergus early on, and a plausible explanation for what had happened to him, she probably would have abandoned the search. As it was, it made no sense to her that someone as loud and rambunctious as Fergus would be completely unknown in any of the Irish bars. If anything, this only added to the mystery that surrounded the strange bread merchant who had saved her life and then disappeared to nowhere.

Panic engulfed her. What if she never found out what became of him? What if she never knew whether he had truly been behind the attacks or not? She remembered his words, that she was good enough. Also his cocky assurance that she would quit her job and fall desperately in love with him. And he was just as convincing when he told her she would die if she went to work that morning. Maria had to know. She *had* to know what the fuck this guy's deal was.

She walked as far as the corner of Norfolk and Delancey in the hopes of getting a cab heading downtown, and briefly debated which side of the six-lane road to stand on, before deciding to stay on the eastbound side. Of course Murphy's Law had it that about six cabs went past on the westbound side. She was about to give up and take the subway, when a voice at her shoulder made her jump.

"Them Micks ain't never gonna tell you shit, you know."

"Excuse me?" she turned and saw the old man who had been in the bar earlier. He now had on a faded blue New York Rangers jacket, with his newspaper tucked under his arm and his hands thrust into his pockets.

"They're all illegal. Every one of 'em. Scared as shit you might be a Fed or somethin'. Maybe you gonna send 'em back to the Old Country? Whadda they know? Rule number one of bein' Irish. Never tell nothin' to no one who might be a cop. Comes from bein' ruled by the Brits for so long."

She looked at him skeptically. "So then why are you talking to me?"

"Because, number one, I'm third generation. Born right here in New York City. Ain't nobody gonna deport me nowhere. Number two, I know you ain't a Fed."

"How do you know that?"

"'Cos you don't look like a Fed. More important, you don't *smell* like a Fed. You know what you smell like?"

"Tell me," Maria said, before realizing she really didn't want this revolting man to tell her what he thought she smelled like.

"Like a lawyer."

"So are you telling me the barman back there knows Fergus Malone?"

"Maloney. His name is Fergus Maloney. And yeah, sure Blawndie knows him. I know him too. Everybody knows Fergus. It's impossible not to. Used to come in to Duignan's Bar with his little wheelie contraption and share out his pigeon food like he was Jesus feedin' the fouwr thowsan'. Then he'd tell jokes and get people to buy him beers all night."

"So where is he?"

The old man sniffed at the air. Maria waited for a response and then asked the question again.

"Sorry I didn't understan' the question. I don't hear so good sometimes."

"I asked you *where*—"

"Naw, I still can't hear nothin'."

"I ASKED YOU WHERE—"

"I've been savin' up for a hearing aid, you see. But they're real pricey."

Maria stared blankly.

"*Real* pricey ..."

Only then did she get the message, and took out her purse. "Twenty is all I've got." The little man whisked the bill out of her hand with a claw-like fist that retreated back into the sports jacket before she could blink.

"So now tell me where—"

"He disappeared. Nobody knows where he went. One day he was in gettin' drunk like normal. Next day he's gone."

Maria paused and looked at the wretched old man as he cracked a malicious, decaying smile. If there was a sense of fraternity and community among the Irish in New York, this creature clearly did not share it.

"Maybe he went back to Ireland?"

"You think so?" He sneered and turned abruptly, visibly enjoying his dramatic departure from the conversation. Maria overcame her repulsion enough to ask him one final question.

"So then what?"

"Do I look like Dick Tracy to you, lady? Go hire a PI." And with that he turned and crossed the road, whistling a tune to himself.

At that minute a cab appeared in front of her and Maria threw her arm out instinctively. She had the rear door open and was about to hop in when a different thought struck her. She apologized to the driver, closed the door again, and retraced her steps to the Irish bar.

The blond barman looked surprised when she appeared again. Now she had more confidence in her stride. With the old man gone, it was just the two of them.

"Now listen," she told him. "I know you lied to me. And I know you think I'm with the government. Well, I'm not. Here ..." she threw one of her business cards on the table, "... I'm a lawyer. I have never worked for the INS and I have no intention of reporting anyone. You have to trust me on this."

The blond man's countenance remained unmoved.

"I need information about Fergus Maloney. Fergus Maloney: black hair, blue eyes, about six foot two. You know who I mean."

"Why?" the barman asked after a moment's reflection.

"Because," Maria started to answer, then realized she didn't have a good explanation. "Because I'm afraid he might be in trouble."

"Well and if he is," the man said, with both stocky arms now planted on the bar, "what's that to you?"

"I'm ... I'm his lawyer."

The barman considered this for a moment. He picked up the card and examined it, then gave her a hard look. Finally, he nodded slowly. "What do you want to know?"

"Was he a regular here?"

"Fairly regular. Some nights he drank in Brooklyn, mostly in The Purple Shamrock. Occasionally a few bars uptown. But this was one of his preferred spots. He'd got to the stage where he was, you know, settled in."

"And then?" she asked.

"And then he disappeared."

"Do you know where he went?"

The barman just shook his head.

"You think he went back to Ireland?"

The barman shook his head again. "Wouldn't say so."

"Why not?"

This time he gave her a long look. She was tempted to take out another twenty, in case he too was expecting some lubricant. But before she had made up her mind to do so, he reached underneath the counter and produced a letter.

"These keep coming for him. Two a week." The envelope was squat: the sort used in Europe. It was addressed to '*Fergus Maloney c/o Larry Cullen, 1342 West Riverside Drive, 07024 Fort Lee, New Jersey*'. On the back was a return address: '*Clodagh Brogan, 23 Harlech Crescent, Clonskeagh, Dublin 14, Ireland.*'

"She's either an ex-girlfriend, or else she's his sister."

"So, would you have any idea where he did go?"

The barman shrugged. "He used always to be talkin' about going to Cuba. Just a fancy of his, I reckon. Never thought he'd actually make it there. But that's the only place he ever mentioned."

Maria took down the address and thanked the barman. As she sat in the cab on her way back to the office, she thought about the possibility of a man like Fergus just leaving on a whim and heading off to Cuba. How likely was that? She had no idea, really. What did she know about him? Nothing. And why did she even care so much? Another question she couldn't answer.

12

Whatever hope Fergus had entertained of going out to the Purple Shamrock that Friday night evaporated in the long, boring hours he was forced to spend back in his cell. They had mentioned something about 'processing', but that was ages ago. How much time had passed? He could hardly tell. Was it midnight? Two in the morning? The corridor light streaming through the little window at the top of the door gave him no indication of time. Only the fact that the footfall had lightened in the corridor suggested it was a quieter time of night. And his body clock was heading towards system shutdown. Eventually he drifted off to sleep.

Fergus woke up with a start at the sound of screaming. A sharp bang on the wall followed, then it turned into a steady pounding. He heard a cell door open and voices calling something in a foreign language.

"Stand down!" a guard's voice commanded. There was a thud, followed by a crash. "I said stand down, motherfucker!" More thuds. The screaming continued in the foreign language until, amidst a successive reign of thuds, it petered out to silence.

At some stage, after what seemed like an eternity, Fergus fell back onto the bed. As soon as he put his head down the cell door groaned. When he looked up a prison guard was already entering the cell, baton at the ready. A second man entered and once they had him spread against the wall, they handcuffed him and led him out by the elbows, without a word.

They led Fergus past the interrogation room, up a set of stairs and along a corridor into another room: one with a glass-fronted window that looked out onto an office area. On the other side of the glass, guards and agents in suits milled about everywhere. A team of men and women at desks were taking phone calls. Beyond the office area was a number of large plate-glass windows, through which Fergus could see the light of a rising sun illuminating the façades of other office buildings across the street. It was a cold, crisp, Saturday morning in late September, and the sky was blue. The sight of the outdoors, of free people going about their business, lifted his heart and made him sing with longing to have the handcuffs removed and get the hell out of there. It was strange, but Fergus found himself thinking that losing his liberty—even for a little while—had made him realise what a precious thing it is to be free. He became increasingly anxious for the guards to come to take him for 'processing'.

The door leading to the office area opened and a little agent in a white, short-sleeve shirt and tie popped his head into the room and stared at Fergus.

"Who are you?" he asked. Before waiting for an answer, he turned back into the office and asked someone else the same thing. "What's he waiting for?"

"They said I was to be sent for processing," Fergus shouted over to him, but the little man ignored him.

"Oh, Code 94, really? He's like the whitest Islamic terrorist— What? Oh, Irish, huh? Well, do we have anyone from INS here? Not this early? Then take him back downstairs or something! What? No shit! Has he even had breakfast?" The man's head turned back towards Fergus. "Have you had breakfast? You understan' English?"

"Ah, yer grand," Fergus nodded, "I'll get some food once I'm let go."

The man laughed at this, and instantly Fergus went from liking him to hating him. "He'll get some food once he's let go! Hey, Bonzo, BONZO! Get over here. Can you feed this guy or something until INS gets here? No, he's not going downstairs ... because, apparently there's no more room down there ... I dunno, because they had to put the Afghanistanis in different cells from the, uh, Iranians or whatever the fuck they are ... I know, it's like a fuckin' zoo ... yeah, really ..."

The door closed again, and Fergus watched the little man in the short-sleeve shirt disappear into the confusion of the big office on the other side of the window.

The ultimate insult came an hour later when a bearded man, whom Fergus assumed was 'Bonzo', arrived with some doughnuts and another Styrofoam cup of coffee, which he left on the table in front of Fergus.

"Hey, the handcuffs!" Fergus said.

The man looked back at him and shrugged. "Sorry, I'm not authorized to deal with that."

"You're not authorised to ... Aw, fer fuck's sake, I can't fuckin' eat with my hands behind my back, can I?"

Bonzo left without another word.

Fergus sat for a second, looking at the doughnuts and the coffee left tantalisingly close to his mouth. He could feel the rage building up inside of him. The sleeplessness, the hunger, the absolute pointlessness of this whole daft charade were too much for him, and it all exploded out at once. "FUCK!" he shouted, lifting himself out of the plastic chair and kicking the table so hard it flew onto its side. Coffee and doughnuts went everywhere. "Let me the FUCK out of here right now!" He ran at the door which led into the big office and kicked it furiously. It was about to break off its hinges. Several people stopped what they were doing and turned to look at him.

A second later the guards, who had been standing outside the door, were upon him. They pulled him to the ground. As his head hit the carpeted floor he saw a baton wavering high in the air above him. It came crashing down on his chest. Everything flashed red. The impact consumed his every sensation and turned it to searing pain. As the red flash faded, Fergus could see the slick, black stick above him once more. This time pain seared across his temple.

Blackout.

A thin man with a gaunt face was looking at Fergus leeringly. He had one green and one brown eye, brown skin and a single, good tooth which glistened as he smiled. He was speaking. As Fergus attempted to understand what the man was saying, a drum began to beat inside his head and stars danced in front of his eyes. The man poked at something orange which Fergus had been using as a pillow. He climbed up onto his hands and knees in a desperate attempt to regain control of his body, but this only made him nauseous. The nausea got worse. His body tightened, his back arched, and a jet of vomit hit the orange thing on the floor below him.

Laughter erupted from all around him. The thin man was holding his shoulder, rocking him gently back and forth. Other men came into focus behind him, seated on a metal bench. They were all dressed in orange suits. He looked around at the walls and the metal door. It was a cell of some description. One of the men, also brown-skinned but, unlike the others, with short hair and no beard, was staring intently at him. Fergus had noticed him right away, perhaps because he was the only one not laughing.

"You gotta put that on. Use your dirty T-shirt to wipe off the vomit first. Then put it on."

Fergus looked at the orange thing and realised it was a set of prison clothes. An orange shirt and a matching pair of baggy trousers.

"I'm not wearing that," he said in words that came out unexpectedly hoarse.

"You fucking better," the quiet man on the bench said, without changing the tone of his voice. "I want this to end as quick as possible. So everyone here is going to cooperate and be polite. Including you. I heard what you did in the FBI office, Irish boy. You're not gonna do that again, or, so help me God, I will give you a reason to puke like you never puked before." The short-haired man said something in a language Fergus could not understand. In response, the gaunt man and another, who had risen from the bench, grabbed Fergus from the floor and threw him against the wall. They handed him his orange clothes. "Now put it on."

Fergus nodded, and they released him. He slowly undressed. The men stared at him indifferently as he did so. He put on the orange clothes, stepping gingerly forwards into one trouser leg, then gingerly forwards again as he stepped into the other.

"I don't know what your deal is, Irish boy. But everyone else in this cell is innocent. So if we all stay calm, do as we are told, we'll—"

The beardless man's words were interrupted by the ball of Fergus's foot, which connected with his clean-shaven chin as the Corkman delivered a swift push-kick straight up into his face. The force of the kick caused the beardless man's head to knock against the wall, and he began to slump sideways.

"Now who's gonna give me a reason to puke? Don't threaten me, ya little fuckin' prick, you!"

Instantly, three men were upon him. He attempted to sidestep them, but the surge of rage had caused him to overestimate his own strength. He was jittery with lack of food and still quite nauseous. As they grappled him, his balance failed, and he was quickly wrestled to the ground. A punch landed on his stomach. Someone else was kicking at his legs.

"You fuckin' cowards. Fight me man to man. Fuckin' four against one, you cowards. Fuckin' cunts!" As he struggled to free his pinned arms, he was screaming as loudly as his hoarse voice would let him. So loudly, he almost failed to hear the cell door open.

"Stand down," a voice called. There was a hissing sound of gas escaping and fine vapour filled the air above Fergus face. His attackers released him instantly, and cowered to the corner of the cell, furiously rubbing their eyes and gasping for breath.

"You! Get up!" the voice shouted at him. He attempted to do so, but by this stage the pepper spray had floated downwards and into his eyes. The room streaked and smeared, and he coughed. A guard took hold of his arms. Fergus offered no further resistance as he felt the plastic ties bind his hands behind his back. He was pushed out through the door. A blurry corridor swam past as he was marched into a different room. He was pushed into a chair, but he missed it and fell sideways to the floor. Eventually, he crawled back into the seat; only then did he cop a man was sitting at the other end of the table. With eyes still blurry from the spray, it was all Fergus could do to see that the man was bald and wore a military uniform.

"You're trouble, aren't you?" The man asked. There was something intensely unpleasant about the way he spoke.

It was on the tip of Fergus's tongue to repeat his request for a lawyer and a contact with his embassy, but, for once, he decided to keep quiet. Instead, he held the man's stare, which was hard to do with the pepper spray still causing his eyes to stream.

"And not only are you trouble for yourself," the man continued, flicking through a file that was open on the table before him, but never looking away from Fergus, "but you have a tendency to get others in trouble too. You got Karim

Saunders in trouble. And you were trying to get those Afghani guys in trouble, weren't you?"

Fergus looked down. He watched the military man's hands shuffling idly through the file. Underneath papers, he saw a streak of burgundy which his teary eyes identified as his Irish passport.

"So, Irish boy. Would you like to save the United States government a whole lot of expense and trouble and just tell me all you know about the September 11 attacks?"

"Nothing."

"Nothing?" The man's smile of disbelief fell away quickly.

Fergus hesitated. "It was a misunderstanding."

"The way I heard it told, you knew the attacks were gonna happen before they happened."

Fergus winced. "Just ... just say it was a lucky guess."

The man leaned closer, never looking away. Revulsion built up inside Fergus, until he had to look away. "A lucky guess?"

"That's right."

"Well then see if you can guess where you're headed next."

He rose abruptly and nodded to the guard, who opened the door. "Get him cleaned up. Food in his cell. I want him in solitary until he ships."

13

Cindy was a grueling taskmaster. They had been running for what seemed to Maria like hours already, and her friend gave no sign of wanting to stop for a breather. They were on their fifth circuit of Meadow Lake, near Cindy's house in Flushing Meadows. Hardly anyone else was out at this ridiculous hour of the morning. When they reached the parking lot of the boat club, Maria decided she'd had enough.

"I need pancakes," she groaned, putting her hands on her thighs and watching the steam of her breath hang in the frozen air, as she panted like an old dog. "Lots of pancakes. With maple syrup."

It was the first really cold morning, the second Sunday in November, and Maria had wanted nothing more than to stay in her bed and sleep in. And that's what would have happened, if the incessant ringing of her doorbell at 6:45 a.m. hadn't forced her to shrug on her bathrobe and stumble to the apartment door. It was only when she saw Cindy, standing there in her full marathon gear, her powerful, athletic body covered top to toe in Spandex, that Maria remembered she had agreed to go jogging with her friend. 6:45 in the morning! Why had she agreed to this?

"C'mon girl, we gonna miss a *sick* dawn if you don't hurry your ass up!" Cindy looked like she'd been awake for hours. Her car was double-parked; its lights revealed a little smokestack of exhaust from the tailpipe.

And here they were, two hours later. Day had broken, but so what? Maria was still tired, except now every muscle in her body was aching. The sprained ankle had kept her from doing any real physical exercise for two months, and she was badly out of shape. To make matters worse, her ankle was not yet fully healed. Once she stopped running, she realized how much it was throbbing.

Cindy turned back, still jogging in place. She looked as though she was about to crack the whip, then seeing the look on Maria's face, she took pity on her.

"All right, I hear you." She glanced at the state-of-the-art mile tracker strapped on her wrist. "Eight-point-five. Not bad," then added with a big smile. "Let's get showered up and go get us some reward."

Later, over what could have been the best pancakes in Queens, Cindy told her about her latest *pro bono* case. It was a young black man, David Arthur Smith, from the Bronx who had been badly beaten by two white cops. According to the police report, he had 'resisted arrest'. The cops had acted 'in defense of their lives'. Yet none of the physical evidence supported this claim. Smith had been unarmed and neither cop had as much as a scratch on him. Worse still, the public defender whom Smith had been appointed had previous ties with a white supremacist group. Smith, who read at third grade level and had a few priors for possession of narcotics, ended up pleading guilty to all charges. He was brought to jail in a wheelchair, with both legs broken. Cindy had taken the case on appeal, and would argue Smith had not been given a fair trial. They were also planning a civil suit.

"Course, David's just one drop in an ocean of institutionalized discrimination," she told Maria in between bites of her blueberry pancakes. "There's so many men of color in this country who get shafted and end up in jail, it's no wonder I can't find me a decent boyfriend."

Maria thought about what she had been reading on the Patriot Act. "Bush is doing everything he can to further undermine civil liberties, isn't he?"

Cindy shook her head. "Is' not just Dubya. After all, wasn't Bush who passed the Crime Bill, it was Clinton. Big smilin' Bill! He all down with African Americans when he needs our votes, playing jazz on his saxophone like he was one of us, but then he turns around the next day and talks up to the white folk and all the sudden we all *super-predators*. Racism in this country ain't about who's President and who isn't. It's '*a moral catastrophe, rendered invisible in public discourse.*'"

The quote belonged to Dr. Cornel West. Maria remembered it from Dr. West's course in Harvard Law School on institutionalized discrimination, where she and Cindy had first met. Back then, they had shared a passion for civil liberties, and had even attended meetings of the American Civil Liberties Union. That was before Maria had met Jeff.

"Cindy, I need your advice about something. There's this guy," she said spontaneously, and proceeded to tell her friend the whole story of Fergus. At the end, she asked, "Do you know anyone who could take on a case like that?"

Cindy reflected for a minute, swishing the dregs of her third cup of coffee. "Actually, I do. She's this drop-dead gorgeous Latina I went to college with. And she got the brains to match. Full scholarship to Harvard Law. Got an A in Professor Jordan's Constitutional Law class. I never seen anyone who could write a better brief."

Maria smiled. This was not the first time Cindy had tried to convert her to the cause. "You know I don't do civil rights law."

Cindy was in full '*I'm-playin'-with-ya*' mode. "I'll tell you what I know. I know if Darth Rosenthal hadn't offered you that internship with Rosenthal, Roberts & Greed, you would be doin' civil rights law as we speak. Him and that scrawny-ass storm trooper, Jeff Laurence, are what lured you over to the Dark Side of the Law."

"Cindy!"

"But you know I love you anyways. I always will."

"So I guess that means you don't know anyone who could take this case?"

Her friend swallowed a final lump of pancake before asking, "Where'd you say this dude was from?"

"Ireland."

"You know, that reminds me of the quote from a great Irish statesman—"

Cindy didn't need to finish her sentence. It was Maria's favorite quote from college, attributed to the Irish philosopher, Edmund Burke. A quote Maria had used in her closing remarks the day she'd won the Harvard Debating Championships:

"The only thing necessary for the triumph of evil is for good men to do nothing."

Maria did not hear Jeff entering her office. She had turned her desk so that it faced the window and was busy opening a letter from this morning's mail. In front of her was an open folder containing a pile of papers which included the final draft of the now infamous USA PATRIOT Act of 2001. This piece of law had been passed almost unanimously by Congress, with no significant amendments. She jumped as Jeff touched her lightly on the shoulder.

"Hey," he said. "Whatcha doin'?"

Like a naughty schoolgirl, Maria buried the unopened letter amongst the papers and closed the file. "Nothing," she answered.

Jeff grinned and tickled her ribs, forcing her to buck.

"Holy crap, Jeff!"

Then he tore open the file's sleeve and revealed the guilty documents.

"So this is what you're reading on company time, huh?"

"I'm not billing right now."

"Well you should be."

She opened her mouth to say something, but no good arguments came out. The truth was she had been obsessing about the Patriot Act for days. This single piece of law was providing a legal basis for what was already happening: the US and its lapdog—the United Kingdom—were paying the Northern Alliance in Afghanistan to hand over 'suspected terrorists'. Where these prisoners of war were being kept and under what conditions was unknown. Already Amnesty International was asking questions.

What was even more worrying than the situation in Afghanistan were the reports coming through of extraordinary renditions by the CIA from a number of different countries. Yesterday, it was claimed a German citizen of Iranian descent had been attacked by mysterious agents in suits, in broad daylight, on a busy street in Hamburg, in front of a dozen witnesses. They had stunned him, bound his hands with plastic ties, put a burlap sack over his head and threw him into the back of an unmarked Mercedes. His German wife had reported it, but the cops had not so much as taken a statement. Meanwhile, unverified reports were coming through of detention centers being operated by the CIA in Poland, Uzbekistan and Turkey.

Jeff plumped himself down on the edge of the desk in front of her.

"Didn't you get reassigned to the Malcom Lewis & Son account?"

"Yeah, but—"

"They're specialists in farm machinery financing and insurance, aren't they? Merger deal with one of Brightwell's subsidiaries?"

Professional pride caused Maria to redden. "Actually it's with Agricola Limited. The FTC killed the Brightwell deal last year." This account was the sort of stuff she was handling two years ago. Not exactly a step forwards. It felt like she was being punished for the crime of getting her clients blown up by terrorists.

"So, I take it you're reading the Patriot Act because ... these rednecks need to know about counterterrorism? Another war broke out between the farmers and the cowmen in Oklahoma, huh?"

Maria glared at him.

"Jeff this isn't a joke. This stuff is horrible. With the exception of the internment of Japanese Americans in the 1940s, there's never been a time when we were so quick to throw our libertarian principles out the window."

"Not true," he countered. "You're forgetting about the Sedition Act, which was passed in 1918 and made it illegal to criticize the government over war decisions. Then, of course, we had the McCarthy anti-Communist witch hunts of the 1950s. The systematic oppression of black extremism in the 1960s. Kent State happened in the 70s. And then there was the Iran-Contra stuff in the 80s. Fact is, we have a long and venerable history of violating our own lofty principles.

"Or," he went on, lifting a thin, rhetorical finger, "you could choose to look at it differently. You could see these aforementioned examples as being so striking precisely because—unlike most other nations—we *do* have such lofty ideals, which most of the time, we successfully defend. But there's a balance needed between idealism and pragmatism, and that's what you don't get. Maria, we're in a state of emergency right now. These Islamic terrorists, they'll stop at nothing, including suicide bombing. You want us to respect the Geneva Convention? Tell me, has the Taliban signed it? The old rulebook quite simply doesn't apply any more. This," he pointed to the text of the Patriot Act on her desk, "is the new rulebook. And, yes, people are going to get hurt. Right now that's what we need to do. Hurt some people."

Maria found herself wondering how he would react if someone grabbed him off the streets, threw a burlap sack over his head, chained him to the floor of a military plane and flew him to a CIA detention center. No lawyer. No formal charges. What if Jeff was one of those people who needed to get hurt?

"Hey, don't look at me like that," he said. "I only came here to take you to lunch."

"Sorry, I don't have time."

He shook his head, picking up her copy of the Patriot Act. "Maria, this isn't about civil liberties, is it?"

"Of course it is. What else could it be about?"

His small grey eyes hung on her, and only the slightest quiver of his cheek betrayed any deeper emotion.

"I dunno," he answered. "Maybe an Irishman named Fergus Maloney?"

"I already told you—"

"Tell me again."

A part of her wanted to open up to him right then and there. Nothing, in fact, would have been easier. To tell him that, yes, she had been obsessing about this guy, and that it was a reaction to a situation which had just been so extreme. And then to reassure him that nothing had happened between them. That she still loved him, Jeff, and only him.

But that last part would have been a lie, however much she might want it to be true. And so the only thing Maria said was, "I need to get back to work."

He stopped at the door. "Oh, I forgot to say, I canceled the Thanksgiving ski trip."

She looked up.

"Well, you know, your ankle is all messed up. Not gonna be doing a whole lot of skiing, are we?"

"My ankle's fine. I even started running again."

"Well, whatever. I'm not in the mood for a big trip. I need some 'me-time'. Maybe go to my parent's beach house, eat turkey and hang out with my family."

Ouch. They had been planning that ski trip for a half a year. The timeshare was their one joint asset, bought under intense pressure from Jeff because he had wanted to teach her to ski. And this year they had the season's most sought-after slot—the Thanksgiving weekend—in Vermont's premier ski resort. Now he was canceling and, to rub salt in the wound, was planning a family Thanksgiving. With *his* family, and without her.

A feeling of solitude hit her. Her mom went away every Thanksgiving. That left Maria with nowhere to go on America's most important holiday. She thought of her estranged brother, and even of her father, then dismissed them just as quickly. Sure, her best friends, Sam or Cindy, would happily invite her to celebrate with them and their families, but that would be embarrassing, especially last minute. This was a slap in the face precisely because it was the ultimate reminder that her family was broken. And Jeff knew it. He was doing this to punish her.

Maybe this is exactly what I deserve. To lose my boyfriend for a guy I'm never going to see again. A sickness pervaded her and an anger at the injustice of it. *I'm not good enough, am I?*

That thought, the old thought that always came back, was almost enough to make her capitulate. Jeff was standing there waiting for the usual surrender. This was her cue to say she was sorry for being so distant, to throw herself into his arms. Then he would relent and the trip would go ahead as planned. *Not this time*, she thought. *Not anymore.*

"That's fine," she said. "I've got work to catch up on anyway."

When he'd gone, she forced herself to look again at the file on her desk. She searched for the letter and finished opening it. It was from the FBI, a response to her request for access to documents pertaining to Fergus Maloney under the Freedom of Information Act, Title 5, Section 552. It concluded: "*Request denied, as the information sought is currently and properly classified in the interest of national defense and foreign policy.*"

It wasn't until sometime later that it occurred to her that Jeff had said the name "Fergus Maloney". *Maloney*! *I never told him Fergus's last name. How did he even know it?*

Jeff wouldn't return her calls, and was gone from his office for the afternoon. It could have waited until the morning, perhaps, but some impulse inside Maria wanted the showdown to happen sooner rather than later. If he had defied her, and used his father's connections in the State Department to get Fergus arrested, it was more than simply a breach of the man's civil liberties. It was a breach of trust in their relationship. *Trust and mutual respect.*

The more she dwelled on it, the angrier Maria felt herself getting. The anger sat on the subway next to her all the way up to midtown, where Jeff's apartment was situated. From the sidewalk, she could see there was a crack of light in the living room window, which meant he was home. And yet he refused to answer his phone when she called once again. *Coward! Well, he isn't getting off this easily.* She fished around in her handbag for the spare key to his apartment which she kept for emergencies.

As Maria passed into the building lobby, the doorman Travis looked up from his paperback and gave her a bored nod of recognition. She took the stairs down to the basement. Though Jeff lived at the finest of addresses—East 61st Street, off 3rd Avenue—the actual apartment was nothing but a jazzed-up storage cellar with tiny windows tucked up against the ceiling.

Through the door, Maria could hear loud music playing. After a brief round of knocking, she turned the key in the latch. Her eye fell on bags piled up at the door. Also *two* pairs of ski boots and matching skis. The thumping of the music drowned out her calls. "Jeff? Jeff?"

She peered down the hall and saw there was a light on in his bedroom. The door was ajar. A smell of perfume flooded her senses. Before pushing through, she already knew what she would find.

Jeff was lying in bed with another woman.

"Maria! What the fuck? What are you doing here?" Jeff shouted, as he decoupled. Maria could only stare. Though she was the only person in the room with clothes on, the sight of him there, the very indignity of his actions, made her feel as though she was the one who was exposed. As though every intimacy they had shared was debased, sullied, and cheapened.

How long? How long had he been screwing someone else and at the same time acting jealous? Was his jealousy a ruse, a deliberate smokescreen? Or was it the old truth that the guilty were always the first to cast suspicion on others?

There was enough 'jilted lover' left in Maria for her to look at the other woman a little more closely. As if to complete the cliché, she was younger: maybe in her mid-twenties. At first, Maria didn't recognize the girl. Her long, blond hair half covered her face. Maybe she was some bimbo Jeff had picked up at the bar? But then the hair shifted, and Maria knew who it was. She was an intern with the firm, fresh out of Stanford.

What was her name again? Maria remembered her because she had dressed up as Cat-woman for the firm's annual Halloween party. It was a look this girl had the body to pull off, and that had not gone unnoticed. Jeff had made some stupid comment about her being a slut. And now here he was, a cheating slut himself. Everything made sense. The sudden cancellation. The ski equipment at the door. *Family Thanksgiving, my ass.* The trip to Vermont was happening, but with a different woman!

That was when Maria remembered the girl's name from the one time they had shaken hands.

"Liz..." Maria murmured.

"Um...Sorry I guess," Liz, the 24-year-old intern, replied.

But Maria wasn't speaking to her.

"...is short for Elizabeth," she finished her sentence.

The intern managed a half smile. "Right."

"*Elizabeth in the basement.*"

A chill ran down her body. Now she was sure of two things: That Jeff had reported him, and that Fergus Maloney was innocent.

The phone rang on the other end. The ringtone was the European style: two little solid beeping sounds, then a pause. Then repeat. On the fourth cycle, it picked up.

"Hello?" It was a child's voice.

"Oh, hi. Can I speak to ... um, Clodagh Brogan, please?"

In the background she could hear the boy screaming "*Muuuuum. Phoooooone!!!*" Footsteps. And then a woman's voice.

"Hello?"

"Hi, is this Clodagh? Clodagh Brogan?"

"Yes. Who's this, please?"

"Hi, my name is Maria Da Silva. I'm calling about your brother, Fergus."

Silence on the other end. Then the words "*Go get ready for bed. I'll be up in a minute.*" Then, into the phone, "Who is this?"

The sound of Clodagh Brogan's voice stirred in Maria that strange feeling which Fergus had awakened in her. Up to a few hours ago, she had been frightened by the power of it, confused, guilty for feeling it. Now it was a delicious sensation, and she was already afraid of it fading away, of losing it.

"I'm ... a friend of Fergus's. From New York. I'm searching for him. You're his sister, right? Have you heard from him? Is he there?"

And if he was? If Clodagh Brogan put him on the phone right now? What would she say to him? Maria looked down at the files on her desk and reminded herself there was almost no chance of that. Something had happened to Fergus, and wherever he was, he was not in Ireland.

"No," the Irishwoman confirmed. "It's been a while now and we've heard nothing from him. We're very worried. His mammy is very worried. There's a man in New York called Larry Cullen, who he used to work for."

"I've spoken to Mr. Cullen already. And to other people too. No one has seen him. He ... he's disappeared. I think he might have been detained. There's some evidence he was held by the FBI and may have been transferred into ... I don't know. Military custody, maybe."

"Oh my God ..."

"I'm sorry."

"Where is he? Who's taken him? Why?"

"That's what I'm trying to figure out. Listen, I'm a lawyer. I ... I 've been doing a lot of research and what's going on here is not right. Fergus needs help." From the silence on the phone line, she had no way of knowing whether the woman in Dublin was shocked, or angry, or crying her eyes out. "Is there any way you could come to New York City?"

"I can't. Not now. There's too much to do here. Did Fergus get my letters?"

"I don't think so. No, not since September."

"Will you be speaking to him?"

"I'm not sure. I will, if I can. What about someone else in your family? Your mother, maybe? Or father? Could one of them come?"

When Clodagh spoke next, her voice was choked with emotion. "No," she replied, in something like a gasp. "I have a letter for Fergus. It's mostly from his mother. She's very sick now. And she wants so badly to speak to him. Please, if I send it to you, can you see he gets it?"

"Sure. I mean I can't promise anything but I'll try. Let me give you my address. It's 215 Hicks Street. That's H-I-C-" A sudden impulse seized Maria. She looked at her watch. "You live in Dublin, right?"

"Yes."

"OK, I'm coming to you. I'll be there tomorrow morning." It was four fifteen. There was a red-eye from Newark to London which she could catch if she hurried. She could get a connection there. So much for Vermont, Maria thought as she booked the flight on the Internet. She was going to be spending Thanksgiving in Ireland.

14

At 4:30 p.m. on November 28, 2001, just as Maria Da Silva stepped into a cab bound for Newark Airport, Lieutenant Brandon Zeiss left his office at Andrews Air Force Base, two hundred miles south in Maryland. By 6:30 p.m. he was an hour north of Baltimore, on Interstate 83 heading to his home town of Carlisle, Pennsylvania. He had done this drive a hundred times before. First, in the Chevy pickup truck his dad had given him as a graduation present, and, more recently, in his current vehicle, the minivan he and his wife, Mandy, had bought together now.

Traffic was heavy, which is exactly what you would expect on the Wednesday before Thanksgiving. As the long procession of holiday travelers slowed to a crawl for no apparent reason, Brandon inched past the '*Welcome to Pennsylvania*' sign. Someone had decorated it with multiple Stars and Stripes. A particularly bored patriot had stuck a '*We're comin' to get ya, Osama*' bumper sticker across the state speed limit sign a hundred yards further on.

Brandon let his gaze drift up the highway embankment and into the desiccated foliage of Penn's Woods. The last of the brown and gold leaves clung tenaciously to the branches, shivering in the breeze. Winter was on its way again. Brandon found himself wondering how much of the coming winter he would get to see. Not much, he guessed. A pang of regret and fear shot through him as he remembered the form he had signed and left in the Mail Out tray earlier that day. He was afraid of having done the wrong thing. But mostly he was afraid of what Mandy would say to him when he told her.

Mandy already headed up with the kids that morning to beat the traffic and help her mom prepare for the onslaught of the North family. "The Norths come from all directions; east, south, west and, yup, even north!" her dad would inevitably say at some stage after dinner tomorrow, placing his hands on his belly and leaning back in his chair to survey with pride his Irish clan of six children and eleven grandchildren, who gathered every Thanksgiving in the North family home in Carlisle.

Brandon knew he ought to have called Mandy when the offer letter came, and, at least, have the conversation on the phone. He had sat there at his desk, staring at the piece of paper marked '*Confidential*' and '*Urgent*'. He had wanted to call her. But he couldn't. She was going to be pissed that he didn't call her, because it meant he had taken a decision that would affect her too, without consulting her. That was the thing she always hated the most. *So the mission begins with a screw-up*, he realized.

Instead he called his brother, Zack, who had told him without a second's hesitation that he should accept the offer to participate in the new Joint Task Force 170.

"Dude, in life you never regret the things you do. On the other hand, you always regret the things you didn't have the balls to do. Plus, if you want to make colonel before you retire, you gotta shine, right? This is your chance to shine, bro. No way you're beating the curve with your ass on a chair at Andrews. Don't take this the wrong way, Bran, but for an Air Force officer with zero flight hours on the clock, you ain't getting any younger."

"How'm I gonna break this to Mandy?"

"Dude, better question: how you gonna break it to Dad if and when he finds out you turned the offer down?"

But his real decision was made when he remembered watching that blip disappear off the radar screen in the operations room in Andrews. That was the moment forty-four innocent people lost their lives on United Flight 93. If America had had better intelligence, Brandon thought grimly, those people would be heading off right now to celebrate Thanksgiving with their own families.

Nearly two hours later Brandon parked on Franklin Street as close to the North house as the backlog of cars would let him. The procession of license plates told the tale of that family spreading its wings across the great United States: Illinois, Massachusetts, New York (Bob's disintegrating '85 Honda Accord),

Virginia, and a rental that meant Jill was home from California. Not to mention Mandy's blue Corolla with the Maryland plates. The Norths had all arrived home.

As he walked up the side path to the back of the house, the same thought hit him as hit him every time he visited his in-laws. How in hell did they all fit in there growing up? It was a four-bedroom, but only if you counted the attic. And it had only one bathroom. His own parent's home was a five-bedroom Dutch colonial over on Fleetwood Drive, with just the four of them living there: his mom, dad, himself and his brother Zachary.

Mandy's dad, George North, had been a mailman who took early retirement due to back problems. Now he was active in the Carlisle Lions Club. His wife worked part-time at the supermarket and did this and that at craft fairs and the local boys' and girls' club. They lived frugally, and despite never having much money, they were never in debt. Growing up, the North kids had struggled to get ahead, putting themselves through college with loans and part-time jobs or else—like Bob—just not going. They were not a military family. The opposite in fact – staunch Democrats with liberal leanings and some pretty weird ideas, as far as Brandon was concerned.

Politics was something Brandon avoided talking with them, especially with his brother-in-law, Bob. Although they were nice people, they were in the category Brandon referred to as the 'bleating lambs'. That was his first category of people. The second category was the grunts: the GIs; the enlisted men; they were what he called 'the sheepdogs'. And the Zeiss family, with its proud military tradition, and its four generations of distinguished officers in the US Armed Forces? Well, they belonged to the third and most important category: the shepherds. Brandon often reflected that if he had not happened to fall in love with Mandy, sheep like the Norths were the sort of people he would never hang with.

It was Bob's voice that drifted into his ear first, as Brandon pushed open the storm door and entered the kitchen. Bob was sitting at the table, surrounded by bowls and chopping boards piled up with carrots, Brussels sprouts and yams waiting to be peeled. His mom had put him on veggie prep duty, which he had obviously abandoned in favor of strumming the guitar that was now in his lap as he crooned the lilting, plaintive tones of 'While My Guitar Gently Weeps'.

He looked up at Brandon and pushed a tuft of greasy hair out of his eyes.

"George Harrison, Rest in Peace," he said, by way of greeting. From the way he spoke, Brandon could tell he was stoned.

"What, the guy from the Beatles? He died?"

"His body died two hours ago," Bob answered solemnly. "But in a deeper sense, there never was a time when he did not exist. Nor will there ever be a future when he shall cease to be."

"I thought somebody shot him in New York, like, back in the Eighties."

"No, man, that was John Lennon." Bob's long, dirty fingernails plucked the wisp of a tune out of the guitar strings, and soon he was lost in his music again.

Brandon forced a smile and said, "It's good to see you, Bob," before entering the living room to be greeted by the rest of the flock.

Scott Zeiss, Brandon's pride and joy, broke free from playing with his cousins and ran to his daddy's arms.

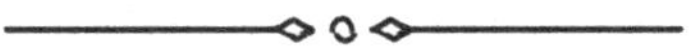

"I'm walking as fast as I can, Brandon. It's hard with the baby!"

"I know; I didn't say anything."

Before he reached the car, Mandy caught him by the arm and pulled him to a halt. When he turned to face her, she was smiling. "Honey. It's okay. We're, like, five minutes late. I'll take all the blame, OK?"

Her smooth, beautiful features, her soft, round eyes, the long brown hair woven into a braid that hung over her shoulder in the front across the kangaroo-style baby carrier containing their daughter Linda; these exquisite details of his wife were almost lost on him in the stress of the moment. Because it wasn't okay. And they weren't just five minutes late.

They were *eleven* minutes late. Not acceptable in the Zeiss family. Father took it as a mark of disrespect.

"You don't have to take the blame, Mommy" Scott said, tugging vigorously on his mother's dress. "It was Uncle Bob's fault. Right, Dad? I'll tell Grandpa whose fault it was."

Brandon grinned at his son in pride, and his anxiety melted away. Scott was a Zeiss, through and through. A shepherd, born to the loveliest lamb-mother in the world.

It took Brandon only four minutes to cross town and pull up in front of the house on Fleetwood Drive. Mother was already waiting at the door. When they got out of the car, she waved them in. Scott ran into his grandma's arms, but there was no time for greetings. They were ushered through the hall into the elegant dining room, with its wood panels and heavy curtains, in which, as a boy, Brandon had listened to the sound of his soup spoon, as each agonizing contact with the elegant Lennox china soup bowl broke the artificial silence of their austere family dinners. Nothing had changed in that room. Not the military insignias on the wall; not the portrait of Johannes Zeiss, their noble German ancestor who settled in Philadelphia in the mid-1800s. And in the center of this antique room, the polished cherry dining table was set with the Lennox china and the Tuttle sterling silverware, waiting for them. At its head, Father sat, as polished as the knives and forks, reading a book.

He rose slowly when they entered, and took off his reading glasses. But not before glancing at his pocket watch.

"Amanda, you're welcome here, as always." A stiff nod, then he turned to Brandon. "Lieutenant." Another stiff nod. "And YOU, young man," he pointed down at Scott with mock ferocity. Up to last summer, Scott used to hide behind his mother's leg whenever his grandfather stared at him like that. Scott's grandmother would scold her husband gently for scaring the child, to which Colonel Zeiss would reply, "Nonsense! He's a Zeiss, not a coward!"

But now Scott held his ground, stood to attention, and simply replied, "Hello, Granddad," the way his mother had advised him to. Once again Brandon's heart filled with pride. He himself had never been able to stand up to Father like that when he was a boy. Scott had his Uncle Zack's boldness of spirit. In time he would be a formidable shepherd, a good husband, and a valuable asset to the United States military.

The atmosphere over dinner was cold and quiet. No alcohol was served in the Zeiss household, not even for holidays. It always felt eerie and empty to go there after the raucous joy that was had on Franklin Street, with Bob and his guitar leading the merriment, and a bottle of Irish whiskey slowly disappearing, as the cards were dealt for another round of nickel-and-dime poker.

When the food was eaten, Mother made some small talk, asking Mandy details about how Linda was sleeping and eating and so on. Without Zachary there to lead the discussion, there was not much chat on the men's side of the table. Zachary, Father's golden boy—the one he referred to as the True Soldier—was on special assignment with his Alpha Company of Army Green Berets and could not get leave for Thanksgiving.

"Any more word from Zack?" Brandon asked at one point.

"Captain Zeiss and his Alphas shipped to Afghanistan last Tuesday. Operations are already underway. The rest is classified."

Brandon gave a silent nod. Scott began playing with the saltshaker. Brandon was about to ask Father how things were at the Army War College where Father taught, but thought better of it. He knew from Zack that there had been problems. Father was not happy with the new command, which he felt was too soft, too liberal.

"So," Father said at length, breaking an awkward silence, his eyes focused on the ornate silver sauce bowl in front of him. "When my second son went into the Air Force, I have to admit I was skeptical. We Zeisses never have had a love of the Air Force. Cowards in cockpits, that's the way we always saw them. When it transpired he wasn't even going to be a pilot, I was downright disappointed. A paper-pusher in the Air Force! Five years later and I find my own son has still not made the rank of captain; well, quite frankly, I was beginning to wonder where I'd gone wrong.

"But I must say," And with this he turned and looked Brandon directly in the eye. "This latest news is a welcome development. The Joint Task Force, huh? From what I heard, it seems you'll be back under Army command. When do you ship out?"

Brandon's heart dropped. The women stopped their conversation and stared. Even Scott abandoned the condiments and looked up.

"Not for three weeks."

"Ship out where?" Mandy asked in a tiny voice that nevertheless filled the bigness of the dining room.

Father's look grew even sterner. "You mean you didn't tell your wife, soldier?"

"Ship out where, Bran?" she asked again.

It took him an eon to reply. "I can't say. It's part of OPSEC."

"You can't say?" Mandy whispered in disbelief.

Brandon's face went red. Somewhere on the table a fork clattered against a plate. He tried to look Mandy in the eye, but she had already diverted her gaze.

"Excuse me," Mandy rose and left. Mother rose too and followed her upstairs. Scott hesitated, unsure to which group he belonged.

"I... I only just confirmed today," Brandon explained to no one in particular. "There was no time to tell her."

"But you managed to tell Zachary," Father insisted.

"Is that how you knew?"

Father didn't answer the question. Instead he narrowed his eyes to slits and said, "Look at me, son. I've been married for thirty-five years. My marriage is rock solid. Always has been. There have been exactly two reasons for this success. The first one is that I married a woman of my own faith.

"By marrying a Roman Catholic, you have already fallen at that hurdle. Catholicism is a faith incompatible with our own. They believe salvation comes from pouring water on a baby's head, not through faith alone in Our Lord and Savior Jesus Christ. Marrying a Catholic was a mistake, if not an outright sin, and I told you so at the time. The Good Lord knows I have not changed my opinion on the matter, nor will I ever.

"But the second thing I always did with your mother was tell her the truth. No matter how painful. No matter how much I knew she'd rail against it. And in the end she thanked me for it. Because it meant she knew she could depend on me. Which is the most important quality a commanding officer can have. So you get up from this table, you go upstairs right now and you speak honest words to the woman you made your wife and the mother of my grandson. Dismissed, soldier."

Brandon held Mandy in his arms as she cried. And cried and cried. He wished she would get angry and hit him. Punch him in the face. Shout at him, call him a bastard. He was not a coward. Not physically, at least. He'd withstand a whole battery of blows rather than witness her wordless pain.

Only after what seemed like hours did she speak, in a voice still choked with hurt.

"You remember the night you proposed to me? You said you loved me above everything else and you'd be the happiest man alive if I said yes? And I said no, I wouldn't marry you. And you were shocked. You asked me if it was because I didn't love you, and I said 'No, Brandon, it's the opposite. It's because I love you so much.' Because I knew you'd join the military. And the day would come when you'd leave me alone with our children, and I would—" here Mandy broke down again "—and I would be destroyed.

"You promised me right then; you said you would give up the military if that's what it took. But I couldn't ask you to do that. Not if I loved you. Because I knew who your father was. I knew it was your destiny. And ... and, you remember what happened next?"

Brandon sat in silence, his gaze fixed past her silhouette. He remembered it as if it were yesterday. "I told you maybe we could find a compromise. I told you I'd get a desk job."

"You told me you would do *intel*. You told me that was the one job in the Air Force which was always done on base. Everything could be done from a computer screen, you said. You promised me you'd never leave me on my own like this."

She broke into sobs again.

"Sweetheart, that was before 9/11. Everything has changed now. Our country is under a whole new kind of threat. The military no longer needs paper-pushers who are only good at thinking. And it doesn't need men like my father either, who are only good at acting. It needs men who can do both; think *and* act."

Her reply came as a whisper, so low he could pretend he didn't hear it. "And what about men who can feel?"

15

The cab which bore Maria from Dublin Airport into the city wended its way down the left lane of a heavily-trafficked road, lined on both sides by identical red-brick row houses. A railway bridge with a large Guinness sign read '*Welcome to Dublin*'. Further along, they passed streets of houses with storefronts on the ground floor, over which hung garish signs that clashed even more completely with one another because of the sameness of the buildings they covered. There was a griminess to this part of Dublin that made Maria think of her home town of Fall River, the butt-end of Eastern Massachusetts.

The taxi driver had a bloated, red face and chattered on in his heavy, nasal accent, pointing out to her various details of local interest, and telling her about his brother who was a fireman in Boston. Maria did her best to feign interest and stay engaged in the conversation, but the jet lag was taking its toll. The only thing that ran through her brain was how much this cabbie possessed the infamous Irish 'gift of the gab'. Fergus had it too.

When they entered into what Maria guessed was the center of town, the man interrupted his own anecdote to point out a number of grand old buildings. "That's Trinity College Dublin, that is. On the other side is the Bank of Ireland, what used to be the Irish Parliament back in the day." As they paused at a red light to let a stream of office workers walk across, Maria observed how strangely busy the city was for Thanksgiving Day. Then it occurred to her that for Irish people it was just another day in November.

They left the downtown area along roads that gradually grew more affluent. "The Southside," her guide informed her. "This is where all the posh folks live."

And indeed, the avenues were now lined with trees, and the bookies, old-style pubs and Chinese takeaways Maria had observed on the other side of the river had been traded in for Italian delicatessens, French brasseries and boutique clothes stores. Clodagh Brogan had done well for herself, Maria thought.

"What can you tell me about Clonakilty in County Cork?" Maria asked him.

The driver shook his head indifferently. "Not a bleedin' thing. Only that it's down the country. I've lived me whole life in Dublin. Never been down that far."

At length the taxi stopped on a quiet road of well-tended suburban homes.

Before Maria could even ring the bell the door opened. The physical appearance of the woman who answered the door gave Maria a shock. For a second she felt as if she was looking at a female version of Fergus. The same mouth, the same startling blue eyes, the same wavy black hair, the same pale skin. Only the sister was older and her manner was much more reserved, making her seem older still. When she smiled, it was with none of the warmth Maria had remembered from Fergus.

"Please come in," Clodagh Brogan told her. Her accent was softer than his too, possibly from living in Dublin.

The house was comfortable; tidy, but lived-in. Clodagh led her into the kitchen, where Maria sat and looked out at a well-used backyard of trampolines, soccer goals and a little patio with a barbecue on it. A soccer ball lay in the wet grass.

"Thank you," Maria said as a cup of tea appeared in front of her. "How many children do you have?"

Clodagh smiled at the question, "Three. Two boys and a girl."

A thought flashed through Maria's mind. It was the strangest thought possible; so strange it caught her completely off guard. *If Fergus and I had kids, Clodagh's kids would be their cousins.* Maria pushed it out of her mind by opening her briefcase on the table.

"This is what I know so far," she explained. "Fergus was taken from his home in Harlem. He was interviewed by the FBI and an emergency extradition procedure was opened. Beyond that we have nothing. He just disappeared."

"What did they arrest him for?"

Maria shrugged. "As far as the records show, he was never arrested." Maria fished out another file. "This is a statement from the FBI confirming no formal arrest was ever made."

"So ... where is he? What's happened to him?"

"I've sent out more information requests, but so far no answers. And here's the real kicker. Technically, I don't even have the right to be asking these questions. I can't legally represent him because I have no authority to do so." Maria sipped her tea and continued. "But I can represent you."

"What do you mean?"

"There's a provision in US law that allows for what we call 'next friend' status. What that means is someone can legally represent someone else if that person is incarcerated or incapacitated. We just need to prove there's a close relationship. Not necessarily a blood relation, though that helps a lot. What matters more is that the relationship is close."

Clodagh Brogan looked down into her own mug of tea.

"Are you and Fergus not close?" Maria asked.

"I've tried to be close to him," she said. "I've written to him. I've asked him to come home. I've even paid his debts. But he won't talk to me."

"Well, is there another sibling he gets on better with? Another sister? A brother maybe?"

Clodagh's eyes flashed. "We had a brother, but he died when we were children. It's only us who are left now."

"Why won't Fergus talk to you?"

The Irishwoman didn't answer. Maria reflected on the letters, unopened, which had been sent to Barry Duignan's pub.

"Did something happen between you?" Maria found herself asking. The woman's body language had changed. Maria sensed she had to be cautious. "Clodagh, I'm not trying to pry. But if I'm going to help you, I need to understand the background to this case."

Clodagh shook her head. "I don't know why he's the way he is. He was always a difficult child. Ever since ..."

"Ever since what?"

"Ever since we were children."

The woman's blue eyes were wet with emotion now. "And you know, it breaks his mammy's heart. He made the decision to turn his back on her. He turned his back on all of us. His own mother, whose only wish now is to see her son before she dies. And if only for that," Her blue eyes flashed with something like defiance, "I'll do what I can to help. For mammy's sake."

"Well, the best way we can make her wish come true is by giving Fergus the chance to stand trial. Is there any way I could talk to your mother?"

Clodagh was quick to shake her head. "She's much too sick. She's in a wheelchair now. The cancer treatment has her in bits. I doubt she could take the shock of all this."

"What about your father?"

Clodagh shook her head again. "He died years ago."

"Will you be able to come to New York, at least for the main hearing?"

"I don't know. Mammy needs me daily. I'm her only support."

"It would really help if you could."

"I'll do my best."

Maria tried another approach.

"We'll need to be able to document your mother's illness. Medical records, a statement from her oncologist."

"I can let you have copies of her nursing home statements. But I'll need the originals back. For our taxes."

"OK, no problem. You said earlier you paid Fergus's debts. Did you keep any receipts?" Maria asked.

"I don't know ..."

"We'll need everything we can muster in order to prove next friend status," she said.

"I'll have a look upstairs. Is there anything else?"

"I'd like a picture of him." Clodagh gave her an inquisitive look, which prompted Maria to add, "Not for myself. It's for identification purposes."

When Clodagh left to fetch the documents, Maria wondered why this interview was not going according to plan. In her mind, Clodagh would be heaping praise and thanks on her for the efforts she was making on her brother's behalf. *Is this just me being praise-hungry?* Maria strolled around the kitchen and into the living room. She gazed absently at the plethora of photographs on the walls and on the mantelpiece. The Brogans sure liked their family photos. There were shots of the children winning sports prizes or celebrating birthdays; of a husband, who was obviously some kind of successful businessman, accepting an award or else playing golf. The husband's father and mother were everywhere too. The little girl was pictured riding a pony. In the back of her jet-lagged brain, Maria registered that something was missing. What was it?

After the exchange of papers, Maria asked if Clodagh had any questions for her.

"I suppose I'd better ask about your fee. I've the nursing home to pay for. And the schools for the children. We're not rich, you know."

Maria nodded, struck by the tone. Yet why should she be surprised? Money was money, after all. Even over here in Ireland. "Don't worry," she said. "I'm not asking for a fee." And in answer to Clodagh's unspoken question she explained, "Your brother has already saved my life. The least I can do is try to save his." They parted promising to talk again soon.

It wasn't until Maria was in the taxi heading towards her inner city hotel that she realized what was strange about the pictures in the living room. There were none of Clodagh's mother. None of her father. None of Fergus. And yet the husband's parents, brothers, sisters, were in a dozen of the photos. *Why would a woman who cared so much about her family not put up even one picture of them?* Even stranger: there was not a single picture in that house of Clodagh herself. Maria shivered at the realization that she didn't trust this woman. *Okay, but why don't I trust her?*

The misty Irish rain shrouding the view of Dublin's suburbs provided no answer to the question. To her left ran a low, curved stone wall which formed the entranceway to an institutional building set in grounds. As they passed it by, Maria noticed a plaque mounted on the wall bearing the inscription, '*Clonskeagh Hospital*'.

Maria's heart jumped. "Can you stop right here?" she asked the taxi driver.

"This isn't the Gresham Hotel ..."

"I know." Maria opened the file she'd been given and fished through for the nursing home receipts for Mary Maloney. There it was: *Clonskeagh Hospital.* "Can you wait here, please? I'll be right back."

There was a surprising lack of security in this nursing home which called itself a hospital. Maria half-expected she would have to charm, bribe or lie her way passed a severe matron and into the rooms where the old people sat around. In fact she was able to waltz right through unchallenged. Actually, she had the opposite problem: finding someone to direct her.

"I'd like to see Mary," Maria asked the one nurse she finally managed to track down.

"Which Mary?"

"Maloney."

The nurse gave a look of surprise.

"This way, follow me. I don't suppose you're Clodagh. Not unless you were adopted, you're not."

"What? No, I'm ..."

"Ah, well, it's just Mrs. Maloney keeps asking for her. Clodagh, Clodagh, Clodagh. Where's my daughter, Clodagh? And we've never had sight of her. Not in over a year of Mrs. Maloney's being here. And I know for a fact that woman's house is only up the road. I've a mind to call up to her myself and tell her would she ever come down and visit her mother! So if you're not Clodagh, what are you to Mary Maloney, then?"

"I'm ... her niece. From America."

"Her niece?" The nurse stopped and gave Maria a frank stare of disbelief. "Well, whatever you are, she'll be glad of a visitor at last. Right through that door. Mary's the one in the wheelchair by the window. Mind, she hasn't had her pills yet."

"Wait," Maria called, for the nurse was already on her way to another ward. "There must be some mistake. Her daughter, Clodagh, comes here every day. She told me so. Maybe you're confusing her with another Clodagh ...?"

The nurse smiled coldly. "Clodagh Brogan?"

"Yes. Clodagh Brogan. She comes here every day."

A wry smile formed on the nurse's lips. "Is that what she told you? Well, I work here five days a week as I have done for years, and I can tell you that woman's never been next, nigh' nor near her mother. Of that there's no mistake."

As Maria approached the woman in the wheelchair, she could see Mary Maloney's body was wasting to nothing. Her face was gaunt, deeply lined and pockmarked with what appeared to be open flesh wounds. Her abdomen was swollen, as if she had a basketball stuffed under her night-gown. That was the liver cancer.

"Mary? Mrs. Maloney?"

She turned slowly and squinted at her visitor with eyes glazed, probably from morphine. If there was family resemblance to Fergus or Clodagh, Maria couldn't see it.

"Is that you, Clodagh?" Mary Maloney asked her weakly.

"No. My name is Maria. I'm a friend of your son."

The sick woman squinted. "No," she answered softly. "No, you're not."

For a moment Maria was at a loss for words. "Yes, I am. That's why I'm here. It's because your son—"

"My sons are dead. Both of them."

"Your son Fergus—"

"Is dead! Fergus is dead, just like Darragh! Where's Clodagh? Where's my daughter, Clodagh? I want to speak to her? Nurse! NURSE!"

Maria blushed and turned to see several of the other residents peering over at the scene. She resisted the urge to flee before the nurse arrived.

"Mrs. Maloney. Please calm down. I want to ask you about Fergus. He's not dead, he's in prison. And I'm trying to help him."

Mary Maloney was clutching her face now, pulling at the pocks until bloody pus made her stumpy fingers glisten. "John," she said in a tone of reverence and supplication. She was staring into space. "Come sit with me, John, would you ever, and we'll watch the *Late Late Show*. Leave them, sure, they've gone to bed. They're only children. They're only *children*, John. C'mon an' I'll make you a nice cuppa tay."

"Mrs. Maloney, Fergus needs help."

She turned abruptly to face Maria and her voice changed into something vile and almost demonic. "You're a LIAR!" she screamed. "You're a feckin' little LIAR! Get out of my house and don't ever come back!" Then she was soft again, "John, are you all right, John? Come up now and sit into your chair. Mind, I'll make you a cuppa tay ... I know. Sure, t'was only ever lies. Wasn't he always tellin' them lies? Just like his brother before him. Desperate, like! Ne'er mind that now, and we'll have us a nice cuppa tay. The *Late Late* will be on in a bit ..."

"What lies, Mrs. Maloney?" Maria forced herself to ask, "what lies did Fergus tell?"

In silence the old woman stared out the glass door where dead leaves collected rain in a courtyard. For a while Maria couldn't be sure Mary Maloney had even heard the question. Until at length, she turned to face her. In that eerie way such people have of suddenly returning to the present, she looked Maria right in the eye and said,

"My John was a good man. I won't have you saying otherwise. You're not my daughter. You're not my Clodagh, you lying little bitch. Get out of here. Get out, do you hear me? GET OUT OF MY HOUSE!"

Maria retreated out of the room, with the old woman calling, "Clodagh? Is that you, Clodagh?"

She ran out as fast as she could to the waiting taxi. Once inside, she slammed the door shut. "Please, go. Just drive."

"Gresham Hotel?"

"No, the airport."

On Monday morning, after the group meeting with the senior partners, Seth Rosenthal grabbed Maria's arm and asked her to step into his office for a moment. When she did so and they were both seated, he let a moment pass in which he enforced a power silence, coupled with a small smile.

Seth Rosenthal was a little man, but he had long ago mastered the art of projecting an image of himself much larger than the physical space his body occupied. His features were chiseled and distinct. They drew your gaze into every nook and crevice, every bump and dimple. For Maria, he had always held a fascination beyond the professional respect she had for him. There were times she imagined what her life would have been like if Seth Rosenthal had been her father, instead of a deadbeat loser, whom the records of the Rhode Island state prison system named as Jorge Silvestre Cruz.

"How's everything with the Lewis deal?"

"Fine," she answered. Seth was hard to read, and that always made her a little uneasy. Plus, she knew he didn't call her into his office to discuss the Agricola Investments merger.

"I heard about you and Jeff," he began. Maria's heart leapt. How had he found out so quickly?

"Seth, it's okay, really. I mean, we ended things like adults. He wants to date another woman and that's his decision. I accept that. Period."

Seth studied her in silence. "Period?"

"Period," she confirmed.

"Are you sure it's not more of an exclamation mark than a period? I heard what happened. You have every right to be angry."

Maria sighed. "Wow, news really travels fast around here."

Seth smiled. "An exclamation mark is okay too. What I don't want, given that you both work for me, is a comma, or even a semi-colon. Or a question mark."

Maria nodded. "Don't worry, it's over. As far as I'm concerned Jeff Laurence is just another guy in the office."

"Maria, I know you've had a hard time since 9/11. Losing your client like that wasn't easy. It's only natural you would feel confused."

"I'm fine."

He just gazed at her, and it felt like he was able to see right through the shields of professionalism she put around herself.

"Is there something else?" she asked.

At length he answered. "Putting you on Lewis & Son wasn't a punishment, you know."

She nodded.

"You know, Maria, it's counterintuitive, but what makes someone a champion isn't winning. What makes a champion is learning from your losses."

She forced a smile. "Right."

16

Dear Dubya, hello, this is your old friend, Fergus. You'll *remember me from that night we spent snorting cocaine at the rodeo in Texas back in '68. Remember the way we got busted by the coppers and your dad pulled some strings to get us off the hook? Ah, those were good times! Do you remember that very drunk cowgirl, the one with the plaid shirt and the enormous knockers? Remember how we took her into the back of the Chevy Van and we ... well, anyway ... enough about that.*

Listen, I'm in a bit of a bind again. Your lads here at the FBI or NSA, or I frankly don't know who the fuck they are anymore. Anyway, they seem to think I was involved in some kind of terrorism, which you and I both know is rubbish.

Now, I know our lives took very different paths. I ended up travelling the world and having amazing adventures and sex with beautiful women, whereas you're stuck married to some bible-thumping teetotaller, doing a boring desk job down in DC. But like for old times' sake, I need to ask a favour of you. I'm talking Presidential Pardon here, Dubya.

I wouldn't be coming to you like this looking for dig-outs, only I'm going out of my fuckin' mind in here. I've been in this fuckin' cell now for I don't know how long. Actually, I do know. Forty-two days. That's how long. No lawyer. No contact with my embassy. I get to walk around a yard once a day in circles with some fuckin' ape of a guard watching me. I'm losing my fuckin' mind here, George. I'm starting to write letters to the Presidents, imagining they were my mates. Last week, I wrote one to Clinton. This isn't normal. This is fuckin' madness. Why are you doing this to me? You cunt. You insane fucking C-U-N-.

Fergus started hacking the final 'T' into the wall with increasing violence, before giving up and throwing his metal scratching implement to the floor.

"FUCK ME!!!" he shouted at the top of his lungs. Shouts came back. Metal pipes clanked on metal.

In the nothingness of the cell, Fergus took up his scraper and began another composition, this one a poem. He called it: "To Clodagh":

The rot that's planted in your skin
No make-up can conceal
The lies that you live in
Never turn to something real.
Only oxygen and stinging salt
Can cleanse our wounds and wash our face
Admission of fault
Come with me to the sea, the secret place
And let us weep for our brother
And we'll forgive each other,
And then we'll live.

No sooner was it done than he started scratching it out. Not a letter could remain visible. Even the full stop after 'And then we'll live' had to be changed.

Fergus changed it into a question mark.

17

The plane about to take off from Pensacola Naval Base in Florida bound for Gitmo was going to have to describe an arc around the island of Cuba, because US military aircraft were not authorized to cross into Cuban airspace. They would trace a flight path just off the Mexican coast, near Cancun. Then they'd cut east, flying over the Cayman Islands until they reached the very end of the 'Upside-down Shark', as Cuba was known by the Air Force guys who planned the flight routes. Right where the shark had its eye, that's where the Guantánamo Bay Naval Base was situated. It was a small enclave of US-controlled land in an otherwise hostile, communist country.

This was one of the things Brandon knew well from his former job. Mapping non-friendly airspace and planning flight paths for military aircraft was a huge part of intel in the Air Force. Even if it was mostly boring logistics, it was all strictly classified.

The Navy pilot was a chief warrant officer who introduced himself as Beane. Technically Brandon outranked him, but inside the plane, it soon became clear who was in charge. As an Air Force officer, Brandon was not only welcome, but, in fact, encouraged to take the co-pilot's seat in the C-12 Huron light cargo plane. As soon as the doors closed, Beane's co-pilot snatched a porno mag from a side pocket in the wall and said he was going into the otherwise empty passenger compartment to 'relax'. Brandon strapped himself in and stared at the dazzling array of controls in front of him. After five years in the Air Force, this was the first time in his life Brandon had actually sat in the cockpit of a real plane that was about to take off. The ground handler on the scorched tarmac waved them clear, Beane engaged the thrust and the plane jolted forward with a roar. Seconds later they were airborne.

Brandon watched as the Florida coast began to recede behind them, off to the left.

"You fly this way a lot?" he asked by way of making small talk.

"Every day," Beane answered. "Three hours there, three hours back. That's my gig. Usually just shippin' SRs and supplies. But lately's been gettin' busy. Black shoes, brown shoes. Army, Marines. Butter bars. Gold leafs. Silver leafs. Stars and bars. We even got Air Force guys comin'. Word is, if things get much busier, they gonna start flying in commercials from Jacksonville.

"Now, you'll know better than me why that might be so. I'm just a plain ol' non-commissioned flyin' squid. Say, you wanna take the stick for a while, Lieutenant? She's easy as pie in the sky to handle."

"I ... uh .... naw."

Beane chuckled. "I'm joshin' you. I got the 'sup on you back at base. You a regular Remington raider! Air Force's finest ground pounder. Gonna have to hope and pray me and John-boy back there don't have no double heart attacks, 'cos then you gonna have to learn to fly *real* quick. I'm talkin' Tom Petty and the Heartbreakers at 5,000 feet of alt-i-toode!"

This was coming very close to insubordination. No enlisted man in Andrews would speak to an officer like that, and it was starting to make Brandon's blood boil. He considered pulling rank here and ordering this CWO to fly the plane in silence, but he did not want to start this mission off with bad blood. Not until he knew the lay of the land a little more.

"We all have our jobs to do, Chief. Yours is flying an aircraft. Mine is classified."

Beane chuckled again. "I hear ya, Lieutenant. I don't mean no disrespect. It's just my way of shootin' the breeze. I spend six hours a day staring at nuttin' but sky n' water. Man needs some form of distraction. Johnny back there, well, he got his tittie mags and a lifetime supply o' Kleenex. All's I got is humor."

Bran nodded and relaxed back into his seat. The steady buzz of the engine made him want to go asleep, but that didn't strike him as behavior befitting an Air Force officer. And so he watched the sun stream uninterrupted across the vibrant blueness of the Caribbean Sea, a striking contrast to the cold grey December he'd left behind in Maryland. Tropical islands appeared on the horizon. It was all so beautiful out there. If he didn't know better, he'd have thought he was going to some kind of luxury resort.

It was an even more striking contrast to the barren mountainous terrain his brother Zack was facing, together with his 'A-team' from the Seventh Special Forces Group. The last reports they'd gotten were vague. Brandon only knew his brother was deep in hostile territory, one of a handful of Americans directing a ragged band of pro-US fighters called the Northern Alliance. His men called him Capt'n ZZ, and he had a reputation for being tough, but fair. Already a saying was going around the fresh recruits for the Green Berets, as they speculated on where they might be assigned: "You can have it easy, or you can have it ZZ." Tough though he was, they respected Zack, because he led from the front, like the fearless shepherd he was born to be.

In honor of Zack's sacrifice, Brandon pushed weaker, self-indulgent thoughts of the long goodbye he had had with Mandy out of his mind. *Focus on the mission*, he told himself. *The intel we gather here might very well keep my brother alive.*

As the plane came in to land, Brandon's pulse picked up in anticipation. He saw the clear blue water of the bay first and knew the base stretched across both sides of its elongated mouth, with the airport on the left and the main camp across the water on the right. The beaches along the coast coming in were rocky—not the clear white sand he was expecting. On the airport side, which they were fast approaching, there was no sign of fences or cell blocks or anything like that. Only a few scattered camouflaged vehicles. More was going on across the bay, but it still didn't look anything like Andrews, in terms of scale or significance.

So this was the mighty Gitmo, Brandon thought to himself. "A tick bite on the asshole of a rat" was how one of his pals back in Maryland had described it to him. Or, as he would now be able to call it for the next two years, 'home away from home'. Despite his determination not to be sentimental he realized it was Christmas Eve. He would not get to watch Scott unwrap his presents. He would not be there for his daughter's first Christmas. His heart was sick with regret.

Then he thought of Zack. And of his father's parting words to him. Mandy would come around, just like Mother had come around. And when he got his promotion and stood with pride in his captain's uniform, she would be proud of him too.

When Beane had taxied as far as the airport, a group of MPs came out to meet them. Brandon stepped out the door and was nearly flattened by the heat. His feet hadn't even touched the tarmac and already he was sweating.

The MPs led him into a waiting area not far away. IDs were checked and he had a short wait before an army sergeant attached to Joint Task Force 160 arrived to take him to the ferry landing.

It was on the ferry that the contrast struck him forcibly, the disconnect between the breathtaking tropical beauty surrounding him, and the gravity of its military purpose. Perhaps it was just the general mood post-9/11, but it seemed to Brandon that there was a distinct edge to everything here, an expectation of things to come. And yet, if you away from the barbed wire, you could be forgiven for mistaking it for a beach resort. You needed only to add some of those little straw huts and a cocktail bar.

On the windward side of the bay, an almost identical army sergeant met him with a lazy salute and a wave towards the waiting jeep. Brandon noticed his crumpled uniform and poorly-polished boots. There was a slovenly feel to him, and maybe that too was part of life in Gitmo.

Brandon enjoyed the breeze of the open jeep as it sped along a road which had the bay to its left and the dry scrubland of the island to its right.

"What the fuck was that?" Brandon asked, as the jeep swerved to avoid a large, possum-like rodent that darted across the road.

"That there was a banana rat, sir. They's the official Gitmo mascot. Reckon' if they ever did get the upper hand on us, they'd gladly eat us all alive. Word has it, they flock to this here base from all over Cuba 'cos we feed 'em scraps. Over on t'other side, the commies roast 'em on a stick for supper."

"Charming," Brandon noted, as another one darted across the road up ahead. "So how long have you been stationed here?"

"Too long, sir!" the sergeant replied. "I chose to become a hunk."

"Excuse me, soldier?"

"We have a little saying here, goes like this: 'When you come to Gitmo, you gonna leave as one of four things: a chunk, 'cos all's you do is eat. A hunk, 'cos all's you do is work out. A monk, 'cos all's you do is read books. Or a drunk.' I don't figure that last one needs no explanation."

Brandon smiled and flexed his muscles. He reckoned he'd go the hunk route himself. And for the first time, he began to think he might actually enjoy life in Gitmo.

"Lieutenant Brandon Zeiss, reporting for duty, sir!"

The man behind the desk, Colonel Benjamin Rhodes, did not respond immediately. Nor did he look up. He was sipping coffee, and taking his time about it, too. Brandon observed his shining, bald head, which reflected the glow of the ceiling light fixture almost as if it was a mirror. Brandon maintained a crisp salute to his forehead, waiting for an acknowledgement which seemed an eternity in the coming.

"First rule around here, Lieutenant, is we don't salute and we don't call each other 'sir.'" The bald man looked up and his face assumed a sour expression. "Drop the fuckin' salute, Brandon."

Brandon did so, rather deflated.

"Second rule around here is sit the fuck down in that there chair."

Brandon followed this order too. He was shocked at the Colonel's use of language. His father, also an army colonel, would never have cursed like that while on duty. Rhodes seemed more like a gangster than a military officer.

The Colonel was nose deep in paperwork, which Brandon soon realized was his own personnel file.

"Did you have yourself a merry little Christmas?"

"It was fine. I've been finding my bearings around the base."

Rhodes nodded absently, absorbed in the file he was reading. "Air Force Academy *Magna Cum Laude*. And you choose a desk job in logistics?"

"Tactical support, sir. Logistics was part of our work. But mostly we did classified planning, mapping flight paths to support forward military positions, including ones close to hostile territory. We were also part of the Code Red defense shield. On 9/11—"

"Like I just said: logistics. Care to explain to me why the grandson of one of World War Two's most celebrated generals ends up on his ass behind a computer screen instead of going for glory in the cockpit? Says here you got 20/20 vision so that wasn't the problem. What it is Brandon? You scared chicken-shit?"

"No, sir. I ... wanted to be close to my wife. Close to home."

"Is that right?"

"Yes, sir."

Colonel Rhodes guffawed. "Small town boy from Pennsylvania falls in love with his high school sweetheart and promises her he won't fly away into the sunset. Touching."

He looked up and fixed Brandon with a dead stare. "And, yet, here we are, three days after Christmas. 1,500 miles from Pennsylvania. God Himself doesn't know the next time you and Mrs. Brandon Zeiss will be getting busy in each other's arms. So what happened to you, boy? You fall out of love?"

Brandon swallowed a lump in his throat. Rhodes was baiting him, and he knew it. "No, sir," he replied.

"Says here you suddenly attacked the Arabic language like you were a *Mohammedan*. Scored straight fours in Arabic in the DLPT in an improbably short space of time. How come?

"9/11, sir."

"Don't tell me that, Brandon. You started studying Arabic two years before 9/11 happened."

"I ... took an interest, sir, ever since Dar es Salaam. But I intensified my studies after 9/11."

"Why? Was it because your marriage was falling apart?"

"No, sir."

Rhodes smiled. "C'mon Bran. I'm your commanding officer here. You can tell me what it's like. She spend all her time with the kids nowadays? What are their names ... little Scott and Linda? Maybe things got a little dull in the bedroom, huh? How 'bout her tits? They starting to sag a little, maybe? What about her ass? That nice booty you used to admire so much back in high school—is it starting to look a little bit flabby after she finished squeezin' out them kids?"

Brandon could feel his ears burn. His fists clenched. But he said nothing.

Rhodes—watching him all the way—burst into sudden laughter. And then his face fell serious just as quickly. He looked at Brandon with something akin to hate. It was a fearsome stare. Involuntarily, Brandon unballed his fists.

"This isn't going to work unless you're completely honest with me, Zeiss. So now let's start again." He banged the table and leaned as far forward as the desk would permit. Brandon could feel the Colonel's breath. "Why the fuck are you here?"

"My family is military, sir. My brother's on track for major in the Army. My father's a colonel. As you know, my grandfather was a general. I'm lagging behind. This is my opportunity to get ahead."

Rhodes stared at him hard. Slowly he nodded. "Okay," he said quietly. "Now you're talkin' my language. Listen up, the JTF is the military's prize project right now. Promotion is almost guaranteed, if you do what I say. In ten days, the first fifty prisoners arrive from Afghanistan and three more are on their way from Europe. And they're just the tip of the iceberg. In six months, I fully expect we'll be hosting hundreds of detainees and we want a command structure in place. That's gonna mean multiple camps—maybe as many as ten. And a captain in charge of each one of them. You're gonna be my first captain. If you play your cards right, you'll be leaving Gitmo in two years as a major. How's that sound to you?"

"Sounds good, sir."

"All right. Now drop the fuckin' 'sir.'"

Brandon smiled and nodded.

"I want you to familiarize yourself with the camp. You've got clearance to go everywhere in the base that's under JTF command. Sniff out every corner of this shithole, from Alpha right up to the Cuban fence. Get to know the interpreters. Get to know the guards. You'll need them. That's your first mission. You have until New Year's Day. Any questions?"

"When do we get our interrogators?"

Rhodes looked at him and smiled.

"How much interrogation have you done so far?"

"I completed the Army's standard—"

"No. I didn't ask you how many courses you completed. I asked you how many interrogations you done. Of actual enemies."

"None, sir."

"Right. So how could you possibly command interrogators? You'll get your specialists when you're able to train them. Right now, you are the interrogators, Brandon." Rhodes flipped through the manila files on his desk and selected one. "What's your opinion of the Irish?"

Brandon paused before answering. "My wife is Irish ..."

Rhodes nodded. "That's right, she is. That means you're gonna have to confront your conscience early on. Best way to test your suitability for this job, as far as I'm concerned." With this he tossed the file across the desk to Brandon. "Here's your second mission. His name is Fergus Maloney. He's gonna be your test case. I want you to read his file very carefully and be ready to start interrogation as soon as he arrives."

"But, sir, I'm trained in Arabic ..."

"Yeah. I know. But you're gonna practice on one of your own. That's how you know it's real. Don't worry, you'll have plenty of time to hone your language skills. Once this place kicks off, we'll have absolutely no fuckin' shortage of sand niggers, I can promise you that."

18

"**Next case please, Peter," Judge Victor Manuel said,** even before he was back in his seat. It was 4:29 on a Friday afternoon, high time to finish the day's hearings in the second chamber of the United States District Court for the Southern District of New York. Maria knew Manuel still had to do his paperwork before he could call it a week. She also knew he lived in Connecticut and would have a long commute to get home. He rubbed his temples, obviously hoping this would be something for which he could order an adjournment and be done with quickly. She must not let that happen.

"Brogan versus Mueller, petition for the release of information," the clerk read, before handing a file up to the bench. Manuel put on his reading glasses and settled in, asking the clerk, "Are the parties present?"

Maria rose, "For the prosecution, Your Honor. Attorney Maria Da Silva. I represent Ms. Brogan."

A lawyer with slicked-back hair and wire-rimmed glasses rose and said, "Attorney Sheldon Rubenstein. For the Federal Bureau of Investigation and the office of the Attorney General of the United States, Your Honor."

"What information is your client seeking, Ms. Da Silva?" the judge asked.

"Your Honor, my client, Ms. Clodagh Brogan, is the sister and next-of-kin to Mr. Fergus Maloney, formerly of 3887A Broadway, New York, NY. Mr. Maloney was taken from his home and placed into FBI custody on the night of Thursday, September 27, along with a Mr. Karim Saunders. The Bureau has failed to produce charges pertaining to Mr. Maloney's arrest. No information has been provided as to the conditions of his detention, nor the place of his detention nor has he been given a fair hearing in a court of law. My client is in the dark concerning her brother's welfare. I have filed no fewer than three Freedom of Information requests pertaining to the arrest and detention of Mr. Maloney, and have been told that this information is vital to national security. The FBI's illegal detention of my brother's client is in breach of the US Constitution."

"OK, I didn't ask about the Constitution. That's a debate for another day. I asked what your client wants to know."

"She wants to know where her brother is. What he has been charged with and when he will be released."

"Mr. Rubenstein?"

"Your Honor, the current whereabouts of Mr. Maloney are unknown to the Bureau. Mr. Maloney was invited by FBI agents in New York City for questioning in relation to suspected terrorist activities of his associates in Harlem. He attended for questioning on September 27, but was not, as Ms. Da Silva suggests, arrested at that point in time.

"During the course of the questioning, certain inconsistencies between the evidence he provided and that provided by another witness led the agents in charge of the interrogation to consider Mr. Maloney was withholding information vital to national security. On this basis, he was detained as a material witness for a number of hours. This is in accordance with the United States Code, Your Honor.

"In the course of further interrogation, the material witness admitted to being illegally resident in the United States. In order to avoid the launching of an extradition procedure, he agreed to a voluntary transfer into the custody of the Immigration and Naturalization Service, which took place on September 30. With the assistance of the United States Air Force the detainee was offered a place on a flight to Ramstein Air Base in Germany with a view to repatriation to his native country of Ireland. From there, the Bureau has no further information of his whereabouts."

"So he went to Germany," Manuel repeated. "Have you checked with the German authorities, Ms. Da Silva?"

"Yes, Your Honor, I checked." Maria intervened. "But the point is Ramstein isn't officially part of German territory. He never entered the Federal Republic of Germany. Mr. Maloney never returned to Ireland either."

"So what happened to him?" Manuel asked Rubenstein in a tone that clearly conveyed that he didn't really care.

"The Bureau has no further information concerning this individual."

"But you're the Attorney General," Maria insisted. "You know where he went. You must."

"Right now I'm representing the Bureau," Rubenstein countered, with a certain degree of smugness. "The petition was filed with respect to information held by the Bureau concerning their material witness."

"Counsel, are you satisfied with this?" Manuel asked Maria, who was anything but satisfied.

"Your Honor," Maria said. "The petition includes a list of detailed questions concerning Mr. Maloney's detention in FBI custody which my client would like to have answered. All these questions were included in the original FOI request, and all were refused response on the grounds of national security interests. In line with the current petition, I would like to seek judgment on how this, mostly personal, information could possibly be deemed vital to national security."

The clerk handed the judge a wad of papers stapled together. This was Maria's annex, which she had had the foresight to prepare. The questions ranged from the obvious: '*What was the nature of Mr. Maloney's questioning?*' to the downright trivial: '*Were Mr. Maloney's dietary requirements respected during his period of detention and, if so, can the Bureau detail what medical procedures were applied to ensure this was the case*?' At the time she had put the list together, she had no idea they might prove useful in court. But a good lawyer always equips herself with as much ammunition as possible. "If you ever do have to file an FOI," her boss and mentor Seth Rosenthal had once told her, "make them say no a thousand times to the same question asked a thousand different ways. Version 999 of that question might end up being the one you can use in court, and if nothing else, you will have forced them to waste a lot of time."

Maria had done just that, and now she was glad of it. It would take Judge Manuel an hour at least to go through each one and make a judgment on whether the information could be excluded from the provisions of the Freedom of Information Act on the grounds cited by the FBI. Maria knew it was a risky strategy: pissing off judges was never something you did unless you had to. But right now, she had nothing else.

Manuel looked at his wristwatch and let out a sigh. "Approach the bench please."

When they got to the bench, Rubenstein stood in Maria's personal space. Maybe it was a sort of power play, maybe he was coming on to her. Either way, the smell of his hair product was sickening. Something like Peach Melba. Manuel leaned forward and asked Maria in a tired whisper, "Do we really have to go through this? Seems to me you just want to know where this guy ended up, am I right?"

"Yes, Your Honor. My client's primary concern is the current whereabouts and condition of her brother."

Manuel turned to Rubenstein. "Can't you just tell her, Counsel, and we can all go home?"

"Your Honor ..." Rubenstein began and then paused, clearly struggling for words. He wanted to perjure himself and claim he didn't know, but it was too late for that. "... this is a question of national security."

"Why? I'm not suggesting you reveal classified counterintelligence information. All she wants to know right now is where this man ended up. I fail to see how that compromises the security of this country. Unless you think Attorney Da Silva is going to stage a jailbreak?"

"No, Your Honor, but ..."

Maria suppressed a smile. This was playing out nicely. If Rubenstein refused now, it was the same as telling the court, "*Look at me, Your Honor, I clearly don't have a date tonight. Hell, I'm prepared to plead on every single one of these questions for the rest of the evening. Right until Jay Leno kicks off on NBC late night.*"

"Counsel," Manuel said to him in a less conciliatory tone. "If you make me miss my train, I'm going to rule against you on every single one of these questions. Got it?"

Clodagh Brogan wasn't really looking to sue the FBI for improper procedures during a detention which had ended a month and a half ago, but from the Bureau's point of view, that was the risk here. Maria knew the FBI had run the equivalent of pogroms in the wake of 9/11. Procedure had been tossed out the window. Rubenstein would surely get heat Monday morning if the FBI was forced to provide written answers to all these detailed questions.

They returned to their places and Rubenstein fished around in his briefcase, eventually extracting a letter for an envelope deep within it. He read out loud.

"On October 1, while passing the clearance gate into Ramstein-Miesenbach, Mr. Maloney was apprehended by Military Police as an enemy combatant, under powers provided by the Authorization for Use of Military Force. The following day he was transferred to a temporary detention facility at a classified location, pending the normalization of a procedure for military interrogation at a more permanent location."

"Where?"

Rubenstein shrugged. "That a question for the Department of Defense. And it's classified."

"What has he been charged with?" Maria asked.

"That's not how the AUMF works," Rubenstein countered. "It's not a criminal procedure. It's a military one. Mr. Maloney is classed as an enemy combatant."

"But Mr. Maloney was transferred from the territory of the United States into military custody outside the country!" Maria insisted. "The Fifth Amendment of the U.S. Constitution provides for due process—"

"OK, that's enough," Manuel interrupted. "I'm not going to sit here while you two debate the Fifth Amendment. I think we can all agree you've got the information you were looking for here, Counsel. So this request—all the stuff about whether the FBI gave him toothpaste—can I consider it dropped?"

"Yes Your Honor," Maria responded.

"Excellent. Case dismissed."

So the FBI was out of the picture, which meant that as far as the legal context for Fergus's detention was concerned, the whole game had changed. The new basis of his detention, possible trial and release would be conducted in accordance with the Uniform Code of Military Justice, Article 2 (a) (9). Criminal Law was not something Maria had spent much of her career on, much less the highly specialized sub-area of military criminal law, so this was going to take time. The first order of business was to read through both the Code itself and the jurisprudence surrounding it.

Maria stared down at the notes in front of her, which were mostly lists of thing she would need to research further and documents she would have to get from the Law Library. When she looked back up at the laptop on the desk of her home office, the characters on the screen refused to come into focus until she'd rubbed her eyes and forced her tired brain to concentrate. It was only then she noticed the little clock on the toolbar read 2:35 a.m. She had worked well into the night and would need to get some sleep.

But as soon as her head hit the pillow, her heart rate went back up and ideas for how to pursue the case ran through her mind.

Fergus is part of a machinery now. This machinery is currently buying up people like him—what they call 'assets'—for the purpose of interrogating them.

Maria pulled a newspaper report out of her file. It was the British newspaper, *The Guardian*, and it told of how the Northern Alliance was sweeping from victory to victory with the support of the Allied Forces. They were grabbing Taliban men who surrendered. Some were killed indiscriminately, but most were being sold for a bounty to US forces. According to the journalist, these bounties were the Northern Alliance's main source of income. And what was the US getting in return? Assets to interrogate.

But they have no facilities for these assets, Maria reasoned. *They will put them in places, such as the detention center in Cuba, and then they will systematically interrogate them. Right now, there are no legal challenges. So they have not yet had to confront the fact that there is no legal basis for what they're proposing. The Code sets out a procedure for military tribunals, but there's broad discretion for Executive Procedure to define how and when those trials occur.*

This got her thinking about jurisprudence. Right away this posed a problem. Most of the cases would concern US military personnel, not prisoners of war. Prisoners of war! That was it.

Her eyes sprang open. Article 2 (a) (9) of the Code applied the military justice system to prisoners of war, not to 'terrorists'. In order to have a war, you have to have a state. Fergus was not a combatant, nor did al-Qaida possess a state. Therefore, he did not qualify as a prisoner of war and there was no way he could be tried in a military court. His detention and interrogation thus were in violation of the Fifth Amendment, which stated that '*No person shall be held to answer for a capital, or otherwise infamous crime, unless on a presentment or indictment of a grand jury, except in cases arising in the land or naval forces, or in the militia, when in actual service in time of war or public danger.*'

So, Bush and Cheney were going to have to write a new law quick. In the meantime, the hawks would have to keep things out of the Federal Courts. *Of course*, Maria thought. This was what the new detention center in the Guantánamo Bay naval base on Cuba was about. It was being opened not on US soil, precisely because they were afraid of the legal grey area they were creating. They knew this was not going to fly in the Supreme Court. The sooner Maria got the ball rolling on a petition at District Court level to have Fergus tried back on US soil, the better.

The finality of that resolution was exactly what her mind needed in order to be able to let go and get to sleep.

Maria awoke at 8:15 a.m. to the sound of a garbage truck on the street outside. She had not even thought to set her alarm. *Fuck.* She was going to be an hour late for work.

Maria was halfway through writing her request to the Department of Defense for information pertaining to the detention of Fergus Maloney. She would recycle a lot of the material from the FOI request she had prepared for the FBI, but the wording had to be different, because the endgame was now a challenge to the legality of their entire operation.

The information request was of course only the appetizer. The main course was going to be the writ of *habeas corpus*, the legal instrument that would challenge the military's jurisdiction over a civilian accused of capital crimes. That was going to take time to write and Maria was going to need to get a few more details. In fact, she wasn't even sure if she would be able to do it on her own. She might need to ask a few old friends for help. After all, there was no point in going to court and having the judge issue an adjournment because she had not dotted all her i's and crossed her t's. Every delay meant Fergus's period of incarceration would continue, longer and longer.

Maria allowed her mind to wander onto what that incarceration meant. She thought of her trip to Harlem and how the neighbors at 3887A Broadway had seen the cops dragging Fergus out of the building and into an unmarked black van. She thought of Clodagh and the bizarre encounter in the nursing home with their mother, Mary Maloney. The lying, the deceit. They had given up on him, just as they had given up on each other. *I'm all he has in the world right now*, Maria thought.

The phone rang. It was her PA, Barbara, on the line.

"Your two o'clock is here. Should I bring him into the meeting room or do you still need a few minutes?"

"My two o'clock?" Maria shuffled through her diary and saw an entry written in Barbara's careful handwriting and customary green pen, then she looked down at her hand, on which she'd scrawled a 2:30 meeting with the ACLU guy.

"It's Mr. Lewis," Barbara reminded her. "To discuss the preparations for the merger."

Oh shit, Maria realized. She had completely forgotten about this meeting. *I'm going to have to bluff.* "Tell him I'll be right in. Can you get him a coffee while he waits? Thanks, Barbara, you're a star."

She hastily dialed the number of the ACLU contact Cindy had given her, a guy by the name of Clarke.

"I'm sorry, I don't think I'm going to be able to make our two-thirty. Can we reschedule?"

The other end of the phone was silent for a second. "*OK. I can do eight-thirty tomorrow morning*," Clarke said in a voice that implied he was none too impressed with how this was starting off.

"That works," Maria answered, before checking her diary and realizing it really didn't. Seth had called a touch-base meeting for tomorrow morning. Maria was still thinking about how she was going to juggle this as she entered the meeting room and greeted her client.

"Mr. Lewis, thank you so much for coming in today!"

"Ms. Da Silva. Or should I call you 'Attorney' Da Silva? I never know what to say." This remark was delivered with a limp, moist handshake and an overenthusiastic laugh that made his jowls shake.

"You can call me Maria," she told him, and not for the first time. "Please, have a seat."

"So, *Maria*," he began, as an effusive smile stretched across the dewy, nervous face. "How are we doing with our merger?"

"Well, I have been working pretty much non-stop on it since our last meeting, but there are a number of issues I wanted to raise with you, and I thought it would be better to use this time to discuss them face-to-face, rather than have to do it over the phone. I know you don't come to New York very often—"

"Actually, I'm here every week." The jowls shook again. He crossed his legs while placing his hands inside his thighs, in a posture that was at once decidedly beta-male and vaguely obscene.

"Right," Maria smiled. She threw open the files and buried her head in the paperwork. Some of this material she was reading for the very first time. Fortunately, she was a fast reader.

"So the capital structure of Lewis & Sons in preparation for the merger will need to be modified in order to ensure full compliance with GAAP ahead of the SEC submission."

"Right," he whinnied. "We want to get it right with the SEC. Remember what happened to the Brightwell deal?" Spoken in a playful but accusatory tone, even though Maria had been nowhere near that deal, and anyway she knew the client had acted against best legal advice.

"That was the FTC submission, to do with market dominance. The SEC looks at your fiduciary obligations around the share conversion plan. But that's another point we want to be clear on..."

Maria went on, talking on autopilot, reading one sentence ahead of her speech. She was good enough to get away with it, even if her client had been paying complete attention. Which he really wasn't. Instead, Malcolm J. Lewis III was busy devouring her body with his moist, flickering eyes. He did this every time they met. Maria was never quite sure if he heard anything she was saying to him. It didn't really matter. Once he'd given the okay, the box was ticked and she would be free to push the papers under the noses of his senior accountants. There was a lot of work to do on it, though, and she was far behind schedule.

Her mind wandered back to the meeting she had had with Fergus's sister in Dublin. Shunned by his own dying, deranged mother. Abandoned by his family, he was now sitting somewhere in a prison cell. The worst of it was, she was convinced there was no good reason.

At the same moment in time, Malcolm J. Lewis III, heir to a farm machinery leasing empire worth $200 million he did nothing to create, was reaching for the candy bowl on the side table opposite his chair, because he liked to eat candy, but mostly because it allowed him to peek a little further up his lawyer's skirt.

19

Before leaving the cell, they covered Fergus's head and blindfolded him with some sort of goggles. He was left standing for minutes. Or was it hours? Then they walked him down a corridor that seemed to go on for miles. He tried to count his steps to get a sense of the distance, but couldn't get past twenty. Bolts clanked and hinges squealed. A blast of cold air hit him in the face, and he was pushed forward. He must have been outside, although the goggles rendered everything as dark as a locked cellar. Snow crunched beneath his feet. His bare hands, still bound by the shackles, began to turn numb in the cold. They marched him forward again. At one point, his feet stumbled on something, and he was guided up what he figured was a set of metal steps. The air changed. It was less cold and the wind was gone. They were inside now. A metallic smell hung in the air.

A guard forced him to his knees. They secured his wrist shackle to a rail that ran along the metal floor. This made it impossible for him to turn over onto his back or move more than about a foot. Hands grabbed the elastic waistband of his trousers. They were trying to pull down his trousers. "Hold still," a voice told him.

Uncontrollable panic seized him. Fergus twisted and writhed with all the force he possessed, but many strong hands held him steady. He screamed, blocking out the voices of the men, the crows, the cold October wind that blew the rain of memories through his hollow being. Then the face of the Geegaw Man came, as clear as if he was still a boy. As sleep overtook him, the face didn't so much fade away as scatter, in a nightmarish echo of images. He was in something like a state of sleep.

Maybe there was another reality, whose sound was a constant humming, whose taste was metal against his lolling tongue. Shivering in the cold.

But the next reality Fergus was to remember was this: A blast of heat and the noise of boots pounding on the hollow metal floor. More hands were upon him and the wrist shackles loosened. He was led—almost carried—out, having lost all sense of balance. Sun was burning his face now, and a faint, reddish tinge around the edges of the goggles told him there was bright light beyond the blindfold. The air was thick with a heat he would not have been able to imagine only a few minutes ago. He heard the sound of a jeep; voices all around him. The roar of an engine; this time, a big vehicle: like a truck or a bus.

"Stay on your feet!" an American screamed at him. Fergus had no idea why he should be told to stay on his feet. Then he realised why. He had collapsed back onto the ground without even feeling it. Someone made an attempt to pull him back up, but they weren't strong enough, and he fell again. Without any sense of vision to guide him, his head was spinning out of control. It lolled backwards and hit hard tarmac. The movement caused his stomach to churn and he vomited. His cheek was against the steaming hot gravel and when he tried to expel the vomit from his mouth, gravel stuck to his tongue. It tasted of petrol.

When he awoke again, there was a man staring at him. Thin, with a beard and a hooked nose. He said something to Fergus in a language the Irishman could not understand.

Fergus blinked.

The man spoke again. And again, this time gesticulating madly.

Fergus was lying on a metal bed, similar to the one he had spent the last sixty nights on, and staring out through a chain-link fence. The man looking back at him was sitting on the edge of an identical metal bed, two chain-linked fences away. He was pointing at a sheet that hung on Fergus's side of the fence. Fergus decided to ignore him. He turned his head and saw that he was in a cage composed entirely of chain-link fencing. It reminded him of one of those kennels where TV reporters would uncover half-starved greyhounds, except that there was a hole in the floor for a squat toilet, and the bed had sheets.

The heat was unbearable. Fergus realised he had been lying directly in the sun. On the floor was a metal bowl containing food and a metal cup containing water. The food held no interest for him, but the water he drank greedily. He drank again and again. He touched his orange prison suit, to find it was soaked through. With trembling fingers, he drank again.

The water did something to his body: a rumbling sensation ripped through his bowels and he made it over to the toilet just in time to let out a burning stream of diarrhoea. It ran on and on, like an express train with no brake.

Halfway through his uncomfortable shit, he looked up to see a soldier in camouflage standing outside his cage, staring down at him, with his hands on his hips. *Her* hips. Fergus realised it was a woman soldier. She had been standing there, watching him drink. Now she was watching him shit. And the expression on her face was unchanged.

"If you want privacy, turn the screen," she said, without the least attempt to divert her gaze. She licked her lips as she said this, but her facial expression remained stony and impassive.

The screen she was referring to was a sheet of metal attached to a pole at the edge of the toilet area. It covered a small area above the thighs and below the abdomen, provided whoever was on the shitter positioned himself correctly and was of average height. Impossible to do now, given that Fergus was already in the squat. And so he finished up, looking for, and failing to find, any toilet paper. He pulled up his trousers and returned her stare.

She watched on. "Place your hands in the slot," she said at length, referring to a compartment in the metal door just wide enough to pass food through and into which Fergus could fit his hands. When he'd done so, she opened a cover on the other side and reached into the compartment. Her face appeared on the opposite side of a mesh panel. She had plain features under short hair of a nondescript colour. If he had seen her on the street, he would have assumed she'd be the quiet, deferential type. Her most striking attribute was a pair of beady, green eyes, which seemed capable of fixing themselves upon him without the need for blinking. Fergus felt her small, nimble fingers caressing his wrists, tickling him. At first, he thought it was her clumsy way of fastening the tie, but he quickly realised she was massaging him: rubbing his wrists in a way that was almost sensual. It was the kind of touch he had been without for so long, and, despite himself, it sent a tingle down his spine. All of the sudden, her nails dug into his flesh and he let out a cry. Then, with remarkable dexterity, she fastened the tie upon him, all the while her plain, pale little face remained on the other side of the mesh window: expressionless, vacant.

Once his hands were bound, a male soldier opened the cell door. Fergus was taken out and led along a corridor between two rows of wire mesh cells exactly like the one he had been in. In each he saw a man—invariably Arab—and always dressed in the same orange suit he had come to know so well from his previous detention. At the end of the cell block, they emerged into an open space that was slightly less stiflingly hot. Next came a series of drab, green tents lined up next to the camp. On entering the first of these, he thought for a second it might be the International Red Cross, but his hopes fell when the army doctor introduced himself.

What followed was a full medical examination. The doctor began by asking if Fergus spoke English, then proceeded with a battery of questions – did he drink, smoke, did he have any known allergies, did he need any specific medication. Fergus was tempted to say, "Sure if I had, I'd be fuckin' dead by now, given your crowd's kept me for two months and never asked me any of this shite." But once again his powers of speech failed him. It had been weeks since he'd had a conversation with another human being. It was surprisingly difficult to connect the thoughts in his head with the words that came out of his mouth.

Towards the end, he did manage to speak.

"Doctor, I'm innocent. I need to get out of here. You have to tell them to let me go."

"Are you from Ireland?" the doctor said, with an air of surprise. Fergus nodded.

"What part?"

It took him a second to remember. "Cork."

The doctor smiled, "I was there with my wife on vacation last summer. Beautiful. We did the Ring of Kerry."

The thought struck him hard - that this world was the same as the one where American tourists rented cars and drove around the West Coast of Ireland. The innocent banal reality of this doctor as a tourist, someone Fergus might casually chat to in a pub. Now this same man was here, in this place, fulfilling this role. It made him shudder.

The doctor smiled sympathy, as if he understood Fergus' thoughts. "The best thing you can do," he said after a pause, "is cooperate fully with your interrogator."

"They don't listen," Fergus insisted. "You have to tell them—"

"I can't help you," the doctor said. "Just cooperate with them. In the meantime, please stay out of the sun. I appreciate it's hard, especially in the evening when the sun's in the west, but do the best you can. You've got a hell of a sunburn already. I'm giving you these. Please drink all of them. You're dehydrated and your body needs salt and carbs." Fergus inspected the three aluminium cans he'd been handed. It was some kind of energy drink called *Ensure*. "Don't worry, they're halal," the doctor said. Then he turned to the male soldier who had escorted Fergus in and said, "Write him up for another medical visit tomorrow, please."

"Yes sir," the soldier responded. "Sir, Captain Harris requested to know if this terrorist was authorized for transfer to JTF-170?"

"Already? He just got here."

"Yes sir. I believe he's priority red, sir."

The doctor cast another eye over Fergus, then nodded briskly and filled in an extra line of text on the report he had attached to his clipboard.

"Tell Captain Harris he's clear. But make sure he's had the *Ensure* first. And if he wants food, make sure he gets extra food."

Between the chain-link fence at the back of the cell block and the larger perimeter fence—topped with the coils of razor wire—was a no man's land. The baked, bare earth was cut with tractor tracks. Dead weeds spoke of a time—a long time ago—when rain had come. The only significant object between the fences was a wooden post onto which a green arrow had been nailed. Fergus stared at the post for the best part of an hour trying to guess its significance. Was it some perverse implement of torture? His guessing was interrupted by a wail of voices that kicked off all around him. Through the mesh, he could see the other caged men kneeling on mats or blankets. They were all facing in the direction of the green arrow. Mecca, he thought. But was that east or west? It depended on where the fuck they were: a question he had meant to ask the doctor, but had forgotten. More than likely the fucker wouldn't have answered him anyway.

Fergus tried to look beyond the razor wire, in the direction of Mecca, to what he imagined was freedom. Well, there was probably another fence beyond that, but at some point it had to end. The Yanks didn't own the whole world, after all.

Freedom, or the way to Mecca, did not look particularly appealing. It was brown-scorched earth with tufts of weeds growing against a hill. To one side, though, he thought he caught the glimpse of blue ocean. In the empty space between the two fences, an extremely large rodent—something like a possum—crawl without fear across the dirt, wending a path that took it right past the Mecca signpost. The men on their carpets prayed on, oblivious.

As the sun sank further, it reflected off the razor wire, creating a dazzling explosion of light. Impossible to look out at the fence, so Fergus turned and faced back into his miserable little cell.

He picked up the little tinfoil ration he'd been eating and tried a nibble, but the food wouldn't stay down. With a heave of sick, he let it glide out of his trembling fingers onto the concrete ground.

Weeks had gone by. And still the Yanks made no attempt to ask him any real questions. He had had conversations with them in his head, explaining to them how fucking mad it was to keep him in this cell, for nothing; for no reason. How he was innocent. Innocent. *Innocent.* How they'd got the wrong man and broken a half a million laws along the way to getting him. How he would fill out any forms they wanted, if only they'd let him the fuck out. Then he'd get angry and imagine telling them how he was going to sue them so badly, they'd end up handing him the keys to Air Force One. All these things—threats, pleas, promises, rank insults—he wished he could say to someone in charge. But there was nothing and no one to say them to. It was maddening. Then he had that cunt of a doctor telling him to cooperate with the interrogator. Well, what fucking interrogator?! Here he was, in another cell, with nothing but wailing Arabs on all sides of him.

As the sun went behind the hill, a noise roused him. Soldiers stood at his door again: a different pair of them. Two male soldiers this time. Apparently, there had been a shift change.

"Hands in the slot," one of them said.

"Where am I going?" Fergus asked.

"You'll find out. Just put your hands in the slot."

Fergus put his hands by his side. "I'm not cooperating until you tell me where the fuck I'm going and why."

The two guards looked at each other uncertainly. "To meet your interrogator," the other soldier replied.

Okay, Fergus thought, and put his hands in the slot. This was his chance to set things right.

20

Brandon's new quarters were in a small trailer converted into a two-bedroom 'house'. His housemate was a Seabee Second Lieutenant, a Texan kid named Walter with an impeccable pedigree in civil engineering and a whiny voice which had earned him the nickname 'Buzz'. Not a terribly original nickname for a Seabee, Brandon thought, but, OK, he was Navy, after all. Not a branch of the Armed Forces known for their cutting wit. Buzz was part of a team that was organizing the construction of the new detention facility that would replace the current Camp X-ray. Which was strange, Brandon thought, given that the camp had only come into operation that week. No one even knew how the current procedures were going to work. How could they effectively plan for a new one? In another way, it was good because it meant he was getting in on the ground as part of an operation that was going to grow. Just as Colonel Rhodes had said. More importantly, it meant President Bush was as good as his word. He was taking military intelligence seriously.

Buzz had been granted Christmas leave, a rare treat in Gitmo, so it was several days after Brandon's arrival that they got to meet. But when they did, they hit it off pretty much right away. The first night they cracked a beer and, within a week, they were on their way to being good pals. The night before Brandon's first interrogation, Buzz really opened up about his work.

"We're making plans for up to 2,000 detainees here," Buzz told Brandon. "This is going to be a colossus."

There would also be new, permanent housing for the officers and dormitory-style quarters for the enlisted men. New facilities were to be put in to support the population surge, including a few new restaurants beyond the current

McDonalds and the steakhouse, which was already getting busy. Also a new pool, a bigger gym, and a new NEX the size of a Walmart.

Buzz was the kind of officer who liked to take his work home with him. In answer to one of Brandon's questions, he literally showed him the plans.

"You guys are gonna have your hands full building all this," Brandon said, taking a slug out of his second Budweiser.

"Not really," Buzz said. "Most of the work is being done by outsiders. Contractors."

"You say that like it's a bad thing?"

"Oh, I dunno," Buzz said. He looked down at his beer for a moment as if considering whether or not he should open up to Brandon. "It's just ... the way the contracts have been handled. I mean, man oh man!"

"What?"

"This company who we're working with. I saw some of the tender documentation. Brandon, man, it stinks to hell and back. Their estimates are way out. I just don't see how they could win the contract. And every time we point out a problem, some three-piece suit in DoD tells us to shut our traps, sign off, and pretend like nothing happened."

Brandon wished he hadn't heard that. He took a big swig from his Bud, finishing the can, and tapped Buzz on the shoulder.

"You want my advice? Keep that stuff to yourself. We're just soldiers. We can voice our concerns, sure, but only within the chain of command. After that, it's heads down, and get to work. Listen, I got a 0600 start tomorrow, so I'm gonna get some shut-eye. Thanks for the beer."

"Good morning, sir!"

"What did I tell you about the 'sir' bullshit?"

"Sorry. It's a reflex."

Rhodes rubbed his face and nodded. "So, you read the file on the detainee with Internment Security Number 51?"

"Yes, s— Yes, I did."

"Gimme a summary."

"The subject's full name is Fergus Patrick Maloney. He was invited for questioning by the FBI on September 27, following an anonymous tip-off that he was warning people about the 9/11 attacks the morning before they happened. When questioned, the suspect claimed—"

"Wrong."

"Excuse me?"

"You just made your first mistake. You said 'suspect'. At this point he wasn't a suspect. In fact, he has never been a suspect, and if we have our way, he never will be. Care to tell me why?"

"Because he ... I don't know, sir."

"Because to be a suspect, *sir*, you need to be accused of a crime."

Brandon was puzzled. "But ... isn't harboring information about a future terrorist attack a crime?"

"Not here it isn't. Here it's an enemy action. We don't take criminals who were arrested on US soil and stick them in detention camps in Cuba. The detainee with ISN 51 is an 'enemy combatant', otherwise a 'detainee'. If we call him a 'suspected criminal', we have to contend with the US Constitution. Call him a 'prisoner-of-war' and we have to contend with the Geneva fuckin' Convention, which is almost worse. The detainee with ISN 51 was invited for questioning, in the course of which he became what the US Code calls a 'material witness'. Never more. Continue the briefing."

"The ... witness ... claimed he used clairvoyance to predict the attacks on the World Trade Center, claiming he has always been empowered with a psychic gift. His attitude to the investigating agents was one of flippancy, belligerence and, at one point, during questioning he became physically violent and had to be restrained. On September 30 he was transferred into the custody of the Immigration and Naturalization Service, at which point he signed a document allowing for his voluntary transport to Ramstein Air Base in Germany. From there, he was apprehended by Air Force Intelligence in collaboration with the CIA and taken to a detention facility with a classified location."

"It was Poland," Rhodes muttered, with his eyes closed and his head buried in his hands. Before he spoke, Brandon had begun to wonder whether Rhodes had fallen asleep. But apparently this was the Colonel's way of listening intently.

Brandon continued. "No information was included in the file in relation to his detainment at the CIA facility, except we know that under pressure from a foreign government—which I now presume was Poland—the facility was closed on January 9 and the 36 detainees were transferred back into Military custody. Detainee ISN 51, together with detainees ISN 52 and 53, was sent here on January 10."

"Good. What about his priors?"

"He has no prior convictions. Police records provided to the Bureau, under condition of strict confidentiality due to diplomatic sensitivities, reveal that in Ireland he had one suspended arrest for drunk and disorderly behavior. He was also charged with welfare fraud, but the charges were suspended upon his departure to the United States. He arrived in the US on a tourist visa on July 1, 1996 and has overstayed his visa, working illegally in a series of odd jobs, mostly in construction. The subject has never traveled to Afghanistan, Pakistan or the Middle East, but FBI interviews with people who knew him in the Irish community in New York reveal he may have had communist sympathies."

"Known associates?"

"There are no verifiable links between the subject and any known al-Qaida operatives. Although his former roommate in New York, Karim Saunders has been under FBI surveillance since Maloney came to attention, and was also taken in for questioning, though soon thereafter released. This man is an African American, born and lived his whole life in New York City. Name at birth was Patrick Saunders, at twenty-two converted to Islam and changed his name to Karim Saunders."

Rhodes nodded, rose from his desk, and filled a cup from his coffee machine.

"That was a damn good brief, Brandon," he said. "Deserves a cup of coffee."

"Thank you, sir ... I mean, thank you."

"So, why do you think it is the file contains no information about his detainment in Poland?"

Brandon shook his head to indicate he didn't know. The coffee tasted as good as it smelled.

"Because the first rule of intel," Rhodes explained, "is nobody tells anyone else what the fuck they are doing. It's actually astounding we even got this Joint

Task Force together at the level we did, and with as much internal cooperation as we've had. As for the cooperation we've been given from the Bureau, well, let's just say they're being humble 'cos they've got an awful lot of egg on their face right about now. As for the CIA, well, don't hold your breath waiting for them to tell you anything."

"Why not?"

"Why not? Because it's a turf war, that's why not. The Capitol has hundreds of millions of dollars to throw at intel right now and nobody's too sure who's gonna get what slice of the pie. Everyone's trying to be the first to make the breakthrough that nails bin Laden. Including the Joint Task Force. *Especially* the Joint Task Force. Now, the guys in the Senate Committee are busy telling us we gotta work together, and everyone nods like bobbleheads. Oh yes, Senator, we're all cooperating fully. Of course, Senator. We're like the fuckin' Brady Bunch, Senator! Then, on the ground, the exact opposite happens. Which is why we have a 40-day gap in our file right now."

"You're saying they might already have interrogated him and got some useful information but they won't share it with us for fear we would be the ones who got the credit?"

"I'd put it like this: the CIA would rather watch half of New York City burn to the ground in the next successful terrorist attack, rather than admit they are not the right people to protect America from terrorists. Unfortunately, we'll be hearing a lot more from the CIA. We'll also have to continue to work closely with the Bureau, which is easier, but still not easy.

"So," Rhodes continued, leaning forwards to take a booklet out of a desk drawer. "That's the scale of the challenge we're facing. The pressure's on, Brandon."

With this he threw a manual on the table in front of Brandon.

"You familiar with this?"

"Yes, I am."

It was the FM 34-52, the US Army Field Manual on Interrogation. Brandon had studied it extensively in preparation for this mission. He could recite every page.

"First and last thing to say about this book," Rhodes said, "it's made by and for Boy Scouts. Ignore every piece of shit propaganda written therein. This thing is good for one purpose and one purpose alone: talking to the press, which is something we will no doubt be doing when they come a-knocking. Which will be real soon. But as for actual practice, those are not our rules."

"What are our rules?"

"We're here to write the rules, Lieutenant." Rhodes looked down at his watch. "I'm afraid I have another meeting now. Feel free to take the rest of that coffee with you. We reconvene at 2100 hours in the Crucible. Make sure Detainee 51 is fully prepped for questioning."

As Brandon was leaving Rhodes shouted. "I suggest you take a nap. It's gonna be a long night."

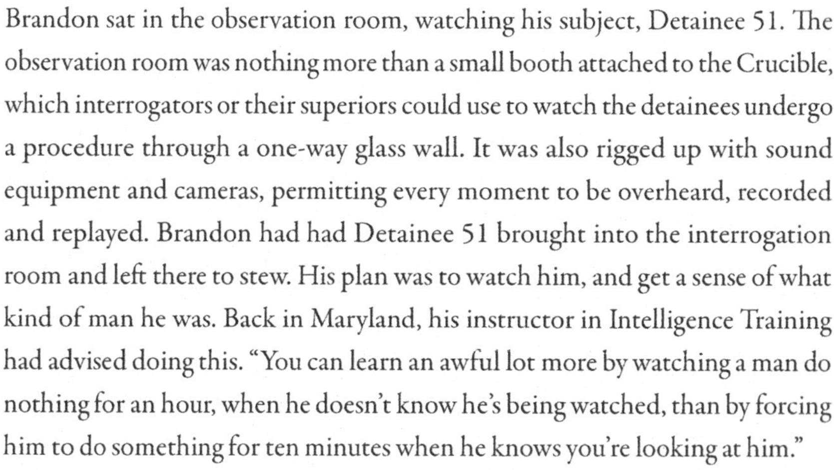

Brandon sat in the observation room, watching his subject, Detainee 51. The observation room was nothing more than a small booth attached to the Crucible, which interrogators or their superiors could use to watch the detainees undergo a procedure through a one-way glass wall. It was also rigged up with sound equipment and cameras, permitting every moment to be overheard, recorded and replayed. Brandon had had Detainee 51 brought into the interrogation room and left there to stew. His plan was to watch him, and get a sense of what kind of man he was. Back in Maryland, his instructor in Intelligence Training had advised doing this. "You can learn an awful lot more by watching a man do nothing for an hour, when he doesn't know he's being watched, than by forcing him to do something for ten minutes when he knows you're looking at him."

Detainee 51 was tall, muscular, and moved like he probably had good reflexes. Almost involuntarily, the Brandon flexed his arm muscles, dropped his chin slightly, and simulated a right uppercut against a phantom adversary.

Brandon was not small himself—six foot even and weighing in at a buck eighty-nine—but growing up in the shadow of Zack, who was always bigger, stronger, faster, he never felt confident when he measured himself against other alpha males. The philosophical side of him would say this was a normal reaction to male-on-male conflict: every alpha had doubts and sought to control them in his own way. The real issue was what you did with that fear; how you best channeled it. Into aggression? Yes. But smart aggression. He remembered a professor of his in the Air Force Academy saying once, "If you find yourself in a fair fight, you didn't arm yourself well enough in advance."

Other than his physical size, he noted Detainee 51 had a bad sunburn on one side of his neck and face. This was common in Camp X-ray, one of the MPs had told him when he did his tour. Because of the construction of the cage cells, it was possible to fall asleep in the sun and not realize the burn until too late.

As the waiting went on and on, 51 grew more and more impatient. He tapped the desk. He burst out spontaneously into song. All of this Brandon noted carefully, until finally, he was ready to conduct their first interview.

As soon as Brandon entered, the Irishman rose and spoke.

"I'm innocent," he said.

That's what they all say. Brandon ignored him, pointing him instead back into his seat.

"My name is Clyde. I'm gonna be your interrogator. How well this works depends on how you cooperate with—"

"Ah, well, then we've no problem at all. Sure, I've every intention of cooperating with you."

Brandon dropped his voice and stared the Irishman in the eyes.

"Don't interrupt me when I'm speaking." This was the first test. Brandon knew he had to assert authority—absolute authority—from the first moment they met.

Detainee 51 held Brandon's stare with his own blue eyes. As he did, a little smile twisted its way onto his lips. "Whatever you're into, Boss. As long as I can get outta here, I don't mind one bit."

"Fine, then we understand each other. Now, first some ground rules." Here Brandon paused and placed the recording device on the table. "You'll see this is red. Whenever it's on and lit up, you're being recorded. When I switch it off, then what you say is just between you and me. OK?"

"Yeah, grand, whatever."

This was of course a lie. In reality every word would be recorded. But it built layers of confidence and was a key part of what Brandon hoped would be his interrogation strategy. Subjects must feel they had different spaces. A confidential space, and an 'official' space.

"Now, let's get down to business. What I want from you is simple. I want you to tell me everything. Starting with the moment you arrived in the United States of America."

"I've already told all this to—"

"And now you'll tell me."

"Ah, here, that isn't fair. If I'm not allowed to interrupt you why can you interrupt me?"

"Detainee 51, this process—"

"My name's Fergus."

"—can go as easy and or hard as you want. You can cooperate and get special privileges, maybe even release. Or you can not cooperate, and we can make your life hell. It's up to you. So now, what's it gonna be?"

51's only answer was another smirk. "Your name's not really Clyde, is it?"

Brandon rose suddenly. "OK, that's enough! I'll come back in an hour when you're ready to talk. Meanwhile, you just sit here and stew for a while."

"No wait!" 51 called. Brandon didn't even turn around. "I have to go to the toilet!"

Tough shit, Brandon thought and left without another word. Outside, he told the guards that under no circumstances should the detainee be allowed to use the toilet.

Outside, the temperature had fallen back into the high seventies, but the air was still muggy. *Now I've got an hour to kill.* He drove home and went for a quick run down by the beach. A full moon hung over Guantánamo Bay. Brandon's feet sank into the sand as he ran and within twenty minutes he was out of breath. By the time he had showered and returned to the interrogation facility, an hour and a half had passed.

Inside the observation booth, Colonel Rhodes sat staring through the glass, and smiling. His presence was unsettling: he had given no warning that he intended to be present for this interrogation.

As Brandon greeted him, a sound came through the microphone. Like a stream of piss hitting the metal chair. When Brandon turned, that's exactly what he saw the Irishman doing.

"Goddamn!" Brandon called one of the MPs.

"Sir?"

"He's pissing on the chair, do something!"

"Do what, sir?"

"Well, stop him, for Christ sake! Restrain him."

"Yes, sir."

In a second the two soldiers were inside the Crucible, grabbing 51 by the arms and forcing him to the ground above the D-ring: the curved piece of metal bolted to the floor which was used for restraining prisoners. The Irishman cursed violently in protest and tried to fight, but the MPs were very professional. Once he was back in 'the Squat'—the secure position in which subjects were fastened by the arm and leg shackles to the D-ring—Brandon turned towards Rhodes in panic. *What the fuck should I do now?* But Rhodes wasn't giving anything away. This was Brandon's first test.

"Looks like this has started pretty well already," Rhodes said.

"Sir, the subject—"

"Urinated on your chair. I know. I'm right here. I saw everything. I watched you allowing it to happen," Colonel Rhodes sighed. "The question you have to ask yourself is why he did that."

"He said he needed to go to the toilet and I thought—"

"I don't give a fuck what he said," Rhodes answered in a dry, low tone. "And that's not the right answer. The right answer is: he did it because he thought he could get away with it. So now the next question is, what are you prepared to do about it?"

Brandon thought for a moment. He tried to remember something from the Manual, before realizing that Rhodes wouldn't want to hear any of that stuff. Eventually, he gave up.

"I don't know."

"There are many times in a man's life when that's the best answer you can give. Unfortunately, now's not one of them. So, I tell you what. I'm gonna sit here, and look at you for as long as it takes until you figure out a way to deal with the fact that your subject just pissed all over your chair, all over your authority, and all over the United States Armed Forces."

Brandon's mind was racing. All the excitement and anticipation were gone. This terrorist piece of shit from Ireland—through this one act—was going to ruin everything. What would Zack do? What would his father do?

The seconds ticked eternal. Rhodes said nothing, as he had promised. This was all the clue Brandon was going to get that he was doing it wrong. Brandon thought for a second. Which turned into a minute. *Fuck*, he thought, panic engulfing every inch of him. *What if I'm just not cut out for this? What if I this is the moment I fail, like Father always felt I would*?

No, Brandon thought, *I'm not going to let that happen*, and he stormed back into the Crucible.

"Detainee 51, you have defaced United States' property, you have insulted my country and you have insulted me personally. If it's a pissing competition with the United States of America you want, well, it's a pissing competition you're gonna get."

Brandon positioned himself above 51's prone body, unzipped his pants, and whipped out his dick. Two seconds later the first stream hit the orange sleeve of the subject's shirt. Brandon lifted his dick a little and the stream rose up the detainee's arm. He pissed on his ear, on his neck, on his head and as close into his face as he could get.

All the time his heart was pounding, both in fear of what he was doing, and in fear of whether this would be beyond what Rhodes expected of him. It was this latter fear that gripped him when, a moment later, he re-entered the observation room. *I might have blown it right here.*

Brandon opened the door, braced for the worst and ... nothing. Colonel Rhodes was already gone. But on the desk he had left a fresh cup of coffee. Under it was a note that read, '*Good work*'.

21

Maria almost called Jeff by accident. A minor incident triggered it: her VCR was acting up and no matter what she did, the tapes kept getting stuck in it. Jeff would know how to fix it.

As she reflex-dialed his number she starting pre-playing in her head the first few exchanges they would have.

"Hey, I need you to come over and do that thing with the VCR again. The tapes keep getting stuck", she would say.

"Why don't you just get a DVD player?" he would say, "No rewinding, no tapes. Discs last literally forever. It's the dominant technology. In a few years, video cassette tapes won't even exist."

"Because I have all my favorite movies on VHS, and because— "

Shit, what am I doing? Maria slammed the receiver down before the phone started to ring. He was probably fucking the blond intern with the big tits—'*Elizabeth in the basement*'—at that very moment. After all that had happened, how could she forget they had broken up over two months ago? Did this mean her subconscious was still in love with him?

No. It wasn't that she loved him. And yet the loss visited her, particularly in moments like now. She had lost not only her boyfriend. She had lost her place in the Laurence family. She had lost a whole vision of the future, which, however limiting, had provided her with certainty and structure.

Maria looked around her living room: the video machine on the floor, with a slightly bent butter knife sticking out of the front slot; behind her, a tray with the bottle of rosé and chocolates on the ottoman. Here she was on a Saturday night, stuck in her apartment, watching old rom coms because she basically had no social life, and without Jeff in her life, the only other thing she knew how to do was work. The most pathetic part of it was, she wasn't even watching old rom coms, because she wasn't able to operate her own VCR.

I'm like a crazy cat lady with no cats.

She thought of calling her girlfriend Sam, and asking for the number of the guy Sam had wanted to hook her up with, until it occurred to her how desperate that would seem. Also, did she really want to go out with some guy just because she was feeling sorry for herself?

Maria crossed the length of the apartment on autopilot. She stopped at the spare room where she kept her home office. Her desk was cluttered with papers relating to the Fergus Maloney case. The sight of them reminded her of the conversation she'd had with Sam at the New Year's Eve party, five nights previous.

"What's all this about?" Sam had asked, interrupting the details of the case Maria was painstakingly explaining.

"Well ... what do you mean? It's about justice."

Sam bit her lip and stared down into her glass of champagne.

"Why, what do you think it's about?" Maria asked.

"I don't know, honey," Sam said at length. "It's only that you've become so obsessed by this. And it's coming on the heels of Jeff being a total asshole. It feels like a reaction. Which, you know, would be totally normal. You've been through a really shitty time. You have the right to a reaction. I just don't think you should get too carried away with it. Does your boss even know you're doing all this stuff?"

"Well, I mean ... not exactly ..."

"Oh Maria!"

"But, Sam, this guy, Fergus, he's got no one else in the world who can—"

Sam smiled and took her hands. That was when she'd told Maria about her brother's friend from college: six-foot two and an ex-hockey jock from Michigan, who had just moved to the City, was *bona fide* single and looking to meet new people.

"He's only 29, but so what? It's not like you have to marry him or anything. Just go out and have a good time."

"I appreciate what you're trying to do," Maria had told her. "And I know that it probably looks like I'm obsessing over this guy because I need a date or something, but that's not it."

"So what is it?"

"I ... I honestly don't know."

Sam smiled. "Okay. But if you change your mind, call me, and I'll give you his number. His name's Nathan. He really is cute. I'm warning you, if you don't start having fun soon, I'm gonna get Cindy on the case. She will *make* you have fun." This forced her to smile. The threat of getting Cindy on the case was kind of scary.

"That's it," Maria announced, throwing down the butter knife. "I'm officially giving up on trying to relax. I suck at it."

And that was the truth. She had spent all day working on the Merger. Meanwhile there was a foot-high pile of *habeas corpus* documents on her desk, which Clarke had given her to help her get up to speed on civil rights law. She hadn't even looked at them.

Next to these files was a folder marked '*Stuff from Dublin*'. In it was the photograph Clodagh Brogan had given her of Fergus. He was a good bit younger in the picture, topless but for an orange life jacket. In one hand he held a sea kayak by the lip of its cockpit, while, with the other, he was waving a paddle. A boathouse was visible in the background. That was the early 1990s, somewhere in Ireland. *Where was he now?*

That question—the question she had been asking herself for weeks now—compelled her to sit down into her office chair once again. She picked up the file where she'd left off. Despite the promise she had made to herself not to work on it anymore that evening, she began to pore over the draft of the writ. Within minutes, she was once again in the zone, wrapped in her cocoon of words and ideas. This had been her comfort, her family, her safety, ever since high school. Maria wasn't able to fix VCRs, but she did not graduate *Magna Cum Laude* from Harvard Law for nothing. Fergus might not know it, but he would have the best defense attorney he could possibly get. Whether or not that would be enough, only time would tell.

The cold rain of a snowless New York winter pattered against the window as Maria worked on, deep into the night.

"Well, here we are, like old friends," Judge Victor Manuel said with a wry smile. "I'm thrilled to see you here again so soon, Counsel."

"Thank you, Your Honor," Maria said without looking up. She found it was best to ignore sarcasm in situations like this.

"You may proceed," Manuel said, putting on his reading glasses.

"The petition for writ of *habeas corpus* herewith presented on the basis of Article 1 Section 9 Clause 2 of the United States Constitution concerns the illegal arrest and detention of my client's brother, Fergus Maloney.

"I cite evidence presented by the defense in a previous hearing before this court concerning the particular circumstances under which Mr. Maloney was brought into military custody. While my client reserves the right to dispute certain aspects of these claims at a later stage in proceedings, this is not material to the current case. Defense testimony in this regard is sufficient to establish a basis for the arguments presented in the petition.

"In essence," Maria went on, "Mr. Maloney's rendition to the detention facility located at Guantánamo Bay Naval Base in Cuba which took place in January of this year, as confirmed by the Department of Defense in response to the informational request submitted by my client two weeks ago, has denied him any due process which is his right under law. Mr. Maloney is entitled to—"

"Ms. Da Silva," Manuel interrupted, turning a page and reading on, "before we even get to the substance, what I am currently having difficulty with here is the jurisdictional issue. And the *locus standi*. Where does Ms. ... Brogan stand in relation to Mr. Maloney?"

"Your Honor, she's his sister."

"But not next-of-kin?"

"Mr. Maloney's mother, Mary, is incapacitated and is suffering from terminal cancer. My client is seeking to be recognized by the Court as a proper Next Friend."

"And she resides in ... Ireland?"

"Correct."

"But, from your summary, it would seem she hasn't even spoken to him since well before the ... uh ... September 27, when he was taken into FBI custody? The last record you have here shows a reverse-charge phone call from a payphone in Manhattan, dated March 2001. Is that the most recent confirmed contact between brother and sister?"

"Yes, Your Honor. Ms. Brogan sent her brother numerous letters since then, but we are unsure if they have arrived. We have requested to be able to arrange a phone call, but the response from the Department of Defense in their letter dated February 3 indicates this is not possible. On these grounds, my client refers to the precedent under *Morris* v. *United States* in relation to Next Friend status being granted in cases where incarceration acts to constrain—"

"So, tell me this," Manuel took off his reading glasses and fixed his stare on Maria. "What happens if I grant this writ? The United States Government throws its hands up in the air and says, 'Okay, we try him in New York for conspiracy to commit terrorism?' Then what? They fly an illegal alien back into the US in order to stand trial? And what if he objects on the grounds that he would have preferred a military tribunal and was denied his constitutional right to plea on his own behalf? This frankly sounds like a legal mess." Manuel turned to the bank of defense attorneys lined up on the Government's side. "What's the position of the United States?"

A slick African American from the Solicitor General's office named Dwayne Johnson stood and stepped forward. He wore dazzling cufflinks and had all the hallmarks of a freshly-minted Republican appointee. Maria wasn't sure, but she thought maybe she had met him once at a Beltway fundraiser Jeff had dragged her along to, a few years back.

"Your Honor, the Government rejects Ms. Da Silva's plea," Johnson said. "On the subject of standing, the Government asserts the Plaintiff to this case lacks standing as she has not been in communication with the subject in detention. Furthermore, even prior to his capture, our sources in Military Intelligence have reason to believe that brother and sister were not close. It's doubtful if the subject would accept a petition filed on his behalf. On these grounds, we plead that the case be dismissed.

"On the subject of the writ of *habeas corpus*, we fail to see that the protections afforded in law could apply to enemy combatants who are aliens captured in the field of combat—"

"Field of combat?" Manuel asked, "he was 'captured' on the doorstep of an air base in Germany, Counsel, as he disembarked from a Continental jet chartered by the US government. That the INS put him on in the first place. Not in the mountains behind Kabul. Last I checked, Germany hasn't been a 'field of combat' since 1945."

Dwayne Johnson was unfazed. "Under the powers granted to him by the US Congress through the Authorization for Use of Military Force Against Terrorists, the Commander-in-Chief is authorized to use all necessary and appropriate force against those who he determines have planned, authorized, committed, or aided the terrorist attacks that occurred on September 11, 2001."

For Christ's Sake, Maria thought, *this guy is like a drone. He's literally quoting the text of the AUMF!*

"Right," Manuel said, coughing vigorously to clear his throat. Maria hoped he wasn't coming down with a cold. Sick judges meant delays. "I'm focused on standing for now." Then, turning to Maria, he said, "Counsel, can you present any more evidence in support of your client's claim as a proper Next Friend?"

"Yes, your Honor," Maria replied, "I refer to the fourth Folio." The clerk handed Manuel a file. "These are receipts showing Ms. Brogan provided financial assistance to Mr. Maloney in the form of payments on overdue beer tabs at establishments where Mr. Maloney was a regular customer: namely the Purple Shamrock, Dicey Toner's and Barry Duignan's Pub. In addition, there are three rental payments made in arrears to a landlord in Queens; the purchase of a pair of Caterpillar brand hiking boots, and a payment made to an unnamed moneylender operating out of Harlem in the period between April 1996 and June 1999. I refer to *Lehnard* v. *Wolff,* 443 US 1306 (1974) in regard to the principle of beneficial financial interest used to establish Next Friend status."

"Fine," Manuel looked through the papers, before lifting his glasses once again. "Anything else? No? Good. I will defer the ruling on *habeas corpus* pending a decision on standing. Expect my decision in a week. Court is adjourned. Peter, find them a slot in two weeks and meet me in my chambers. I believe I owe you lunch."

A whole week to rule on standing! Christ, this judge was slow. Maria considered the possibility that he was dragging his heels deliberately in order to give the Government a chance to muster its forces.

The truly shocking thing was that the inclusion of the fourth Folio in her submission was an afterthought—one she had very nearly overlooked. Without it, there was no doubt she would have lost before she had got going. It was easy to make mistakes, especially when you were operating on your own, moonlighting after a stressful day job. Which reminded her, she had exactly twenty-three minutes to get back to the office in time for her next meeting.

Before leaving the courtroom, she looked across at the bank of Government attorneys—all men—with Dwayne Johnson leading the huddle. Every one of them and their assistants and secretaries were working full-time on this. Her heart sank when she saw the bald spot of the Deputy Solicitor General himself poking out of the back of the huddle. This was not a good sign.

Maria Da Silva had known she was badly outgunned. But it was only now she realized by how much.

A week later, snow came to Manhattan. It started to fall the day Maria had arranged one of her meetings with Clarke. As she left the meeting, the streets were wet and heavy with slush; the sidewalks already looked like a melting nightmare. It would not stick around for long—just long enough to make her late getting back to the firm. Cindy, who had come along to the meeting to pressure or cajole the ACLU into giving Maria more resources, refused to unlink her arm until she promised to go for another merciless run next Sunday morning. *Now I'm seriously late,* Maria grumbled to herself.

As soon as she closed the door of her office she felt something wasn't right. Maria turned slowly and looked—truly looked—at all the items in her office, searching for the one thing that wasn't right. *There!* It was the key in the lock of her top desk drawer: a double set of locker-style keys on a flimsy wire key ring; one key sticking in the lock, the other dangling in the air beneath the drawer handle. Except that Maria always kept the key in the horizontal 'open' position for ease of access. Now it was vertical: in the 'locked' position. She never, never did that. Someone had been rifling through her stuff.

She went back out to her secretary's desk and asked, "Barbara? Was anyone in my office today?"

"Only the lady who cleans," Barbara replied.

"Okay, thanks."

She tried to push it out of her head by opening the Merger file she was working on. The phone ringing made her jump.

"Yes, Barbara?"

"Mr. Rosenthal would like to see you in his office. Right away."

Her boss was seated in his big chair when she opened the door.

"Maria, have a seat. Close the door behind you, please."

Once again, Maria's instincts told her something was wrong. And yet when Seth Rosenthal turned to face her, his expression was as difficult as ever to read. Was that disapproval in his eyes? In that instant, her heart was sick with regret. She wished she could have undone the Maloney case. But it was too late for that.

"You know," Seth said, after a while, "I was in the Harvard Club this week. I go every week. They have a sauna, which helps me relax. I was sitting in the sauna with my eyes closed, lost to this world, and then someone started talking to me. This is not normally what happens in the sauna, so I looked up in surprise, only to see that it was an old friend of mine. We actually went to college together. And it was strange to see him there, because he moved out to Connecticut, so he isn't in the club much these days. Perhaps you know him? His name is Victor Manuel. He's a Federal District Court judge."

Maria's heart dropped. "Seth, I know what this is about—"

"Don't!" He spoke in almost a whisper, but with a sharpness she had never heard directed towards her before. "Don't interrupt my story. I like telling stories." When he spoke again his voice had regained its normal tone. "So Victor says to me, 'Seth, I wouldn't have bothered you, except I'm in a little bit of a pickle and it concerns the case your firm filed. Something about a writ of *habeas corpus* for a suspected terrorist in military custody.'

"I said 'Victor, I honestly have no idea what you're talking about.' And that, *that*, was the truly embarrassing moment. Because you know, despite being very good friends, Victor looked at me as if I was telling an untruth. Which, of course, I wasn't.

"Now, as you can imagine, when I got back to the office, I endeavored to find out what was going on. After all, it's my personal reputation at stake. That led me to a case called *Brogan* v. *Rumsfeld.* At first I could not believe my firm was taking on the Attorney General of the United States without my knowledge. But, sure enough, counsel for the plaintiff was listed as Rosenthal, Roberts & Sleete represented by Attorney Maria Da Silva. You can imagine my surprise, Maria."

"Seth, I can explain—"

"No," he hissed, once again dropping his voice. "I'm not finished yet. When I checked the file, I really couldn't believe my eyes. Because I assumed the suspected terrorist in question would be one of my billionaire corporate clients. Turns out he's not. Turns out he's a penniless vagrant; an illegal alien with a penchant for alcohol and pub brawls. This defeated all my powers of reason and even common sense. So I figured I'd get the story from the horse's mouth." Seth leaned forward and planted his elbows on the desk. "Now I'm finished. It's your turn to speak. Explain yourself."

"It's *pro bono* work."

"*Pro bono*? Are you kidding me?"

"This man, Fergus, he was taken from his home. He was abducted from US soil and sent to a detention center in Poland run by the CIA. Heaven knows what they did to him there. Now he's one of fifty three detainees being held in Camp X-ray. There have been no charges against him; he has had no access to an attorney. And ... and his family! He has no family. It's ... it's quite simply a horrible miscarriage of justice."

"Maria, when last we spoke I told you that you could come to me if you were having problems. I told you I was here to listen. Instead, you chose to go behind my back and make a fool of me in this ridiculous way."

"I ... I ..."

"There's nothing more to discuss. Here is what you are going to do. You are going to withdraw this petition. You are going to forget this ever happened. You are going to return to being the excellent young Mergers & Acquisitions specialist

I saw in you when I drafted you out of law school six years ago. And you are never going to go on solo runs in my firm ever again. Do we understand each other?"

"Yes," she said in a small voice.

"Good," he answered, "I'll see you at the weekly meeting tomorrow."

When Maria returned to her desk the mail trolley was pulling away from her section. A letter was waiting for her on her desk. It was from the Southern District Federal District Court of New York.

She opened it with fingers that still trembled from the strength of Seth's rebuke.

In one sense it was good news. There would be no need to withdraw the petition. Clodagh Brogan had no standing. Case dismissed.

"I'm sorry, Fergus," Maria said, "looks like I failed."

In her heart was disappointment, and yet another part of her—the cowardly part—was relieved. She wouldn't never let Seth Rosenthal down like that again.

22

Once he was done pissing on Fergus, the square-faced interrogator with the dirty blond crew-cut, who had called himself Clyde, exited the room they called the Crucible. For a long time after that nothing happened. Fergus could look about the room, but there was not much to see. Three walls were breeze block and the fourth a giant mirror, which Fergus was sure was one-way glass. Besides, the act of looking up required him to bend his body in an uncomfortable way, because the manner in which his legs and wrists were strapped to the metal ring on the floor meant he was half crouched over. It was much easier to look down at the floor of uneven concrete, into which the pools of the interrogator's piss now gathered. The stench of urine burned his nostrils.

Behind him the air conditioning whirred, and he found himself growing cold. There was—once again—nothing to do but the thing he hated most: thinking.

For some reason it was Maria the Lawyer who came first to his mind. He tried to push the thought away – after all she was the reason he was here. But Fergus had never been very good at controlling his thoughts. She was cold. Her toes pinched into shoes that slipped on wet, slushy streets. Now a blast of warm air hit her on the face and warm light followed. Now she was sitting, and the glow of a computer screen illuminated her face, still flushed from the frosty outside air. He watched her as she worked on, through the night.

Fergus wasn't aware of falling asleep. But he became aware of hands unfastening him from the floor, and that woke him up.

"Let's go," one of the guards said. They led him back out through the short corridor and outside. As the hot air hit him, Fergus felt sure they were taking him back to the cell.

How wrong he was. They marched him around the building multiple times. He stared at the breeze block walls of the shed-like structure he had just come from. Opposite it was a fence topped with curls of razor wire. Strobe lights cut the night open, creating near daytime conditions in the little margin of weedy ground between the building and the fence. Eventually the guards brought him back and chained him once more to the ring on the floor of the Crucible.

This happened again. And again. And each time he grew more tired and was more inclined to drift off to sleep. But they never let him. Sometimes it was by making him walk outside, sometimes by shining a torch into his eyes. Sometimes they blasted rock 'n roll music in through the speakers overhead.

At the final procession around the building, a faint pastel pink had crept into the sky. How many times had it been? How long the night? Fergus had no clue. Still on his feet, he blacked out.

When he awoke the next time he was back in the Crucible, once again in 'the Squat'. The sound of the door opening roused him. ET came in and stood in front of Fergus's prone body. ET was short for 'Electrician's Tape', the name Fergus had given to 'Clyde', because for one thing 'Clyde' wasn't his name, and because the little ID badge on his battle dress uniform was covered with a length of electrician's tape. Also, in his own mind, Fergus had been captured by aliens.

"Are you ready to cooperate this morning?"

"Yeah," Fergus said without hesitation.

"Good."

A moment later the guards were back and his shackles were opened. *Thank fuck for that, at least!* He rubbed his sore wrists as they led him back to the chair, where he could sit across from ET. A cold metal chair never felt so comfortable.

ET hit the button on the recording device. "Now let's do what we should have done yesterday. Let's have you talk, and me listen."

In a haze of exhaustion, Fergus recounted to ET the details of his time in New York. He told him as much as he could remember, and surprised himself even by remembering things from years back which, when rested, his mind would have been unable to recall: details of pubs he used to frequent; job sites he worked on. Places he stayed. Women he had sex with. And then to the more recent stuff. His flat in Harlem. The bread oven. Karim. And the day he met Maria the Lawyer.

Let them know what they want to know, the fuckers, he told himself. *As long as they let me the fuck out of here.*

"So who told you about the 9/11 attacks?" ET asked him, out of the blue.

Fergus paused. "Sure amn't I just after tellin' ya? I had a vision. A psychic vision."

"But who told you about the attacks?"

"No one told me about the attacks."

ET sighed. "Fergus, I'm trying to help you here. But you don't seem to want to help me."

"Do you want me to lie to you?" Fergus snapped. He was gone a bit cranky from exhaustion. "OK, then I will. Osama bin Laden rang me on the night of the tenth of September; 'Fergus,' says he, 'we're gonna blow the shite outta the Yanks. Be so kind as to not tell anyone, there's a good lad.'"

ET slammed his fist on the table.

"You think this is a joke, you Irish son of a bitch? Two thousand Americans died that day!"

Fergus watched the soldier-boy all the way. His anger was only half real. The other half was a bluff. Fergus had faced men like him many times before.

"You're scared, aren't you?" he asked the Yank.

ET hesitated. "What?"

"You're scared 'cos you don't know what to make of me. You're scared you mightn't have the balls to stare me down." The thrill of the fight lent him fresh energy. Fergus stared at ET hard, challenging him to look away. *Go'on ya Yankee bastard. Look away! I dare ya!*

And he did. Fergus laughed as ET got up and said to the guard, "Get this son of a bitch out of my face before something bad happens. Take him back to JTC-160".

Outside the weather had once more grown unbearably hot. Fergus was already missing the comfort of the air-conditioned Crucible. *That's the way the Yanks have it rigged,* he thought. *Make people comfortable so's they'll want to talk.*

At the entrance to the kennel-like cell block, there was a sort of changing of the guard. The ones they called 'JTC-160' took over. They led him along the narrow corridor between the double row of cell blocks. As before, the

Muslims started to go ballistic and readied their weapons. This was the 'splashing' the guards talked about: the prisoners' only retaliation against the guards. It amounted to them collecting their piss in their drinking cups or whatever receptacle they had handy and firing it at the *kafer*, the infidels, through the gaps in the cages. He supposed they still regarded him as an enemy, for they made no distinction between Fergus and the Yanks as they threw their piss out into the corridor.

"I didn't touch your fuckin' book, did I?" he had screamed the first time it happened. But that didn't matter. Most of them didn't understand English anyway.

Once back in his cell, he was too knackered even to strip out of the piss-drenched clothes, and instead lay down on the bed, the strong smell of other men's urine wafting around him, and the late morning sun now penetrating in through the gaps in the fencing and cutting into his eyes. Didn't make a blind bit of difference though: within seconds he was asleep.

"My name is Farouq," the voice behind him said. Fergus had been watching the banana rats eating the bits of food he'd thrown through the wire into no man's land in the hopes of communing with them. When he turned he saw the voice belonged to the pudgy Arab from the cell directly across from him. The one with the little neat beard and the light skin.

"Mine's Fergus," he answered.

"Why do you not eat, Fergus? Is it a hunger strike?"

Fergus shrugged. He hadn't really thought of a hunger strike. It was more that his appetite was gone.

"I have decided," Farouq said, "that you are not a spy, after all."

"That's mighty generous of you, Farouq." A week ago, Fergus would still have had the energy and mental space to tell this fella to go *Farouq* himself.

The Arab was staring at him. "Do you believe in God, Fergus?"

"No," Fergus answered.

"How can you say that there is no God?"

He wanted to say something witty, like, "*How? I contract the muscles in my diaphragm; air is pushed up my throat; then I use a unique combination of muscles in my vocal chords, tongue and lips and—pop! —out come the words 'There is no God'. Simple as that.*" But he was too fuckin' knackered for that craic. So he just shrugged and mumbled, "I dunno."

"You should pray with us. God is the only path to salvation. They will kill us all, of course. But if you embrace Islam before you die, you have the chance to be saved."

It made no fuckin' sense really. Why not believe in a giant spaghetti-shaped monster that rode a red tricycle and spat ice cream cones from the sky? But Fergus was beyond even caring about whether it made sense.

"I can't speak Arabic."

"I will teach you the prayers. In this way you can learn the Qur'an. That is the most important thing to learn in Arabic."

Who knows, maybe there was a God? And so Fergus prayed. He got down on his knees on the little mat they'd left in the corner of his cell, and prayed to God, mumbling the meaningless words which Farouq called out to him. From the corner of his eye, Fergus was aware that the other men stood crowded against their own wire cells, staring intently across at the white man engaged in this holy act.

A memory came to him of the last time in his life he had prayed. He was in his sister's bedroom, kneeling on her bed, pressed up close against her. It was when he was seven years of age. They could hear Mammy's voice floating up from the sitting room, trying to keep the drunk bastard downstairs in the hopes that he'd fall asleep. It was her usual tactic, trying to coax him into watching *The Late Late Show* or else have a cuppa with her. But he just told her he'd go up and check on the children. And wish them good night. That was when Fergus and Clodagh started praying, begging God to spare Fergus that night. To *not* let *him* come upstairs. But it hadn't worked. He'd come in anyway. God had been powerless to stop it.

Abruptly Fergus rose and threw the prayer mat at the fence.

"Leave me alone, all of you. Fuck off and leave me alone!"

"Detainee 51," the guard said, passing something through the food slot. "You got mail. Straight from Ireland."

Fergus took the letter from the slot. With trembling hands and a cocktail of emotions, he managed eventually to get it open. It was from his sister Clodagh.

Dear Fergus,

I don't know if you've received my previous letter, but this one is to tell you how much we miss you and are rooting for you. Tom, Cian, Eimear and Nessa have all said prayers and send their wishes. Just so you know, we are doing everything possible on our side to have you freed.

Mammy is very bad. She's confined to the wheelchair the whole time and is not eating very well. The morphine helps with the pain, but the radiation drugs don't seem to be working. The cancer is progressing. The doctors say she has between one month and three months. But I honestly think she'll hold out as long as it takes for you to come home.

Which brings me to the main point of the letter. Mammy's one wish before she dies is that she might see you, and you might tell her you love her. If you would just stop this bitterness and come back to her, it would mean the world to her. Mammy is a good person and she loves you. I don't know, I will never know, what it is you are holding against her, but you are running out of time to make your peace. I can only do so much, Fergus.

If you can write back, at least promise you'll come when this mix-up with the Americans is resolved, which I expect it soon will be. I will pay for your flight home.

Your sister,

Clodagh

It was a lie. Every fucking word of it was a lie. He tore the letter into a million pieces and buried his face in the bed, trying to shut out the memories. Trying to shut out everything.

23

"Hey baby," Brandon said.

"Bran? Are you okay? It's so early ..." Mandy sounded sleepy. No wonder. It was 5:06 a.m.

"Yeah, I'm fine. I just ... I wanted to hear your voice."

"Is everything okay over there?"

No, it's not okay. I can't sleep. I can't eat. I'm drinking way too much. I hate myself, and I hate this place, and I hate the terrorists because of what they are and what they are making me do. I wish I was my brother, Zachary, out fighting the good fight, like a real soldier should. I made a mistake leaving you and Scott and Linda. A big mistake. But I'm too much of a coward to admit it.

"Yeah, everything's fine. How are the kids?"

"Asleep. Scott was in our bed 'til like three. He's still having nightmares."

"I'm sorry, baby, I know it's early. I just really miss you, that's all."

"Don't, Brandon, you're gonna make me cry again."

"I'm sorry, babe ... Hey, I got some good news."

"Really?"

"Well, it's not one hundred percent confirmed, but it looks like I might be coming home soon."

"Oh, thank God. When?"

"Next week. I have to go to some meetings in DC. But I'll be home in the evenings. Well, one evening, but at least I get to see my beautiful wife."

"Will you still get your leave in April?"

"I hope so, baby. It depends on the mission, but I hope so."

"That's ..." she broke down and started to cry.

"Mandy, please. Don't."

"I can't help it, Bran," she said between sobs. "This is so hard for me."

Brandon listened to her sobs on the other end of the phone. The MP on duty next to him in the communications hut was doing his best to pretend he was paying no attention. Brandon became aware of rain pattering against the metal roof above him. This was the first rain he'd seen since Maryland.

"Mandy, I have to go. This call is costing us our life savings."

"I know," she said.

"You gonna get some more sleep?"

"Yeah."

"I love you, baby," he told her.

"I love you too. Wait, Bran? Are you still there?"

"Yeah."

"One last thing, when you talk to Scott, don't say anything about the nightmares, okay? He made me promise I wouldn't tell you. He's still trying to be the man in the house until you come home."

"Okay," Bran said and hung up. He turned his head and squinted away the tears. The MP made absolutely no sign of having heard every word of the conversation.

Detainee 23—the Yemeni, Omar el-Mahani—made one final, useless attempt to break free of the hold the MPs had him in and lunge at the female soldier, before they dragged him out of the Crucible and into the short corridor that led outside. The man was still screaming in horror, cursing them in a primitive form of Arabic that amounted to little more than fragments. To judge by his face, the pain he suffered was physical. A look from Brandon was enough for the interpreter in the viewing booth next to him to understand he was not required to translate these last few profanities.

As the man's screams faded into the distance towards the cell blocks of Camp X-ray, Brandon watched the female soldier left standing in the Crucible. She had short brown hair, beady little eyes like a stray tomcat, and the gangly body of a teenage boy. Her name was Lucille Meyers, the only female guard at JTC-160, and the only female soldier who had volunteered for this duty. She buttoned up her BDU's, covering her lingerie-clad body at a leisurely pace. Private Meyers made no attempt to turn away from the one-way mirror, evidently not caring whether Brandon or the other men were watching. Brandon's gaze fell on the blackened, reddish stain of 'period blood' still on her hands. Only moments ago she had reached down to her crotch, pulled the hand out covered in 'blood' and smeared it on Omar el-Mahani's face. This was the most outrageous blasphemy they could commit against a devout Muslim: to touch him with the menstrual blood of a woman. Private Meyers, a Texas girl, had been only too happy to strip down to her underwear, and to taunt him with her sexuality. To rub her breasts against his arms and his back. And then finally, on Brandon's cue, to reach down and squeeze the chicken blood into her cupped right hand. Brandon wondered, *if she was having her period for real, would she have used actual menstrual blood?* Something in her eyes made him think she might.

"It's way better than that shitbag even deserves," she had said when it was over. Brandon looked her in the eye and cringed inside. The guy was a shitbag, but that had nothing to do with her willingness to make him suffer.

Brandon looked down at his notes, then flipped back through Detainee 23's file. The period blood had achieved nothing. Nothing useful. No safe houses. No names. Just the same old bullshit. Detainee 23 was either an amazing liar, or he really and truly didn't know anything of any military significance. Whatever his role in the Taliban had or had not been, one thing was sure: he was in no way implicated in the planning or execution of 9/11. And yet he, Brandon, had just ordered a 19-year-old Texan girl to smear her menstruation on this man's face. Not so much ordered, as allowed. But did that even matter? He was the commanding officer. He decided what did and didn't happen in the interrogations.

When Brandon looked up he realized the interpreter was still waiting to be dismissed.

"You can go. The next detainee speaks English. Tell Private Meyers she's dismissed too."

"Yes, sir," the young man said. His name was Abdul, a Syrian American and a Muslim, who had come to Gitmo as an Army Reservist. Brandon watched him closely as he turned to leave. He was one of the JTC-170 specialist linguists whose loyalty was being tested by the increasingly brutal interrogation techniques which his team had started to employ. Placing the Muslim soldiers in situations like this was an explicit part of Brandon's mission. 'Stress-testing the men', Rhodes called it. "Especially the fucking sand niggers."

The sound of the door into the Crucible opening made Brandon look up from his notes. The MPs brought in Detainee 16, supporting him by his limp arms, his lifeless legs dragged along the floor. As per Brandon's orders, 16 was put in the Squat, chained to the D-ring by his legs and arms. This was technically only supposed to be done for the safety of the interrogator, but Rhodes wanted to test a policy of routine Squat restraint as a means of 'softening' them.

"*What we're doing here,*" Rhodes had explained, "*is based on the theory of 'learned helplessness' developed in the 1960s by Dr. Martin Seligman. It was first tested on dogs in Seligman's laboratory. The animals were chained in the tightest of strictures, beaten for no apparent reason, deprived of food and then 'rewarded' for no reason either. What they learned was to unlearn the relationship between their actions and consequences. They become in every sense utterly helpless, and therefore compliant with any command. They forgot how to obey even their most basic instincts. A learned-helpless dog could be made to eat lump of ground glass; to jump off a cliff; to bite its own leg off.*"

The approach when applied to detainees should be one of continuous moral and emotional subjugation. They must be made to feel inferior, subservient, forced to be docile. The physical position they assumed was but one means of achieving this.

Sleep deprivation was another.

"*Ever try to run a marathon when you're out of breath, Brandon?*" the Colonel had said. *It's impossible. Doesn't matter how much you want to, how well trained you are, how strongly you believe God is on your side. Without oxygen going into your blood, you can't run. Period.*

"*Sleep is kind of the same thing. If someone asks you a question you don't want to answer, it requires energy to resist your inquisitor's force of will. Take away someone's sleep, you take away their ability to resist.*"

'*What are the limits?*' Brandon had asked.

"*After 48 hours you start having to monitor them carefully. After 72 hours, you're moving rapidly into brain damage territory. Which is fine, as long as it allows us to get at the information we need. Of course, if we damage them beyond the point of usability, we have failed the mission. But at this stage in your training, I would very much encourage you to push the limits. Especially on 16. He's one resistant son of a bitch."*

This was the second full cycle for Detainee 16, which meant, if the MPs had done their job, he hadn't slept more than ten minutes in two days. Brandon entered the Crucible and shone the pocket flashlight into 16's soft brown eyes. The response time—how long it took the pupils of his eyes to dilate—was a good indicator of how far gone the Detainee was, and how elevated was the risk he might suffer permanent brain damage and slip into a coma.

It took the pupils nearly two full seconds to dilate. That was bad. It was also sickening to watch. It meant his brain was not reacting fast enough for him to be able to protect his vision. If Brandon wanted, he could twist the focus on the flashlight and burn 16's retinas until he was blind. This man was effectively dying.

And yet Rhodes had been quite clear that he should be pushed further: kept awake for one more cycle. Brandon released the grip he had on 16's ear, the only handhold left on his shaved skull, and the head slumped back down. One of his legs was twitching. It was possible he was suffering brain damage at that very moment.

Something within Brandon surged up and he had to leave the Crucible. He retreated into the observation room and resisted the urge to vomit. *What the fuck have I become?*

He then resorted to the only trick that worked. He forced himself to remember what Detainee 16 had done to America. This man was a direct associate of Osama bin Laden and had conveyed bin Laden out of Kabul on the night of February 14, 1999. If he had been caught and interrogated back then, how many innocent American lives could have been saved?

He remembered the words his brother, Zack, had spoken the last night they were together. It was one week before he shipped. "*Truth is, our guys are just point-and-shoot grunts,*" Zack had told him. *"It's you who has the tough job now, Brandon. You're the one we're counting on when we're out there."* He could almost feel his brother's strong hand on his shoulder as they bumped foreheads in that final clasp of fraternity.

"I want to talk to you about the 9/11 attacks, Abu," Brandon said in Arabic, walking around the lifeless body. "Because I know you want to rest. You don't just want it. You *need* it. And I want you to rest. I want to help you, but I can't, unless you start helping me.

"Everyone else in the camp has spilled the beans, you know. Even the guy from Yemen who wants to be your friend. He's the one who told us you have contacts. He ratted you out, Abu. Some friend he is, huh?

"So, now, what's it gonna be? One simple conversation, and then you get to go to sleep. Otherwise this goes on, and on, and on. Forever."

Abu gave no response. It was very likely he wouldn't have been physically able to respond, even if he'd wanted to.

The red light flashed on the wall above the door. That indicated a signal from outside. Brandon stepped out, instructing the MP to shine the flashlight into his eyes in another few minutes, then douse him with water. They would have to add noise disruption to the cycle as well.

A sergeant was waiting in the hallway. "Colonel Rhodes is in the viewing room, sir."

Shit, Brandon thought. He hated it when the Colonel surprised him like this. And it happened often.

Rhodes had his feet up on the desk and a toothpick between his teeth. The smell of good coffee filled the room.

"I just watched the video on 23's last session," Rhodes told him. "Damn that was good."

"Thanks," Brandon replied.

"Still no progress though, huh?"

"I'm afraid not."

"But the thing with the menstrual blood. I liked that shit, Brandon. That was good thinking. How'd you come up with that?"

"It was Private Meyers' idea. I felt it would work because I've studied Islam as well as the Arabic language. But without her ... initiative ... I never would have been able to test it. That was a stroke of luck. And it's got me thinking; I reckon we need more women interrogators."

Rhodes nodded, "I think you're right." But the Colonel's thoughts were clearly elsewhere. Brandon followed his gaze through the one-way mirror and onto 16.

"So," he said, "how's our favorite Saudi today?"

"Lifeless. Reaction times are really slow. He's on the second cycle," Brandon tried to sound neutral. He didn't want his tone of voice to betray the reservations he was feeling. Especially as Rhodes was so damn good at reading his thoughts. "He's not responding."

"But he's listening," Rhodes insisted, abruptly changing his posture to reach for the coffee he'd left on the control desk in front of him. "And he's more resilient than you think. He can take a lot of punishment before he cracks."

Really? Brandon thought. *How can you be sure of that? What if he just dies? We're gambling with a man's life here.*

Colonel Benjamin Rhodes fixed Brandon with a stare from over the rim of his coffee cup.

"Are you prepared to do a third cycle, lieutenant?"

Brandon hesitated a fraction of a second before answering. "Yes, I am." But Rhodes wasn't prepared to leave it there.

"What about the Irishman? Detainee 51? I see you've taken him off the sleep cycles."

"I don't think sleep dep is the best approach for him."

"What's the matter? You can do it to the sand niggers, but if it's one of your own you lose your nerve? That's what I call racism, Brandon."

"It's not that. I just think we're doing this the wrong way. Before you told me we're here to make the rules. Well, I want to try a different approach. I want to try to get him to talk. Willingly. I want to try a much softer approach. No sleep dep, no Mauler. Just talk."

Rhodes fixed him with a venomous stare. Brandon had no way of knowing whether the Colonel was about to blow. Whether this could cost him his entire career in the JTC. But when he did speak, Rhodes was still calm, measured. The question that followed gave nothing away.

"What makes you think it would be any different than before? The FBI, the CIA, they all tried that with him. He keeps sticking to his hocus-pocus story. He's a fortune teller, remember?"

"Because I want to spend more time with him. Learn about his childhood. His family. His background. After all, he didn't just become a terrorist overnight. Something must have led him down that path. That's what I want to figure out."

Rhodes stared him deep in the eyes. "Tell it to me straight. Is this change of approach because you genuinely think it might work? Or is it simply because you lost your fucking nerve?"

"I think it can work, Colonel." Brandon held his stare. It was a stare with just a hint of challenge in it. Brandon let the hard words shoot like silent lasers from his eyes: "*I know General Achelson asked for me to go to Washington DC and not you. I know you didn't approve it. I know you didn't even recommend it. And I don't know—but I suspect—that Achelson has you figured out for the sadistic son-of-a-bitch you are. So, while I absolutely respect the chain of command, the reality is my upcoming trip to Washington represents a subtle shift in the balance of power in our relationship. This stare is my way of telling you I know this. And I know you know it too.*"

Rhodes shrugged and stood up. "OK." He shuffled through a file on the desk and took out a piece of paper. "Then you might find this is a good starting point. Take a look."

Brandon did so. It was a photocopy of a letter written by a woman named Clodagh: evidently 51's sister. It had been delivered last week, and Brandon hadn't even been told.

"He's been getting mail. It's from his sister in Ireland. We redacted the part where she asks him to give assent to the lawyer she hired. Otherwise it's all straight from the goddamn heart. And so, so touching. Good luck, Lieutenant." As Rhodes was leaving, he patted Brandon on the shoulder. "I'm glad to see you're finally starting to take some initiative and act like an officer. If I don't see you beforehand, give my regards to General Achelson."

Once he was gone Brandon breathed deeply. He had agonized over whether to do that. And for the moment it looked like his bet had paid off.

He grabbed the sergeant on duty and told him to take 16 back to his cell. "Cancel his next session. Let him sleep."

It was 0800 hours. There had been one more interrogation scheduled for that morning, but the detainee in question had been involved in a 'cell incident' that night—his Qur'an had been 'accidentally' spat on by one of the JTC-160 guards on night duty, triggering a riot. The net result was that the detainee ended up with a concussion and four broken ribs. Interrogation canceled. This was the latest example of the lack of discipline and chaos that was undermining their entire work here. And so Brandon had some spare time. He could maybe fit in a run on the beach before his scheduled meeting with the NCOICs.

It was only after his shower, while he was on his way to the briefing room that he remembered it was Mandy's first day back as special ed teacher in her elementary school. Her maternity leave ended today. Brandon had forgotten to buy her a card. He had even forgotten to wish her good luck on the phone.

24

As they jogged side by side along the Brooklyn Promenade, and even up the stairs into Maria's apartment, Maria told Cindy again and again that she definitely wasn't going to the party. But Cindy was not the sort of person to give up easily.

"You gonna go to the party dressed like *what* exactly?" Cindy asked, as Maria emerged, post-shower, from her bedroom, in sweatpants and a baggy sweatshirt. Her hair was still wrapped up in a towel.

"Cindy, Please! For the tenth time already: I'm not going. All I want right now is takeout and a movie. I'm exhausted."

"Is it because Jeff will be there? Are you seriously going to give him that power over you? For real??"

"What power? It has nothing to do with power."

"Yes it does," Cindy insisted. "You're effectively censoring your social life because you're afraid of confrontation. Which jus' don't make no sense. After all, he's the scumbag around here, but he got no qualms about confronting you. You need to stand tall, girlfriend."

Cindy grabbed Maria under the arm and pushed her back into the bedroom. "I was the Ohio State Girls Wrestling Champion when I was a senior in high school, I'll have you know. And, so help me God, if you tell me once more you're not going to that party, I will use my wrestling skills to force you into the tightest, sexiest dress I can find in that wardrobe; then I will apply sultry red lipstick to those pretty lips of yours and drench you in enough bling to make Mr. T look like a Cistercian monk."

"Cindy!"

"Then I will DRAG your ass across to this party and ply you with booze until you finally, finally, snap out of this rut you're in and start having a good time."

"You're bullying me!"

"No, I'm not. I care about you. Bullies don't care about the people they bully. Big difference."

To make her point, Cindy finished with one of her smothering hugs. It was impossible to argue with her.

"Fine, you win. I'll put on a dress, okay? Now go! The shower's all yours. You don't want to be late for your big date tonight."

Getting press-ganged into a party is one thing, but Cindy isn't able to force me to enjoy it, Maria said to herself, before realizing how petulant that sounded. She was in an industrial elevator which led to a fourth-story studio loft. The steel walls were decorated with a dazzling light display. Fluorescent pop art images flashed alongside Eastern Orthodox iconography. As soon as the elevator door opened, Maria found herself staring out into a sea of yuppies dressed in eveningwear. The floor quaked to the beat of oppressively loud music.

She propped herself against one of the pieces of art: a marble statue of an ancient Greek torso with plastic nipple rings, that was topped off with the plastic head of Ronald McDonald stuck onto the marble neck. Utterly hideous, but good cover for a wallflower. From this position, Maria scanned the room. She saw the usual crowd of young attorneys from Rosenthal, Roberts & Sleete mixing with their corporate clients. Before, she had always taken these parties at face value: a casual group of the firm's young lawyers and their clients letting off some steam. Dancing, flirting. A little cocaine in the toilets, maybe. It was living the Big Apple dream, and up until now it had always given her a thrill to think she was so much on trend – socializing in the Greenwich Village studio of one of New York's most celebrated abstract artists, a Bulgarian who went by the name of Dizzy Petar.

Now it all looked so disgustingly fake. What was Dizzy Petar, after all, other than a product bought by the firm? His idiosyncratic, sanitized, artistic hospitality was a gimmick solely designed to prove the firm's cultural credentials to its mostly out-of-town clients. These events served one purpose and one purpose alone: to soften up the client base, thereby ultimately making more money for the firm.

It didn't take her long to spot Jeff. He was really in his element, surrounded by three adoring female interns and engaged in banter with a very drunk-looking male client. Maria watched him work the group with a strange fascination. All the years of dating him, she never saw what a false, empty turd he was. Now, with the aid of some physical and emotional distance, it seemed strikingly obvious to her. She couldn't imagine buying a used car off Jeffrey Laurence, much less having his babies.

"The guy he's buttering up right now is his ticket to making Senior Partner."

Maria turned her head. The voice belonged to Tom Greene, one of her least favorite colleagues, who was standing next to her. He was holding an orange juice with a sun umbrella in it, wearing a smile that announced how happy it made him to catch her watching Jeff.

Greene was a small, unassuming tax lawyer, the sort of colleague who, if he ever got tragically struck by a crosstown bus and you had to attend his funeral, you would have almost nothing to say about. Except perhaps that he knew everything about everyone else in the firm. Aside from being a master in the fine art of tax avoidance, gossip-mongering was Tom Greene's only real skill.

"His name is Hale," Greene continued. "*The* Hale. Of Burton & Hale."

Maria only vaguely knew who that was, but Tom Greene didn't need much prompting to go on telling her.

"Looks like Jeff bagged the deal to represent Burton & Hale as they negotiate a whole raft of defense contracts with the government."

"What sort of contracts?" she asked.

"Technically, it's classified. But from what I heard, they're going to be building a whole new military complex in Afghanistan. Word is, it's gonna be the biggest military base outside US soil. Plus, they're building a new prison in Guantánamo Bay."

Maria instantly perked up at this.

"Oh, yeah," Greene went on, warmed by her interest. "Military detention centers are big business these days. And when it comes to getting a sweet deal on government contracts, Burton & Hale don't take prisoners. Hundreds of millions are up for grabs here. Jeff must have really rubbed them the right way to nab this one for the firm. Of course, it helps when your dad is the Secretary of State's right-hand man."

Maria's thoughts flew to Fergus. He and fifty-two other men were the grist in this very lucrative milling operation. *And I gave up on him.* A sick feeling of shame, of revulsion, overcame her.

"So," Greene continued. "I heard rumors you might have a special kind of interest in Guantánamo Bay. Is that so?"

Tom Greene was measuring her reaction with his pigeon-like eyes, magnified in size and intensity by his Coke-bottle glasses. He was fishing for gossip. This was the *quid pro quo*. He had given her a morsel of news, now he expected something in return. But Maria wasn't interested in playing along.

No, she thought. *I'm done with these kinds of games. It's not who I am. It's not even who I ever was.*

"Tom, it really doesn't matter," she told him flatly.

Greene nodded, sipped his orange juice and then tossed another fishing line into the lake. "I notice your client isn't here tonight," he said. He was referring to Malcolm J. Lewis III, the portly and socially-awkward son of the Kansas City agricultural leasing magnate, Malcolm J. Lewis II, whose company's merger she was handling.

"I think he had other plans." The truth was, Maria had no idea if he did or not. She hadn't invited him to the party, and the wry look on Tom Greene's face told her he knew it full well.

"Well," Greene said with a sigh, as he toyed with the paper umbrella in his drink, "I better go mingle. I hope you get yourself sorted out, Maria. Been nice talking to you."

When Tom Greene drifted back off into the crowd, Maria pondered his parting words. *I hope you get yourself sorted out.* What was that supposed to mean? Had he heard something about her? Idly, her gaze returned to Jeff and his little posse. He had exactly the right level of body contact with this Hale guy: friendly, but respectful. Jeff knew how to pretend to be more drunk than he actually was. Yes, it was a disgusting game, and he played it only too well. And, yes, he had probably used his dad's position in the State Department to ensure the firm got the deal. But why was she surprised? That was half the reason Seth Rosenthal had hired Jeff in the first place.

What was shocking was not the way Jeff played the game. It was the realization that she herself had played the exact same game, in the exact same way, only a few months ago. This was what she had done to court Peterson Investments Inc. before Osama bin Laden had put a brutal end to that company's New York operations.

Had Fergus Maloney not saved her life, she would have perished playing that game. And now, because of that, he was inside the very prison whose expansion was going to earn hundreds of thousands of dollars in bonus money for Jeff, and millions for the firm. It all sickened her to the core.

The pounding of the music grew louder in her head. For a moment she felt nauseous, and steadied herself against the hideous statue. There was no air. *I have to get out of here.*

Maria fled. The booming music and the dazzling lights and the fake yuppies danced away in a blur of nausea. Next she knew, she was alone in the cold rain of a New York winter's night. When she'd made it as far as Washington Square Park, the sickness in her stomach erupted. She ran to a trash can and vomited into it. Trembling fingers took out her phone and dialed Cindy's number.

"You okay, baby girl?"

"Yeah ... um ... sort of. No, I'm not. Are you in the city?"

"East Village. What happened? Did Jeff Laurence diss you? I swear to God, I will stick my foot so far up his—"

"No, Cindy, no. It wasn't Jeff. I know this is a bad time, but I really need you right now. Can we talk?" Maria knew Cindy was in the middle of a first date with this mega-handsome guy she'd met on the Internet. But she also knew Cindy was already on her way out the restaurant door. That's the kind of friend she was.

"Where am I going?" Cindy asked.

"There's a coffee shop on the corner of Washington Square East. The corner where University Place starts. Do you know it?"

"I'll be there in five. Order me a latte decaf."

When Cindy arrived there was zero judgment. Just a big, big hug, and some pocket Kleenex to wipe the mascara streaks caused by tears Maria hadn't even remembered shedding.

"Ready to tell me what's up?" Cindy asked eventually.

"I ... I ... feel like such a fucking *coward*." Now, as she vocalized it all, the emotions became clear to her, and therefore more intense. "He has no one, Cindy. No one in the world. And now I've given up on him. I've left him there to rot. Why? So I can go to parties with ... Tom *fucking* Greene? I feel so ashamed of myself."

There were some more tears to dry up. When that was done, Cindy took both her hands.

"Honey? Maria, baby? Look at me." She did. "I didn't wanna say it before but you know what you gotta do."

Maria nodded in reply. It meant an appeal of the decision on standing. It meant taking the fight for Fergus to the next level: the US Circuit Court of Appeals. It might even mean going further.

"That's why you called me, isn't it? 'Cos you knew exactly what I was gonna say."

Maria nodded again, then asked, "But what am I gonna do about Seth?"

"This ain't about Seth. This is about your soul."

Now that the decision was made, Maria calmed down. Only then did she think to ask about the first date she'd just busted up.

Cindy dismissed it with one sweep of her long, graceful hand.

"You 'member how I told you in his picture he looked like Shemar Moore? In real life, he was a whole lotta Forest Whitaker."

The following Wednesday, when she returned home from work, a letter from the United States Court of Appeals for the Second Circuit was waiting for Maria in her letterbox. It confirmed the case of *Brogan* v. *Rumsfeld* would be heard. Another letter from the same court, also in the letterbox, confirmed the date for the emergency preliminary hearing to take place that very Friday to consider the motion for expedited hearing which she had also filed. In this motion, she argued that the conditions of Fergus's detention were so urgently grave that any delay in process pertaining to the underlying motion would cause grievous harm to her client. A third motion, a motion to shorten time, was also referenced in the documents received from court. This would be heard in conjunction with the underlying motion and would aim to force the court to expedite the deliberation period, thereby leading to a quicker ruling. Copies of everything had been sent to the Solicitor General's office by registered mail.

It was an impeccable appeals architecture she had built up in a very short space of time: one the Solicitor General's office was going to have a hard time breaking down. Maria let herself indulge in a brief glow of pride as she paced through the slush-filled streets of a late-winter storm, on her way into the office Thursday morning.

There were really only two problems. The first, she was supposed to be meeting on Friday with Malcolm Lewis and his senior staff, who were flying in from KC especially for the meeting. Getting their whole team to reschedule was going to be a big, big problem. And the second problem was even bigger: she had failed to confront Seth about this, despite promising herself, Cindy, and Sam that she would. The rational part of her brain knew this was a really bad idea, but the emotional part had managed to convince herself that somehow the whole thing could be managed quietly without creating a stir. When she called Sam on Wednesday and admitted as much, her friend had gone nuts.

"Maria, you *have* to tell Seth! What you are doing is outright insubordination."

"Okay, I'll call him first thing in the morning."

On Thursday morning the sun was out, and despite the melting mess lying on the sidewalks, there was a feeling of spring in the air. The sunshine filled Maria with optimism. She would reschedule with Lewis first, then have the discussion with Seth, which meant technically she was going to be calling her boss second thing in the morning. *It's gonna be okay,* she told herself.

Barbara's greeting as she entered was unusually nervous. With the phone to her ear, Maria spent a moment reflecting on the strangeness of Barbara's greeting, as the line to Kansas City rang through.

"*Hi, Attorney Da Silva,*" Malcolm's slimy voice called out through the phone. "*Or can I call you Maria?*"

"Ah ... Maria's fine, Mr. Lewis, I'm afraid we have a little problem."

"Oh?"

"It's just that I have an absolutely unresolvable scheduling conflict, and I'm afraid I'm going to have to postpone our Friday meeting. I'm really sorry about this. I can do absolutely any time on the weekend or Monday. I can fly to Kansas City if you need—"

"Wait, cancel? Are you sure?"

"I'm afraid there's no other option," she told him.

"I'm confused. I got a call twenty minutes ago from Mr. Rosenthal. He told me from now on he would be handling the merger personally. Now, don't get me wrong, you are *great,* Maria. Really the best. But Mr. Rosenthal is a legend. Having him working with us personally is A-OK by me. No way Agricola will try a fast one with Seth Rosenthal across the table!"

"Um ... okay ... I ... there's some confusion here. I'll call you back."

Maria was stunned. It took her a second to recover before she picked up the phone and dialed Seth's number. His PA answered.

"Mr. Rosenthal's not available, I'm afraid."

"It's me, Jen. Maria Da Silva. I really need to speak to him. It's urgent."

"Mr. Rosenthal's not available." *Click.*

When Maria looked up Barbara was standing in front of her desk with a letter in her hand. Right at her back was a security guard with his arms folded across his chest.

"I'm really sorry, Maria."

Maria opened the letter. The subject line read: '*Notice of Termination.*'

25

Fergus was back in the Crucible. They kept him hours waiting for the sound of the door to open. Every click and rustle made him look up to see if someone had entered. This was hard to do, because he was in the chained, prone position in which his head naturally pointed down, and the effort of craning his head up had given him a neck that was beyond sore. It felt as if the muscles were worn through. This pain was the only sensation keeping him conscious.

They would always come at perfectly random times. Sometimes within ten minutes, some-times it would take hours. And in between, there was a tantalising array of strange noises—creaks and bumps, clicks of the air conditioning or Fergus didn't know what the fuck—all designed, he was sure, to drive him fucking bonkers. They wanted him to lose his mind. That was *all* they wanted. This was all about fucking with his head.

He could feel the panic rising up within him and tried to fight it back. And in the effort of doing so, his lips quivered as one desperate, unanswerable question echoed through the cavity of his mind: *Why?* Tears welled in eyes which were already red and swollen from lack of sleep. *Why?* The tears were about to fall, but still Fergus held them back. *Don't let him see you cry,* Clodagh told him.

He closed his eyes, which caused him to momentarily drift away from consciousness. When he awoke he crouching in the small space at the bottom of the wardrobe in Clodagh's bedroom. She was with him. *If you don't cry, he can't hurt you*, Clodagh had said. And she was right, he decided. He wouldn't let the Geegaw Man see him cry. Not now, not like this. They hid themselves in the secret place where he was safe from the Geegaw Man. Or so he thought.

In the next moment, a rough, cold hand lifted the top of his Batman pyjamas and touched his back. It fumbled under the elastic band of his bottoms. The Geegaw Man had found him. Fergus's knees and fingers sank into mud which had not been there before.

Fergus screamed and opened his eyes. His body shook and strained, but he was held tightly.

It was the chains. He was in the Crucible, in the prison, surrounded by the Americans.

"Detainee 51?"

He craned his head up, unsure if this was a real voice or another phantom.

But this time it was real. ET stood before him, in his army fatigues.

"It's me, Clyde. Are you OK?"

ET kneeled down in front of him and his square face came into view. The man's cold grey eyes observed him keenly.

"Sorry they put you into this. You wanna sit down with me now?" Fergus flinched at the words, spoken gently, and without a trace of menace.

He managed a weak nod. Seconds later the restraints opened and he fell limply to the ground.

"You're covered in sweat. Are you thirsty?"

Yes. Yes, he was. He tried to say as much, but his throat was still hoarse from the screaming. When the water came, he drank it in big gulps, and it burned its way down his gullet.

"Can we talk now?"

Fergus nodded again. He fought off the soreness and managed to get himself over to the chair. ET sat across from him and waited. When Fergus was ready, the American switched on the recording device.

"We've had some contact from your family," ET told him. Fergus remained silent, clutching his knees. He tried not to show the panic he was feeling. But it was impossible. His heart was exploding.

"They are very concerned about you, you know. Your mom especially is real worried ..."

Fergus didn't move. Ever so slowly he said, "Leave my family out of this."

"... she told us she wants more than anything to see you, one last time, before she dies. She says she forgives you and just wants you to come back home to Ireland. She—"

Fergus slammed his fist on the table. The reaction was instant. MPs appeared on either side of him, batons at the ready. Fergus cringed down into his seat. But ET stayed cool. With a hand motion, he called the guards back without taking his eyes off Fergus.

"Why don't you tell me what that was all about?" ET asked him.

"Because it's none of your fuckin' business."

"Okay," Clyde said. "Let's start all over again."

"With what?"

"With you. With Fergus Maloney."

"What?"

"You heard me. I wanna know what your deal is."

Before Fergus would have told him to fuck off right back where he came from. Now his brain was too slow, and he only managed to stutter, "What does that matter to you?"

"On the eleventh of September, my country was attacked," Clyde told him. "Two thousand people lost their lives. And the asshole who did it is still out there, hiding. We believe that because of the scale of the operation, there are enough leads and people in his network for us to find him by tracing the threads, one node at a time. It's just a question of connecting the dots. Now, there is reasonable evidence to suggest that you had some prior information about this attack and you have not to this point in time provided a credible explanation for how you came to acquire that information. The United States of America will not be satisfied until we know every single detail about you. Either you're going to lead us to bin Laden, or else you're one more name we can cross off our list. So I'm starting at the beginning and working forwards, right up to the time you were taken into custody by the FBI. You will account for every day, every second, and every hour.

"Meanwhile, so you know, we already have a lot of shit on you. Your records. We have a statement from your family. We have the cooperation of the Irish police. If you are found to lie, and I mean about anything, things are gonna get a whole lot worse.

"But if you cooperate, I promise you on all that is sacred, that I will do everything in my power to help you get the hell out of here, and to make sure they don't hurt you anymore. So you can be reunited with your family. Trust me, I want to be able to cross your name off the list. I want you to get the hell out of here. OK?"

ET leaned forward and placed a proprietary hand on Fergus shoulder. The hand felt like a knife cutting through him.

"So. Have we got a deal?"

Fergus nodded. He'd have agreed to anything. He just needed to get some fuckin' sleep. He felt the American's hand on his shoulder again. "You have my word, Fergus. If you're straight with me, boy, I'm gonna be straight as an arrow with you. Now get back to your cell and get some sleep. We start first thing in the morning."

In the stillness of the night, Farouq's whisper was as loud as a shout. When Fergus turned, he saw the silhouette of the Yemeni, sitting on his bed on the other side of the wire, staring across at him.

"They are trying to break you, my friend," Farouq whispered. "They want to destroy you completely."

"I don't have anything to tell them," Fergus whispered back. "I've told them that again and again and again."

"They don't care," the Yemeni answered. "Don't you see? This is not the purpose. They wish to make us crumble. To watch us suffer."

He looked at the little bearded Arab, or as much of him as he could make out in the half-light, until a tingling of something came to him. A whisper of Destiny. A warning. "Did you do it?" Fergus asked spontaneously.

"Do what?"

"Attack America. Plan 9/11. I don't know what. Whatever it is they have you in here for?"

Farouq laughed. "I left my country to seek work, three years ago. I travelled to Afghanistan to work as a mining engineer in the marble mines of Nangarhar. I was working there at the time when the Americans invaded. The mine we were working on was destroyed by American bombs, because they suspected it might be used to harbour terrorists. We feared for our lives. The road through Jalalabad was closed. There was no safe way to return to Kabul. So we tried to flee east into Pakistan. We made it to the border. A local man agreed to shelter us, for a price. He told us we could wait until the snows melted, when we would be able to descend into the next valley and onwards to the capital.

"But we never made it that far. Because what we did not know, the local man had local enemies. His enemy, another farmer, reported us. In the night, soldiers came across the border. They were with the Northern Alliance. We were carried, through the snow, back into Afghanistan and sold to the Americans for a thousand dollars each.

"They say I was storing weapons for Osama bin Laden. It is foolish lies! I have never met any Saudis in Afghanistan. I doubt he is even in Afghanistan. I have told them this countless times. But they will not listen. Because they do not care. They are evil."

The sound of banana rats scurrying in their nightly scramble for food interrupted their conversation. A mosquito defied the anti-malaria barrier of chemicals that surrounded the cell block and buzzed across Fergus ear. He hadn't even the energy to swat at it.

"I can't take much more of this," Fergus told Farouq after a pause.

"If only you would pray to God. In Allah is strength, my Irish friend. God is great. Greater than evil. Always remember that."

Fergus closed his eyes and tried to imagine a God who was stronger than evil. Nothing came but the sting of the mosquito biting him in the neck.

26

Maria looked across the table at Clarke, the ACLU man, who was absorbed in reading her brief. He was a balding, bearded white guy of vegan thinness and complexion, with a nervous tick. Clarke was too young to be a hippy and too old to be a hipster. He wore a granddad shirt, jeans and canvas loafers. If it had been summer, Maria did not doubt but that Clarke would be wearing sandals and white socks. His office was small, crowded with paper, and totally unpretentious. But despite his unprofessional appearance, Clarke was to the world of civil rights law what Seth Rosenthal was to corporate: a guru.

In his little bony hand, he clutched a red pen, clearly with the intention of marking up her brief like a bad high school assignment. There were even times when Clarke's pen wavered dangerously close to the text, causing little ripples of wounded pride to flare up in Maria's heart. But the pen never actually reached the paper.

When Clarke looked up from his reading his face wore an expression of admiration. "Cindy was right about you. This is one of the best briefs I've ever seen."

"Thanks. That's ... very flattering."

"I don't think you're going to have a problem with the legal arguments, Maria. You are as good, if not better, than anyone we've got."

"Um ... thanks again."

"As for the substance. You're going to win the appeal on standing easily. I don't know what that District judge was even thinking. It's an open and shut case. But the *habeas* writ is a different story. That's where they'll start to fight back. Have you ever taken a case against the United States before?"

"Mostly just the SEC, the FTC, a couple of times against the DOJ, but only the antitrust division, and only civil. I've never even touched criminal before. Unless you count the District Court hearings that just happened—"

Clarke waved his hand. "District doesn't count. Until you get to Circuit, Uncle Sam doesn't even blink. Circuit's where the real battle begins. The Solicitor General is gonna have teams of really good lawyers going over every detail. They will intimidate you. They will intimidate the judges. If there is a single weakness in your arguments, trust me, they will find it. Everything you write is going to have to be as good as this brief. You'll need every bit of help you can get."

"Okay. So ... is the ACLU on board?"

Clarke nodded. "We'll do what we can."

"Which means ...?"

"You can use our offices. We've got two admin assistants, three in the mornings, 'cuz now Sarah's back part-time. Oh, and we have free photocopiers. And coffee."

Maria exhaled disbelief. "I don't need a photocopier, and I can buy my own coffee. What I need are lawyers. Trained civil rights lawyers. The United States will have truckloads of them, you said it yourself. I can't do this on my own."

Clarke paused for a second. Wordlessly, he got up and went into another room. When he returned, two young looking people followed him in.

"Maria, this is Anca and Ralf. They're studying at NYU, focusing on civil rights law. They've agreed to help you prepare for the hearings."

Anca smiled as she offered a handshake. She still had braces on. All she was missing were the pigtails. Ralf looked positively gangly. Maria imagined him living in the attic of his mom's house and hiding a *Playboy* under his mattress.

"Last semester I did my term paper on *habeas corpus*," he told her. "It got an A." When she failed to immediately react, his face erupted into a blush.

"That's great, and no offense to you guys, but what I need is a little experience on my side."

"Right now we are pursuing hundreds of cases," Clarke said. "We're on the ground in thirty states and at Federal. Wrongful arrest. Wiretapping. Entrapment. You name it. We simply don't have a half dozen experienced lawyers hanging around who can work for free." He glanced down at his watch.

"I'm sorry, but I have to go. You guys feel free to use my office to get acquainted. I'll work on getting you some space you can call your own. We'll talk tomorrow about arranging press. Press is important now."

Maria turned and looked at her new 'staff'. *This is going to be a fun ride.*

Clarke's prediction proved accurate. The appeal on standing went almost uncontested. Almost. The United States pushed pack on the motion for expedited hearing, arguing they needed additional time to put together a defense, citing the unprecedented nature of the situation; the changed legislative context, and the rapidly evolving situation with respect to national security. It pushed the substantive hearing out for almost three weeks, which Clarke still felt was a good result. What followed were newspaper interviews. Dozens of them. A spot on national TV was being organized too.

On Clarke's suggestion, Maria even tried to reach out to the Irish media. The idea was that if they could excite outrage in Ireland, this could trigger a political response through the back door. The Irish Prime Minister was due to visit New York for a special ceremony on St Patrick's Day. That could be just in time for a last-ditch diplomatic intervention, Maria thought. She tried all the main newspapers, and even the TV, using every one of the ACLU's contacts.

Yet to her total surprise, the media appeals in Ireland went nowhere. It was like they didn't want to know Fergus existed, and she couldn't figure out why. One journalist, who seemingly owed Clarke a big favor for some past story, gave Maria more than just the polite shrug-off.

"Listen," he told her. "It's not the way things are done here. The Maloneys of Clonakilty...And as well as which, we depend on America for loads of things."

"Wait, what? What did you say about the Maloneys of Clonakilty?"

"Well, let's just say they haven't got the best kind of associations."

"What's that supposed to mean?"

"I'm sorry, I really can't help you any further. Give my regards to Clarke when you're talking to him."

On the US side, though, she was getting a little more traction. Pretty soon the story was in the national papers.

A few days later, at the convenience store near her apartment, Maria got the first taste of what this new media exposure meant. Jerry, the old Italian guy who worked the night shift, was used to serving her whenever she came home late, which was always. They were on small-talk terms.

"Are you all right?" she asked him absently, when he failed to respond to her friendly hello. He was sullen somehow, and she thought maybe his wife was sick again. It was only when he looked right at her that Maria realized this was personal.

"I saw your picture in the paper." He was fishing her change out of the cash register.

Maria smiled. "Guess I'm famous now." She held her hand out for the change.

Jerry nodded, placing the 73 cents on the counter next to her hand. "Lotta people died, you know. Lotta good people died."

"I'm well aware," she replied. "I knew a half dozen of them personally."

"Makes it even harder to understand how you wanna defend the sons 'a bitches who done it."

The encounter bothered her more than it should have. When she got home, Maria closed the blinds in her living room and put on the TV for comfort. The news was on, and she did a double take when her own face appeared in an inset box on the screen.

"*.... is taking a case to have one of these terrorists, named Fergus Maloney, released from the camp and brought to face trial in the United States. Some feel this could jeopardize national security at a time when Osama bin Laden—America's public enemy number one—is still at large.*"

Holy God, this was happening quickly. She wanted to call Clarke, but at that moment, her cell phone rang.

"Who is it?" she asked.

"My name is Karim. I'm a friend of Fergus's." The voice sounded African American. Then it clicked who he was: Karim Saunders, Fergus's old roommate in Harlem. She had looked for him before, but with no success.

"How did you get my number?"

"I called your office. Someone called ... Anca ... gave it to me."

Oh, for Christ sake! Maria thought. Words would be had tomorrow morning, that was for sure. If Karim could get her number just by asking, so could every right-wing nut job in New York City.

"I just wanted to say, you know, he's one hundred percent innocent."

"I know he is."

"If there's anything I can do to help him, I'm down with that."

"Maybe there is. I'll take your number just in case." She took it down.

"One other thing," Karim said. "There's a box of his stuff I still have. I haven't looked through it, 'cos you know, respect for a brother, but if it could help his case you can have it ..."

"It possibly could. I'll get someone to come by tomorrow and collect it."

The next day, when Ralf returned with the box, Maria went through the personal items. There were clothes. There were various trinkets. A very small Buddha statue, a few Irish coins. And in the bottom were poems. Maria hesitated at first, because it felt so personal. Just like Karim she couldn't bring herself to invade his most private space like that. *Except I'm doing this to help him*, she told herself and began reading the poems.

By the time she finished with them, her hands were shaking. Tears ran down her face. *How could any human being endure this much pain*?

Maria lifted one of his T-shirts to her nose and inhaled his scent. She would never stop fighting for him. Never.

27

Brandon set the recording device on the metal table and hit the button. The little red light appeared. Detainee 51's eyes, still woozy from lack of sleep, seemed to focus on the red light.

"Are you going to talk now?"

"Sure."

"So talk."

"I already told you, I don't know anything—"

"No, not about 9/11."

"Then what?"

"Tell me about your childhood?"

"What do you want to know?"

"Where'd you grow up?"

"You know where I grew up."

"I want to hear it from you."

"In Ireland. A place called Clonakilty. It's in County Cork, by the sea."

"Was it a farm?"

"No, we lived just outside the town. In an ordinary house."

"Did you have a happy childhood?"

A silence. Brandon repeated the question.

"Why does that matter?"

"I ask the questions around here. You answer them. Now, did you have a happy childhood?"

"No worse than most, I suppose."

"That sounds like a 'no' to me. What was wrong with it?"

"I didn't like school."

"No? Why not?"

"I dunno. Just didn't."

"That's not good enough, Fergus. Now, what was our little agreement?"

"I answer, I sleep."

"That's right. So now, try again. Why didn't you like school?"

"I hated the teachers. I hated authority."

"Why?"

"Because, it's always the same. Some fella thinks he's better. The brutality of power. Exactly the same shit as is happening right here, right now."

"So you rebelled?"

"Yeah."

"And they threw you out?"

"Yeah."

"What about your home?"

"What about it?"

Brandon noted his emotional reaction at the mention of his home. Stiff body language, flickering eyes, forced breathing. This is where the puzzle was. This is what it all came down to.

When 51 finally did respond, the words were choked and stilted. "I'd a brother and a sister. I was the youngest. We weren't what you'd call a perfect family."

"Why not?"

"We were left to ourselves. And there wasn't much in the way of money. Nothing at all really."

"What about your parents?"

"My mother gave up on us."

"Is that why you're so mad at her?"

"Who said I was mad at her?"

"Well. Are you?"

51 fell silent again.

"You mention your mom a lot. And your brother and sister. But what about your father?"

"He was gone by then. He died when I was a baby."

"And she never remarried?"

51 shook his head, just a little too abruptly. Brandon probed further.

"Why do you blame your mother? Sounds like she had a tough ride, raising three kids on her own—"

"Because she was the one to blame." He came out with it suddenly, in a voice full of irritation.

"For what?"

"For everything."

"What's everything?"

51's body tension was now extreme. He was unable to sustain eye contact. Goosebumps had appeared on his neck and a bead of sweat made its way down his forehead, even though the air con was on full blast.

"Answer me, Fergus."

"Why are you doing this to me? Why are you making me do this?"

"What was your mom to blame for?"

"For what happened to Darragh!"

"What happened to Darragh?"

"He died, all right? Is that what you want to hear me say, is it? He died!" The voice was strained, barely audible in fact.

"How did he die?" Again no answer." Detainee 51! I asked you a question, now answer me, goddammit! How did your brother die?"

Fergus—Detainee 51—was beyond the point of reasoning. Beyond the point at which he could be approached. His face was buried now in his hands and his body shook and shivered. Still, no reprieve, no mercy. This would go on. And on. And on.

"I'm gonna sit here until you answer my question."

For what seemed like an eternal twenty minutes, Brandon made good on his promise. It felt like they'd stay there for even longer, until, eventually, 51 lifted his head. The expression on his face had changed. His mouth was open. His eyes drifted away from the interrogation table and focused on something outside the Crucible, as if he was looking through the cinder block wall.

"You'll find out for yourself," the detainee said.

"Find out what?"

"What it feels like."

"Excuse me?"

51 turned now and looked Brandon straight in the eye. His tone of voice had grown more distant. "Can you not hear it? It's calling to you."

"What are you talking about?" Brandon asked. And yet his skin was beginning to crawl. "Who's calling to me?"

"The crow," 51 said. "It says they're coming for him."

"What? Who are they coming for?"

51's lips curled into a deranged smile. "For the *shepherd*."

The file from the Irish police was listed as '*Secret*', the second highest level of security which could be placed on documents. This was not on account of its contents—mostly just records that could have been obtained locally from government offices—but rather the very fact that the Irish government was cooperating with the US military in this way.

The articles in the British press were having an impact in Ireland too, with some forces on the left of Irish politics talking of closing access to Shannon airport for all US government aircraft. Brandon knew Shannon from his time in Air Force logistics: it was a useful support point for all kinds of military and special purposes missions, due to its convenient proximity on the Atlantic seaboard. If the engagement in Iraq was to go ahead, as was currently being talked about, it would become even more vital to ensure a US presence on Europe's closest landmass. Any suggestion that the Irish were now cooperating fully with the American Military Intelligence in Guantánamo could seriously damage US interests on the European Atlantic fringe.

The most worrying (and embarrassing) part of the file on Fergus Maloney was the handwritten note clipped to the cover. It was from an Irish Special Branch police officer, advising them in not-so-subtle words that this was the third time his office had sent this file to "*colleagues in various US government offices*", and a suggestion that *"it might be more efficient for yourselves if you looked a bit at your own internal information sharing systems."*

The file contained the official records from Fergus Maloney's high school, verifying the account he had given of himself as a dropout. There was also an arrest record dating from 1995, following an incident described as a 'physical altercation' at the *Widow Scanlan's* pub in Dublin. Maloney was released without charge. After that came several records from the Irish welfare office, tracking unemployment benefit paid out to him for a number of months and ending in a copy of a letter sent by the welfare office to an address in Dublin explaining that his benefits had been suspended due to a breach of Section 213 of the Social Welfare (Consolidated) Act 1993. The next document was a photocopy of an expired dog-eared Irish passport with an entrance stamp for Newark Airport, marked August 3, 1996.

Below that there was a death certificate dated January 6, 1987. The name of the deceased was listed as Darragh Maloney. Inside the space headed '*Certified Cause of Death*' the doctor had handwritten: '*Haemorrhage caused by incisions in the wrists and throat.*' And below that: '*Suicide.*'

Brandon slammed the file shut, determined not to have any sympathy with Detainee 51, and even more determined not to be sucked in by the man's bogus voodoo, which quite frankly made his skin crawl. He needed to get out of here before he lost his mind. Brandon glanced at his watch. It was nearly time to catch the ferry. Time for his flight home.

Brandon almost forgot to salute when General Achelson walked into the room. Gitmo had its own strange rules for how things were done, and without realizing it, Brandon had allowed himself to become slovenly.

"Sir!"

The General acknowledged his salute and ushered him into a seat.

"Welcome home."

"Thank you, sir."

"I understand you're a fellow Pennamite?"

"Huh?"

Achelson smiled. "Someone from Pennsylvania..."

"Oh right. Um, yes sir. From Carlisle. Sir."

"I grew up in Johnstown myself. Are you Steelers or Eagles?"

"Eagles, sir."

The general nodded and said with a smile, "I won't hold that against you. Now tell me frankly, Lieutenant, how's it going down there?"

It's a complete fucking mess, sir. We treat the prisoners like dogs. Unsurprisingly, that's how they behave. They throw piss in our faces and riot all the time. The enlisted men are at breaking point. The Arabic interpreters—themselves mostly Muslims—are ready to go native. Our own morale is in the pits. And none of this would matter a damn if we were getting the intelligence we needed to win in Afghanistan and find bin Laden. But the truth is we've got zip out of them so far. Nada. Nothing. Half of them are probably innocent—sold by the Northern Alliance to the US for the bounty or to settle some petty tribal score. But if they didn't have al-Qaida sympathies before now, sir, I can assure you they will be our avowed enemies if and when we ever let them go. Unless we shoot every single one of them and bury them in a mass grave—Auschwitz style—we're breeding a fucking army of terrorists down there. Bin Laden couldn't do a better job if he was running the place himself.

"Very well, sir. The mission is progressing according to plan. We're building capacity and interrogating the high value assets in a routine and methodical way."

"But the issue is results," Achelson insisted.

"It's a slow process, sir. We have to be patient."

"Lieutenant Zeiss, the American public wants to see results."

"I understand sir. But if we act too precipitously, we risk losing intelligence and undermining our own efforts. We have to proceed in a methodical yet determined manner."

General Achelson nodded gravely.

"Are we treating the detainees with dignity?"

"Yes, sir. All detainees receive routine medical treatment, healthy nutritious meals, clean bedding and their religious needs are being seen to."

"What does that mean in practice, 'their religious needs are being seen to'?"

"They have access to a US military imam who is attached to Camp X-ray. We insure they have their prayer time and they're issued with prayer mats. We also respect the sanctity of their religious Qur'ans."

"You mentioned capacity? Do you currently have enough resources to complete the mission?"

"It's frankly a strain. With more and more detainees arriving every week, we lack men, we lack facilities. Operationally speaking, Camp X-ray is at its limits."

"So what would you recommend?"

"Sir, it's not up to me to decide, but I believe the current plans to build an expanded facility known as Camp Delta would be most welcome."

General Achelson nodded and rubbed his chin. "OK, let's try a different line of questioning. What about the reports from the press? The British newspapers? There's talk of flagrant violations of human rights. Some journalists are even using the word 'torture'. What's your honest experience?"

"I can't comment on what journalists might or might not write, sir. I can only honestly relate my experience as an officer in charge of interrogations. I have seen no prisoners being treated disrespectfully, nor have I seen any evidence of anything that could be considered as torture. All interrogations are being carried out as per the FM 34-52, the US Army Field Manual on Interrogation."

General Achelson nodded and smiled again.

"OK, good, and be prepared to recite it, chapter and verse. That's basically all you have to say to them. Any other questions, I'll answer. If they ask any specific details about prisoners, tell them you're not authorized to disclose that kind of information." Achelson clasped Brandon's shoulder in a firm grip and looked him square in the eyes. "The United States Armed Forces appreciates you coming here, Lieutenant. To a soldier like you on the line of scrimmage, it might seem like pointless horse crap, but, believe me, it's mission-critical work." He patted his shoulder again and said, "I know your grandfather was a legend in World War II. One of the best generals to ever serve in the US Army. I'm sure he'd be proud of you if he were here today."

Brandon nodded. "Thank you, sir."

A pretty, young Congressional staffer knocked and poked her head around the door.

"Gentlemen," she said with a smile. "The subcommittee is ready for you now. This way, please."

On the way into the Congressional hearing room, Brandon swallowed hard and prepared to lie his sorry ass off, in a way he knew would shame his noble grandfather to the core of his very being.

Disorderly lines of small children crowded the sidewalk space between the bus stop and the red brick steps leading up to the main entrance of Bingham Elementary School. The children were corralled in by the arms and shouts of teachers, directing them along marked lines in the designated stopping areas. From there they filed into the big yellow buses that would take them to their suburban homes. Behind them were the fenced-in yards with sports facilities, now empty. A forgotten basketball leaned against a gutter at the edge of the fence. And in the foreground, among the children, Brandon caught sight of Mandy.

"Dylan! Don't run. Wait in line until your row is called." Mandy's voice trailed off as she turned and said something else to the teacher standing next to her.

Children and teachers. Prisoners and guards. Bingham Elementary School ran on the same basic model as Gitmo, Brandon thought. Even the fences looked the same. Except here in Maryland there were no banana rats and no orange prison suits. And no one was being tortured.

He pushed the idea out of his head. How could he even think something like that? A chill ran through his body. Was it a chill of disgust in himself or was it just the shock of temperature? He had the car's heater turned way up, but the fresh February air had still managed to cut into his bones and make him shiver. He was acclimatized to tropical weather now, and even though the sun was shining and the car's thermostat displayed 53 degrees, Maryland felt cold as ice.

He could have got out and walked over to greet his wife, as she stood directing the last of the kids into their buses. He could have thrown his arms around her and kissed her passionately. And the kids would have pressed their faces against the windows of the bus and laughed, and the other teachers would have made jokes, and Mandy would have gently scolded him for his indiscretion, but secretly been overjoyed by it. And if anyone noted the impropriety, well, it would be remembered that Mrs. Zeiss's husband was a brave soldier: sacrificing, serving far away, keeping America safe.

But Brandon chose to remain in the car and wait and watch, in a detached, almost voyeuristic way. It was she who spotted him, and with a final goodbye to her fellow teacher, she strode briskly over to the car, her smile growing bigger with each step.

She pulled the door closed and turned to him wordlessly.

When the hug came from across the passenger seat, Brandon tried hard to focus on the pressure of her body against his, to feel it and acknowledge it as something that was real. Her softness. Her smell. The slight spasms of her soft body against his, which told him she was crying.

"I missed you so much," she said. He answered something similar, and was finally able to break the embrace and put the car in drive.

"Take a left here, honey," she said. "We're going straight home."

"But Darlington's that way. Scott's school—"

"Scott's at home already. Bob's here for a few days and he already picked him up a half hour ago."

Brandon swallowed an irrational feeling of anger and discomfort, something close to jealousy. What the hell was Bob North doing in his house, getting his son from school? He might have been Mandy's brother, but he still had no business taking Brandon's place. It was a stupid thought, and probably didn't last more than a millisecond, but Mandy was watching his face.

"I asked Bob to come, Brandon. Dad's back is bad again and Mom needed to go home and take care of him. And I can't deal with everything here on my own. Bob was the only one who could find the time."

'Course he could find the time. It's easy to find time when you don't have a job.

Brandon smiled. "Sure, honey," he said. "I understand." And he tried hard to.

Scott beamed up at his father from his place on the carpet between Bob's knees, smashing, with all his heart, the drumstick into the Irish drum he held with his other hand. They were singing a song which Bob had taught him. It was some Irish ditty about a soldier returning home from the British army. As they sang,

Brandon watched his brother-in-law's face and thought of all the ways he resembled Fergus Maloney. What separated them? Bob maybe had a better family and the good fortune to be born in the USA. That was all.

"Guys! It's nearly seven o'clock!" Mandy called from the kitchen.

"Seven o'clock. Daddy's going to be on TV with the Con-dress!" Scott shouted, jumping up and down.

Mandy laughed. "Con*gress*, honey. Not Con*d*ress."

"Can we watch you on TV, Daddy? Please, can we?"

"Wow, Bran," Bob said, his fingers still tracing wisps of chords on the guitar strings. "You managed to get a five-year-old interested in watching C-SPAN. Now *that*'s a heroic feat!"

Brandon fixed Bob with a stare. "What's that supposed to mean, Bob?"

"Nothing. It was just a joke."

An awkward silence descended. Mandy turned from the kitchen and looked in at them. Scott's little voice filled the silence, "Can I watch you with the Con-*gress* on TV, Daddy? Please?"

"No," Brandon answered. It came out harsher than he wanted. Mandy looked at him in surprise.

"But Mommy said—"

"Don't talk back to your father!" Brandon said, snatching the wooden drumstick out of the boy's hand with a violence he hadn't intended. He looked at Mandy and tapped his watch. Scott, unsure how to react, dropped his mouth and stared at his daddy.

"Come on, baby, it's time for bed," Mandy said, scooping the boy into her arms. "Say goodnight to Daddy and Uncle Bob."

Brandon winced as Scott leaned in and kissed Bob's bearded cheek. It was symbolic of everything that was going wrong in his home. Men in the Zeiss family did not kiss one another, irrespective of age.

When the woman and child were gone upstairs, a silence fell between the two men. Bob returned to the oblivion of his guitar, his filthy fingernails dancing noiselessly over its strings, refusing to touch them by a fraction of an inch. There was something in the very absence of sound that annoyed Brandon. He found himself thinking once again of Detainee 51, Fergus Maloney. An image came to him of the Irishman's prone body, of cold air conditioning, and water dripping from the detainee's forehead. Heavy metal music blasted inside Brandon's head. It was the music they used for the noise disruptions as part of the sleep dep cycles. Now it rang out in supreme contrast to the deafening silence produced by Bob's long, dirty fingernails strumming inaudible chords in the air.

"I don't want you taking drugs in my house, Bob," Brandon announced. His voice drowned out the heavy metal music and the silence. No reaction from Bob North. "And I don't want you kissing my son either. He's not a sissy."

Bob looked up at him. For an instant, Brandon's muscles flexed, and he imagined doing physical battle then and there. It took him a second to register Bob's look as completely unthreatening, whereupon his muscles relaxed again.

"Sure thing, Brandon." Bob put down the guitar, grabbed his pack of cigarettes and headed out to the back porch. Before he left he added, "I'm glad you're home safe. Mandy really misses you."

Brandon caught up to Mandy as she was coming out of Scott's bedroom.

"I want him out," he hissed into her face in a venomous whisper.

"What? Who?"

"Bob North. I don't want him in my house."

Mandy's expression was pained. "He's my brother."

"He's a drug addict."

"He's not a drug addict; he just smokes a little bit of—"

"Marijuana is an illegal drug. I could call the cops right now. I don't want him in my house and I don't want him near my son. Is that clear?"

Mandy stared in disbelief. "I don't know who you are anymore."

Later Brandon listened from his bedroom window as the engine of Bob's old Honda Accord fired up and—fan belt slipping—rumbled out of the driveway and off into the night. Brandon lay waiting in the dark for Mandy to come to bed, until eventually sleep overcame him.

He awoke in the middle of the night and had one of those moments of not knowing where he was. Slowly it came to him. He listened to the sound of Mandy's gentle breathing next to him. There was enough light from the cracks in the blind to illuminate the shape of her breasts as they rose and fell in the motion of her sleep.

He touched her. He ran a hand across the silky material of her nightie, then up along the breasts themselves, lifting them up onto her chest fully, as if to reverse the sag which two children and ten years had inflicted upon them. He continued playing with her breasts in a way that slowly became sexual. The nipples stiffened under his touch. She stirred. Her hand was upon his arm and she turned towards him. In the half-light, it was impossible to tell if her eyes were open or not, and, to dispel the discomfort of that uncertainty, he leaned in and kissed her. Soon they were entwined, and his arousal grew physical.

Her nightie slid up over her backside. Pushing the sheet away, he rose to his knees and positioned himself between her legs. He looked down at her, focusing on the curves of her body, allowing himself to grow yet more aroused. She reached up and traced a pattern on his chest, which was more muscular now. His fingers tugged at the elastic of her panties, and she lifted her behind ever so slightly to help him get them off.

Only then did he notice the blood. It was gushing out of her panties, coating her inner thighs. He touched his own hands one against the other, and realized they too were covered in her blood. The clean satin sheets ran slick with it all the way down to the indentations made in the mattress where he knelt. In horror, he looked at her face and saw it was no longer his wife who lay before him. Another woman had taken her place. It was Private Lucille Meyers, the JTC-160 guard who assisted in the interrogations.

"Fuck me, Brandon," the mousy, short-haired Texan girl whispered in a hoarse, lurid voice. "Fuck my blood-wet cunt as hard as you can." She licked her full lips, and they too ran red with blood.

Brandon awoke screaming. The heavy metal music was still playing, ringing in his ears. Somewhere in the distance of his own body, he could feel Mandy's hand on his back, gently stroking him.

"I'm sorry," he muttered, then climbed out of bed beyond her reach.

It was 5:13 a.m. His flight back to Gitmo left at 0600 hours.

As he left the bedroom, he saw out of the corner of his eye how Mandy sat in the bed, clutching a pillow to her chest, watching him.

28

The little red light went on above the camera. Kelley Mann, the presenter of *America Now* turned towards it, then lifted up her notes. Her heavily made-up face froze into a smile as she waited for a hand signal from one of the producers. Sitting a few feet away from her, Maria thought her makeup looked simply awful—way too heavy and garish. Her dyed-blond hair was held into position with a styling agent that might have doubled as superglue. Yet Maria had watched some old episodes and knew that on camera, Kelley had a killer look. *This isn't journalism,* Maria reminded herself. *It's entertainment.*

Then the text on the teleprompter began to scroll.

"Good evening, USA! I'm Kelley Mann, welcome to another edition of *America Now*. On today's show, the hunt for Osama bin Laden. In a few minutes we'll be taking you on a virtual tour inside the complex of caves located in northern Afghanistan where American troops now believe the terrorist mastermind is hiding out. Also our security expert, retired Army General Bradley Sampson, will explain why the new airport security measures might still not be enough to protect us. He's calling for state-of-the-art 'body scanners' to be installed at airports around the country. But before that, we'll talk to Maria Da Silva, the new face of the campaign to free suspected terrorists being held in Guantánamo Bay. She's in our studio to explain to us why she thinks these men deserve a trial here on US soil. Not doing so, she argues, could lead to more terrorist strikes in the future. Maria, welcome."

"Thanks for having me on the show."

"You've come to the civil rights area on a very different path?"

"That's right, Kelley. Up to recently I worked as a corporate lawyer in a totally different area. It wasn't until I became aware of what was happening in

Guantánamo and in other detention facilities operated by the CIA that I became alarmed at the direction our country was taking."

"So what is it you want done differently?"

"What we're looking for is that these men, who are prisoners of the United States of America, either be granted status as prisoners of war under the Geneva Convention, or else tried under a civilian jurisdiction. But right now, they're in a sort of legal limbo. Most of them haven't even been charged with any crimes. We tend not to see it this way, but the reality is, with the Patriot Act now in force, the US Government can—without any justification—put a bounty on the head of anyone, anywhere on the planet, then take them into military custody in a place like Camp X-ray and torture them—"

"Torture them? Do you have any evidence to support that claim?"

"The International Red Cross visited Camp X-ray and were denied access to a number of prisoners. While their exact findings cannot be made public due to the terms under which the Department of Defense granted them access, we know that they expressed grave concerns at the manner in which detainees were being housed and interrogated."

"But that's not the same as saying they've been tortured?"

"Depends on your definition of torture. There have been reports of waterboarding—"

"But these are all unverified claims, right?"

"Because the military won't allow us to verify them!"

"So your accusations are based solely on worst-case assumptions about our military?"

"Well—"

"And your key argument, if I got it right, is that *not* releasing these men might actually increase the risk of a terrorist strike. That seems counterintuitive. After all, if they're terrorists, letting them go creates another risk for our country, doesn't it?"

"You said '*if*' they're terrorists. And that's just the point. We don't *know* they're terrorists, because we never got a fair trial. The risk is we are detaining innocent men. Nothing is surer to turn people against our country than knowing we're imprisoning innocent people. It undermines everything we stand for as a nation. And it's our good reputation around the world, which we fought so hard to establish, that's likely to keep us safe. Not these detention camps."

"But you're implying the military would have some motivation for holding innocent men? Don't you believe the men and women who proudly serve our country want to find the bad guys? Why would you assume our soldiers aren't able to make that judgment? After all, they're the ones on the ground."

"It's not even a question of that; it's a question of civil rights. We need to make sure—"

"You also have a very personal reason for pursuing this case, isn't that right?"

"Well," Maria hesitated a second, "the case I have taken on is about one person in particular—an Irish citizen by the name of Fergus Maloney. In some respects, his case is unique, because he was for all intents and purposes extradited from the US into a CIA detention facility outside the US, then brought to Gitmo. But, in another sense, every case is unique. And what we are looking for here is to establish a principle in law. That the United States must grant equal justice to everyone—"

"But is it true that you have a personal relationship with Mr. Maloney? That you knew him before the attacks? You two were friends?"

"We met once or twice."

"And is it true that you were actually the one who gave the testimony to the FBI which led to his arrest? It's an extraordinary story!"

"I ... no, that's not true! And anyway, it's beside the point. The point is, he hasn't had the opportunity to stand trial."

"But isn't it true that you yourself thought Mr. Maloney was a terrorist? Do you still believe that?"

"That's ... no! And that isn't even the point!"

Kelley Mann glanced down at her notes. "What about the connections Mr. Maloney's family has to the Irish Republican Army? I mean, we can both agree that the IRA are terrorists, right?"

Maria was dumbstruck. "What?"

"Well, according to local sources in Ireland, several members of Fergus Maloney's family were under investigation by the Irish anti-terrorist police."

"I ... I don't have any information about that. That's circumstantial at best. And ... and it's not the point!"

"I think for many Americans watching, the question 'is he a terrorist or not?' is very much the point. So, do you, or do you not, believe Mr. Maloney to be a terrorist?"

"If you put it like that, the answer is no. Because the principle of law in this country states that everyone is innocent until proven guilty. Until Fergus Maloney is given a *fair* trial—which means not behind the military's closed doors and not on national airwaves—and until a jury of his peers finds him guilty, he's innocent. I believe that because I believe in due process. And the case I'm taking right now is about making sure that fair trial happens."

"And how would you respond to those who accuse you of working against the United States in our quest to win the War on Terror? Some people claim your case, if you win it, could compromise national security and ultimately allow al-Qaida to stage another 9/11-style attack."

"I think that's nonsense. A functioning justice system is one of the values that makes us strong, not weak. If we compromise our values, we let the terrorists win. And these quasi-legal facilities across the globe are not helping to win us any friends. Already there are reports coming out of Gitmo and other places which suggest the men we are holding there are becoming more radicalized while in US custody. These detention centers are breeding grounds for future terrorists. We have to shut them down."

"So where are you in the Maloney case right now?"

"We're getting there, I think. I've just won the support of the American Civil Liberties Union and that's a big boost. In terms of process, we passed the first hurdle last week when the Federal Appeals Court overturned an earlier ruling which said we didn't have standing to take the case. The substantive hearing is next week."

"Well, I think I speak for a lot of people when I say, I hope justice is done, but in a way that keeps Americans safe. Thank you for speaking to us, Maria."

"My pleasure, Kelley."

No part of that ordeal was her pleasure. She left the TV studio and was met in the lobby by Anca and Ralf, her new ACLU interns.

"That ... could have gone worse," Anca said, and showed off her braces with a sympathetic smile.

"Yeah, it totally could have!" Ralf agreed, before exchanging glances with Anca. He stuck out his hand as they emerged out onto Madison Avenue, and—amazingly—a taxi stopped for them right away. The first good thing that had happened all day.

"Yeah," Maria mumbled, "the only way that could have gone worse would have been if I'd socked her in her smarmy, botoxed mouth. And actually, at least then I would have got some satisfaction. Oh my God, that was awful. I was awful." Maria grumbled. "She made me look like a petty blow-in with an ax to grind, bulldozing through America's safety in order to do her friend a favor. Who even put that rumor out there that I reported Fergus? And what the hell was that stuff about the IRA? Who told them that? This is rigged. Did you hear her at the end? *I hope justice is done, but in a way that keeps Americans safe.* That's code for 'set up a bogus military tribunal to provide a veneer of justice, just make sure nobody actually gets found innocent.'"

Ralf and Anca exchanged glances again as they all piled into the cab and Maria gave the driver their office address.

"What?" Maria asked.

"The ACLU has some friendly sources inside the DoD. It seems that's exactly what they intend to do. They're just trying to figure out a way to make the Tribunals legally watertight."

"I suppose they need some time to appoint the kangaroos," Maria mumbled. "Although on the bright side, at least it means they're reacting. They're taking this seriously now."

She watched the traffic swish past. Somewhere inside her, a feeling started to bubble up. Something was not right. But what? She glanced in the driver's direction. He was black, a big man, well-groomed, maybe in his early 40s.

"There's one other thing," Anca said, flicking through her notes which she had opened out onto her lap. "Clarke says there's someone you have to meet. It's one of our sources, a British journalist. He's been hounding us for an exclusive interview and we've been putting him off 'cos we know how busy you are. But Clarke says he has something you might be interested in. According to Clarke, this guy has been following the whole Gitmo thing, especially the plans for the new Camp Delta. He thinks there could be something useful for *Brogan* v. *Rumsfeld* in this."

Maria was about to ask for more details, but the feeling of unease stopped her short.

"Clarke told me to tell you—"

Maria silenced her with a sharp hand motion. "Sorry, Anca, I ... I have a splitting headache. Can we talk about this later? Right now I just need to de-stress." She had figured out exactly what was bugging her - the driving. Too smooth, too perfect. New York cabbies came in all races, creeds, and sizes. In fact, they only had one thing in common: They were all shitty drivers. But not this guy. This guy was smooth as silk.

When the cab arrived at their office on West 44th Street, Maria let the other two get out before leaning forward to pay. She opened her purse and pretended to search for some cash.

"How much is it?" Maria asked.

"Fourteen dollars." The driver's voice was cool, and he spoke well, in measured tones.

"Are you sure about that?"

"Says so right on the meter."

"I think that's kinda hefty. We only went a few blocks. Maybe your meter's broken."

Behind her she could see Anca and Ralf looking uncomfortable. "Maria, I can take care of—"

"No," she cut him off. "It's a point of principle. I hate getting ripped off. Even for a few dollars. I'm willing to bet money this meter is rigged. Let's see what the NYPD has to say about this." She looked the driver hard in the eye as she flicked open her cell.

The driver nodded coolly. "Just forget it, lady. I don't need trouble."

She sat staring at him for a second.

"Get out of the cab, lady."

When she was out, he put the car in drive and cruised off before Maria could even dial 911.

"Maria, why did you do that?" Anca asked, "it was like ... borderline racist."

"And frankly not reasonable," Ralf added, "I mean, fourteen dollars wasn't even a lot!"

Maria stood on the street and watched the cab pull away into the distance, making a mental note of the license plate. "That's the point," she told him, "it was actually five bucks too cheap."

That had proved her suspicions. No real NYC cabbie would have let her off that easily. And no NYC cabbie drove that well. She was willing to bet her right arm the car that had just driven them across lower Manhattan wasn't a registered NYC taxi cab at all.

Damn right they take this seriously.

29

The Englishman was tall, with smooth, even features and a bright smile. His name was Chris Delafonte. He introduced himself as a freelance journalist, though Maria had already checked him out on the Internet and knew he wrote primarily for *The Guardian* and *The Independent*, England's two left-wing newspapers. When she shook his hand, his grip exuded the perfect confidence of a man who knew how to control his own body. It was just a momentary thought—nothing that would make her lose professional focus—but Maria couldn't help thinking this was the first time she had even looked at a man since ... since Fergus.

"I have to say, it's quite a pleasure to meet you in the flesh," he began. "Your story is incredible. This whole case is incredible. If nothing else, I really hope you'll do me the honor of an exclusive interview."

Maria nodded. "I don't know how 'exclusive' but sure, we're doing lots of press. In a way, it's our best weapon. Public opinion matters in this case. And frankly, it's against us right now. At least in this country."

She poured out two coffees and handed him one.

"I'm really flattered you came all this way just to interview me."

"Thanks," he said as he took the coffee. "But to be honest, I'm chasing another story too. It's a related story, in fact."

"Yeah, Clarke mentioned something to me. I'm curious."

"Well, it could be nothing, or it could be a major scoop. Depends on the source."

"Now I'm really curious."

"It's to do with the handling of the contract for the new detention facility in Guantánamo Bay."

"Have you seen the plans?"

"Yes. Which is shocking in itself. It seems they're creating a detention facility capable of housing thousands of prisoners. The current intake is nothing more than the tip of the iceberg. But that's not the half of it. Seemingly the contract was won on tender last week. According to my source, the handling of the tender process was nothing short of scandalous. Confidential information was given by the Department of Defense to the privileged bidder, tender specifications were shared with the privileged bidder. The privileged bidder, it seems, even rewrote the tender to suit their own bid."

"And this privileged bidder was Burton & Hale?"

"So you knew?"

"I guessed. My old law firm was handling the negotiations on their behalf. When Rosenthal, Roberts & Sleete gets involved in the bid for a contract, their client usually wins. By any means, fair or foul."

Delafonte shook his head. "From what my source is telling me, foul."

"So publish it. Expose it. That's what you guys do, right?"

"I'm afraid it's not that simple. Our source refuses to go public."

"Can't you protect him? I thought journalists did that all the time."

"Not if he refuses to let us even identify that there is a source. He's afraid that if he blows the whistle, no force on earth will be able to protect him. And given the current climate, I have to say I've some sympathy with those reservations."

"So ...?"

"So, the only way we can print this is if we get copies of the original documentation. The contracts. The accepted tenders and the rejected ones."

"And your source has these?"

"Oh, he has them. The problem is getting them out. You see, he's stationed in Gitmo. All channels of communication into and out of the base are tightly controlled. For him to get anything out, he'd have to smuggle the papers out in his personal luggage. Highly risky."

"So will he do it?"

Chris shrugged. "I'll find out tomorrow. He says he'll be in Washington for work and if he can manage it, he'll come to me."

"Well, here's hoping. From my point of view anything that discredits this operation is a good thing. I wish you luck with it." She could have added "*You'll need it given who you're up against.*" "But, and I mean I'm flattered you would confide in me about this, is there anything you think I can do about it?"

"If I do get the documents, I'll need someone to talk me through the legalese. You are the only corporate lawyer I know in New York who's not in the direct employ of the Dark Side, shall we say."

"Count me in. Day or night."

He smiled. "Thanks. Stay tuned for my call, then. So ..."

"About the interview?"

"Right. Listen, my flight isn't until the morning. I'm still in New York tonight and I haven't any plans. Is there any way I can do this interview with you over a drink? Perhaps even dinner?"

Maria paused. The come-on line was so direct she almost didn't see it coming.

He followed up with a smile. "I understand if that's a no, but you can hardly blame a bloke for trying. As far as I'm concerned, you're Woman of the Millennium."

She stared down into her coffee. "That's kinda faint praise. This millennium's only two years old."

Delafonte laughed. "So what do you say? Dinner tonight?"

She could almost hear the voices of her friends Sam and Cindy, like two little cartoon angels appearing on either shoulder, "*Let's see ... should you? Or should you not? Well, he's six foot a million tall, super-gorgeous, intelligent, has an English accent to die for, is probably also rich, your wedding reception will be in the tasteful gardens of a British mansion and we will get to be your stunningly dressed bridesmaids ... you sooo should!*"

But in the end she shook her head. "I'm sorry. I'm way too busy right now. I'm really sorry."

"Oh no, not to worry. But I hope you've still got time for the interview now?"

Maria looked at her watch. "Fifteen minutes."

"Perfect," he said. A Dictaphone sprang out of his pocket and into his dexterous grip. He had hands so finely sculpted and features so handsome, she found herself wondering why on earth she had just turned this guy down.

The interview questions began, and Maria waited for the pat responses to roll off her tongue.

"What made you want to give up a successful career with one of New York's best law firms to take on a *pro bono* case?"

"Well, it's a question of justice. If a man can be taken from his home without even being arrested, taken to a prison, yet not even be called a prisoner. Tortured, for all we know. Be denied access to his family, to a lawyer. And the temptation is to say, well, he's an illegal alien, homeless, a rough case. But you know, first they come for the undocumented, and we do nothing because we're not undocumented. Then they come for the civil rights lawyers..."

Midway through the *spiel*, Maria knew why she said no to a date with Chris Delafonte. It hit her like a brick: she was in love with Fergus Maloney. Completely and utterly in love with him.

His dreams became a place of refuge. A certain coherence had emerged among the cacophony of voices, increasingly in the form of Maria, the Macy's bag girl. Night by night, she loomed bigger in his thoughts, until eventually, being awake was a severance from her. There was now no more doubt in his mind. She was the key to everything. She would save him as he had saved her. There was no other way.

A rough hand shook him awake. It was the middle of the night. The torch illuminated the beady green eyes belonging to the female soldier. And behind her, it was *him*. It was the Mauler. Fergus hadn't even heard them come into the cell. The drumming of the rain against the iron roof that covered the cell block had been incessant, enough to drown out the noise of the cell door opening. He was a child again, and the Geegaw Man had found him.

"No," Fergus begged, "please, no."

"Shut the fuck up, you terrorist piece of shit." Her voice was low, an icy whisper that cut into his brain. He curled, forming a ball, pressing his body backwards against the wire wall. But there was no escape.

He closed his eyes, then tried to close his mind to the feeling of the plastic tie around his wrists. The Mauler dragged him down onto the concrete floor, where thin rivers of water ran in from the heavy rains outside.

"You wanna taste my pussy or his cock?" the female guard asked. Her breath was hot and moist on his throat.

Please, no.

The Mauler spat into his face as he spoke. "Which is it gonna be, Lucky Charms? Pussy or cock?"

Fergus closed his eyes and tried to think of the beach where he passed his dream-time. The feeling of sand running through his fingers; sunlight dancing atop the waves and beach grass blowing in the breeze. But they were gone. There was nothing but the steady rhythm of the rain against the metal above him. The heavy, husky breath of the woman behind him, and the wet hardness of the concrete under his knees. Then he heard the man unzipping his fly. The pressure of the female guard's sharp nails increased, digging into the back of his neck.

"Pussy," he tried to say, but his voice broke and he just spat a 'p'. They only laughed.

"Open wide, Lucky Charms. It's time for your breakfast."

30

When Brandon opened the door he caught sight of his roommate Walter, aka 'Buzz', shuffling through files on the coffee table in the living room. The Navy Second Lieutenant hastily crammed the papers into a bag and treated Brandon to a guilty "Hello".

"Hey, what's up?" Brandon called out on his way into the kitchenette.

"I didn't think you were due back until tomorrow."

"Seems I couldn't wait to get back to this tropical paradise."

On his way back from the fridge, can of Bud in hand, Brandon glanced at the bag into which the Seabee had just shoved his papers. It was the same file case he took home every night: the one Brandon knew contained sheaves of architectural drawings—the final design specs for the new Camp Delta. If that's all that was in there now, there was no reason for Walter's sudden furtiveness. After all, Brandon had a higher security clearance than the Navy Second Lieutenant. Probably the kid was looking at a porno mag or something. He was kind of a dweeb that way.

"Well, not much has changed since you were gone," Buzz said. "Oh, except they stocked up on Frito-Lay at the NEX."

"Yum, high-carb junk food. Just what us soldiers need to stay lean and keen. Gitmo's finest, right?"

Walter nodded. "Right." His pleasure at having steered the conversation in this more innocent direction was written all over his pasty face.

"So," Brandon asked, plonking down on the couch next to him, "how goes the plans for our shiny new gulag?"

"Yeah ... I mean, it's all on track. They're flying me out to DC tomorrow for the last round of technical meetings. Unless there's some last-minute glitch with the contract, we should be breaking ground by the end of the month. "

"By 'we' you mean the contractors, right? The ones you said were trying to screw Uncle Sam. What did you say they were called?"

"I didn't. Listen, sorry, but I gotta go back to the office and do some stuff. So, I'll, like ... see you when I get back."

Brandon shook his head and took a long drink from the can. Buzz was an okay roomie in terms of keeping clean and keeping quiet, but socially he did nothing to dispel the isolation. Brandon looked around at the bare, uninviting living room of their two-bedroom cottage. This was it: full-on Gitmo, right in his face again. In all its splendor.

Dark thoughts swirled in his mind about how he had wasted his precious time back home. Waves of guilt struck him when he thought of Mandy: of how incapable he had been to comfort her, to be there for her, even during the short few hours of their time together. And that too was Gitmo's fault ...

When he set the beer can down, something caught his eye. The surface of the coffee table was made of a corky material with a cheap wood-effect grain along it. It was covered in the graffiti of previous tenants, tattooed with beer stains and pockmarked with burn holes from other people's cigarettes. A true piece of US military furniture.

But it was the part of the surface that was right next to him—a relatively unblemished part—that caught his attention. It was right where Buzz had been sitting. The light reflected the indentations of lettering. Obviously the Seabee had been writing something on a piece of paper and had pressed a bit too hard, causing the impression to bleed through onto the soft, corky wood. Curiosity got the better of Brandon and he tilted his head until the grooves in the surface caught the full glint of the lamplight. '*Chris Delafonte, Topaz Hotel, 1733 N Street NW.*'

Topaz Hotel. Brandon knew where that was. It was a new hotel in Washington DC. He and Mandy had seen a comedy show there last October, shortly after it had opened. He shook his head at the thought of Buzz hooking up with some guy in a hotel.

Whatever. It's none of my business.

⸻◇○◇⸻

When Brandon next found Detainee 51 he was cringing in the corner of the Crucible, shaking.

"Has he been undergoing sleep dep, sergeant?"

"No, sir, no procedures."

"Fergus," Brandon said, approaching him. "What's wrong with you?"

"Stay away from me."

Brandon reached out a hand and Fergus recoiled.

"Don't let them touch me. Please. I'll tell you anything. Anything at all."

Brandon went back into the observation room and checked the logs. Sixteen interrogations took place while he was in DC. All routine. None involving Fergus. The files were all in place. Wait. There! An entry page was missing. Yesterday at 1500 hours. And in the check-in sheet, the interrogator's time slot was initialed '*BR*'. Benjamin Rhodes. Brandon checked the tapes, but of course they were missing too. He looked through the glass at Detainee 51, still cringing and shaking in the corner, like a beaten dog.

He slammed his fist on the desk. Anger rose up within him. What the fuck was going on here? What the fuck was Rhodes doing? Never before had Brandon doubted his purpose. Never before had he put in question the high and lofty principles of the United States, values which he was proud to fight and—yes—even to die for.

But this was something else. It felt like some sick worm had crept inside the wire of Gitmo, and was infecting their brains. *His* brain. It was making them do things that were not only an insult to the flag of the United States of America, but an insult to common human decency. Making them—no, *him*—do things that were...

"Evil," he said out loud.

He snatched the receiver from its cradle and dialed an extension.

"*Colonel Rhodes' office, can I help you*?"

"Yes, can I speak to the Colonel please?"

"*He's not available, can I take a message*?"

"This is Lieutenant Zeiss. I'm afraid it's urgent."

"*The Colonel is in a meeting, Lieutenant.*"

"You'll have to disturb him. It's urgent."

"*Just a moment.*"

The blood was pounding in his temples. Brandon recognized it as one of those moments when you became conscious of the fact that you're losing control, but in a sort of detached way, like watching someone else about to do something really stupid, and you have no power to stop it from happening.

"Rhodes," the Colonel's voice came on the line, husky as usual and clearly annoyed at being interrupted.

In a split second, Brandon slammed down the phone. His courage abandoned him. *I'll call Rhodes back, but not right away.* He needed to think.

"Check 51 back to his cell," he ordered the sergeant. Make sure nobody goes near him. Not even the JTC-160 guards. If anyone so much as talks to him, I want to be informed."

He drove the jeep back home at breakneck speed, put on his jogging gear and went for the longest, hardest run he could, along the main road and down as far as the beach.

When Brandon returned, he resolved to go straight to Colonel Rhodes' office and meet him face-to-face. He felt calmer after the run, though his determination had not diminished.

"Oh, there you are," Rhodes said to him when he walked in. "I went looking for you. Couldn't find you at your post."

"I was running."

"No shit. You disturb me in my meeting, prank called me, and then you decide to go do some sports in the middle of a work day? Care to explain yourself?"

Brandon could feel his determination fading under the iron stare of his superior officer.

"You were interrogating my asset, Colonel."

"Is that so?" Rhodes asked with a sort of sneer on his face.

"Detainee 51, Fergus Maloney."

"You mean the high-value asset you've made zero progress on? Your little friend and buddy?"

"He's not my friend and he's not my buddy. What he is, is the clearest example of how wrong this mission has gone. I've been over his file. I've been interrogating him. Deeply. For days now. I know this guy inside out. And I can tell you, he has no intelligence. He's innocent. Yet we keep him classed as a high-value asset. Why? Because we think a guy like Fergus Maloney is going to lead us to bin Laden? Or because we need to keep the statistics clean in order to justify the wad of cash our government is spending on this new Camp Delta? Or is it just pure sadism? And it's not only Fergus Maloney. There's dozens of guys inside the wire just like him."

Rhodes did not respond. The Colonel knew how to use silence as a way to make a statement. When he eventually spoke, it was to give a command. "Sit down, Brandon."

Brandon sat. In that magical way he had, Rhodes managed to switch the pace of the conversation. Now it was calm.

"So you've been digging deep down into 51, huh?" he asked, almost whimsically.

"Yes, I have. My report records over three hours of interrogation using my new, less coercive technique. I've had a lot of success getting him to talk."

"I know. A lot of success. I actually just read your report."

Brandon didn't like the sneer. His tone sharpened ever so slightly. "Then you'll know that I also obtained a fresh, original copy of the file on him through our contacts in Ireland."

Rhodes nodded. "Wouldn't look anything like this file right here, would it?"

Brandon stared in surprise at the file the Colonel pulled out of his desk drawer and held in the air. It was identical to the one he had in his own office, the same blue with a gold harp logo on it. This was supposed to have been given to the CIA months ago, but JTC had never been allowed to see it.

"Where did you—"

"I've been playing this game a long time, son. I have my contacts. The more important question is this: did you read it?"

"Yes, I did."

"All of it?"

"Yes. I mean, almost—"

"Because in your report you note that Detainee 51 and his two siblings were raised by their mother, Mary Maloney, and that the father died when 51 was still a boy."

"That's right."

Rhodes put on his reading glasses and began flipping through the contents of the file. "So then, how do you explain this?"

It was a piece of paper right underneath the death certificate for Darragh Maloney. On it was a report dated 1997 from the Special Branch of *An Garda Síochána*: the Irish police force. It contained information on one John Maloney of Curraghlan, Clonakilty, County Cork, aged 64, husband of Mary Maloney and father of two children who was under investigation on suspicion of sedition.

"Looks like they were about to charge him under the ... '*Offences Against the State Act*' for membership of an illegal paramilitary organization better known as the Irish Republican Army," Rhodes said. "That was right before they signed the big peace deal in '98, brokered by Clinton. Lucky for John Maloney, or he'd be in jail right now.

"Look what else our Irish counterparts magicked up," Rhodes shoved another piece of paper at Brandon, the last one in the pile, "a phone bill from three months ago. John Maloney is still alive and kicking. He was making phone calls even as NYC firemen were digging dead bodies out of the rubble of the Twin Towers.

"Yet your report says he died years ago," Rhodes sneered.

"I don't understand how this could b—"

"I'll tell you how it could be. You got duped, son. You let a very clever man play you for a fool. To the point where he had you eating out of his fucking palm. To the point where you, a senior interrogator in the US Military, wrote an unverified claim into your report, that a man with a close family connection to the detainee, who you said was dead, is in fact, a living, breathing *fucking suspected terrorist*. If he can fool you on something so basic, something that's written, black on fucking white, in the background file we got on him, WHAT THE FUCK ELSE HAS HE FOOLED YOU ABOUT?"

Rhodes went on screaming, "And then you have the *gall* to storm into my office and tell me we're doing this all wrong? You fucking halfwit cocksucker!"

Rhodes stood up and walked over to Brandon. His forefinger bored into Brandon's chest, and every hard consonant he spoke sent spit into Brandon's eye.

"You listen up, son. The ante just got upped on 51, big time. Seems like some do-gooder lawyer in New York is pushing hard to get him out of here. Which means we have to turn the screw on him and get at the intelligence he's withholding before he slips through our fingers.

"Now, I'm giving you one last chance to prove to me that you are not a fuck-up, Zeiss. And I don't give a shit who your granddaddy was, 'cos if you get tripped up like this again, so help me God, your career in the Armed Forces is over. Do we understand each other?"

"Yes."

"That's 'yes, *sir*'. From now on you call me 'sir'. You've just been demoted. Now get the fuck out of my office."

31

The American Civil Liberties Union had their New York headquarters on Broad Street in Lower Manhattan, one block from Battery Park. The office they eventually managed to find for Maria was a fraction of the size of her old office at Rosenthal, Roberts & Sleete, and she had no personal assistant anymore. The slick barista coffee service in Royal Dalton china cups was gone too. In its place, she had a cheap vending machine that spat out coffee in Styrofoam cups with creamer made from some substance that had never seen the inside of a cow's udder.

None of that mattered to Maria anymore. This building was safe and the ACLU security team had it regularly swept for bugs: something she wouldn't have believed was necessary in modern America. But if even half of what Clarke told her was true, it was more necessary now than ever before.

It was the day of the substantive hearing, just before eight in the morning. In two hours' time, Maria would be in front of the United States Court of Appeals for the Second Circuit. She finished prepping her team and was pouring one final time over the text of the brief that would be the basis for deliberation. In particular, the case of *Ex parte Quirin* was the most significant in terms of legal precedent. This was a Supreme Court ruling dating from 1942, which upheld jurisdiction of a military tribunal, and was the basis of the Government's case to keep Fergus in custody. If the Solicitor General could argue that Bush's proposed system of tribunals in Gitmo was being done the same way President Roosevelt had done it during World War II—and the two Executive Orders were nearly identical—then this would provide a pretty watertight defense for their actions.

"Our job," Maria had told her team, "is to remind the court of a little thing our country signed right *after* the war. This little thing right here," she held up one of the ACLU's well-worn copies of the Geneva Convention, "Bush likes to forget it's part of US law too."

In truth, Maria knew they would have to do better than wave around the Geneva Convention. The issue was whether the treaty was, in and of itself law, or whether it imposed obligations on the legislature to write laws consistent with it. And then there was the POW issue: the protections of the Geneva Convention only applied to "prisoners of war". DoD was careful never to use the word prisoner in any of its documents on the 100 men currently being held in Camp X-ray. Donald Rumsfeld had already gone on record as saying that detainees in Gitmo were 'enemy combatants', not POWs. To qualify as a prisoner of war, he insisted, you had to be wearing a uniform.

Prisoner of war! The whole idea of it was ludicrous, of course. Fergus was no more at war with the United States that the dozens of homeless guys whose sleeping bags lined the floor at Penn Station. In the twisted way of the law, she was going to have to argue he was being held as a POW in order to prove he was nothing of the sort.

She finished re-reading the text of her brief for the fifth time, and was gathering the papers together, when there came a knock and the office door swung open.

"Hi."

It was the last person in the world Maria expected to see: Jeff Laurence.

"What are you doing here?"

"I came to talk." He was trying on his usual arrogant swagger, but there was something different about him now.

"I'm busy," she said.

"Getting ready for court?"

Maria didn't reply, so Jeff tried again. "How's your mom doing?"

Again, no reply.

"You know, Maria, I'm really worried about you."

This got her to look up. "What?"

"You're throwing away your career. I mean look at this place. It's a shit hole. You're drinking coffee out of a ... what is this? Is it even a Styrofoam cup?"

"It's bioplastic. Made from elephant grass."

"My point is, you were our best attorney. Think about everything you worked for. Think about all your dreams. All our dreams. Don't you remember when I first met you? You were waitressing in a burger joint in Harvard Square. Look how far you've come. Do you really want to give it all up for some worthless illegal alien?"

He advanced. His hand reached out for hers.

"I ... I know I've acted like an asshole. Fact is, I was jealous of him. I know, I know! I'm a hypocrite. But that thing with Liz, okay, you got me. It was all wrong. And it's over now. Maria, can't we try again, baby? Can't we just go back and start over?"

Despite herself, Maria felt the vaguest stirring of emotion at the sound of these words. Comfort and security beckoned to her, like a sugar craving.

"Just ... just drop the case, Maria."

"What?"

"This Fergus Maloney stuff. It's a reaction, isn't it? Because deep down, a part of you is still in love with me. And you're angry. You're doing it to make me jealous; to take revenge. I can understand that. I was an asshole. I probably deserve it. But there's no need to drag the entire US government into our love life. We can talk about it. If I hurt you, *tell* me. I'm here to listen."

Maria could hardly believe what she was hearing.

"Are you seriously asking me to drop the Fergus Maloney case?"

"Yes."

"No. Really? Is that really why you came here?"

"I came here because I'm still in love with you."

Maria began to laugh. "You came here because the firm sent you. Or else Burton & Hale. Or else your dad. I don't know which. Actually I don't care. Get out of my office, get out of this building and get out of my life. You come near me again, I seek a restraining order. Capito?"

"Maria, you are being ridiculous."

She pushed his arm away with a force that startled him, then grabbed for the phone. "Hi security? I need you to come to my office, please. Yes, Maria Da Silva. Third floor." That got him moving.

When he was gone, Maria allowed herself a little moment to enjoy the feeling. A feeling of freedom and control that was new.

The morning sidewalks were slick with night rain. A steady wind cut Maria as she crossed Fifth Avenue and strode towards the midtown hotel where her client was waiting. Maria wore her blue Prada heels. *Maybe for the last time,* she told herself.

As she approached, she saw Clodagh Brogan standing at the entrance, behind the brass revolving doors. It was their first meeting face-to-face since Dublin.

"Did you sleep all right?" Maria asked her as they shook hands in front of the hotel, then climbed into the cab that was waiting for them. That was all she could think to say.

"Fine thanks."

Clodagh's hands clutched her handbag, so hard the knuckles went white. "Do you have any last minute questions for me before the trial starts?"

"Will there be press outside the building?" Clodagh asked. Her face bore every hour of the sleepless night she had spent in her hotel room; the eyes bloodshot and the skin pale under the makeup.

"Probably."

"They're asking questions about our family. About me. It's none of their business."

"I need to know," Maria said suddenly. "Why did you lie to me?"

Clodagh's clear blue eyes never changed their focus. Save for the motion of the taxi cab, she was as still as a statue.

"Why did you tell me you frequently visit your mother?" Maria persisted. "The fact is you don't. Why did you pretend your mom asked to see Fergus? She thinks he's dead. Or at least she pretends to think that. And why didn't you tell me your family had connections with the IRA? It's all been lies!"

Still the blue eyes stared. The only reaction was in the fingers clutching the handbag. Her nails clawed and gripped at the leather with tremendous force.

The taxi turned the corner onto Worth Street. Almost there. Maria could feel her own heart pounding. This was not the time for a confrontation. And yet she couldn't help herself.

"What happened to him, Clodagh?" Maria remembered the poems she had read. "Who hurt him so badly?" But Maria knew the answer, for that too was in the poems. "Who was the Geegaw Man?"

"Stop!" The Irishwoman hissed, turning her blue eyes, now wet with tears, upon Maria. Her mouth trembled. There was a fierceness in her countenance, like a cornered animal. "Stop it. Just stop it!"

At 9:25 a.m., the taxi pulled up in front of the Thurgood Marshall Building. The two women got out on opposite sides.

To say there would be press outside the courthouse was the understatement of the week. The entire area from Centre Street to the grand steps which led up to the entrance doors was crowded with a chaotic mix of protesters, reporters and camera crews, all jostling for space behind the blue police barriers erected by the NYPD. They were greeted by two plainclothes policemen and escorted through a passageway of metal barriers. Cameras flashed in their faces. Arms holding microphones poked out from the crowd all along their path.

In front of the revolving doors, another policeman checking ID detained them briefly. This distracted Maria's attention, and when she looked again Clodagh Brogan had taken a step away and was staring, bleary-eyed, at a particularly persistent Fox News reporter.

"Come on, Clodagh," Maria urged gently. She avoided looking into any of the cameras, but the image of her catching Clodagh's arm, and the slight tension that gesture implied—lawyer pulling client into courthouse—would be exactly what the press photographers were looking for. *Fuck,* Maria thought. She had just made the cover of tomorrow's *New York Times.*

"All rise!"

Justice Lisa Colworth entered the courtroom amid the din of bodies shuffling to their feet. Maria threw a glance across at the respondent's bench. The

Solicitor General himself was in the front, leading the charge. Rarely if ever did he appear before any court with a lesser address than 1 First Street, Washington DC. She thought back to the taxi-driver spy the other day. Whatever spin Jeff might want to put on it, one thing was clear to Maria, the United States government was not fucking around with this case.

"We'll hear argument on number 07-176, Clodagh Brogan versus Donald Rumsfeld. Ms. Da Silva, you may proceed."

"Justice Colworth," Maria began, "may it please the court, what is at stake in this case is the authority of the federal courts to uphold the rule of law. Respondents assert that their actions are absolutely immune from judicial examination whenever they elect to detain foreign nationals outside our borders. Under this theory, neither the length of the detention, the conditions of their confinement, nor the fact that they have been wrongfully detained, makes the slightest difference. Respondents would create in the Guantánamo Bay Naval Base a lawless enclave, effectively insulating the executive branch from any judicial scrutiny now or in the future."

Judge Colworth began her first question: "How long has your client—or more properly your client's brother—"

"My client was awarded standing under a ruling of this court—"

"Yes. How long has Mr. ... Maloney been in detention?"

"Two months in the custody of the United States Armed Forces. Previous to that he was held in an unspecified extraterritorial location by unnamed US intelligence operatives."

"What do you suppose, Ms. Da Silva, is the minimal period of detention before a *habeas corpus* entitlement becomes valid?"

"It's not a question of that, Your Honor. The question we're asking is whether the government's response that the detention is legal is an adequate response. They'll tell you they don't need to give hearings required by the Geneva Convention, but if we are to treat it as a binding United States treaty—"

"But it is not self-executing," the judge pressed. She glanced over at the dark-suited, grey-haired personage of the United States Solicitor General, who may or may not have hazarded a sober nod in reply. Maria's heart sank into the pit of her stomach. She fought back a defeatist feeling that this case was somehow completely unwinnable.

"I would argue," Maria said, forcing her mind back into focus, "that the question of whether it is or is not self-executing is a straw man. Since 1813, if a treaty provides a rule of decision, even if something else provides a cause of action, the treaty nevertheless provides the rule of decision. That was several—"

Colworth waved her long elegant hand. She was in her sixties, but her hands had lost absolutely none of their vibrancy. "Forget about the Geneva Convention for a second. I mean, we know from Johnson—"

"—Your Honor, I would caution against inferring from the Johnson case—"

"—What I want to know is this: If your client had been given a review of his status as enemy combatant in the way set out by an Executive Order, would there be a form and process possible which would satisfy your claim?"

Maria paused for the slightest of seconds before replying. A cough echoed from one of the benches behind her. "That would depend on the manner of the review. If it were held in accordance with the Geneva Convention—"

"I'm confused as to whether you're arguing on the basis of the Geneva Convention alone, or on the basis of the *Habeas* Statute?"

"Both, in fact."

"Can the *Habeas* Statute even apply?"

"In Guantánamo, yes. The enclave is unique. It is the only place outside of US territory where the United States has complete civilian and military control. I reference the case of *Bridge* v. *Pitman Enterprises 1999* in which a civilian employee of a McDonald's franchise restaurant operated in Guantánamo was charged with damages resulting from an alleged arson attack on the premises."

"He tried to burn down the McDonalds?"

"Allegedly. After failing to win the 'Employee of the Month' award."

Everyone broke into a chuckle, even Colworth.

"The point is to demonstrate that the jurisdictional precedents—"

Colworth nodded. "We can leave that point, I'm satisfied. Thank you, Ms. Da Silva. General Carter, we'll hear from you."

It was then that the Solicitor General directed the fullness of his person to the court. His pulverulent voice barely carried to the bench, yet Maria was sure the whole court hung on his every word.

"The United States is at war. Over 10,000 American troops are in Afghanistan today in response to a virtually unanimous congressional declaration of an unusual and extraordinary threat to our national security, and an authorization to the President to use all necessary and appropriate force to deter and prevent acts of terrorism against the United States.

"It's in this context that the Petitioner asks this Court to assert jurisdiction that it is not authorized by Congress to exer—"

"What if the war was over?" Colworth cut across him, "would there be jurisdiction then?"

"No, there would not be."

"So the war is irrelevant to your argument. Your argument is that the *Habeas Corpus* Statute simply does not apply."

Maria suppressed a smile. Colworth was a rookie at Appeals, fresh out of the flesh-mill that was the Federal District Court system. By contrast, the Solicitor General was as close to a Supreme Court justice as a lawyer can get. In squaring up against the legal personification of the United States of America, Maria had expected Colworth to kowtow a little. Maybe even a lot. But this freshly-minted Circuit Court justice was not showing any signs of intimidation. She was exactly as Maria had hoped she would be: direct, clear and good at her job.

"The context provided by the war adds extra force," Carter graveled on, in response to Colworth's point.

"Mr. Carter, I have another question. A hypothetical one. If Mr. Maloney were a citizen of the United States, being detained under identical circumstances, would the Statute apply?"

Here Maria detected the slightest of pauses before the grey-haired United States of America Solicitor General answered. "It would apply, Your Honor."

"Interesting," she said. "And again: if Mr. Maloney had been detained on US territory, would the Statute apply?"

"Most certainly."

"But at the doorstep of a US airbase in Germany, these protections cease?"

"That's outside the jurisdictional context covered by the Statute."

"But it's hardly a war zone?"

"Your Honor, here we come again to the context of the War on Terror. The very nature of the threat posed by these enemy combatants suggests conventional definitions of the war zone no longer apply."

"Just so I understand you, you are in effect arguing that the diffuse nature of the enemy threat is such that we can interpret a 'war zone' to mean anywhere outside the jurisdictional territory of the United States; yet given the fact that the 'enemy combatants' did not wear uniforms, they are not subject to the protections afforded to prisoners of war under the Geneva Convention?"

"The position is consistent with *Quirin*, Your Honor," the Solicitor General replied, with something like a sneer in his voice. It was unbecoming of a man of his station to talk in this way. *Good*, Maria thought, *it means he's rattled.*

"If I take a step back and consider the essence of the petition," Colworth resumed, "the Petitioner is in effect saying 'Look, we are claiming that our man is innocent. And for the purposes of this proceeding, we must assume that. And all we want is some process to determine whether he is indeed innocent.' How would you respond to that?"

"Firstly, by noting that the detention period has been exceedingly short—"

"Two months without any kind of a review or hearing? Longer if you count the extra-territorial detention. I'm not sure I'd call that short."

"—and secondly, by noting that a 'Combatant Status Review Tribunal' has been convened and is in advanced preparations to conduct the review in question."

"When is it to take place?"

"Preliminaries commence tomorrow morning. I understand the detainee's Personal Representative has just been appointed."

A bustle of noise erupted through the court. Clodagh's imploring eyes met with Maria's, and in the background, court artists furiously rushed to finish the outlines of their sketches.

"There's no mention of this in your brief, General Carter."

"It's a rapidly evolving situation on the ground, Your Honor."

"I see ..."

So did Maria. Crystal clear, in fact. They had slopped together this Tribunal last minute: as a panic response to this very court case. Whatever Carter's bluff might be, the government was scared to death of losing this case on appeal just as Congress was about to vote to approve a massive facilities expansion in Cuba and Afghanistan.

"For the record, the United States government would like to assert and argue that the convening of this Review is not in respect of any obligation imposed by the Geneva Convention or other legal instruments, as those cover prisoners of war and not enemy combatants. The Review is not judicial in nature, but purely a standard part of military procedure in combat situations. Its findings and the evidence disclosed will remain classified until properly declassified."

"Is it the intention of the United States to hold these Tribunals for all detainees?"

"Other Reviews will be conducted in due course, but this particular Review was expedited by the fact that the detainee in question does not require interpretation or translation of the transcripts of the evidence against him. His native language is English, which makes things much simpler."

Bullshit, Maria thought. This particular Review was expedited because of *Brogan* v. *Rumsfeld.* That's the only reason. He just had the good fortune of having me on his side.

Colworth's long, elegant hands folded her papers and let her reading glasses fall from the bridge of her nose onto the beaded lanyard that kept them around her neck. "Thank you, Mr. Carter. The case is submitted."

Maria's heart rose with a new hope, one she dared not express to Clodagh Brogan: that the government had set this military tribunal review to take place during the deliberation period on purpose in order to pre-empt the decision and kill the case. *By releasing Fergus!*

32

The man who stood over him in his cell was not the Mauler. It was not *her*; it was not even Clyde. This man wore a suit and gold-rimmed glasses. The big, mad, fleshy thing that moved slowly in the air towards Fergus's face was his hand. It was soft, with a line of golden hair that ran along the back of it, and a plump wedding ring on its second finger. Fergus recoiled from the touch, wedging himself deeper against the chain links of the fence. Though the rains had passed and it was hot, he drew the thin blanket tighter across his body, like a child shielding himself from monsters.

"Mr. Maloney," the man's voice was soft, like his hand. "Can I call you Fergus? My name is Lieutenant Gabriel O'Brien. I have been assigned to act as your Personal Representative before the Combatant Status Review Tribunal that you are to attend next week."

The hand with the golden hairs wavered in the air in front of Fergus's face. The big fat wedding ring caught the light. Vile and plump. Moist. A column of cold shot up through Fergus and he clenched his body. The fence at his back would be making patterns, he knew. Like diamonds digging outlines into his skin.

"Fergus, the purpose of this Review is to determine whether you qualify to be treated as a civilian; whether you might be granted the status of a lawful combatant, or whether you will continue to be detained in accordance with the rules pertaining to *unlawful* combatants. My job here is to assist you in participating in this process—"

The sound of the words weighed on Fergus, pushing the air out of his lungs. He closed his eyes and the plump golden-haired hand disappeared. Where was the beach? Where was the feeling of sand? Where was the cool breeze in his face? Gone. All gone. His mind raced further and summer was ended. Hard rain fell on the beach, leaving deep pockmarks everywhere. And the sea was violent.

He left the beach and ran. The grass that grew up along the middle of the *bóithrín* out of Curraghgrane was long and damp. He followed along a mossy path that cut further to the right, keeping the harbour to his left, where he knew, without looking, that the fishing boats would be tilting against the sandbanks as the sea slowly abandoned them, and white gulls would be fighting the wind, swooping and flapping, in thrall to the eternal rhythm of the tide.

His path took him inland now. He crossed a field where tall scutches of sedge punctuated a carpet of short grass, a sort of poor man's pasture. At the end, he climbed a fence up, over, and onto the main road. Once past the high hedge, a filling station came into view on the right.

"...now it's important that you understand that this Review is not a judicial procedure, but rather it is an administrative one. Testimony will be presented by representatives of the Joint Task Force in relation to the allegations that have been made against you. Now, you yourself are not required to testify before the Tribunal though you may do so at your own discretion ..."

For as long as anyone could remember, the bus stopped at Murphy's Filling Station on the Cork Road. It wasn't an official bus stop, really, because of course the coach wasn't operated by Bus Éireann. It was Ken Barry's Coach Service out of Skibbereen and it only made one stop in Clonakilty: at Murphy's Filling Station outside of town. The Ken Barry coach only went once a day at 11:15 a.m., and it stopped in Cork, Youghal and Dungarvan and a half dozen towns beyond–meaning it took ages to get you to Dublin. But it was half the price of the Bus Éireann coach, so of course everyone took the Ken Barry's. Except the tourists.

"... and the Tribunal President will rule on whether or not such documents are relevant to the allegations that stand against you. Fergus? Are you listening?"

Fergus had said to himself he wouldn't go that way until after Clodagh was well gone—half three at the earliest—and yet the way of his walking had somehow brought him to that spot, where five or six people were waiting, some with suitcases, at the slip road that led into Murphy's Filling Station.

And there she was. At first, she didn't see him, and he thought he might walk away unnoticed. But at the last minute she turned her head and caught his eye. He quickened his pace, back down the road towards town. Emotion bubbled up inside him. Anger, mixed with fear and despair and, somewhere, below all that, a desire still to be loved.

"Fergus?" she called after him.

"Fergus? Are you listening? If so, can you please make some sign of recognition that you understand what I am saying to you?"

He wanted to keep walking—out of spite. Just to show her, like. But he didn't. He turned and looked. And when she beckoned him to her, he even travelled back.

"What?" he said sharply.

"I thought you might come to say goodbye."

"Well?" he asked.

"Well?" she answered. "Well, will you not miss me?"

"Why the fuck would I miss *you*?" he hissed, and waited for the hurt to make her eyes cloud over. Good if she was hurt. It was no more than she deserved. The bitch. And yet his sister was unmoved. Her cold blue eyes just stared back, and she spoke with a distance: a politeness that was a thousand times worse than her giving out.

"You can come, you know. And visit me in Dublin. Not right away, like, but once an' I've myself a bit sorted, you know."

"This isn't going to work, Lieutenant. He needs to be able to sign the Detainee Election Form."

Visit her! Running away and leaving him on his own was what she was doing. And Clodagh knew it! She knew he was on his own. And she'd the cheek to say he could visit her? What use was that to him? He clenched his fists in anger and squinted away the tears. He wanted to tell her to fuck off, but instead he said in a voice that was weak and pleading, "Don't go."

Clodagh smiled and nodded, as if he'd said something else. "Ah, sure, I'll be grand. Look after Mammy and tell her I'll be home for Christmas, won't you? The bus'll be here any minute. I'll ring you from Dublin once I've meself sorted, like."

"He won't be able to answer questions— "

"He doesn't need to answer questions. But we need to have his signature on the Detainee Election Form."

"Just grab his hand. Make him sign it."

"I tried that. He keeps assuming the fetal position. He's like a hurt animal or something."

"Maybe we can administer something to him. Look, he's shaking. Don't we have some kind of tranquillizer for situations like this?"

Fergus watched the Ken Barry's bus pull in. He watched Clodagh board it. He watched it drive off, lost over the hill at the top of the road. Still, a part of him thought she might change her mind; tell the driver to stop, and soon she'd come walking back. And so he waited there, staring at the empty road, as the hours passed and a fine September rain filled the sky. Until the day expired.

"Is he crying?"

"Wait, he just said something. Fergus? Did you want to say something to us?"

"He said 'Don't go.'"

"Lieutenant, this man needs some kind of treatment. There's no way we can put him before a Tribunal like this."

"OK, I'll call the doctor and see what we can do. In the meantime, stay here and see if you can get him to sign the form."

"Why'd you lie to me, 51?"

Fergus felt Clyde's hands grabbing roughly at his face. He opened his eyes. "Look at me when I talk to you, boy! Why the fuck did you lie to me?"

They had done a full sleep cycle again. Now, chained to the floor of the Crucible, Fergus reclined forward into the Squat, too limp to control his body, too limp to respond.

"I told you if you were straight-up with me, I'd be straight-up with you. But you fuckin' lied your ass off, and now what happens? All your privileges are gone. All of them. Because you lied."

"I didn't lie," he stuttered, in a voice that would have shouted, if it had had the force.

"No? Then who is this?"

A blurry picture was thrust before his face. He closed his eyes, but the voice above him boomed the command.

"Look at the fuckin' picture, you lying son of a bitch! Who is it? Do you want me to call the Mauler in here, 51? Because I will, if I have to. Now look at the goddamn picture and tell me who you see there."

Fergus tried to look and eventually the image came into focus.

"It's my father."

"You told me he was dead."

"He's dead to me."

"That's not good enough."

A crow called out in one hideous caw. The sound blended into the opening of the door, and in stepped the Mauler.

"Take off his pants," the Mauler commanded. "I'll show you the punishment he responds to." Clyde obeyed. Instinctively, Fergus clenched his buttocks. With new-found force he shook and railed against the shackles.

"No, please," Fergus begged. He closed his eyes as the piercing screams of the darkest familiars—crows, crabs, biting insects—sang out in a chorus of doom: Destiny's fiercest and vilest composition conducted by the Geegaw Man.

The Crucible disappeared, and Fergus was a child again.

Outside Clodagh's bedroom window, Fergus could see the stars set in a clear black sky. The night was cold. The moon lit up a sheet of frost that covered the grass in the field behind their house. He knelt on her bed, pressing his knees into the sheets, the ones that were patterned with little pink flowers. Fergus shivered from the cold in his pyjamas; his bare feet, like blocks of ice, were still gritty with the dirt of outside. Clodagh clasped his hands in hers, pressing his fingers into the right position for prayer.

"Now look up at the stars. Those ones there!"

"Why do I have to?"

"Because that's where God is."

"But I can't see Him."

"Because He's invisible, ya little eejit!"

"Well then, how do you even know He's there?"

"Because He *is*! And Darragh's up there with Him. Now do as I say before the ..." here she stopped and mouthed the words '*Geegaw Man*', before continuing her sentence, "... gets here."

That was enough of an argument. Fergus touched his prayer-shaped hands to his nose and looked out the window up at the little patch of stars. He felt Clodagh's breath against his neck as she spoke. "Now say this: 'Jesus, God and the Holy Spirit, I know I've been bold an awful many times—'"

Fergus broke off and looked back at her. "But I *haven't—*"

"You have, ya' little liar. And God knows the truth, and if you lie to Him, He'll only ignore your prayers. So say it!"

Fergus mumbled it, vaguely calculating that—seeing as he hadn't in fact been bold at all— God would know this confession was only Clodagh's words, and He wouldn't hold it against Fergus in any way.

"'... but I am praying to you tonight to ask you to protect me against *him*.'"

"... but I'm prayin' ta ya' tonight for to ask you to—"

"You have to speak proper or else God won't listen. He hates when people speak to Him like an' as if they were tinkers."

"... to protect me against the G— Against *him*."

"'... and if the ... *you-know-who* were to have an accident on his way home from the pub tonight, that would be OK by me.'"

"...and if *You-know-who* were to fall out o' th' pub and break his dirty ol' neck in five places, that would be OK by me."

At that moment a black form crossed the break in the hedge, on the road outside. Fergus turned to Clodagh and saw from her face that she had seen it too.

They heard the door open. And froze in their places. No more words were permissible, even if said in a whisper. The danger was too great.

The Geegaw Man's voice called out and Mammy answered him something. Fergus felt the cold all along his body and longed to get into Clodagh's bed; to hide under the covers, and press his nose into her long, black hair. But he daren't make a sound. He daren't move.

"Where iss'ee?" the Geegaw Man's jocular tones sounded out from downstairs. "Where's de li'l *slíbhín* hidin' hisshelf?" The words were slurred with drink, infused with sick lust.

It was silent for a moment. Then the heavy boots made the painted wooden boards on the stairs outside creak. They counted the steps. *One, two, three ...*

Fergus risked a final whisper, thinking God might perhaps be more willing to heed a plea spoken out loud. "Please God, you might still make him fall and smash open his dirty oul' neck!"

... four, five, six ...

"Would you not have a cuppa and sit with me? Gay Byrne'll be on the telly," Mammy's voice called weakly from the kitchen. But the steps continued.

"I'll jus' wish a goodnight to the children."

... seven, eight, nine ...

"Where iss'ee?"

... ten, eleven, twelve ...

A creak on the landing outside. They heard the door to Fergus's room open.

Clodagh grabbed Fergus and pulled him to her chest. "Please, God," she mumbled a hot whisper in his ear. "Please, tomorrow if it has to be, but only just save my little brother for tonight."

"Where's that cute li'l hoor hidin' hisshelf?"

"Please, God," Fergus whispered, as the dread engulfed him. The door to Clodagh's room swung open and the threshold was filled with a dark shadow. The stench of booze and tobacco and damp night air wafted into the room.

"Wazz'ee doin' in his sister's room? Did ye ever see the like? Are ya a girl, are ya? Puttin' on her dresses, are ya? Hehehe. Putting on her frilly li'l knickers? C'mere, Fergus an' I'll tell ya' a good-night story ..."

The big thick hand of the Geegaw Man clasped his wrist and led him into the other bedroom, the one that had belonged to Darragh ...

"Noooo!" Fergus screamed, his body bucking against the restraints that held him, shackled, to the floor of the Crucible, in the Interrogation Facility of Camp X-ray, Guantánamo Bay Naval Base, Cuba.

33

It was four o'clock in the morning when Brandon awoke from the nightmare. His face was dripping with sweat. Outside the rain had stopped and the heavy, wet air hung in a stagnant halo around the lamppost in their 'back yard'. Iguanas scurried and scratched their way across the road. Nothing else moved.

What's wrong with you, son? his father's voice asked, screaming to be heard over the heavy metal music that played in Brandon's head. It had become a permanent soundtrack, like a sort of musical tinnitus. *Get up out of bed.* As he walked, he felt increasingly dizzy.

Can't you even be man enough to do your mission?

He found himself in the kitchenette and stumbled against the sink.

Pull yourself together, soldier.

He drank hard from the faucet, forgetting the tap water wasn't potable, then splashed his face until the spinning stopped. The living room behind him came slowly into focus. Against the wall next to the door, Buzz had left out his kit for the trip to Washington DC. Probably the early flight, so he'd be getting up in an hour and, like a good soldier, he had everything packed before going to bed.

Brandon knew he wouldn't be getting any more sleep, so he pulled on his running clothes and hit the road, determined to pound out a few hard miles. Sweat and adrenaline were the only antidotes left to him. *And booze,* he thought.

As his sneakered foot kicked off the wooden stoop and onto the gravel path outside, he planned on going down to the beach, but somehow his route took him past the site they had already marked out for the new Camp Delta. From there he jogged onwards along the main road to Camp X-ray. An MP jeep patrol stopped him halfway along the road and asked for ID. Absently, he held up the ID card that was attached to the dog-tag chain around his neck.

When he made it to the wire, he stopped, identified himself to the gate guards from JTC-160 but did not enter. Instead, he began jogging around the outside perimeter, along the rough track the MPs drove when they did their loop patrols around Camp X-ray. Halfway along, he paused to catch his breath. He peered in through the wire at the floodlit cinder block wall that was the back of the interrogation building. Under the floodlights, clear as day, he could see the three guards accompanying Detainee 51 for his "wakey-wakey" stroll around the block. At the corner of the building, before disappearing out of view, Fergus collapsed from fatigue. The guards took turns kicking him, and then hauled him back up to his feet so that he could continue his unsteady march around the building. Just as Brandon had ordered them to do. Involuntarily, Brandon's mind returned to what the Mauler had done to Fergus that afternoon. And to what he had done himself.

"Tell us everything," Clyde had told the Irishman, hitting the red button on the recording device and sliding it under the man's prone, dangling body. And Fergus told them everything. The transcript of the interrogation played itself in Brandon's mind. It was a recording of every single detail of Fergus's long, painful history of sexual abuse. Brandon fought to dispel the images of a young boy, somewhere in Ireland, burying himself in blankets and pillows, to drown out the sound of his older brother in the bed beside him being raped by their own father. Again and again, night after night, until one day, his brother kills himself. And then the piece of shit turns to his youngest son and the rape goes on.

Fergus had told them everything: of his flight out of Clonakilty; his years living on the streets of Dublin: stealing, fighting, drinking, playing music to forget. Every gory detail. Everything, that is, except what really mattered. On the subject of Osama bin Laden, the Twin Towers, 9/11, Fergus kept up the pretence of knowing nothing.

Brandon punched the wire and his mind screamed.

"Why won't you confess, you fucking bastard? You fucking shit, piece of crap! Why are you making me do this?"

His fingers dug so hard into the wire, he thought for a second he might break the skin. With one mighty kick against the fence, he let go, stumbled back and fell against an embankment.

The anger passed, and there was only the moon and stars above him. And in front of him, the overwhelming brightness of the strobe lights that illuminated Camp X-ray in all its ugliness. The heavy metal music returned into his brain. Or had it ever gone away?

He closed his eyes and fought back the tears.

"Mandy," he said out loud. And he knew he had to speak to her. Brandon broke into a sprint, and fifteen minutes later he was at the Comm shack, flashing his ID at the next GI on duty.

As the ringtone sounded, he prepared his apology for waking her up. His excuse would be that he needed to hear her voice. Then he would apologize for how he behaved when he was back home on leave the week before. And for not calling her all week long. He would tell her how difficult it was; how much pressure he was under.

I should have confided in her from the beginning, he thought. That was a big mistake.

It was only then he realized the phone had been ringing for a really long time. This was strange because Mandy was a light sleeper. She always answered the phone. Maybe she'd gone back to Carlisle. But no, it was the middle of the week. A school day...

He hung up and signed out.

Nothing was open at this hour in the morning, so Brandon reluctantly returned home. Unable to sleep, he started cleaning up the house, clanking dishes extra loudly as a distraction from the noise in his head. At 0515 he heard Buzz leaving and turned to say goodbye. Buzz was positively furtive, barely acknowledging him. It was this, more than anything else, that caused Brandon to turn and watch him as he walked down to where the squad jeep would be picking him up.

Some instinct seized Brandon then and he went into Buzz's bedroom. Everything in there was impeccably neat, just the way Brandon would have expected. His eye was drawn to the trash can, out of which poked a corner of a newspaper. He lifted it up. It was a British newspaper: *The Guardian*. A strange thing for the little Navy second lieutenant to be reading. Brandon idly flipped through articles about British politics, and something about the new International Space Station. Then his eye caught an article entitled 'Detainees in Guantánamo Bay denied a fair trial' It was all about an American lawyer named Maria Da Silva who had launched a case against the government. His heart jumped when he saw the name: Fergus Maloney. His heart jumped a second time when he saw the byline: *Chris Delafonte.*

"Walter 'Buzz' Prescott, you dumbass," Brandon whispered, jumping up out of his chair. The meeting in a DC hotel room was no gay hookup. "What in hell are you thinking, boy?"

Brandon ran as fast as he could. The site for the new Camp Delta passed on his right. This was the very site which Buzz was responsible for building. Gitmo's newest construction project, all fenced off and shovel-ready. And then it hit him: this was what Walter wanted to tell the British journalist about. He wanted to blow the whistle on the DoD.

Brandon thought about how much his sense of duty meant to him. Yes, he might be pissed at the DoD. Yes, he might be disillusioned by the mission. Yes, Buzz might have a point about corruption in the deal for the new facility. But to break the chain of command in this way? To betray the United States Armed Forces? And to the journalist of a foreign newspaper? It was not something Brandon could let happen.

He caught up to Buzz just as the second lieutenant was about to climb into the squad jeep and head for the ferry. The sergeant who was driving him gave Brandon a nod, then fired up the engine. Buzz waved and smiled as he saw him.

"See you in two days," Buzz said.

"Wait! I need to talk to you!"

"Sorry, man, but I really have to—"

"It's urgent. I have a message for you."

"Still no time. I have to make the 0600 flight—"

"The message is from Chris Delafonte."

Buzz froze. He muttered words to the sergeant then climbed back out of the jeep. If Brandon had been in any doubt before, he knew from the expression on Buzz's face that something was up.

Brandon lowered his voice so the sergeant sitting behind the wheel couldn't hear them. "If you do this, you will leave me with no choice but to report you to my commanding officer."

"Do what?" The bluff wasn't getting any better. Even in the light of the jeep's headlamps, Brandon could see that Buzz had gone red from ear to ear.

"It's treason, Buzz. And it's gonna land you in jail. Now give me the copies of the contracts."

"I don't know what you're—"

"If you don't give them to me, I'm still gonna report you. They'll find them in your luggage and you'll get busted anyhow. So hand them over, right now."

Buzz tore open the attaché case and frantically pulled out the papers, handing them to Brandon. "I wasn't going to—I mean, my mind wasn't really made up—Brandon please don't tell anyone!"

Brandon cut him off with a gesture. "It's all right. So far you've done nothing wrong. Plus I know your heart's in the right place. This stays with me. But from now on, we respect the chain of command, and we do our jobs as soldiers. You promise not to go anywhere near the Topaz Hotel when you get to DC. In return, I promise not to know anything about this. We got a deal?"

Buzz nodded.

"Now go. Don't miss your flight."

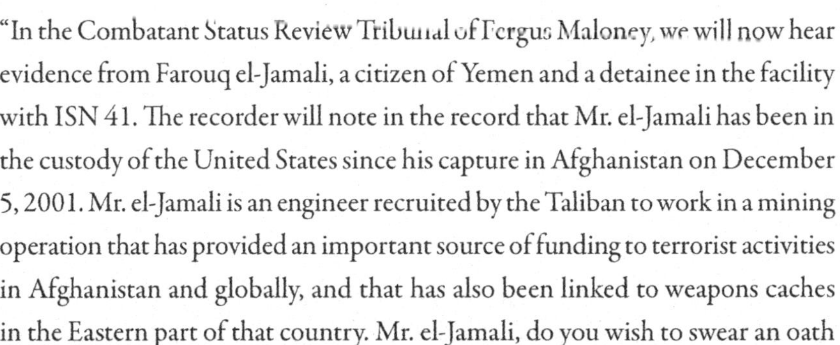

"In the Combatant Status Review Tribunal of Fergus Maloney, we will now hear evidence from Farouq el-Jamali, a citizen of Yemen and a detainee in the facility with ISN 41. The recorder will note in the record that Mr. el-Jamali has been in the custody of the United States since his capture in Afghanistan on December 5, 2001. Mr. el-Jamali is an engineer recruited by the Taliban to work in a mining operation that has provided an important source of funding to terrorist activities in Afghanistan and globally, and that has also been linked to weapons caches in the Eastern part of that country. Mr. el-Jamali, do you wish to swear an oath before providing testimony? If so, a religious leader stands ready to assist you in doing so."

The pudgy-faced Arab's eyes darted from the imam back to the Lieutenant General who was presiding over the Tribunal, back to Brandon. Finally, he sent a sideways glance the way of Fergus himself, who sat, eyes glazed over, with his head slumped against the wall.

"I already told my interrogator everything I know," Farouq said.

"Yes, we have the report. But this Tribunal prefers to hear it, as it were, direct from the source."

"But there was so much, where should I begin?"

"Mr. el-Jamali, can you first please answer the question about the oath?"

"No oath," he said, with guilty eyes darting past the imam.

The Tribunal's president continued. "You can restrict your remarks to factual statements concerning Mr. Maloney. Begin by telling us how you know Mr. Maloney."

"He shares the cell next to me. At least, he did, before I was moved."

"Was this the first time you saw Mr. Maloney, when he arrived in Camp X-ray?"

Farouq looked at Brandon, then over to Fergus, who still appeared not to be listening. Not surprising, Brandon thought. They had him so junked up on Xanax it was a wonder he could still remain seated.

"I wasn't sure at first," Farouq answered cautiously. "And so I engaged him in conversation, to find out who he really was."

"When?"

"In the days after his arrival. A few months ago. I waited until nighttime mostly, then I would ask him questions. We talked a lot, but always in a whisper. I didn't want the others to know I was talking to him."

"And what did you discover?"

"Let's just say, I confirmed my suspicions."

"Your suspicions about what?"

Farouq looked at Brandon again, then shot one final glance over to Fergus, who remained passive, eyes focused on nothing at all.

"I've already said all this to—"

"You're part of a Tribunal now," the president said, a little less patiently than before. "This is separate and distinct from the interrogations you have already undergone."

Another member of the Tribunal, an Army captain whom Brandon did not know, turned over a piece of paper, looked up and said, "Why don't you start your story at the beginning? Explain how you first came to know Mr. Maloney."

The Arab obviously liked the tone of this lesser officer, and addressed only him as he spoke next. "At the time, when I finished my studies, there were not many opportunities in my country. My father had made great sacrifices for me to attend university and it was important that I find a job. I heard from friends that they were paying well in Afghanistan, because the work was so dangerous. You have to understand that I am not political and not—" Here he broke off and looked at the imam warily, "—and not religious either. So I accepted, and two months later I came to Afghanistan. This was in 1999. The man who hired me was a manager, but I knew he was not the owner. His name was Aziz. As I told you many times before, I had no idea he was with the Taliban. He in fact told me the operation was protected by tribesmen. It was not until much later that I found out the truth."

"Mr. el-Jamali, you are not on trial here. We are only interested in information pertaining to Mr. Maloney."

"Yes," he said, sipping from the glass of water they had left on the bench next to him. "One time, a few months after I arrived there, a group of men in jeeps visited the quarry. They were heavily armed with rockets and guns. Aziz was with them, but he seemed to be very afraid. They questioned us in Arabic and in Pashto, asked us whether we were true believers. Of course, we all said we were. After all, nobody is stupid.

"They made us show them the entire site, including the drilling shafts and the explosive equipment. They asked us questions about the structure of the mines, whether we could make it suitable for weapons caches. I tried to explain that this would not be possible without stopping the operations. An argument started between Aziz and one of the Arabs.

"That was when a small man arrived and raised his hand. Instantly there was silence. He negotiated with the fighters and a decision was reached to leave us alone. Aziz was greatly relieved."

"And this small man was Osama bin Laden?"

"Yes. But I did not recognize him at the time. The only reason I remembered his face was because he seemed to be very important. Also, I remember he had a Saudi accent."

"Was he the only person who caught your eye from that group?"

"No. There was one other man who was in the same jeep as bin Laden. A European or American. With blue eyes. I remembered him, and later I asked Aziz who he was. Aziz said he wasn't sure, but that he thought he was the one who was selling them the good rockets. He said the rockets came from America, but no longer directly. He said an intermediary was buying them on behalf of the Irish freedom fighters, the IRA, and selling them on to us. It was these rockets the Taliban needed, he told me. They were the ones that were winning the war for us."

"And this man was Fergus Maloney?"

"Yes. I did not recognize him at first. But once we were in the cell, a suspicion came back to me. And then, when we were talking, I asked him if he had ever been to Nangarhar before. He told me, yes, once he had been there. And then I knew it was him."

"How certain are you that the man you saw in the Nangarhar mines in 1999 was Fergus Maloney?"

"Very certain. One hundred percent sure of it."

As Farouq spoke these final words, he seemed to gain a little in confidence. The Yemeni raised his voice a little and even turned to face Fergus, who sat in the same position, with his head propped up against the wall and a thin line of drool escaping from his mouth.

Brandon thought perhaps Fergus would be roused by this accusation, turn and defend himself. And indeed, at that moment something like words came out of his mouth, though without the lips properly moving. His eyes were still glazed and vacant, only now they were streaming with tears.

"What?" the Tribunal's President said, turning to the recorder. "Did you get what he just said?"

The Lieutenant General turned to Fergus's Personal Representative and asked, "What did he say? Detainee Maloney, repeat what you just said before the Tribunal."

You could have heard a pin drop in the room. Fergus lifted his head ever so slightly and turned, saying to no one in particular:

"Please, make him stop. Make him go away."

The Tribunal broke for lunch after the testimony of el-Jamali, and Detainee 51 was sent back to his cell. Brandon too was released. As he pushed open the door of the OPHQ, that wall of Gitmo humidity smacked him in the face, with all its 95-degree intensity. The rains had stopped now and the sweltering, unmoving, eternal dog days were back, as searing and merciless as before. A stench of jet fuel hung in the air. An engine roared. There was nothing beautiful in this place. Only scorched concrete and the remnants of an American military apparatus that had lost its sense of higher purpose.

Was Farouq telling the truth? It seemed incredible that Fergus could somehow have stolen away from New York and traveled to Afghanistan without any record of doing so. Without any other cross-verification. That he could have withstood the enhanced interrogation techniques to which Brandon had subjected him without cracking, without telling them any of these details. *Especially as he had told so much else.* Other detainees had snapped much more easily. And Farouq was a known liar, who had provided ready testimony on other detainees before, in exchange for the false promises which Brandon and his team of interrogators were so willing to give out.

And yet another part of him refused to believe the Irishman was innocent. It was impossible. It had to be impossible. The FBI were right. There was some connection between al-Qaida and the Irish terrorists.

Even as he formulated the thought, Brandon realized how ridiculous it sounded. The whole case had been stitched together at the last minute, just in time for the CSRT. No one knew that better than him; he was the one who did the stitching! Yet this place had a way of making lies seem like they could be true. It was the very currency of Gitmo, and it bled into your skin like mercury. A shiver ran through his body. *Zack*, he thought, *I'm doing this for you, bro.*

Brandon walked swiftly, hoping to escape for thirty minutes of peace before any of the others could catch up to him. It was, of course, in vain. As he turned the corner to the parking lot where he'd left the jeep, Rhodes was standing, blocking his path.

"Well? How's it going in there?"

The memories of the Mauler came back to him, and he had a hard time looking Rhodes in the eye. "Fine, sir. Farouq, I mean, Detainee 41, was just up."

"And? Do you think they bought his story?"

"They bought it, sir."

Rhodes nodded and stared Brandon in the eyes. He didn't need to be told what Brandon was thinking. The bastard knew. It was like he could read minds.

"By the way, I've approved an internal promotion. The file's already on your desk."

Brandon was momentarily shocked. Was it his promotion, already? And just as quickly guilt consumed him. This was the wages of sin.

Rhodes cracked a sarcastic smile, once again reading Brandon's mind. "It's for one of the guards from JTC-160, who'll be joining us as an interrogator." Before Brandon even had a chance to ask, Rhodes added, "I think you know her already. Private Lucille Meyers." Rhodes left him feeling disappointed, foolish and guilty, all at the same time.

Five minutes later Brandon was inside the Navy Comm shack, seated at an identical telephone desk to the one used by JTC, with an almost identical-looking MP doing an almost identical job of pretending not to eavesdrop. Except this MP was a little sharper, and stood a bit closer to Brandon. Maybe he was imagining it, but it felt like he was now being watched, very closely. It was an open secret that Gitmo was stepping up its internal surveillance. There was talk of strip searches for anyone leaving the base. Everywhere was mistrust, dissension and ill-feeling. As the phone started to ring, Brandon thought of Buzz, and whether he would have had any chance of making it off Base with those stolen documents. More than likely, he had saved the Seabee a court martial.

"Hello?" a male voice answered the phone. He was expecting Mrs. North to answer the phone, as it was the North family home in Carlisle, Pennsylvania, he was calling. Maybe even Mandy directly. Brandon had tried her a dozen times at their house in Maryland. He'd called the school and been told she was out sick. The secretary was weird on the phone when he asked for more details. Now, he was calling the North's house, which was the only other place she could possibly be.

"Who's this?" Brandon asked the male voice.

"Hi, Brandon. It's me, Bob."

"Is Mandy there?"

It took Bob a few seconds to respond. "Brandon, I don't think this is such a hot time."

"Hot time? I wanna speak to my wife, right now. Put her on the phone, Bob."

No reply.

"Put her on the phone, Bob, do you hear me?"

"Brandon, you gotta cool down, man."

"Where is my son? Where are my children? Where is my wife? Is she OK?"

"She just ... I think she needs some time out. Some space to breathe."

Brandon could feel the heat rising into his face. He was only vaguely aware of the MP looking with some discomfort in his direction. "You *think*? You fucking dopehead, you don't decide that. I wanna talk to her, right the fuck now! Put her on the phone. DO YOU HEAR ME?"

A shadow fell over him. When he looked up the bulky form of the MP was looking down at him.

"I think you might have some connection issues, Lieutenant. Am I right? You might want to try the line again later, sir."

In fact, Bob had already hung up. Brandon put the phone down. *I'm losing everything. My career, my family, my soul.*

Anger surged up within him. Fergus Maloney. That's who was to blame. Once he confessed, the music would clear out of his head. Mandy would come back to him. He'd get his promotion and request a transfer back to Maryland. Everything would somehow be OK. He picked up the phone again and called JTC-160 on the internal line.

"Sergeant. Prepare Detainee 51 for transfer to the Crucible. He's gonna undergo another interrogation today."

34

On what was an unusually mild and sunny day on March 17, 2002, Maria watched the St Patrick's Day parade stream down Fifth Avenue. Men in skin-tight green body suits, leprechaun outfits and tweed Scottish hats played the drums, blew trumpets and danced like drunken clowns. Behind them a team of cheerleaders with green face paint and glittering silver halter tops whirled their green-trimmed batons in perfect unison. A shamrock-bespangled banner held up by the smiling vanguard announced they were the representatives of the Irish American Club in Atlantic City, New Jersey. Right behind them was a similar contingent from Yonkers.

The crowd was at record levels on account of the balmy weather, the fact that it was a Sunday, and also as a show of patriotism for the first parade since the 9/11 attacks. Every second spectator held up a homemade sign proclaiming a patriotic slogan: '*We Honor our heroes*' or '*Never forget the fallen.*' For every Irish flag being waved, there were at least two American flags.

It was ironic, Maria thought, that the annual Saint Patrick's Day parade would block her access to the hotel where she was to meet Clodagh on the morning of her return to Dublin. It was ironic too that the celebration of fake, plastic 'Irishness' would drown out the press coverage that might lead to the release of the very real Irishman who was unjustly condemned to rot in a cell in Cuba by this selfsame patriotic fervor. The Irish Prime Minister, who Maria learned went by the unpronounceable title of '*Taoiseach*', had stopped in New York that morning to pay tribute to the victims of 9/11 before his customary visit to the White House to present President Bush with a pot of shamrock. They would shake hands and exchange pleasantries. No mention would be made of Fergus.

His family's connections to the IRA, though of no actual relevance to his case, had proven enough for the Irish government to pretend he didn't exist.

At last Maria spotted an opening in the endless stream of hibernophiles. She leaped over the barrier and sprinted between two blocks of marchers. After a series of apologies to the cop who stopped her on the other side, she managed to wriggle her way through and bee-lined it for the hotel on East 49th Street where Clodagh was staying. She was twenty minutes late, and so it was no surprise that Clodagh was already in the lobby with her coat on, standing in a pool of her luggage.

Clodagh smiled at her in her cold, reserved way, even going so far as to offer Maria a handshake.

"I want to thank you for everything you've done. Fergus's mother and I—the whole family really—we appreciate it. You've done your best. I know you have."

It was as if that cab ride to the courthouse had never happened. The forced pleasantries were somehow grotesque. Maria would have preferred a good, honest catfight.

"I'll let you know as soon as the verdict is in," she said flatly.

"You've done everything you could, that's all that matters." Clodagh answered.

"Clodagh, about what I said in the taxi on the way to court—"

"You tried your best, I know. And on behalf of the family, I want to take the opportunity to say thank you."

"But it's not over. If we win, the United States will appeal. Even if we don't, we can appeal ourselves, as long as the Supreme Court grants cert—"

"No," Clodagh said, in a determined exhalation of air, "we won't appeal." Defiance flashed up in her blue eyes. The caged animal was back.

"What?" Maria couldn't believe what she was hearing. "Why not?"

The other woman blushed and looked away. Her reply, when it came, was halting and nervous.

"I can't ... I have my own family now."

Maria felt a lump forming in her throat as Clodagh spoke. She pursed her lips to stop herself, but the words shot out nonetheless.

"Fergus *is* your family. You hide behind a cloak of lies, Clodagh, but the truth is always still there. Until you face up to it, you will never find peace."

On Clodagh Brogan's face was panic. Snatching up her luggage, she pushed past Maria and scurried towards the hotel door. Maria ran after her, catching up as she was getting into a waiting taxi and taking her arm.

"Clodagh, come back, please! You can't do this! He needs you. Fergus needs you now,"

"I have to go home now." As she spoke, she pulled herself free of Maria's grip and got into the back of the cab.

"To the airport, please," she said to the driver.

"Well, I'm not giving up on him that easily!" Maria bellowed at her. "Do you hear me? I won't give up on him! Not now, not ever!"

Clodagh did not look at her. There was a dull politeness to her tone. "Thank you for your services, Ms. Da Silva. My mother and I are very grateful to you."

"He's not dead! He's not gone!" Maria was shouting now. The taxi began to drive away. Maria followed, breaking into a full sprint. She caught the taxi at the red light on the next block, and banged on the glass. Clodagh's eyes were fixed on the road ahead. She didn't divert her gaze.

"You abandoned him," Maria screamed through the cab window. "That's why he hates you. That's why he won't answer your letters full of lies. Because you gave up on him! And you're doing it again. But I love him! I won't give up on him. I believe in him."

The light turned green and the taxi pulled away.

"I won't give up on him!" Maria shouted, clenching her fists. A horn behind her blazed, but she stood in the road, unmoved, watching as Clodagh Brogan was driven away. She knew that she would never see her again.

A single thought sat with Maria on her subway ride back to Brooklyn: without Clodagh Brogan she would have no standing. That meant no Supreme Court appeal. Which in turn meant everything depended on this one decision. A horrible realization gripped her that perhaps she might lose this case. Intellectually, she had always known it, but emotionally she had somehow never quite believed they could lose, even if Clarke and Cindy and everyone else kept trying to manage her expectations. She remembered Fergus's prediction that they would be married, live on a farm in New Zealand and have 'loads' of babies. He had foreseen it. Just like 'Elizabeth in the basement'. It had to happen. They *had* to win now. It was Destiny.

These thoughts evaporated as soon as Maria caught sight of the front window of her apartment. The glass on the pane of the bay window closest to the stairs had been smashed in, creating a big enough hole for someone to climb in through. A break-in.

Inside the building, Maria's apartment door was swinging on its hinges. She pushed it open and took stock of the damage. Everything was turned upside down. On the wall, in crude red spray paint characters was written '*terorist bitch*' and '*USA*'. They hadn't even bothered to steal anything. There were deep stains on the furniture and on the carpet; the television was smashed in. Maria moved into the office, where every paper was ripped into shreds, and graffiti covered her desk. Thankfully, all of the sensitive files were safely locked up in the ACLU's offices. She walked into her bedroom and saw the most sickening part of all. They had put what looked like human shit on her bedsheets. Every drawer was thrown open and on the bedroom floor was a pile of her underwear, covered in dark stains.

Maria fought back tears and crossed her arms in front of her chest protectively. She took out her cell and dialed Cindy's number. She and Sam were playing tennis. They'd come right over.

In the time it took for them to get there, Maria wanted to leave. This was no longer her apartment. She couldn't even sit down on the furniture. Everything was sullied, destroyed. It was hard to even look at it.

Cindy and Sam arrived a half hour later, still in their tennis outfits. They ran into the apartment and smothered her in hugs.

"Have you called the police yet?" Sam asked.

Maria nodded. "They said they'd send someone around."

Sam stared at the mess in disbelief. "Why would anyone do this?"

"I know why," Maria said. It was the Fox News report from two nights ago: an in-depth 'analysis' of the trial. Their security 'expert' had said with authority and conviction that *Brogan* v. *Rumsfeld* would cost more American lives; that it was more than simply unpatriotic— it was downright treasonous to question the US military at a time of crisis such as this. Sad part was, there were enough angry meatheads in '*Murica* to believe crap like that.

"This is a hate crime," Cindy said, her voice growing angrier with every step around the apartment. "Damn, they real tough! Breakin' into a single woman's apartment when she ain't even home and messin' with her stuff. Big, courageous, USA-lovin' patriots, defending freedom and standing up to terrorism. That's what I'm talkin' about!"

Sam smiled and stroked Maria's arm. "At least you weren't home. You're fine and that's the main thing."

Maria tried her best to smile back. "Am I?"

"You will be."

When the police finally did arrive, they offered little in the way of sympathy and less in the way of practical advice. For them, it was a standard break-in, and despite protestations from Cindy, they found no evidence of a hate crime.

"It's a routine burglary."

When pressed by Cindy that they should "maybe take into account the red spray-painted invectives on the walls, 'cos that ain't the kind of thing the *Hamburglar* usually does when he be snatchin' them Big Macs," one of the police officer mumbled, with a barely suppressed frown, "Maybe you need to take into account that a lot of people in this city lost more than a few pairs of panties 'cos of these terrorist scumbags."

"Okay." Maria called it before things got too heated. "Thanks for your time, officer. Cindy, Sam, let's just get out of here, please. Cindy? Please. Cindy? For me..."

At a local restaurant, Maria did her best to pretend the food and chatter of her friends was working to cheer her up.

"You're going to stay with us tonight," Sam told her.

"Nuh-uh," Cindy cut in, draping a possessive arm around Maria, "I got the guest room all made up already! All Samantha Klein got is a sofa bed. And I know from bitter experience her man likes to walk to the bathroom butt naked at three in the morning and do this weird spitting thing in the sink. Girlfriend, believe me, you do *not* want to get woken up by that!"

Sam laughed, "Oh, it's like that? Well, what if I say she can stay in our room? Me and Clive get the sofa bed. Then I'm the only one who has to look at his naked butt. Which I'm quite fond of, actually."

"What? You upping the ante on me, white girl?" Cindy turned in mock outrage. "Well, I'll let her wear my Japanese silk robe, handmade in Kyoto. And I'll throw in a box of Belgian chocolates!"

This brought her to smile, and pretty soon even laughter.

"You guys are great," Maria said, "and I'm really, really grateful that I have friends like you. But I think I need to get out of the city for a while. I'm going to my mom's place in Fall River."

Both friends gave her a look of unreserved astonishment.

"Don't worry," Maria explained. "She's gone to Atlantic City, on one of those group tours. I was supposed to water her plants this weekend and I totally didn't have time. So in a way, it's a good thing." Maria held up the keys as proof. "She has massive potted yuccas."

"Sweetheart," Sam said, "Are you sure you want to be alone right now?"

Maria looked at her watch and signaled for the bill, but it was too late, Cindy had already paid. *Damn, she was a quick draw.*

Outside, they walked as far as the corner of Montague Street, where Cindy hailed a cab and said goodbye. Sam and Maria walked on through the quiet side streets of Brooklyn, back to where Maria's car was parked.

"I'm worried about you, honey," Sam said, taking her hands. "You're so wrapped up in this Fergus Maloney case. And these people you're up against! They're really ruthless. Don't you think maybe it's time to give this one up?"

"You know I can't think like that. Not after coming this far."

"But what if you lose? Are you going to be able to deal with that?"

"If we lose ..." Maria said, and tried to finish the sentence in a reassuring way. "I don't know. We're not going to lose." She realized how unconvincing that sounded and was about to add, "*There's still the Supreme Court*", before remembering the scene with Clodagh.

"Maria, one way or another, this case will end," Sam continued, "then what are you going to do with yourself? Have you thought about the rest of your life?"

"I'm not sure. Maybe I'll travel. I hear New Zealand is nice this time of year." Even she had to smile at how absurd that sounded.

35

Fergus had fought with Tadgh Coffey and beat him fairly hard, even though Tadgh was eighteen and he was only fifteen. But Fergus was strong, fast and quick. He hit hard and kept focused. Tadgh hadn't really wanted to scrap with him at all, but Fergus had left him no choice in the matter. He'd humiliated him publicly, in front of all the girls. And when the fight happened, well, he had only to dance around Tadgh, dropping punches at will, even singing 'Eye of the Tiger' as he punched.

When the fight was over Tadgh's own gang looked on with a mixture of fear and merriment. Fergus smiled back at them and wiped the blood from his own burst lip: his way of showing that the only lucky dig Tadgh had managed to get in didn't as much as smart.

He knew that Tadgh was the final challenge Clonakilty had to offer. Nothing and no one, not even the Guards, would hassle him again. Grown men were afraid of him. Now there was only one thing left for him to defeat. Fergus flexed his muscles and turned towards home. If it was to be tonight, well, sure, he was as ready now as he'd ever be.

Mammy was back from work when he came home. She saw his knuckles and his lip and looked alarmed.

"You're not bringing trouble into my home again, are you?"

His only answer was to sulk up to his room and put on his Walkman. Red Hot Chilli Peppers.

The screaming started after the hall door banged closed. It was right after midnight, as usual. He heard his mother's angry voice, and then the oul' bastard responded: louder, angrier. But she came back at him. Fergus rose to his feet and stood at the door to his bedroom, waiting for it.

It came. The sound of his open hand against her cheek. Fergus threw open the door and flew down the steps, four at a time.

"Get your fuckin' hands off her!"

She was on the kitchen floor clutching her face. And *he*, still in his cap and coat, surrounded by a film of summer rain. He was smaller than he appeared, with rough knobbly hands imbued with ancient power and evil strength. Even from across the room, Fergus could smell the drink and tobacco off him. The old man's bloated lips spat the usual venom, "Just you mind yoursilf, ya li'l *slíbhín*!" But there was fear in his eyes. He measured Fergus uncertainly and saw that tonight, something had changed.

"Don't you touch my mother."

"Get out of my house," the old man hissed.

Fergus took a step forward and his father retreated. It was only a small step, yet in his lifetime Fergus had never experienced it before. The spell was broken. The Geegaw Man had no more power over him. His father, John Maloney, seemed to shrink before his eyes, an inch a second.

Fergus struck him, and was astonished at how easily the old man fell to the ground, how weak and feeble he was, after all. The Geegaw Man remained on the ground, covering his face, like the coward he always was. Fergus raised his left fist to strike again, less out of rage and bloodlust than out of sheer curiosity and novelty. And again. He would break every bone in his punching hand, and he wouldn't feel it.

Then a blow came to the back of his head. It was Mammy. Fergus fell off onto the ground, himself dazed. Not so much by the strength of his mother's blow, but by the very fact that she had delivered it. Never before had his mother raised a hand to him.

"How dare you," she said. "How dare you strike your own father!"

For a second he was speechless. "He deserves worse than I could give him!"

"He's your *father.*"

"A father, is he? Is that what you call it? You know what he done to me! You know what he done to Darragh! Is that what you call a father, is it?"

"How dare you!"

"He's a bastard. It's 'cos of him Darragh killed himse—"

"What are you talking about? What are you saying?"

"I'm saying ..." Fergus heaved air. His body trembled. The Geegaw Man cowered on the ground, still with his hands covering his face. The next words would cost Fergus every bit of his courage to speak. Even before he spoke them his tears were full of eye and he began to do what no boy with his age and reputation ever should: He cried. "I'm saying ... he *touched* me. And Darragh. And that's why Darragh cut hisself."

"That's a lie."

"T'isn't. And you know t'isn't."

"Liar!" She hissed. "You foul little liar. I'll not have you tearing my home apart with your lies. You've a sick little mind. Get out of this house and take your filthy, perverted lies with you. Get out!"

Fergus shook. He would have said, *I'm not a liar. And you let it happen, and that's why you won't admit it. Your pride is why you let Darragh kill himself.* But his voice choked and only the cawing of crows echoed, over and over, in his brain.

"You're dead to me," Mammy hissed. "Just like your brother. A liar. And like him you're dead. Now go. Get out of this house and don't return!"

When the wooden door with the smoked glass inset and the flaking green paint closed behind him, it was for the last time. He left without his guitar, without his Walkman. Without even a coat on his back...

... and he was inside the room made of cinder block walls and a one-way mirror. Orange prison clothes gathered in a wet heap around the shackles that held his bare legs in place. A voice blasted from speakers high above his head.

Fergus closed his eyes and thought of his brother's body, lying in the ditch behind the houses, with the cut marks running the length of his wrists and across his throat. Darragh had escaped in the end.

And Fergus knew that he could too. All he needed was a blade. *Come to me,* the crow called. And Fergus followed, heading towards the dark ditch.

He was too sore to walk back to his cell, and so the guards dragged him there and flung him on the bed. They closed the metal door. The touch of anything against his skin - the mattress, the metal, even his own arms tucked into his sides - was repulsive to him. He appeared to have lost consciousness. What they could not see from outside the wire cell was the piece of metal he had hidden under his pillow, and now clutched to his throat. He had sharpened it on one end to a fine point. It would serve its purpose well enough.

Come to me, the crow called, watching him with its beady eye. Fergus dropped his satchel full of school books and walked towards the ditch, where a thin rill of water ran and where eternal darkness waited. He would lie down, beside Darragh, in the stank and close his eyes and press the blade against his throat and—

Yet in that moment something happened which the crow had not foreseen. Another voice called out. Fergus turned his head.

His grip on the sharpened metal shard loosened. He lifted his body out of the water and stood.

The voice was calling his name, but at a distance. It was somewhere out beyond the ditch. Out beyond the field. Beyond the town. He turned and listened for it. The crow turned too, fixing its beady eye in all directions, searching. Fergus climbed out of the ditch and began walking away. He let the blade fall out of his left hand and into the wet grass.

Now he was on a beach. The storm had passed and there was not a trace of cloud in the sky. The tide was out. Sandpipers darted across the metallic tan sheen of wet tide, where the water had retreated, disappearing in and out of the sun's reflection. The wind came in off the sea, making the air pungent with salt and brine. Though the sun was lower now and had lost its power over the earth, a warmth lingered in the safe crevice of his hiding place. Fergus leaned back against the bank of the dune and watched as a lithe figure made its way up from the surf, advancing slowly towards him, calling his name.

Maria. A smile danced on her lips. The tasselled hem of her colourful summer wrap was wet and stuck to her calves where the waves had caught her by surprise. Clumps of wet sand clung to her heels and around the edges of her red, painted toenails.

"I told you I'd come back," she smiled. Fergus was once again lost in her big brown eyes. They sat for a long time, saying nothing, just watching the seals bathing in the last of the sun, out on the rocks of an island not far away. "You only needed to wait for me. To keep alive the hope. I'm so glad you did."

Like this they sat and listened to the sea. Their fingers touched. They could have kissed. They could have made love. But it would not have brought them any closer than they already were.

When Fergus awoke, it was morning. The sun beat down through the wire fence. Iguanas scratched the bare earth. The Muslims would begin their prayers soon. Then the guard would come with rations. Fergus's body was sore all over, in places and in ways he daren't even think about. When he moved his arm to rise from the bed, his hand brushed against something sharp and metallic. He threw it on the ground.

She'll come.

The man with the golden hair and the fat, soft hands— the one who called himself Gabriel O'Brien— made one final appearance in Fergus's cell. It was the afternoon. He placed a piece of paper in front of Fergus and offered him a pen.

"Sign it," he said.

Fergus obeyed.

"This is the confirmation of the fact that a Combatant Status Review Tribunal was held in relation to your detention and that the Tribunal's deliberations are now concluded. The statement confirms that the evidence against you has been duly considered, and that you were afforded an opportunity to make statements on your own behalf or through your Personal Representative."

Here O'Brien paused and looked up over the rim of his golden glasses. He made some sort of smiling facial gesture. "That's me."

He continued reading, "Your status as an unlawful enemy combatant has been confirmed. You will remain in this detention facility and may be subject to further interrogations as to be determined by the Joint Task Force."

Fergus looked at the piece of paper the American with the Irish name had left on his lap and tried to read the words. He could not.

Clyde entered the Crucible dressed only in cargo trousers and a white, sleeveless T-shirt. Over the past two months Fergus had grown thin and weak, while Clyde had grown muscular and more balanced. He ran at Fergus without any warning and punched him hard in the stomach.

Fergus doubled over in pain. Clyde's foot spun through the air and caught Fergus on the side of the head. He collapsed, dizzy. Stars danced in front of his eyes.

"Ready for your shower?"

Without even thinking, Fergus cringed, protecting his face with his hands. He knew what was coming. A blast of water into his face so powerful he could not breathe. He turned away from the stream, but another hose was waiting and hit him from the other side, pummelling his head from both directions. The force of the water pushed him along the concrete floor and up against the wall. He gasped at the few pockets of air that became available.

"Please"

The hoses went off. Fergus looked up from the puddle and Clyde advanced. He cringed, but no kick came. Didn't matter. The very threat of it was just as painful.

"Tell me about John Maloney," Clyde said.

"He was my father."

"IS, Fergus. He *is* your father!"

"*Is* my father."

"Why did you lie about him?"

"Because he's a bastard and I hate him."

"Were you in Afghanistan in 1999?"

"No!"

"You lying to me again?"

"No."

"Then why'd you lie about John Maloney?"

"Because he's a bastard and I hate him."

"Did you know he was in the IRA?"

"That's naught to do with me. I hated him. I knew nothing about him. I only wished he would die."

"How did you know about the attacks of 9/11? Who told you about them?"

"Nobody, I told you—"

The water hit him in the face again, knocking his head against the wall. He coughed and spluttered, desperately trying to find another breath. Just as suddenly, it stopped. Fergus stayed in a crouch, and tucked his head under his arms. He remained in that position for a long time. When finally he looked up, the guards were gone. Clyde was gone. The only thing that remained in the cell was a dildo, standing on its base on the floor in front of Fergus. He was alone.

Only he wasn't alone. Someone was watching from behind the mirror. Fergus could feel it. And he knew too, who it was. His breathing became short as the panic gripped him in the chest. Pretty soon the Mauler's voice came through the invisible speakers, high up in the walls.

"*Lie in the puddle Fergus. Lie flat in the fucking water.*"

Fergus did as he was told. The air conditioning had come on and it was cold now. He could feel his kidneys ache. His teeth chattered.

"*Now get on your hands and knees and crawl around like a dog.*"

Fergus did as he was told.

"*Take off your clothes, you sick, little son of a bitch.*"

Again, Fergus did as he was told.

"*Now lie back down in the puddle,*" the Geegaw Man told him.

And Fergus obeyed.

"*Now take the fuck-stick in your right hand. That's right. Grab it around the base. Now rise up onto your knees.*"

Fergus closed his eyes, trying desperately to return to the beach and be with the brown-eyed woman.

36

Brandon stood behind Colonel Rhodes and Private Meyers in the observation room, watching as Detainee 51 knelt on his knees in a puddle of ice cold water and inserted a dildo in his ass. The Irishman's eyes were closed, yet tears still streamed down his gaunt, wasted cheeks. An insect of some description walked across his back, along his neck, across the tight black stubble of his shorn skull, over his closed eyes and—finally—into his open mouth.

"Okay, that's enough," Rhodes said into the microphone. "Take the fuck-stick out. Put it down and walk over to the mirror ... now lick the glass like a good dog."

Without even watching to see if Fergus would obey, Rhodes hit the mute button on the mic and turned to Lucille Meyers. The Colonel's face was stern as ever, but in his eyes Brandon thought he could see a glint of joy.

Shame washed over Brandon, and an inner sickness. He resorted to his mantra. *They drew first blood, not us. They have made their choices. I'm doing this because it's my duty. And I'm doing it for Zack, and for every soldier who's been forced to fight against these sick sons of bitches.*

"This is the Seligman effect I was explaining to you earlier, Private," Rhodes was saying, "whereby the subject has been so utterly broken that he will do literally anything we tell him to. The effect was well documented by Dr. Seligman in the 1960s, albeit only on dogs. What we have lacked, until now, is the thorough and systematic application of the method to human beings. I've always maintained you could break a man the same way Seligman broke dogs. And I think this proves me right. Detainee 51 is a broken man now.

"Now, I know some critics of the method will point to the moral questionability of doing this to a human being," the Colonel continued, "and I sympathize with those arguments. But what they fail to fully appreciate—which we here in Gitmo have learned through bitter experience—is that radical fanatics of Islam, such as these men, are impervious to more humane techniques of interrogation. Just as the War on Terror has demanded that we realign our strategic priorities to face this new kind of threat, so too must we realign our means of procuring military intelligence."

As Rhodes spoke, right behind him on the other side of the glass, not three feet away, Detainee 51 ran his tongue up and down what on his side was a mirror, leaving fat smears and streaks that slowly turned the tortured image of his face into a blur. Not once did he open his eyes.

"Now all you have to do is get a confession out of him," Rhodes said, turning to Brandon. "How hard could that be, Brandon?"

"What if he's actually innocent?" Brandon asked.

Rhodes slammed his fist on the table, startling both Meyers and Brandon.

"No! Maybe you were on Mars or something, but here in Gitmo we just wrapped up a goddamn Tribunal which said he wasn't fucking innocent! Do you even understand what that means? We've doubled down the bet, son. Half the goddamn country is watching the outcome of this case. What if the courts decide this guy should be tried back in New York, and they decide he's innocent? Do you have any idea what it would mean for this operation; for the future of this facility if our most high-profile asset turns out to be a dud? Think, Brandon, about the brave American soldiers whose lives would be put at risk by this piece of shit being found innocent? That's not an option any more, Lieutenant. He needs to confess. Confess or die trying. Simple as that."

Confess or die trying. Brandon recalled the JTC-160 guard he had met earlier, handing him the metal blade that had somehow found its way onto the floor in Fergus's cell. The thought passed through his mind that perhaps the Mauler had left it there, calculating that Detainee 51 might be at the stage where he'd make everyone's life a lot easier. Just like his brother had done.

"My stomach is ... I ... I need some air," Brandon mumbled. He rose and left the observation room, left the interrogation building.

Outside Camp X-ray, he walked through the baking heat of yet another torpid day in Gitmo. The heavy metal music was so loud, he screamed to make it stop. Several soldiers stared at him. He hadn't even realized he was screaming. The rumbling in his stomach started again. Brandon ran as hard as he could around the back of a service shed and dropped his pants just in time for the torrent of diarrhea to pour out of his ass. It burned. Brandon remembered the faucet water he had drunk. A memory came to him of his last day in Maryland, before the mission.

As he was gathering his bags and checking to make sure he had all his papers, Mandy had appeared at the bedroom door. Her brown eyes were still red from crying but she took his hand and, with trembling lips, said to him, "I've been reading up on Gitmo. You have to use lots of bug juice, 'cause the mosquitoes carry diseases. And the water from the faucet isn't potable. Promise me you won't drink it." Brandon smiled and took her in his arms. "I promise." They kissed a final, tear-filled goodbye.

Mandy, he thought, and fresh waves of grief poured into his heart. Up ahead was the Comm shack. He stumbled in and scrawled his name and ID on the sign-in sheet.

His finger bashed out the number of the North household again. Mrs. North needed to answer. He needed to talk to Mandy. He would apologize; he would tell her everything. It didn't matter that the guard was listening.

But there was no answer. The phone just rang and rang. And rang.

In utter desperation, Brandon dialed up his own parents. His mother could drive over to the Norths' house and intervene on his behalf. Seconds later the phone was answered, and, mercifully, it was not Father who picked up.

"Mom?"

When she spoke there was strain and hurt in her voice. *So she knows already.*

"Brandon, I'm so glad you called. Your father wants to be the one to tell you the news. He's just gone up to his study. Hold on a second and I'll get him."

When Father came on the line, Brandon was braced for a lecture about how he had lost control of Mandy. How it was a mistake to marry a Catholic in the first place. How he needed to be more of a man in order to win her back.

But when the old man started speaking, it seemed he didn't even know Mandy was back home. His manner was distracted, bizarre even. His stern voice was faltering.

"Is something wrong, sir?" Brandon found himself asking, with a growing sense of dread.

"Yesterday your mother and I received confirmation from the United States Army that while leading a special op mission in Helmand Province, the armored Hummer vehicle transporting Captain Zeiss and four other men from his Alpha company was hit by an Improvised Explosive Device. Shortly after the explosion, and thanks to the heroic efforts of an Army rescue unit, the men were taken to safety. But only one man out of the crew of five survived the impact."

Brandon's heart stopped. One breath. The feeling of the phone's plastic receiver pressed against his ear harder than was necessary. Then a sound, that might have been his Father trying to speak—and for the first time ever—unable to find the right words.

"My son, Zachary, is dead," Father's voice came eventually, choked with emotion. "My True Soldier is dead."

Brandon put the phone down. When he lifted it again, it was for an internal line. He dialed the Crucible. "Sergeant," he said. "Is Detainee 51 still in the Crucible?"

"Yes sir."

"Get the waterboard ready."

The board was placed on two saw horses of slightly different heights, so that it was angled downwards on one side. It had black restraints for the hands and the feet. Fergus did not try to resist as they pushed him on the board and fixed the restraints in place. A blindfold was placed over his eyes, though it was hardly necessary. He never opened them.

The bucket of water was placed on the floor underneath his head, which hung out over the board at the level of the neck.

Brandon placed a black towel over 51's mouth.

"I want you to tell me about the men at the cookout in the church. The ones who told you about 9/11."

Brandon poured water from a watering can onto the towel. For a second there was no reaction. Perhaps 51 was so far gone that he would simply allow himself to drown. But the CIA man who had taught Brandon the technique assured him this was impossible. You couldn't actually drown someone while waterboarding them. They would just *feel* like they were drowning. Still, as he watched Fergus's lifeless body he wondered—what if they were wrong? What if the Irishman gave in to the sense of drowning and stopped his lungs from seeking air?

Ten seconds later Brandon knew this would not happen. Fergus was not giving up. The will to live is a thing so strong within a human being, it never wants to let it go. Fergus began to shake and thrust his feeble limbs against the restraints, to strain against the sensation of dying. The same as the other detainees had done. The same as they always did. There was still life within Fergus Maloney.

Brandon gave the signal and the sergeant lifted the towel. Fergus gasped and spluttered for air. His lips were blue. His face ghostly-white. Yet he clung to life with a force of will that was all too human.

"Are you ready to talk now?"

"P-p-please. I don't. I didn't."

"Tell me about the IRA people, Fergus. Who were they? Where did you meet them and when?"

"I didn't ... I ..."

Brandon gave the signal and the sergeant put the towel back over his mouth. He lifted the watering can and applied more water. This time there was no hesitation in Fergus's struggle. He fought and twisted like a dying animal. Brandon forced himself to count out ten 'Mississippis' before ripping up the towel.

"Are you ready to talk now?"

Fergus's face trembled. The blindfold had slipped and Brandon could see his eyes, bulged open as he stared forwards into space. It was like the only thing his mind could comprehend was the quest for fresh air. If nothing else, the physical strain on his body would kill him, sooner or later. Then it would end. The pressure from Rhodes, the pressure from DoD, the habeus corpus crap the civvies back in New York were stirring up. Maloney would either have to confess, or to die. And in that moment, it sank in that he, Brandon, would have to be the one to do it.

He looked down at Detainee 51, whose soaking wet body was now shivering from the cold. Zack wasn't around any longer to help him overcome his weakness, to help finish the job. *Sometimes the kindest thing you can do is to kill the weak.*

"I can take it from here," he told the sergeant who was with him. "Dismissed, sergeant." Once alone, he returned briefly to the observation room and silenced the recording, both audio and video. He signed 51 out. What was to follow had to be kept strictly off the record, in order to eventually be recorded as a suicide.

Back inside the Crucible, he leaned in close to 51's ear and whispered, "I gave you every chance I could, Fergus, and you refused. Now I'm going to kill you, plain and simple."

Then he placed the black towel over Fergus's mouth, for the last time.

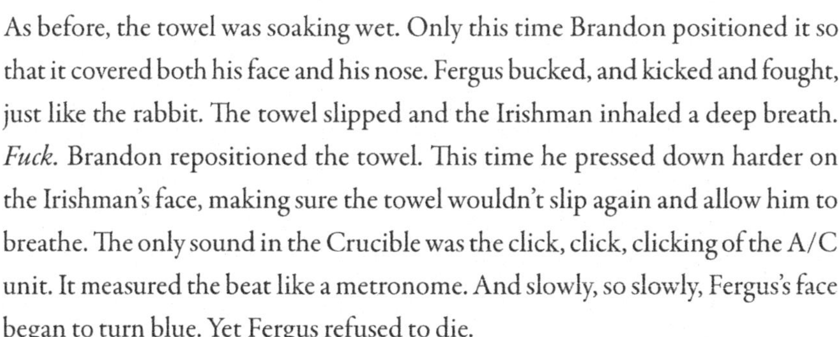

As before, the towel was soaking wet. Only this time Brandon positioned it so that it covered both his face and his nose. Fergus bucked, and kicked and fought, just like the rabbit. The towel slipped and the Irishman inhaled a deep breath. *Fuck.* Brandon repositioned the towel. This time he pressed down harder on the Irishman's face, making sure the towel wouldn't slip again and allow him to breathe. The only sound in the Crucible was the click, click, clicking of the A/C unit. It measured the beat like a metronome. And slowly, so slowly, Fergus's face began to turn blue. Yet Fergus refused to die.

Click. Click. Click. Brandon applied more water to the towel. It ran in heavy drops off onto his knees, and still the Irishman kicked. His eyes stared up at Brandon, helplessly, just like a rabbit. Only his will to live was so much stronger. His soul clung to the wasted, gaunt body and gave him so much strength that Brandon's arm was growing weary from exerting the downward pressure. Yet Fergus refused to die.

Click. Click. Click. The Irishman's bright blue eyes fixed on Brandon, imploringly. *I should have put the fucking blindfold back on him.* His skin was turning blue as well, but it was a darker blue, the blue of dying blood. Without wanting to, Brandon focused on the eyes. They drew him in, captivated his attention, as if he were compelled to witness the moment when Fergus died, when the soul left his body and went to join his brother Darragh in heaven.

I confess.

It was directly from the eyes that the words came, unspoken, emanating straight into Brandon's mind. It sent a shiver through him. He ripped the towel from Fergus's face. For a second nothing happened. It seemed to be too late. Was he already too far gone?

Then, to Brandon's infinite relief, Fergus coughed. Water ran down his cheeks and he began to breathe again. Within seconds the color returned to Fergus's face.

"Do you confess? Do YOU?" Already Brandon was doubting the voice he had heard inside his own head. Had it just been the same kind of weakness which had rendered him unable to kill the rabbit, all those years ago? Was he, after all, just prolonging Fergus's suffering? *The cruelty of cowardice.*

"Yes," the Irishman whispered, in between stunted breaths. "I confess. I confess to everything."

37

The break-in and vandalism of her apartment on Hicks Street in Brooklyn Heights helped Maria make up her mind on what to do with the place. The following afternoon, when she returned from Fall River, she called her landlord and gave notice to quit. The lease had expired years ago, so they were operating on a month-to-month basis. The guy would be only too happy to get her out, given how much he could now raise the rent.

"So when can I start showing the place?" he asked.

"I'll make you a deal," she said after a pause. "If you're willing to clean up and get rid of all the stuff that's in there, you can take back possession starting tomorrow. I just need one backpack and I'm done."

The thought of releasing herself from the furniture, the obligation to pay rent she could no longer afford, the stress of knowing that whoever had trashed the place might come back; it all felt like a huge weight off her shoulders. What nine months ago would have struck her as absolutely unthinkable, now seemed like the most natural decision in the world.

After a moment, Maria picked up the phone again. This time she dialed a number with the country code for the United Kingdom.

"Hello?"

"Chris Delafonte?"

"Yes that's me. Who am I speaking to, please?"

"Maria Da Silva. From New York."

"Oh, hi, Maria, how are—"

"I'm sorry, I'm a bit short on time. I just wanted to ask about your contact in Washington. The military source you were working with? Did he ever come through?"

"He never showed up. The line went cold."

Maria sighed. It was what she had expected him to say; still a good lawyer pursues every possible line of attack.

"Okay, thanks. If I think of anything that might help, I'll call you back."

Maria looked around her little office. It was the last place she could call her own. She gathered the files she would need for their team meeting, the final one before the judgment would be issued. One way or another, this was going to be the end.

And then what? She thought. *Where do I go? What do I do?* A bittersweet memory of Fergus's prediction played in her mind. That she would leave her job, her apartment and go to live in New Zealand.

She fired up the internet and plugged "New Zealand" into the search engine. There were dozens of travel sites, information on how to apply for visas. But as she read, her eyes grew wetter and wetter. A sense of foolishness filled her. Even in her early twenties, when it was the right age for that kind of thing, she had been no good at that carefree, cool young traveler stuff, chasing adventure across the globe. Her work was the one thing she had been good at, and now she'd lost that.

"Maria," a voice woke her out of her reverie. It was Anca. "Time for our team meeting."

"I'll be there in a minute."

She'd need at least five to compose herself and freshen up her make up.

When Maria got into the meeting room, she saw Clarke was in attendance, as well as Anca and Ralf. That was an unusual honor. As per the agenda, they discussed the latest developments in the case, which at this stage were frankly fewer and fewer.

"We got confirmation of the outcome of the CRST," Ralf began.

"And?"

"Well, it's what you would expect," Anca said, "they confirmed his status as an unlawful combatant."

It was exactly what she expected. Still Maria's heart sank at the news. One more possibility eliminated.

"But on process, where are we?" she asked. "Anything around the Tribunal that we can use for the case—the medical report, the testimony? Who was the Personal Representative?"

"Classified, classified and even more classified. They're not even telling us what building it was held in."

"Okay," she paused and looked around at her team. "Well, then ... anything else?"

"I think we need to seriously consider where we go from here in case of an adverse ruling on the substantive points," Clarke said.

Maria shot him a look. "You don't think we're gonna win, do you?"

Clarke shrugged. "I don't know. One thing's for certain. Whatever happens to Fergus, there are plenty of other cases that are coming to our attention. The problems in Gitmo are going to get worse, not better. We need to think long term."

"I'm not going to give up on him," Maria said, before realizing how empty this statement was. She had no apartment, no standing to take another case, and without the support of the ACLU, she had no hope of doing anything more for Fergus. And even if she wanted to, there was no guarantee a legal avenue would open for a Supreme Court challenge.

"Let's just see what the judgment says, first of all," Clarke counseled.

"Okay. We reconvene tomorrow at— When's the mail due? Can we find that out?"

"I already checked," Ralf said. "Seven thirty in the morning."

"Okay then, we'll see you guys back at the mailroom tomorrow morning."

A half hour later Maria was back at the apartment gathering her stuff. She opened her bedroom closet and took out a handful of things on hangers. They were expensive, designer dresses and skirts, still in the protective sleeves that came from the dry cleaners. It was a wardrobe that had taken years to build up, and had cost her maybe twenty thousand bucks, maybe even more.

I don't want any of these things, she thought.

One formal outfit would be enough for the remaining hearings, if any were to happen. For that, she chose the red-and-cream skirt and the silk black-and-white striped blouse. And one pair of heels, which she put in the worn out Macy's shopping bag.

Everything else went into a big bulky backpack. Passport, small cosmetics case, bras and panties. Assorted socks. T-shirts. One pair of sweatpants. One cashmere sweater. Her copy of *Oliver Twist*, still with the stamp from the high school library on the title page.

She paused on the steps before closing the door on her little Brooklyn apartment for the last time ever. It was impossible not to be melancholy as she remembered the excitement of getting that apartment, four years ago. How much she had felt she was on the road to success.

An hour later she pulled up in front of Cindy's house. It was already late and Cindy had changed into her night robe, obviously settling in for movies and delivery food.

"Is that offer of a bed still good?" Maria asked.

Cindy smothered her in a hug and dragged her, bodily, inside the apartment. "Always, honey. Always."

38

After removing the restraints and allowing the detainee to crawl into the corner of the Crucible and curl into a ball, Brandon waited. It took Fergus a full ten minutes before he was physically able to talk. Brandon was prepared to give him this time, but not more than that. He took the opportunity of going to the toilet and emptying his bowels once again, in what he hoped would be the last symptom of the nastiest stomach bug he'd ever had.

Once the recording equipment was switched on, he began the questioning. The same questions he had asked Fergus a thousand times before.

"Who told you about 9/11?"

"It ... it ... was Karim," Fergus said slowly, though his eyes did not regain their focus.

"Karim Saunders?"

"Yes."

"When and where did this happen?"

"We were at the cookout."

"Which cookout?"

"The Mount Zion Baptist Church annual summer picnic. August 2001. In the yard behind the church. There was a barbecue. Karim took me aside and told me there was someone he wanted me to meet. He introduced me to two men. One was named ... Mustafa."

"Mustafa Troye? Shawn Mustafa Troye?"

"Y ... yeah. I think so."

"And who was the other?"

"Jamal. He told me they were going to make America pay for sending armies to the Holy Land."

"So Jamal was the third man at the picnic? Was he an Arab?"

"Yes. Jamal was the Saudi guy. He was the one who told it to Karim. He was the al-Qaida contact. He said the eleventh of September would be a day the Americans would never forget. A day that would change the world."

"Why didn't you tell us this before now?" Brandon's voice hardened as he asked this question. The change in tone caused Fergus to press his body tighter against the wall.

"I don't know. I should have. I'm sorry. I'm so sorry. Please forgive me ..."

"What about the IRA men?"

"Yes. Yes. I knew them. That's how I met Karim."

"Who were the IRA men?"

"There were three of them. One was a Corkman, the other two were from the North. I didn't know the Northerners' names. But the Corkman I had seen before, when he was with my father. He was from Cobh. His name was Sean Hayes. After the peace deal he left and went to New York. They were Continuity IRA. They didn't sign up for the treaty – thought it was selling out. I met him one night in a pub in Brooklyn, just by chance, like. He recognised me and we got talking. He trusted me because I was John Maloney's son. And so he told me what they were up to."

"And what were they up to?"

"Selling arms to al-Qaida. Using their old contacts in the arms black market in the States. He told me the money would be used to fund the campaign for a united Ireland."

"And you supported this campaign? This Continuity splinter group?"

"Yes. I agreed to help them. That's why I ended up in the flat with Karim. My job was to watch, to make arrangements. They gave me free rent."

"Did you ever travel to Afghanistan?"

"Yes, once."

"When was it?"

"I can't remember—"

"Fergus, don't start bullshitting me again."

"I ... 1998."

"You sure it wasn't 1999?"

"Maybe. Yeah, it could have been."

"And when you were there, did you meet Osama bin Laden?"

"Yes. He was the one we were negotiating with. He was the buyer."

Brandon breathed out a deep sigh of relief. He realized he had been sweating like a pig the whole time, his hands balled into fists. Now he released them.

It's nearly over. This was what he had hoped for all along. This was salvation.

He forced himself not to think about Zack, because he had to control his anger, at least until they had the confession. Instead, he hit the red button on the recorder.

"Okay, we're gonna keep going tonight. I want names, I want addresses. I want every detail that is in that head of yours. It's gonna be a long night for both of us. The sooner we start, the sooner we finish."

39

Pretty much the entire ACLU staff was assembled in the mailroom that morning. The US mailman came in wheeling his usual cart with the translucent, white plastic mail bins stacked four high. He handed over the bins, one at a time, just the way he would on any morning. He was too disgruntled in his job to even care why an entire organization's staff would be assembled in the basement, waiting for the mail at seven thirty in the morning. Sid, the zitty kid who processed the mail, was overwhelmed by the pressure of having so many people watch him work.

"I ... n-normally use the wire trays in th-those cubby holes, o-over there." He looked around at the sea of expectant faces and blushed. "I'm sorry everyone, but it normally takes me an hour to—"

"Sid!" someone pleaded. "Just find the letter from the United States Court of Appeals. The one for Maria Da Silva. Literally everything else can wait."

Amid chuckles and a general bustle of bodies, Sid eventually extracted the right letter from the pile. It was handed solemnly from person to person until finally it had made its way into Maria's possession. Someone passed her a letter opener, which they had had the foresight to bring down with them. A few interns climbed atop the sorting desk to get a better view.

Maria closed her eyes and said a little prayer.

A hundred pairs of eyes watched as she opened the envelope. The same hundred pairs of eyes watched as she took out the contents, and unfolded them. Maria read carefully, oblivious to the people around her and their vain attempts to read her expression.

"Petition denied."

Her heart sank. It was only when she heard herself saying the words that it became real. All she could see was an image of Fergus lying in a little wire cell, alone and forgotten.

"The Supreme Court might grant a writ of *certiorari*, Maria," Anca said.

"Yeah," Maria replied. "They might." But without Clodagh Brogan, that would mean nothing. Maria knew it was over.

I'm sorry Fergus. I've failed you.

She ignored the consoling hands that sought her shoulders. She ignored the kind words of support. Passing the letter to Clarke, she left the mailroom and left the building and walked out, into a fresh spring morning where men and women walked freely on the streets of New York City, and never imagined their lives could be any other way.

Her wandering took her down to Battery Park, Manhattan's southernmost green space. From here, she stood at the railings and looked out over the harbor as the milky sun climbed above the water. She was looking due south. Out there, somewhere, across a thousand miles or more of water, was the island of Cuba where Fergus would rot away, maybe for the rest of his life.

Why couldn't you foretell this? she found herself asking him. *You said we'd go to New Zealand together. You told me I'd quit my job, and leave my boyfriend and give up my apartment and go away with you. And look, here I am. I've done everything you said I would. But in the end, it wasn't good enough.*

You were wrong about me. I wasn't good enough.

At 0751, just as Maria was staring out at the Harbor of New York City in despair, Brandon Zeiss burst into Colonel Rhodes' office clutching a logbook and tapes. Private Meyers was with him, and she jumped away from the space behind the Colonel's desk when Brandon entered. If there had been any doubt before, Brandon now knew the Colonel was fucking her. But that didn't matter a damn. All that mattered were the three audio tapes which Brandon placed on the Colonel's desk. These tapes contained a full confession from the Guantánamo Detainee with Internment Security Number 51, Fergus Patrick Maloney. If there was something like elation in Guantánamo Bay, this was what it felt like.

"I got him, Colonel. He's confessed everything. The IRA, al-Qaida, Karim Saunders, even the trip to Nangarhar! Turns out that lying shit, Farouq, told the truth for once in his life. Maloney *was* there. And he *did* meet Osama bin Laden."

Expressionless, Rhodes and Meyers stared at Brandon.

"I have to admit there were moments I was doubtful. I apologize for that, sir. But this interrogation has taught me an important lesson about the need for perseverance in what we do here. It's a lesson I won't soon forget."

For a brief moment, an unreadable silence filled the Colonel's office.

Then they laughed. First the Colonel, then Meyers joined in. Their laughter created its own contagion until eventually they were both in hysterics.

"You stupid fuckin' moron," Rhodes said at last, after wiping the tears from his eyes.

"Sir, I'm not sure I understand—"

"He didn't go to Afghanistan, you nimrod. Farouq's story is more full of holes that a fucking Swiss cheese. Karim Saunders wasn't involved in al-Qaida. There were no IRA contacts in New York. John Maloney's been out of the game since the early 1980s. You seriously think the Bureau didn't already check this stuff out the moment they took 51 into custody? You think they don't already know everything there is to know about Saunders, the Mount Zion Baptist Church, John Maloney's contacts and Fergus's movements while he was in New York? They're stupid, but not even they are that stupid. No, that honor belongs to you alone—" He started laughing again, but brought himself quickly under control.

"He ... he confessed."

"Brandon, seriously. What did I tell you last night? Maloney is a broken man. If you asked him to confess to the assassination of JFK, he would have done that with equal zeal. If you asked him to saw off his dick with a breadknife and eat it in a hot-dog bun with some mustard and relish on top, he'd do that too. That's the Segilman effect. There is no useable intelligence we can extract from a man like that."

Brandon's face went red as the Colonel's words dawned on him. He hadn't slept properly in days. His head was spinning. Yet if this were true ...

"Then why?"

"For the second time in so many days—because we needed a goddamn confession. Gitmo's a part of a wider operation now; an operation that's just gearing up. Fergus Maloney will be a small success story; an inconclusive piece in a bigger puzzle that will allow us to achieve our military objectives. That's why we needed the confession. And having an interrogator who's so stupid he actually believes the bullshit he's hearing is useful in terms of making the confession sound authentic."

"Are you telling me you ordered me to torture a man who you *knew* was innocent?"

At this Rhodes's expression changed. When he spoke next, the mirth was gone out of his voice. "I didn't order you to do anything, Lieutenant. You're the officer in charge of interrogation. You did everything on your own authority. Including directing an unnamed, enlisted man to disguise himself as 'the Mauler' for the purposes of administering enhanced interrogation techniques on high-value assets who were proving particularly intransigent. Techniques which I never approved of or endorsed. I hope that's clear to everyone here." He turned to Private Meyers, whose beady eyes fixed themselves on Brandon.

"That's the evidence I would give, Colonel," she said. "If I would be asked to give evidence, that is."

"How long have you known Fergus was innocent?" Brandon's voice was not quite his own. "How long have you had the extra files from the FBI?"

"That's not important."

"How many others do you know to be innocent too? How many other men are here needlessly, living worse than abused dogs?"

"You're out of line, soldier."

"This isn't even about getting bin Laden, is it? It's about pushing the war from Afghanistan on into Iraq, isn't it? It's about goddamn contracts for private companies, and oil and ... and nothing I ever believed in, *nothing* my grandfather would ever have risked his life for. I ... I ..."

The words ran out. A brief moment of rage passed through him, and with it the image of him leaping across the heavy wooden desk, grabbing the letter opener and ramming it into Rhodes' throat. But the rage passed just as quickly into deep sadness and a sense of his own helplessness. And a tiredness that seemed to Brandon like no amount of sleep would ever lift it. *Why had Zack given his life? What did he die for?*

Rhodes read this too. "You don't look so hot, Lieutenant. Go home. Get some rest." He picked up the tapes. "I've been a little rough with you, but that's just my way. Fact is, you've done good work today and you deserve a break. I'm fast-tracking your April leave request so you can go back for your brother's funeral, starting tomorrow. Dismissed."

The diarrhea was merciless. Liquid shit just kept coming in periodic bouts, long after Brandon was sure his guts had nothing left to unload. He spent the rest of the day and most of the night running to the toilet. Now, finally, as the long night threatened to end, he felt empty. *Empty in every sense.*

It was 0400 hours when he awoke. Awoke wasn't the right word; because the thing he had experienced wasn't any kind of sleep. It was a heavy metal concert that refused to end. He looked around the little bungalow that had been his home for the past four months. Four months wasn't that long, and yet he had a hard time imagining what his life had been like before he'd come to Gitmo. He pushed out of his mind the thoughts of how much longer the mission would last. He tried instead to think of the reprieve which his leave would give him in a few hours' time. Yet that too was tainted – with the loss of his marriage and with Zack's death. And no matter how far he traveled from Gitmo, the memories of the things he had done would travel with him.

That thought made him kick the cheap table in the living room. The heavy metal music boomed on in his head. But there was no escape. Not in the living room. Not in his bedroom where he packed, not anywhere.

When he reached the very last pile of clothes, his hand touched a folder. It was the contracts he'd taken from Buzz. He opened them and began reading. Most of it was legal gibberish. He tried to read it out loud, in order to make better sense of it, but the music in his head was so loud he couldn't hear his own voice.

Brandon closed his eyes. Somewhere in the jumbled mess of thoughts and confused feelings there was a pattern. If only the music would stop! He tried to recall the things Fergus had said to him over the weeks and months of his interrogation, to fit them together. *He had foretold Zack's death.* And the lawyer, Maria Da Silva, she was the one he talked about in his sleep. She was the woman who came to him and gave him strength. She was the woman he kept meeting on the beach.

Brandon went to his desk drawer and took out the newspaper he'd found in Buzz's trash can. The article on Fergus was there, and in it an inset picture of Maria Da Silva. She was beautiful. Brandon closed his eyes and tried to imagine her the way Fergus had done. Then it came to him, and he knew what he had to do.

With trembling hands, he cut out the picture of Maria Da Silva and added it to the pile of documents. In the bathroom he found an old jar of Vaseline. He returned with it to his bedroom, rolled the documents into a tight wad, then taped them closed and sealed them in Saran wrap which he got from the kitchen. He used his fingers to coat the exterior of the document roll with a thick layer of the petroleum jelly. Finally, he opened his fly and dropped his pants and boxers. Bending over, he inserted the greased wad into his anus. Inch by inch it went up into the cavity which the stomach bug had left as empty as a cavern. Right up it went, into the lower intestine, until the butt end was lodged inside his sphincter. When he'd got his pants back on, he practiced walking. It was intensely painful, a discomfort unlike any he had felt before. And yet the pain was nothing against the relief inside his head.

The heavy metal music had stopped.

40

As she handed her phone to the guy in the Sprint store, Maria saw 12 missed calls on the display, all from Anca. Item six on the long list of things she needed to do before she could leave New York forever was canceling her cell phone subscription. Cell phones were for lawyers. And she was no longer one of those.

"For someone who doesn't need a cell, you sure get a lot of calls," the store guy said with an ironic smirk. "Wanna check your voicemail one last time, before I send this baby to the Great Sprint Store in the Sky?"

She was just about to say no when the phone started vibrating and lighting up. It was the 13th call from Anca. Maria snapped the thing open and jabbed at the green button.

"Anca, I already told you—"

"*Maria, please just listen for a second. This is about something else. There's someone I really think you should talk to.*"

Maria sighed. "How many times do I have to say it? No reporters, no interviews. I'm done with—"

"*It's not a reporter. It's something else...*"

She waited for her to continue.

"*I can't tell you on the phone.*"

"Okay, now you have got my attention."

"*He's waiting for you in Washington Square Park, right now! You have to hurry, he can't stay much longer.*"

"Okay, but what's his name?"

"*Just, please, go there now, okay?*"

The Sprint sales guy was waiting patiently for her to finish this conversation.

"I changed my mind," she told him. "I gotta keep this after all."

It was a crisp, bright morning in New York City. Young people, mostly NYU students, sat on the benches of Washington Square Park chatting, while pigeons patrolled the ground looking for crumbs. Maria unstrapped the oversized backpack and let it drop from her shoulders. She scanned the crowd for a full minute, and was just on the verge of calling Anca back when a guy stood up and walked towards her with a sense of purpose. He was in his late twenties, dressed in a black suit, and had his blond hair in a military crew cut.

"Ms. Da Silva? My name is Brandon Zeiss. I'm a Lieutenant in the Air Force, assigned to the Joint Task Force 170."

As soon as she heard Joint Task Force her heart skipped a beat. "Is he okay?"

The military man opened his mouth to say something, but his words faltered. Maria studied his face. Underneath the hardness of his clenched jaw there was a weakness to him, and a watery cowardice in his eyes that spoke of guilt.

She repeated her question.

Finally he answered, "I'm sorry. For what I've done, and for what I've become."

"Is he dead?"

"No. But he's hurt."

Somehow Maria knew: "It was you, wasn't it? You're the one who tortured him."

His silence was all the answer she needed. She would have wanted to hate him. To hurt him. To beat him with fists of rage. Instead, she could only feel the empty futility of it all. In a voice heavy with bitterness she asked, "Is that what you came here for? My forgiveness?"

"No ma'am. I have to ask that of my Maker. I came here to help Fergus." He took out a document case from his backpack. In it were pages and pages of crumpled documents, many with the seal of the Department of Defense on them. Others bore the more familiar letterhead of Rosenthal, Roberts & Sleete. There was also the logo of Burton & Hale. Her eyes scanned through them quickly.

The act of reading contracts calmed her brain, yet what she was reading excited fresh anger. She thought of Chris Delafonte.

"Where did you get these?"

"From a source inside Gitmo. I can't give you his name."

She looked him in the eye. "Are you prepared to stand over their authenticity?"

Brandon paused. For a fraction of a second, maybe, his lips quivered. But then he swallowed and said, "Yes, ma'am. I am."

Maria watched him all the way. "Why are you doing this?"

Brandon's pale eyes waved. He shook his head. "I lost my brother in Afghanistan. Fergus foretold it. His gift ... I think it's real."

Maria nodded. "I know."

"Then it's up to you to save him." He handed Maria the document case. "Go save him, ma'am."

Maria knew even before pulling the rental car in to the drive of the Laurence family beach house in Southampton, that the great and good of the right-wing establishment would be gathered there for the 65th birthday celebration of William Dale Laurence. Among the fleet of cars crowding the driveway and lining the street, she spotted Jeff's, parked right behind his sister's minivan. And, of course, the late model Lincoln Continental with the DC plates that belonged to the birthday boy himself. But it was the jet black Porsche with the Connecticut plates that caught her attention most. It belonged to Seth Rosenthal. *Good*, she thought. *He's here too*. Everything was going according to plan.

Maria was dressed in jeans and a T-shirt, and, as she wasn't on the guest list, the hired doorman showed no signs of letting her in. When she persisted, Candyce Laurence made an appearance at the door, just as Maria knew she would.

"Maria! What are you doing here?"

"I came to wish William Dale a happy birthday, of course!" Maria answered.

There was an awkward pause as the two women faced off, until eventually Candyce smiled and said, "Of course, come on in."

Inside, the crowd of finely-dressed, rich, white people spilled out through the house and onto the deck. She caught sight of young Nathan running down the hall. When Jeff spotted her, he advanced swiftly.

"What are you doing in my father's house?"

"Come on, Jeff, you told me we deserved a fresh start." She smiled, with no expectation he would buy it. "You know what? I've known your dad for six years. It's only normal I should wish him a happy birthday. Plus, look," she held up a carefully wrapped box with a glittery golden bow on it, "I got him a present."

With Jeff trailing behind, she continued through the house, until she caught up with William Dale in the study, standing with a group of tuxedoed men that included Seth Rosenthal. William Dale lost none of his usual aplomb as she gave him a kiss on the cheek and wished him a happy birthday. Seth, too, was cool enough not to react. Jeff, meanwhile, stood behind them and glowered at her.

"I'm sorry to hear you didn't get a result on *Brogan* v. *Rumsfeld*," Seth said, when the greetings were over. "Still, I hope it doesn't dissuade you from continuing in your new chosen field of law. Next time, perhaps, a little more caution in your approach."

"In your words Seth, 'it's not the wins that makes you a champion. It's how much you learn from your losses'. And what I learned was that the system is so badly rigged that you cannot expect justice if you play by the rules."

William Dale laughed, perhaps a little uncomfortably. "I certainly hope that's not true."

"Oh, but you know it is."

An awkward silence fell. Two of the other men in the group excused themselves and went to refresh their drinks. With a muttered excuse me, William Dale turned his back to her too. But Maria grabbed his shoulder and spun him back around to her, with a force that surprised everyone. "I nearly forgot, William Dale. I got you a birthday present."

"Thank you, Maria," the Laurence patriarch replied, and placed the wrapped box down on the desk.

"Please open it now," she implored with her sweetest smile. "A lot of people went to an awful lot of trouble for me to be able to give this to you."

He unwrapped the box.

Inside were papers.

"What is this?" William Dale asked.

"Incriminating evidence," Maria explained, still smiling sweetly. "Copies of memos between the Department of Defense, a private contractor called Burton & Hale and a junior associate of your firm, Seth, whose name happens to be Jeffrey Laurence. These documents provide irrefutable proof that the White House administration, including a certain 65-year-old official in the State Department, rigged the tender process for the construction of new military facilities in Burton & Hale's favor, thereby conspiring to defraud the American taxpayer out of millions of dollars."

She looked around at the frozen faces. "Now, I know most people in this country don't give a shit about Fergus Maloney, or any of the other innocent men rotting away in a prison camp far away from here. But people do care about what happens to their tax dollars. They care an awful lot about fraud at the highest levels of government."

"I think you need to leave my house now," William Dale said. His voice was calm, but the color had already started to drain out of his face.

"Of course, it's not a *unique* present," she continued, now without the pretense of a smile. "Because I'm afraid what you have there is only one copy. The other copy is with a journalist acquaintance of mine, safely in another country, waiting to be published in a leading British newspaper," She glanced at her watch. "It could be on news shelves all over London before this party is even over." She scanned their faces. They were good, but not good enough to hide how scared they were. "Do you still want me to leave your house?"

"You really think you can come in here and intimidate my father?" Jeff screamed at her, with balled fists of rage. "Get out of here before I call the cops."

"Jeffrey." It was Seth who spoke now. "Think for a minute, would you? She didn't come here to intimidate us. She came here to get something. So what is it you want, Maria?"

"You know what I want. I want justice. I want the case against Fergus Maloney closed. I want him released from military custody and declared completely innocent." She turned back to William Dale. "And that's the real birthday gift, William Dale. The chance to do penance. The chance to give an innocent man back his life."

"How do we know you'll return the documents if and when we let him go?" Jeff asked with a sneer.

"You don't," she told him. "Except for the fact that in six years of going out, I never once lied to you. I never once cheated on you. Despite being a lowly, immigrant Spic, I'm what's known as an 'honest person'. And that's a lot more than you can say."

"What if we just get your ass thrown in—" Jeff started, but his father silenced him with a wave of his hand. The two older men exchanged glances, then stepped away. A few quiet words were spoken. Maria watched them in their secret little confab, and saw them as she had never seen them before. These were the two father figures whose approval she had fought so hard, for so long, to win. Now it was laid bare what they really were: scheming criminals huddling in a corner to save their corrupt asses from prosecution.

"All right," William Dale told her. "But it ends here. No more cases against the United States. You disappear. You take your Irishman and you go."

"Deal," Maria said. The knot in her stomach that had been holding her together was loosened. She wasn't sure she'd make it back to her rental car without throwing up.

41

Brandon drove from New York City to DC as fast as he could. Halfway through New Jersey the cloud cover started, and by the time he'd crossed into Delaware, it was raining heavily. He arrived in Arlington exactly on time for the funeral of his only brother, Captain Zachary Zeiss. The dripping wet branches of the trees in Arlington National Cemetery were still bare in late March. They looked like splayed skeleton hands, black in silhouette against a slate gray sky.

Brandon walked through the rain, up the neat path past the rows of white stones which marked the graves of the brave, fallen soldiers of the Civil War. The lines of Zack's comrades in their gleaming green uniforms and all wearing their trademark berets formed the guard of honor up to the plot. Brandon walked straight up to the small group of mourners, clad in black, who headed up the procession. There, under broad umbrellas, were his father and his mother. He stood beside them, and together they waited for the casket to arrive. It was carried by Zack's true brothers, the men of his company, also in their green berets. The holy man spoke some words, among which Brandon heard 'sacrifice' a couple of times. Some guns were fired into the air. Then the box was lowered into the bare, cold earth. More words followed. The men on either side of the grave carefully folded the American flag, while in the distance a brass musical instrument rang out. The Stars and Stripes must never touch the cold, wet earth. Zack's body, on the other hand, was condemned to lie in it forever.

Throughout it all, Mother wept, as Brandon knew she would, and when he took her in his arms to console her, he wondered why it must be him. Why her husband was so unable to do what should have been so natural.

When they turned to leave he saw Mandy in the group behind him. He was surprised how her beauty struck him now, amidst all the tragedy. The idea of losing her was at once unbearable.

"I didn't think you'd come," Brandon told her, unsure for a moment how he should react.

She shook her head. "How could you say that?" The tears that stained her cheeks were soft, yet they struck Brandon like hammers, shattering his steely reserve.

He rushed to her, but stopped short of taking hold of her, as if he were waiting for permission. "Mandy, I'm so sorry. I missed you so much."

She opened up her arms in a kind of quivering exasperated despair. "Then hold me."

When he did, her body went limp, as if all the force she had was used up in the effort of making it that far. From amidst the choking sobs, he heard her say, "I missed you so much."

Despite the cold rain, he felt a warmth he had not once known in four months in Cuba.

"I'm not going back," he told her.

"Don't say that Bran. Don't say it if it isn't true."

"It's true, Man'. I'm home for good."

The meeting with Maria Da Silva seemed only half real to him now, yet he knew that the consequences of that meeting would change his life forever. There was no going back to the Air Force. One way or another, his career was over.

Mandy looked up into his eyes and dared to smile.

"Then come home with me right now, and tell it to Scott. Tell your son you're back home."

Here he was forced to break, and to face her. She had to know the truth. "Mandy, I've done things ... to people ... I didn't ever think I could do. Horrible things. Things you can't imagine."

She looked at him with such wisdom and understanding that for a moment he was scared. "I know," she told him.

"And you don't hate me for it?"

Mandy smiled and shook her head. "You have to trust in God. Confess your sins. Pray. God will listen. He'll show you the way back. You've already taken the first step."

"You don't think I'm a coward?"

Mandy trailed her fingers across his face. "This, right now, is the bravest thing you've ever done in your life."

When they made it to the bottom of the hill, Brandon's father turned from addressing a group of other officers and strode across to meet him.

"Where's your uniform, soldier?" Father asked, his disapproving eye travelling up and down, taking in Brandon's black, civilian suit.

"Is that what matters right now?"

Father's lips curled in disgust. "Duty matters. Today more than ever."

Brandon turned and faced his father, perhaps for the first time in his life. "Why can't you give mom a hug? Why isn't that your duty?"

"How dare you!" Father hissed. His eyes filled with contempt and loathing, he raised his hand to strike.

For the first time in his life, Brandon didn't flinch. "Go ahead. Hit me."

"I wish it had been you," Father whispered. "I wish I'd lost you instead of him."

Brandon shook his head. "You have lost me. You lost both of us." Then he turned to Mandy and said, "Let's go."

Maria strode out into the Arrivals area of Dublin Airport, and saw the expectant crowd of friends and family that waiting to greet their loved ones. She knew before looking that Clodagh Brogan would not be among them. Nor anyone else, for that matter. No bustle of reporters, no civil rights activists. The fact that no one else cared, only made her care about Fergus more. She checked the screen and saw that the flight from Frankfurt had not yet touched down. There was still time to get the tickets.

"Two tickets for the next flight to London Heathrow," she told the woman at the ticket counter. "One way."

"That'll be a hundred and eighty euro, please."

Euros. The last time she had been in Ireland it was 'pounds'. It was a new world now. Everything had changed. Shouldering the enormous backpack, she returned to the Arrivals hall, this time joining the swell of people on the Dublin side of the barrier.

As the Frankfurt passengers arrived, she began to wonder whether he'd be among them at all. Perhaps they had lied? Perhaps Fergus had not been sent from Gitmo to Ramstein and released, as promised?

So painful and so pressing was this thought, that she almost missed him when he did emerge. He had no baggage. His head was shaved and covered in scars. His face and frame were gaunt. The clothes, such as they were, hung on his body as on a wire hanger—a worn T-shirt and a pair of ill-fitting polyester blue pants. He walked with his head down, his hands hidden under folded arms. The crowds, the light and the sudden openness of space seemed to overwhelm him. A few of the meeters and greeters, parents, lovers and friends, paused in their homecoming rituals to throw him a brief, curious stare.

His body shook under the weight of their glare. *Leave him alone!* she wanted to shout at them. She dragged her backpack across the polished floor towards him.

"Fergus."

But he didn't hear her. He made it as far as a corner, in a gap behind the toilets, and collapsed against the wall. He buried his shaved head between his bulbous knees and covered it with his right hand. His left hand was clawing and toying with the tiled floor, as if scraping in imaginary dirt.

She kneeled down before him and watched his hand shifting the empty space, like a child playing in a sandbox.

It's sand, she realized. And as from nowhere she knew what he was doing.

"You're on the beach," she whispered. His movements stopped. He was aware of her now. She reached to the ground and touched the tiled floor, pushing the grains of imaginary sand into little piles before him. "I'm with you now." Tears filled her eyes. "Can you hear the gulls? They're calling to us."

He nodded.

After a while, without another word, she took him in her arms and they left.

EPILOGUE

Maria and Fergus walked hand in hand along the path of wooden ties that led from Abel Tasman Drive over the dunes and to the beach at Golden Bay, where the Cook Strait met the Tasman Sea. Today had been a good day for them. They had eaten at their friends' house, a German couple who ran an organic farm over in Motueka. Six people and three hours. And Fergus had been okay with that. He was getting better every month.

Yet Maria knew the signs. She knew when he had had too much. That was the time to make their polite excuses and go back to where it was more comfortable: into the wild hills where they still spent most of their time, or back at their little house down the dirt lane.

Most days, Fergus worked their four acres of farmland or else made improvements on the house, while Maria ensconced herself in the little attic room which they had fashioned into a home office. Nowadays, via the internet, it was possible for her to stay in regular contact with Clarke and with Cindy. Although on the other side of the world from New York City, Maria remained one of the ACLU's most active civil rights lawyers, fighting for the closure of the Guantánamo Bay Prison Camp, when she wasn't battling for justice for Latino and black men who languished in ever greater numbers in America's prisons. She could easily spend days at a time working on her myriad of *pro bono* cases, were it not for Fergus.

Today she'd decided to take him to a new beach, a hidden one her friend Ulla had told her about. It was a place the tourists hardly ever found, because there was only a single track that led to it, with high bluffs blocking it from either side.

The surf was white today and the sky almost totally free of haze. It was nearly November, and the Southern Hemisphere summer was beginning to make itself felt. The days were getting longer too. But when the sun went down, it still grew bitterly cold on the South Island of New Zealand.

Maria took him to a quiet, sheltered spot, a sort of a hollow between the dunes. It was protected, yet still afforded a view out over the sea. The sun hung low in the northern sky before them, creeping slowly around to the west.

"You don't have to stay with me, you know," he told her after a time. "I know I'm no use with small talk and that. You can go back and join the party. I don't mind. I'll just stay here on me own, like."

She shook her head. "I'll never leave you, Fergus."

When she looked down at his hands, she saw that he was digging into the sand, clawing out the last bit of warmth from the fading sun. Good, she thought, if it kept the nervous shaking at bay.

Today had been a good day. And there were good nights too. But the nights were still the hardest. Whenever Fergus closed his eyes, she knew the horrors would return, and as often as not he'd wake up screaming, covered in sweat. And she'd hold him against her chest and sing to him, until sleep overtook them again.

"Look, Fergus!" she said, after a while. "Out there. There's an island!"

"I know," he said quietly.

"I think there's something moving out there, on the rocks. Like big lumps of something—"

"Seals," he told her. "There's a whole colony of them out there." He said it as if they were something he'd seen many times before.

Maria turned to him in surprise. It was so like Fergus to be able to see seals, without even turning his head. Yet there were tears on his cheeks.

"It was just like you said it would be. Everything has come true for us." Her voice was a whisper. "Everything."

"Not *everything*," he said, and one of his rare little cheeky smiles crept up onto his face. Those smiles were what she treasured most. "Sure didn't I promise you loads of babies?"

Maria beamed at him, her heart exploding with love. She lifted the hem of her shirt a few inches, took his fingers and placed them, one by one, against her tummy.

"Everything," she said.